STRAY CAT STRUT

STRAY CAT STRUT

BOOK 7

RAVENSDAGGER

Podium

*To the imaginative fans creating their own Samura to inhabit
the Stray Cat Strut world—thank you!
The joy you find in my sandbox only makes me want to build bigger castles.*

Cover design by Roger Pinheiro

ISBN: 978-1-0394-8727-7

Published in 2026 by Podium Publishing
www.podiumentertainment.com

Podium

STRAY CAT STRUT

Delilah cut the call with Cat and suppressed a sigh. Catherine was . . . being herself. Which meant she took the news that Earth was about to be screwed over with all of the grace of someone who really didn't give a fuck.

It was almost refreshing, in a way.

Delilah's own worries paled in comparison to how little Catherine cared, because as far as she could tell, Catherine assumed that things would either work out, or they wouldn't and they'd all be too dead for it to matter.

It wasn't a way of thinking that Delilah could ever hope to emulate, but it was still comforting to witness.

She glanced to the side, where Princess was sitting with her knees drawn up to her chest in the passenger seat. She wasn't wearing a seat belt, but Delilah wasn't going all that fast, and she wasn't planning to get into any sort of accident in the first place.

The young samurai . . . worried Delilah a little, especially given the news Cat had just dropped on her. "Atyacus," she subvocalized. "Can you do a little digging into Princess and Knight? Confirm what Cat discovered."

Of course. You must be aware that there is only so much metaphorical digging that I can do. The privacy of other Vanguards takes priority over the curiosity of the one. However, I can let you know what is a matter of public record.

Delilah nodded slightly, a very shallow nod, but one that her AI picked up anyway.

Tiffani Dupont, also known as Princess, has been a Vanguard for a little over three days. She was contracted soon after the death of her father, the previous mayor of New Montreal. Her identity as a member of the Dupont family was sealed until the time of the mayor's death.

"How?" Delilah muttered.

There are certain provisions that members of the political elite can use to keep the identities of family members, the location of their homes, and other confidential information private. One of these was employed on young Miss Dupont until the moment she became a Vanguard. There are traces that the privacy shield was removed by another AI.

So, likely Princess's own AI had removed whatever the mayor had put in place. Did she want to make her public identity easier to find after the death of her father? She wasn't wearing any facial coverings. No mask, no helmet, nothing. It contrasted pretty hard with those samurai who *did* want to keep their identities to themselves. Like Knight.

Delilah sighed again, and this time she noticed Princess glancing her way. "Is everything okay, Miss Gomorrah?"

"It's fine," Delilah said. "We're here."

She pulled *God's Righteous Fury* to a stop on the side of the road. There were a few other cars here, left abandoned on the sidewalk without a care.

Saint-Jérome wasn't all that unfamiliar of a city. Not that Delilah had ever been here, exactly, but she could remember being raised in a much smaller city than New Montreal, before she was sent off to the convent. One city was much like the next. Apartment buildings crammed in as close to one another as possible, with the occasional commercial building, parking lot, or city infrastructure shoved in where they could fit. She'd even driven past a park. A little one, with exactly twelve trees and seven vending machines.

"Alright, all out," she said as she pulled herself out of the *Fury*.

Hedgehog jumped off the roof of the car and landed with a slight bend of his knees. "What's the plan from here on out?" he asked.

Delilah wished, in moments like these, that she had Cat's grace when it came to giving orders and the like. Not that Cat was *good* at it. It was just that her . . . closest work friend had a fantastic ability to bullshit her way through problems that Delilah completely lacked.

"We'll be moving northward and slightly east. Cat's team is following Highway 117 north as well. We'll meet by the far end of the city. There's a Super Dollar there with a large parking lot," she said.

"Got it," he replied. "Well, I'll see you there."

Delilah reached out toward him, almost in time to stop him, but the samurai moved on toward the nearest side street, walking with a quick, determined stride.

She hesitated, then let it drop. The city wasn't entirely swarmed by aliens. If anything, this was as close to an ideal learning ground as a new samurai could ask for. Lots of weaker enemies, with no time to establish themselves or set up traps, and a literal army riding up behind them when things went wrong.

There was something to be said about teaching someone by tossing them into the fire. There was probably a lot more to be said about carefully training a person through limited risk and with careful preparation. But that wasn't how Delilah had grown as a samurai, and she'd turned out just fine.

"Did you want to stay close?" she asked Princess.

Princess nodded. "Yes, please," she replied.

"Do . . . you have any weapons at all?" Delilah asked next.

The younger woman nodded, then reached into the ruffles of her dress and pulled out a rather ordinary all-gray handgun.

"Huh," Delilah said.

"What is it?"

"I was expecting . . . No, never mind." She didn't want to dig into it. Maybe the gun had been bought before Princess secured her whole princess theme? Delilah had tried a couple of things before she decided that she preferred just burning everything to death, and even now she was experimenting with a few different techniques.

Mostly they revolved around fire, but sometimes it was just melting things with powerful acids, or sometimes it involved exciting something's atoms apart.

"I'll take point, then," Delilah said. She reached into the trunk of her car and pulled out a flamethrower. It only took a moment to shrug the pack on and run a quick diagnostic to make sure it was ready to burn.

"I'm used to sticking behind a little," Princess said. "Not, ah, not that I have much experience."

"Oh?" Delilah asked. "Have you fought the Antithesis yet?"

"Yes. The day I became a samurai," Princess said. "Isa—Knight and I were out of the city, at my dad's estate. We didn't kill that many."

Delilah lowered her estimate of the girl's capabilities by a whole lot. This wasn't going to be like when she worked with Catherine, who . . . despite everything, was at least capable of pulling her weight.

"I'll light them up, you finish them off, then," Delilah said. It wasn't much, but a few early points could really set a samurai up. Princess was even working for two, in a way. If the only person she was supplying was Knight, then it wouldn't be all that bad. Delilah had enough cast-off equipment to supply a small platoon, and she'd only been a samurai for a relatively short while.

They started down a road adjacent to the one Hedgehog had taken. Delilah noted the soldiers coming up behind them, trucks unloading men at every intersection.

That was good. Soon enough, they'd have all the backup they could want.

"Atyacus, what's the news saying about Phobos?" Delilah asked. She didn't bother subvocalizing, so Princess was able to hear her loud and clear.

"Phobos?" Princess asked. "Is that a samurai? Or do you mean the moon?"

"I mean the moon, the Martian one," Delilah said.

Not much news has reached the public yet. There are some tidbits on a few astronomy enthusiast websites, but the reports are conflicting and the sites are brushing it away for the moment. Mars has never been easier to see than right now.

"Because it's close?" Delilah asked.

Because the entire surface is currently on fire.

"Oh," Delilah said. An entire planet . . . That must be quite the sight, actually. And with Mars's atmosphere being so light, she imagined it would burn quite strangely. She wasn't averse to seeing it.

The Family and other Vanguard associations are tracking the Phobos Object now. A clearer idea of its projected landing zone should be available by 2130.

"Why are you talking about Phobos?" Princess asked guilelessly. She could only hear half the conversation, which . . . was a very Cat thing for Delilah to do.

"Sorry. I just wanted Atyacus to keep an eye on it for me. You'll . . . learn more about it very soon," Delilah said. "Don't worry about it. For now, let's focus on getting you a few kills, and a few more points."

"Oh, I've been getting a few already," Princess said.

"You . . . have?"

The samurai nodded. "Yeah! My sister is probably killing some already, because I have points coming in. Don't worry so much about me! We've got something good going on, the two of us!"

Delilah wasn't sure she was entirely on board with Princess's big thumbs-up and bigger smile, but she supposed that with everything else going on, giving her a chance wasn't so bad.

They would all need some chances in the coming days.

CHAPTER ONE

FIGHTER, CAT, RANGER

For a fleeting moment, there was a real possibility that technology and weaponry would supplant the need for martial arts. The Antithesis put an end to any such thought. Humanity's foe can be defeated with fist and strike.
—Sensei Mo' Money, opening to his bestselling seventy-eight-part *Martial Guide to Alien Killing*, 2038

"There's the cute little aliens I was looking for," I said. There were only three of them so far, which was actually an auspicious number . . . maybe? "Myalis, what does *auspicious* mean?"

It means something that will lead to success.

Yeah, this was real auspicious. "Model threes. Knight, take the one on the left. Crackshot, take righty," I said.

I was currently busy babysitting . . . No, that wasn't quite the right term. Crackshot was capable enough, and while I hadn't seen Knight at work, I trusted that she was at least minimally competent. I could probably leave and everything would work out just fine, so this was less babysitting and more coming along to make sure no one got overwhelmed.

The three of us were half-hidden by the shadow of a highway that led from south to north through the entirety of Saint-Jérome. It was probably one of those sixteen-way roads, judging by how thick it was.

The majority of the buildings here were apartments. I imagined that a lot of people lived here and drove or rode a bus to get to work in New Montreal. Or something like that. I hadn't done a deep dive into the local demographics, but that made sense to me, and it matched up with the number of apartment complexes out here.

"Alright," Knight breathed out. She reached to her hip, gripped the sword there, then pulled it out without any fanfare to hold it in front of her with two hands.

I knew nothing about sword fighting, even if I carried one around with me. I did it for clout and because it was cool. Knight handled hers like she knew how to use it as more than a metal club.

"I like this," Crackshot said as he tipped his hat back. "Sharing, I mean. But, uh, won't we get a percentage cut of all of this anyway?"

"I don't know, actually," I said. "Does it matter?"

He shrugged. "Guess not. Sixty percent of three-times-ten is more than just a flat ten, ain't it?"

I frowned, trying to work the math out in my head. "Well, whatever, the result is still pretty small, no?"

Crackshot grinned, raised his old rifle up to his shoulder, then casually punched a hole through the head of the rightmost model three. The doglike alien took two more steps toward us before the rest of its body realized that it was dead. Then it flopped onto the ground, greenish blood geysering out of its stump.

I raised my Laser Pointer and took a couple of seconds to line up the sights on the middlemost mutt. A quick squeeze and then a tug to the side to correct my burst, and the dog was dead, two holes punched into its chest—and a third in the asphalt way off behind it, but that was no one's business.

Which left the last one for Knight.

She seemed tense, even through all of that armor. That might've been having two people shooting past her, though. That'd make anyone tense, I figured.

I watched, ready to do something to help if she fucked up, but Knight just stomped toward the model three until the alien started running at her, its claws clicking on the asphalt. It leapt, and Knight simply stepped to the side, then, quick as anything, she lunged back, the point of her sword skewering the dog between two of the unevenly spaced black plates on its side.

While the model three was still reeling, she pulled the sword out, brought it up, and swung it back down in a chop that left the dog headless.

"Nice work," I said. "You chip in something for those sword skills?"

"Huh?" she asked. "No? I did HEMA."

I leaned toward Crackshot. "What's her working in heating got to do with sword skills?" I asked.

He glanced at me. "That's HVAC, or maybe HEPA," he said.

"Huh?"

Knight stared at me, and even through her mask I could tell she wasn't impressed. "HEMA is a broad school of martial arts. It's pretty popular. You learn how to kill things with swords and spears. There's a lot of training to fight Antithesis, just in case."

"Oh, alright," I said. So she'd gotten sword training the hard way. Impressive. "I had lessons on fighting too."

"Really?" Knight asked. She looked at her sword, then casually swiped it clean along the alien's back. "What kind?"

"Brawling, mostly? Scuffling?"

Crackshot laughed. "Roughhousing for me," he said. "Oh, and I'm a black belt at drunken miss."

"You mean fist?" Knight asked.

"I know what I said," Crackshot replied with a grin.

I was just happy that we were getting along well, more or less. Knight was surprisingly nonconfrontational, all things considered. She could have been. Hell, I think she had every right to hate my guts.

I'd be pretty upset if I met the fuck who murdered my parents. Maybe not murderously so, probably, but it had been over a decade since it happened to me. I'd shot Knight's dad . . . was it three days ago? Yeah, that was probably a little fresh.

"Hey, Myalis," I muttered, low enough that the others couldn't hear.

Yes?

"Can you keep an eye on Knight? I don't want to be sworded in the back, if you know what I mean."

I know what you mean. I can try to draw up a psychological profile of Knight, if you wish? Without access to a few key information-gathering catalogs, it'll be rather superficial, based on what social media algorithms and private records have picked up about her, but it should be better than nothing. Or I could ask for Princess's own AI to assist.

"You can do that?" I asked.

It's somewhat strange, but I don't think it's too unusual. This exact situation, on the other hand, is rather unusual. It's only the third time that a Vanguard has been confronted by another Vanguard whose parental figure they killed.

I shook my head. "Wait, this has happened *three* times? Anyway, yeah, do what you gotta. I want to trust her. She seems dependable enough, but I don't wanna be stabbed. It sounds painful."

One moment . . . From what I've been able to gather, Isabelle Dupont is a relatively levelheaded and pragmatic young woman. She has a high level of empathy, specifically for her sister, and a good work ethic. I could pore over her interests and hobbies for you, but I don't believe that would be necessary.

"So, will she stab me or not?" I asked. I clammed up when I noticed Crackshot turn to look my way. That might have been a bit louder than necessary.

As long as you don't threaten her sister, or act in a way unbefitting of a Vanguard, then you are unlikely to be stabbed . . . by Isabelle Dupont. I give even odds of you being stabbed by something, eventually. You are very careless, Catherine.

I rolled my eyes. "Yeah, yeah, okay fine."

We continued to walk, moving past the three model-three corpses. I did notice that Knight nonchalantly stabbed the one I'd shot, as if making sure that it was really dead. It was a casual little display of violence that had my hackles rising, but it was also perfectly pragmatic. The alien I'd killed still had a head attached to its shoulder, so why not give it a poke?

"So, those three were scouts, yeah?" Crackshot asked. He was scanning the area ahead. "We're only a tenth of the way into the city. We'll be meeting more of them, won't we?"

"The outer wall only went down . . . last night? This morning?" I couldn't quite remember from the briefing, but it was relatively recent. "Antithesis are quick to build hives, but we're not going to find anything too intense in the city just yet."

"That sounds like you're trying to jinx us," Knight said.

"Nah, I don't believe in that kind of shit," I said. "I'm mostly talking from experience. Kinda. Bigger models take a while to pop up. We might find some if the hive that hit the north end was bigger than predicted, but I'm expecting a pretty clean sweep of the city. Oh, look! More points!"

A pack of model threes was coming down the road, and I had a suspicion that the birds in the sky above were model ones. In the middle of the pack was a larger model.

It didn't really matter. Crackshot took the big one's leg out with a shot, then planted a couple more holes into it. I sprayed the rest of them down even as the pack started to really put on some speed.

Then they were almost on us, but being plant-brained morons, they focused on the nearest of us, Knight, and soon came to regret that as she started swinging that sword of hers.

Give us an hour or two, and I was sure we could clear out Saint-Jérome.

CHAPTER TWO

IRC IS FOREVER

User Stooopid Princess [2036-02-12]: There are a few samurai who share their powers, yeah.

User Nene [2036-02-12]: Yeah, I want me some samtech bb!

User MierTam [2036-02-12]: Why don't more do it?

User Khorne [2036-02-12]: Would you trust anyone but yourself with god-tier gear?

—IRC Discussion, 2036

"Uh, there's a second group coming in from our right," I said as I glanced that way. I didn't keep my focus in that direction for long, not when we had more pressing issues coming from the front.

The deeper into the city we went, the more aliens showed up to ruin our afternoon. It was . . . actually pretty nice. So far, the biggest thing that had popped up was a trio of quill-covered model fives that Crackshot and I had taken out with a bit of concentrated fire.

The two of us alone were probably more than enough to take care of this whole group. Actually, I was pretty sure I could do it solo. I was less sure about Crackshot managing it on his own, but his way of fighting was more about sitting back and letting the aliens come to him rather than moving into them. He would have managed on his own, I think, just with a bit of effort.

But Crackshot and I had come to an agreement. Well, sorta.

It's not like we sat down and talked about it, so the agreement was mostly built on a few shared looks and some subtle nodding to each other.

Yeah, we could have taken out all of the aliens we'd encountered so far. Crackshot was living up to his name, and I had grenades and a gun that was fully automatic. But if we went all-ranged badass, then the last member of our trio would suffer for it.

Knight swung her sword in a wide arc with a grunt, the blade whistling through the air before it crashed into the lower half of a model-three's head, then kept on going right through. The model three gurgled as half of its head was severed, one of its big mandible-mouth things flying off.

That wasn't quite enough to kill it, though, and it leapt forward toward Knight.

She spun with the momentum of her swing, ducking and weaving right past the alien before she planted her feet and lunged at its side. Her sword went in between two armored plates, then came right back out, stained a greenish black all along the blade.

She was doing pretty well for herself. I wasn't sure what the point split was like for her, but I imagined that even if it wasn't one hundred percent, she was still earning Princess a good number of points every minute.

"Need a break?" I called out.

Knight stood up and glanced around, then shook her head. "I'm still able to keep going," she said. I could tell that she was panting, though, and I imagined that she was probably regretting some of her choices when it came to wearing full-body plate armor.

I nodded, then gestured to the right. There were some twenty-odd model threes rushing toward us from the far end of a side street. They were accompanied by a couple of model fours, the big tentacle boys pulling themselves after the pack like eldritch nightmares on crack. Somehow they were way more horrifying out in the open sunlight.

"Oh, shit," Knight said when she saw the second group. But she flexed her arm a couple of times and looked ready to give it her all.

Then a squad of soldiers came out of an alley somewhere between us and the aliens. They got onto one knee, raised their rifles, and fired. There was a loud-ass cacophony of gunshots for a few seconds before the soldiers paused and all reloaded at the same time.

There was one surviving alien in the lot, a model three that had only been smacked a few times in the side. It started to crawl toward the soldiers when one of them—a sergeant, by the stripes—pulled out a handgun and finished it off.

The soldiers looked our way, and a few saluted before they started to cross the road as one tight-knit group.

I shrugged. It was kind of impressive to see, but I supposed that a dozen guys with fully automatic weapons should be able to fuck up some weaker Antithesis without any real issue.

Crackshot planted a round in the forelimb of the last standing alien in the road ahead of us. The model four stumbled forward, its tentacles grasping out even as a few went back and tried to staunch its own bleeding. The samurai lowered his gun and watched the bleeding monster approach before he turned to study the soldiers. "Looks like they caught up," he said.

Down at the other intersection, I saw an APC slowly move into the middle of the road, its turreted gun swiveling around to face ahead. It fired a quick burst at something I couldn't see. Troops on foot were keeping up with the armored vehicle.

"Yeah, I guess we slowed down a little," I said. "We'll be with the advance from now on, instead of ahead of it. Think we should tell them to hang back?"

"Nah," Crackshot said. "No harm in being with them, I figure."

We both watched Knight fight the model four in close-ish quarters. She took it out by the numbers, slicing apart grasping tentacles before moving in around the monster and slashing it across the side. Model fours were a bit trickier to kill, what with having no heads.

Death by a thousand cuts . . . Well, more like death by a hundred large gashes, but in any case, the big guy went down, and Knight stepped back, not even trying to hide her panting.

"Does your suit have any enhancements?" I asked.

"En . . . enhancements?" she asked in between deep breaths.

"Like, power armor shit," I said.

"Oh," she replied before shaking her head. "No, nothing like that. It's all muscle. But the armor's a lot lighter than it looks. It's titanium and carbon fiber and some other light metals. I've worn formal gowns that weighed more than this." She tapped herself in the chest with a faint *clink-clink*.

I nodded along. "That's still damned impressive. Are you gonna keep upgrading as you go?"

"That's the plan," Knight said. "Princess's AI is keeping track of the points I make. Princess buys me gear with half the points I earn, so as long as I work hard, I'll keep getting better."

That was . . . surprisingly fair. I wasn't sure if I even used half of my own points to improve my gear, not when I spent a lot on other crap.

"You really care for your sis, huh?" Crackshot said. "It ain't just anyone who would step up for someone else like that. Normal folk don't go running toward the aliens, especially not with just a sword."

"A sword is what I know how to use," Knight said. "Never did like guns much. But if that's what I need . . ."

"Eh, don't sweat it," I said. "The first time I saw Emoscythe fight, she had a scythe-sword and she fucked up a bunch of aliens."

Crackshot nodded. "I've seen her fight too. In videos and the like. For research. She mostly uses close-range weapons. Though she also has a lot of mobility."

"Mobility, huh?" Knight asked. She nodded too. "That might be something to look into, I guess. I was honestly thinking of investing more into like, shields? I could carry one, and maybe have some deployable shields too. Princess seems to be okay with guns, so if I can lock down areas and force enemies to come in from one direction or something, that could be sweet."

I could see that working, more or less. Gomorrah actually fought that way a lot. She'd splash fire around and create barriers of it that the smarter Antithesis would gun around. Then she'd nail them as a group.

I glanced at the time. It had been forty-five minutes since we started our stroll. "Let's keep moving," I said. "Have you considered grenades yet? They're *kinda* like melee weapons."

"How is a grenade anything like a melee weapon?" Knight asked.

"Well, you throw it, don't you?"

Knight gave me a look, then shook her helmeted head. "Anyone ever tell you that you're weird?"

"Yeah, a few times," I said offhandedly.

Honestly, I was pretty happy that I was able to banter and chat with Knight like this at all. That whole thing with her father . . . Well, it wasn't the best way to start a relationship with anyone, let alone a more professional relationship.

This whole thing was going well so far, but I couldn't help but feel like I was waiting for the other shoe to drop.

Then again, Gomorrah had mentioned that the mother of all shoes was hurtling toward us from Mars, so maybe that was it.

CHAPTER THREE

COFFEE BREAK-IN

Washington: What about the New Montreal branch? How are you faring?

New Montreal: NM is doing well enough. We have a few promising new samurai. None of them are space-capable yet. Our crop of high-tier samurai are all in Mars's orbit already. We're left with a few mid-tier samurai who have been keeping to themselves.

—New Montreal Family Internal Messaging, 2057

"Hey," I said as I pointed to a little coffee shop on the corner ahead. It looked like the place still had power. Actually, most of this area was still powered. Lights were on indoors, and a few streetlights were still flitting between Coca-Cola red, McDonald's yellow, and Fanta green.

"What is it, boss?" Crackshot asked.

The road ahead of us was littered with dead aliens. Mostly just model threes and maybe a few model fives and sixes to spice things up, but it was overwhelmingly small-fry that we were dealing with. "Let's stop over there, grab a drink, take five."

"It's probably not open," Knight pointed out. She was breathing heavily and covered in a whole heap of alien blood.

"Uh, yeah, I figured as much, but the lights are on. They probably have fridges with drinks, right?" I said.

"I guess?" Knight said.

"Right, so what's the problem?" I asked.

She paused for a moment, then shrugged. "I guess it's mostly just . . . not allowed? Sorry, I'm still not used to thinking like, well, thinking like a samurai, which I'm not, so . . . yeah."

That was fair. "Don't sweat it," I said. "I don't think the owners will be too pissed that we popped in to grab a drink. Hell, if they find out, they might use it for advertising or something."

Knight nodded along, and we crossed the road to the sounds of distant gunfire. We were still a little ahead of the soldiers, having pushed forward while they moved in a more . . . stuttery fashion. They'd cover one road, clear it, then move on to the next with a fresh squad or whatever. It gave those who'd just done some work time to reload and such.

There was a communication network running between the three battalions present, and all of the smaller platoons that made up those battalions. I was privy to it, since some members of the brass were still under the misconception that I knew what I was doing.

The moment I clicked into the command channel, I picked up some chatter. There was a helpful little readout box that popped up in my augs, some secretarial AI transcribing everything that had been spoken so far. People were still talking aloud though, of course.

"East flank reporting in. I have three injured that need moving here. Low-priority."

"West flank, update on the fire situation. We have three trucks hosing it down. Should be under control."

"Keep me posted, west flank," a familiar-ish voice said. The comms transcribed it as coming from Lieutenant Colonel Juno.

I cleared my throat. "This is Stray Cat, on the east flank. I was wondering if we could slow progress down a little on this side? Unless we're far behind the west flank?"

"You're a little ahead of the west flank at the moment," Juno said. "May I ask what the pause is for?"

"Uh, I need to check in on everyone, and the broader situation. Crackshot's still raring to go, but I think Knight needs five. Hell, I could use a bit of water too, you know?"

"Right. I'll tell the sergeants on your flank to hold their next position. We could use some time to reorganize and bring ammo up to the front as well. Some troops need to be moved back."

I frowned at the last part, then refocused on what was happening immediately around me. Crackshot and Knight had moved ahead while I was a little distracted. They were tugging at the predictably locked doors of the coffee shop. Crackshot pulled out the handgun at his belt, some sort of revolver, then blew a hole the size of a melon through the door and its lock.

An alarm went off in the shop, and the two slipped in and started looking for a way to shut it down.

"Are there lots of injuries?" I asked over the network.

"No ma'am," Juno said. "But this is the first encounter with xenos for a lot of our ground troops. Puck Battalion is three-quarters filled with less experienced soldiers. Regulations suggest pulling soldiers back after their first violent encounter if their augmentations detect any major signs of stress."

"Wild," I said. I supposed it made some sense. Needed to ease people into the idea that if they fucked up, they'd be eaten. "Didn't know we were dealing with so many noobies."

"The Seventy-Seventh Recon Company and Twenty-Second 'Maple' Battalion are all veterans," the Lieutenant Colonel defended. "Don't worry, ma'am, we'll handle our part. Let me know when you're ready to move again and I'll unpause the flank."

"Got it, Stray Cat out." I clicked out of the channel, then stepped into the coffee shop with a crunch of glass underfoot. The alarm had been shut down, and I found Crackshot arm-deep in a fridge behind the counter.

Knight was sitting at a table nearby. I slowed down as she reached up and undid a pair of clasps under her helmet, then pulled it off. Knight was . . . a girl. Well, a young woman. Maybe sixteen, seventeen-ish? She wasn't a beauty. Actually, she looked a bit like her dad, but without the facial hair and the weight issues and . . . I wasn't being very complimentary, so I turned back toward Crackshot, who was placing cans on the counter. "What's your poison?" he asked with a grin.

"Eh, anything cold and fizzy," I said.

He tossed me a can and I caught it out of the air with a fumble. Knight caught another with a smack, then looked at it. "Do they have water?" she asked.

"Ah, yeah," Crackshot said. "I don't drink that stuff."

"You don't drink *water*?" Knight asked.

"Fish fuck in it."

I pointed to Crackshot. That was a fair and valid point. Then I had the front of my helmet fold in on itself, letting some fresh air bathe my face for the first time in a while. It was nice. I popped the tab on my drink, then sipped it. "Right, we can take five here. Get some liquids in you, maybe steal one of those doughnuts if they're still fresh-ish?"

"Nah," Crackshot said. "I gave them a poke, they're all hard."

"Sucks," I said. "I'll be checking the news for a minute, don't mind me." I went to a seat not too far from the others, then pulled my legs up and plopped them on a chair across from mine. It was comfortable enough, and it was nice to take some weight off my feet.

Sure, my boots were about as comfortable as could be, but I'd still been standing for a few hours. Also, my skin was still itchy. That whole skin-replacement treatment was probably worth it in the long run, but the moment I was sitting down and no longer active, I could feel the itch returning with a vengeance.

"Myalis," I said, because I needed a distraction, fast. "Can you look into that whole exploding moon thing?"

Certainly. I'm assuming you mean Phobos?

"If that's what it's called," I said. "Big moon over in . . . on? Around? Uh . . . Mars's moon. Probably looks like the moon here, I guess."

Your guess would be wildly inaccurate. Phobos is much smaller than the Earth's moon. Or, it was. I suppose that it would no longer count as a moon of Mars now that it's left the planet's orbit.

"Cute," I said. "So, Gomorrah didn't give me a precise timeline for when that thing would be here. How long do we have?"

"Wait," Knight said. "What are you talking about?"

I glanced over to her. "Phobos is coming to visit Earth."

"The *moon*?"

"Yeah, apparently it's smaller than Earth's moon. Cool facts!" I said.

"Phobos's original path, after its deorbiting, would have taken several months. However, the moon is still accelerating."

"I'm not the educated sort, but I reckon that's not supposed to happen," Crackshot said.

"It's some alien fuckery. Way, way above our pay grade. Or it would be if it wasn't heading to our doorstep," I said.

Given its current course and speed, and approximating the amount of fuel the moon could carry, as well as cross-referencing its movement with the movement of similar large Antithesis bodies in the past, Phobos should be approaching Earth in approximately nine days.

Nine days. A week and change. That . . . was actually a long-ass time. "Bet the Family are scrambling for space-capable samurai right about now."

A general bulletin in that regard was sent out two hours ago, yes. You didn't receive a priority version of it, seeing as how you're still ground-bound. There are ways for you to obtain orbital capabilities with your remaining points, but I'm afraid that it wouldn't be anything luxurious or capable of assisting much.

Right, so I had nothing to worry about, then. "Alright! Two more minutes, then let's head out. We're probably going to want to earn as many points as we can, while we can."

CHAPTER FOUR

BIG CAT ATTACK

A "milk run" was an action that was deemed simple to undertake. The expression came from the routes taken by milk delivery drivers in the past.

Now, with Milk™ being such a luxury commodity, the expression has faded to irrelevance.

—*Oxford Online Dictionary*, Premium Definitions, 2039

"Hey, there's the wall!" Crackshot said. He pointed ahead of him with his free hand, then refocused on plugging alien heads with his bolt-action.

I fired my last few rounds into the crowd of Antithesis in front of us, then stood a little taller while reloading. He was right, over the sea of aliens was a wall. It was some three or so meters tall, made of naked concrete with iron girders at the back, and had plenty of holes blown through it. Some sections had collapsed inward, probably kicked in by the aliens currently pouring into the city.

"Nice! Alright, let's push these fucks all the way back to the wall, then we can plug it up!" I shouted over all the noise.

We were the ones making that noise, mostly. Model threes and the other lower-tier models were usually pretty silent. No roaring or screaming. The only noise they made was when they charged around, and even that was their weird feet thumping the ground.

Right now, the entire eastern front of our operation was squeezing in, following the edges of the outer walls of Saint-Jérome. The city was more or less oval-shaped, so we were just now reaching the end of it.

Highway 117 came swooping down ahead, descending into a line of toll booths at ground level. We were going to have to block those out too, but for now what was important was plugging the gaps in the wall.

I glanced over my shoulder real quick while fitting a new magazine into my Laser Pointer. Knight was hanging back a bit. She had an assault rifle in hand, given to her by one of the soldiers forming a barricade behind us.

Sure, she wanted to kill things with her sword more than anything, but there was a point where that wasn't realistic. With half the Fifth Battalion gathering up in one big line, supported by armored cars and all, the amount of crisscrossing fire into the horde was way too high for one girl to be standing in their way.

So, Knight had been given a gun and was plinking away at the carpet of aliens.

I finished reloading and turned my attention back to the front. This area was mostly occupied by apartment blocks. Not the megabuildings I was used to back home, but something similar in design ethos. These were big, all-white squares, maybe five stories tall, with a recessed entrance on the ground level. It was going to be a bitch and a half checking each one for any alien that snuck off, but that would be a problem for later.

I fired a few bursts into the aliens ahead and grinned as those I hit flopped bonelessly a dozen meters away. We were concentrating enough fire on them now that there was no way they'd be making it, at least as long as our ammo held up and they didn't pull anything funny.

"Myalis, garrotes," I said as I extended a hand to the side.

Here you go.

A grenade landed in my hand and I casually flicked off its spoon before tossing it as far ahead as I could. It burst into action near an intersection ahead, sending sliced bits of alien flying every which way.

I called for a few more garrotes and tossed them out over the heads of the aliens. It created a few spots where the horde was shredded apart. The best bit was that with the aliens pushing themselves forward, they were being pressed into the field of those grenades without time to move around them.

I laughed as I opened fire again. The front of the horde was thinning out. Soon, we'd be able to move up another block, and then it was one more until we hit the kill zone between the wall and the city.

A click in my ear and a flash on my augs alerted me to an incoming message, this one over the command channel. "Stray Cat here," I said as I clicked into it.

"Ma'am," said Lieutenant Colonel Juno. "I'm with Lieutenant Colonel Britannica, of the Twenty-Second armored. He's broken through the outside of the city and is ready to spread out to either side."

I frowned, then put it together in my head. The armored division had gone ahead way at the start of the fight, they had Tankette with them, and they had a fuckload of normal tanks. They were supposed to reach the east end of the city and plug it up for us. Which clearly hadn't happened yet. "Right, I'm surprised you haven't covered the inside of the wall already," I said as I tossed an empty mag aside and called up another.

"Hrmm," a new voice said. My augs labeled it as the voice of Lieutenant Colonel Britannica. "We met more resistance than we expected. We're ready to play the anvil to your hammer."

"Alright. We'll charge up to the wall, then," I said. With the armored battalion on the other side, that should stop any more aliens from coming in, and then we'd just have to double back and send search teams through the city to look for any remaining pockets of resistance. "How's it looking on the outside?"

"Alien numbers are higher than expected, but not beyond what we can handle," Britannica said gruffly. "We're tracing the direction of incoming xenos to pin down the location of their hives."

Hives, plural. Great. We were going to have to take care of that sooner rather than later. "Okay. Hang tight, we'll be at the wall in ten minutes or so. How's the west flank?"

"Samurai Gomorrah has just arrived at the wall there. The other half of the Fifth Battalion is setting up defensive measures now," Juno said.

Damn, Gomorrah had gotten ahead of me. Probably that little break we took. Or maybe we were just moving slower. "Got it. We'll be moving up now. Stray Cat, out!"

Crackshot looked my way. "How're things going?" he asked.

"We're too slow," I replied. "Do you mind if I bring in the heavy shit? We need to speed things up a little."

Crackshot shrugged. "Go ahead," he said.

By "heavy shit," I of course meant my mecha. The giant cat mech thumped its way to the front, then lunged over the row of soldiers walking behind us to land with an earth-shaking crunch next to me. I pointed ahead at the aliens still rushing our way. It wasn't necessary to point, but it felt cooler. "Kill them," I instructed.

The mech's front lowered, then its shoulders unfolded, two multi-barreled guns slipping out from enclosures within the mecha before they pointed ahead. Then they both let out ungodly *brrts*. Two streams of lead flowed out ahead, crisscrossing and spreading out so that they covered the entire wave of aliens.

What they left behind were hole-riddled corpses, some of them burst apart from the shots they'd taken.

I didn't even need to pull out the big guns for this kind of small fry.

"Well, shit, we could have done that sooner," Crackshot said.

"Yeah, but I want you to get some kills, and Knight too," I said.

Sure, I had a few ways of wiping out a horde this small on my own without too much trouble. Hell, I had bombs for days. If I didn't care about collateral, I could turn this end of the city into a series of creative craters, but that wouldn't be fair for the newbies.

They needed a chance to practice their shit and get some early points too.

I suspected that I'd been given the same chance too, way back when I started a few weeks ago.

Deus Ex had been around, and so had a few other higher-tiered samurai. They could have probably wiped the floor with any number of aliens, but I suspected that they had left little "bubbles" of untouched space around any new samurai, giving us a chance to get some early levels in.

I was all for doing the same, especially if it meant less work for me. "Alright, let's move up!" I called out to the troops behind me.

I didn't expect to get a cheer in response, or see some hundred-odd soldiers start charging the aliens, but I wasn't about to complain. I ran along in front of them, the mech charging out ahead and crushing whatever was left underfoot.

The wall came up soon enough, and the entrance there was jam-packed with aliens crawling over each other to get in through a few fallen sections. I don't think the soldiers were expecting a counter-charge, but Antithesis brains being what they were, their only response to seeing an aggressive attack was to attack right back.

Fortunately, we had guns.

I flicked on the command channel again as I slowed down. There were sergeants trying to get things back in order while some soldiers were repeatedly shooting into corpses or stabbing aliens with bayonets. "Hey, Lieutenant Colonel Juno? Yeah, we've made it," I said.

CHAPTER FIVE

105MM ARMOR-PIERCING FIN-STABILIZED DISCARDING SABOTS FOR FUN AND PROFIT

The trees are coming! Oh God, the trees are coming!
—Overheard from a soldier of the Forty-Fifth Heavy Battalion, 2048

Things were going fine, and it was making me nervous as fuck.

The wall was properly defended now. There were tanks sitting on the outer side blowing up anything that showed up, we had mortars being installed, and pre-fabs were coming in from behind. I even checked the reports to see if there was anything going wrong anywhere.

The worst I found was one report about a common sidearm having ammo that wouldn't work half the time, and a second report about a logistics train being ambushed in the city. But the train was defended, so the ambusher was mowed down in short order. More teams were being sent back to comb through every building to look for stray aliens to shoot.

I almost jumped when Gomorrah called me. "We have a problem," she said.

"Oh, thank fuck."

"Pardon?" she asked. "Are you . . . happy that we have a problem?"

I nodded, even if she couldn't see me. "You wouldn't believe how happy I am. I was getting real worried there. What's the problem, and is it the sort that can be blown up?"

" . . . Yes, Cat, it's the kind of problem that you can blow up. Can you meet me at the front? There's an FOB . . . a forward operating base, over by the edge of Highway 117. Princess and Hedgehog are here, as well as Tankette."

"Alright, I'm on my way. See you in five," I said.

"See you in ten," she agreed before cutting the line.

I rolled my eyes. Just because I'd been consistently late in the past didn't mean that I was going to be late again today. I found Crackshot chatting it up with a few soldier types while wiping a cloth over the barrel of his gun. A tap on his shoulder and a point out ahead was enough to get him to follow me. Knight was hanging out by the edge of the wall, her back pressed up against one of its pillars and the visor of her helmet raised so that she could stare at . . . a physical phone.

"Is that a smartphone?" I asked as I got closer.

She looked up and nodded before tucking the phone away in a belt pocket. "It is. My dad . . . kind of insisted that I learn how to use one."

Weird, but whatever. Rich people would want rich people toys, I supposed. They'd gone out of fashion some thirty years ago, but I supposed that fashion stalled a lot for the upper crust. "Alright. Gomorrah said there was trouble, so we're going to go find it and blow it up. Wanna come?"

"Uh, sure," Knight said. She stood up, and then followed as Crackshot and I made our way out.

It was kind of strange to step out past the walls. The space within was all city. Sure, it was some shithole little city, barely worthy of the name, and it probably didn't even have a seven-figure population, but it was still *urban*. The space right outside the walls very much wasn't. It was open, cleared fields for about half a kilometer, then scraggly woodlands that no one seemed to care about clearing.

The tanks of the Twenty-Second were spread out across the space, each one with a dozen meters between itself and its neighbor. There were two companies of heavy armor in that battalion, which made twenty-eight tanks in all, plus another two companies of lighter armor. That made for a pretty long line of heavily armored "Fuck off."

Any aliens coming in from the north were going to be running into a rude surprise. And that wasn't including all of the infantry sitting around, or the APCs and lighter transports that still had guns strapped on because fuck it, why not?

All that to say I was feeling pretty confident when I walked up to the middle of Highway 117 where someone had set up a massive unfolding pavilion tent. I supposed that the mobile bases were still at the other end of the city, so we'd have to handle things without that convenience.

Gomorrah's *Fury* and Tankette's mini-tank were parked off to the side of the tent. We walked past them, then ducked into the tent itself. Gomorrah was there, sitting on one of those shitty foldable chairs next to Tankette. Hedgehog was at the back of the room, minding his own, and Princess was pacing in the corner. Across from them was Lieutenant Colonel Britannica and Lieutenant Colonel Juno, the two of them talking while looking at a tablet held between them. There weren't any fancy projectors, just a normal-ass table in the middle of the room with some maps unrolled on it.

"Hey," I said calmly as I walked over to Gomorrah. "You said there was trouble?"

She glanced up at me, then nodded. "Some. Take a look at this." She made a small gesture in the air, like she was flicking something my way. My augs got a ping at the same time. A video file? I opened it, then enlarged it so that it was just about the only thing I could see.

It was satellite footage. Or maybe drone footage? In any case, it was taken from high above the ground. The video scrolled across a city that had to be Saint-Jérome, then continued northward, following the highway for some ways. There were lots of forests, and a few small towns built up around intersections on the highway.

Then the video stopped above . . . something big. Or lots of big somethings, rather. An uneven line of black splotches. They were moving, but not quickly. The camera fixed on one that was ahead of the rest by a bit, then zoomed in on it.

It was covered in leaves and greenery on top. Actually, if there weren't so many of them and they weren't lined up, I might have dismissed them for a couple of trees, but this thing was moving, and because it was zoomed-in-on, it was easier to make out the small figures around it as model threes.

"What in the fuck are those?" I asked.

"Model twenty-twos," Gomorrah said.

"I'm . . . sorry, but what are those, exactly?" Knight asked. She had moved around the room to be next to Princess. They were both looking at the same video on a tablet held between them. What was with all the handheld shit today?

"Model twenty-twos are also known as mobile hives," Gomorrah said. "They're one of the larger models in the twenty-range of Antithesis. They're six-legged, big, and pretty tough. They're also not an offensive model."

"They do shit out offensive models," I said.

"I . . . wouldn't use that term, but it's not entirely inaccurate," Gomorrah said with a nod. "Model twenty-twos can produce smaller models. Anything in the lower ranges that's smaller than a midsize car. They can produce something like ten model threes an hour, or between two and four model fives in that same timespan. They often produce mixed models."

"How many of them are there?" I asked. I scrolled back in the video, then counted the line. "I see seven?"

"We know of nine," Gomorrah said. "But for all their size, they're relatively hard to spot."

"They're heading this way," Princess said. Then her face lit up in a massive grin. "They're heading this way! We're going to get to see you at work, Miss Cat!"

"Uh . . . uh-huh," I said. That girl still creeped me out something fierce. "We're going to have to roll out the welcome wagon for them, that's for sure. If they are heading this way, will the Twenty-Second be enough to take them down?" That last part was directed to the two Lieutenant Colonels.

Britannica sniffed. "I'd like to see them stand up to a salvo of 105mm armor-piercing fin-stabilized discarding sabots to the face!"

"Myalis, I'm going to assume that that would work?"

Yes. That would certainly be sufficient to take out a model twenty-two.

I nodded. "Cool. So we either sit back and wait for them to get into range, in which case we blow them the fuck up, or we rush out there and mess them up ourselves."

"I think the problem isn't so much the model twenty-twos as it is the number of them, and their origin. There's a hive to the north capable of producing a large number of these. That's a concern," Gomorrah said. "And just because they're coming this way doesn't mean that they won't stop out of weapon's range and just sit there producing more and more aliens to send our way."

"They have a lot of biomass available to them," Hedgehog said. We all turned his way. "I've seen this kind of thing before. They'll sit way back and start pumping out weaker models by the dozen, then by the hundred, then in massive swarms. We're going to run out of bullets before they run out of trees and dirt to eat."

Well, that was a bit of a problem.

CHAPTER SIX

FORBIDDEN BATH SALTS

A river red beneath the moon,
Carves through the land, a sorrowed tune.
It flows where hope and dreams are slain,
In its wake, only shadows remain.
Red River Armaments.
Violence is Poetry.

—Ad for the Red Moon auto shotgun, 2041

"I suggest violence," I said. That had a few of the others turning my way, so I shrugged and decided to explain. "Look, if we sit on our thumbs and spin, then we'll never get anywhere before the aliens gather enough biomass to eventually overwhelm us."

"Sit on our . . . oh, I get it," Princess said. Then her face reddened. "I wish I hadn't."

"Do you have to be so crude?" Knight asked.

She hadn't seemed to mind so much earlier, when Princess wasn't around. Was Knight that bothered about the purity of her sister's mind or something? I could recall a few people who were scandalized by the language we used at the orphanage, but that generally only encouraged us to be even more vulgar.

"Right, point is, if we sit here, we're gonna get . . . fricked? No, I'm sorry, Princess, I'm not censoring myself, that shit's fucked."

"It's okay, Miss Stray Cat," she said. "I wouldn't want you to be anyone but yourself."

That earned her a look from a few of the others. Tankette especially seemed a little worried. "Uh-huh," I said. "So, if we sit here, we die. Or worse, we'll have to call in reinforcements to bail us out in a few hours, maybe a day if we fight hard enough, right? Myalis, can you give us rough estimates here?"

Certainly. Based on the number of model twenty-twos, I can reach certain conclusions about the size and capabilities of the hive producing those models.

These are, of course, very rough. Several factors come into play: The distance from the hives to their advance, the approximate age of the hive, the local available biomass, and the hive's temperament.

I nodded along. The others did too. Myalis was transmitting live, her voice coming from all of the little speakers in the room at the same time. Somehow it didn't sound like shit, despite the varying quality.

On the lower end of that spectrum, it is entirely possible that a relatively young hive has dedicated all of its production to the birthing of the nine visible model twenty-twos. This would have taken a small hive three to four days, less if the initial models started to produce assistants from the moment of their birth. This scenario is unlikely.

"And the high end?" Gomorrah asked.

On the opposite end of the same spectrum, weighing for the currently visible number of Antithesis in the region, it's possible that there is a medium-to-large sized hive that has split its production, creating several model twenty-twos in order to expand faster while also keeping up the production of a variety of other models. This scenario is also unlikely.

"So, what's likely, then?" Crackshot asked. He reached under his hat and gave his hair a scratch.

The most likely scenario is something closer to the middle of these two extremes. A moderate-sized hive producing two to three model twenty-twos a day to assist it in expanding while also producing smaller models in order to gather local biomass and protect its main structure.

I nodded along and started to think of what to say next. Surprisingly, Hedgehog cut in before I could think of anything halfway smart to say. "I know these aliens," he said. "From experience. They're not smart. It's wrong to give them more credit than they are due. Not to say that they're weak. They're not, not when there's enough of them, but they're also not able to *think*. They act on instinct. If this hive's acting this way, then there's something in its environment that's pushing that."

"Myalis mentioned the hive perhaps creating these model twenty-twos to expand further," Gomorrah said. "What would make a hive want to expand?"

This time, it was Atyacus who replied. He always sounded kinda smarmy to me. "*If a hive growing in an environment that is inconducive to its growth is aware of areas beyond it that are more capable of sustaining it, that hive will usually attempt to either move itself, grow toward the richer environment, or dedicate all of its biomass to creating the instruments necessary for a new hive to be born in that better location.*"

"Like a dandelion growing between the bricks," Tankette muttered.

I glanced at the maps on the table. "Are there any shitty places for hives out there?" I asked.

Gomorrah leaned back. "Prévost is to the north and a little west, along the highway. An evacuation was called, and most of the city's population moved out, but there's a militia and some locals still there. They're not reporting anything special."

Lieutenant Colonel Juno's eyes widened. "Oh," he said.

"Oh what?" I asked.

"I . . . shouldn't say," he replied. He looked up, meeting my eyes, then nodded slightly. What . . . what was that supposed to mean?

He wants you to ask him anyway, Catherine.

Oh, he was being fucky. "Tell us anyway," I said.

"Is that an order?" he asked. The other lieutenant colonel was giving him a look, but he wasn't stepping in.

"Yeah, sure," I said.

"In that case, I suppose I have no choice. Echo Lake, to the north of us, east of Prévost. It was purchased from the government by a small private company."

"A company bought an entire lake?" Princess asked.

"The company was co-owned by Baytheon and Bonsanto. They used it for a joint venture, testing a prototype weapon's platform."

"They needed a whole-ass lake for that?" I asked next. Judging by his annoyed look, he was getting pissed at all of the side questions.

Still, Juno nodded. "Yes. They were developing a weapon to assist in the removal of underwater hive structures. They used the lake to test it. It was not successful. The lake and its surroundings were fenced off, and the area is now considered a biohazard zone."

Myalis was kind enough to pull up a satellite image of the lake in question. From above, it was a roughly squarish lake, one that looked like it had dried up a whole lot. The area all around it was yellow, as if all the grass there had been burned away. That went on for a while, too, and I could trace the location of little rivers and shit because of the dead vegetation around them. "When was this?" I asked.

"Some five, six years ago," he said.

There are no public records of this. There are, however, tangential ones. The company's founding, its initial growth and hiring period, and its relatively recent closure. Furthermore, there are reports of a threefold increase in cardiovascular issues in the area, as well as a sixty percent increase in lung and kidney cancers for all humans within a hundred-kilometer radius downwind of the site.

I shut off my helmet's mic. Myalis had sent that last tidbit to me alone. "Isn't New Montreal within a hundred kilometers?" I asked.

Yes.

"And no one's throwing a shitfit over it?" I asked.

Cardiovascular issues kill more humans than the Antithesis do every year. Masking this wouldn't be overly difficult.

"Huh . . . add the CEOs and shareholders of both companies to my shit list, then send it to the Family," I said.

Noted. Sent.

"Okay," I said, then remembered to turn the mic on. "Okay," I repeated, as if I hadn't just fucked up. "So, good odds the hive started in that spot, where whatever hyper-fucked insecticide is messing it up. Honestly, I kinda don't want to bring the soldiers in closer unless they're in full PE gear."

"PPE," Gomorrah said.

"That too. Which means it's just the samurai here. Can you guys hold off any aliens without us while we run up north and blow this hive up?"

"Is using explosives a good idea?" Hedgehog asked. "That's against standard procedures when dealing with any space where the dirt is a carcinogen. You don't want to toss it into the air."

"Ah, right . . . Well, we'll kill it some other way, but it'll be dead in the end," I said. "I'm not anyone's mom, so I can't tell you guys what to do, but I'd suggest some gear to resist whatever fuckery's in the air."

"I *am* someone's mom," Tankette said. "And I'd really appreciate it if everyone took some basic precautions here. Better safe than sorry."

Princess nodded. "I'll do what I can. Knight, too! We made a heap of points today, so it's no big deal."

"Cool," I said. "So, we ready to head out right away?" The sooner we hit the hive, the faster we'd be done. And I didn't want to be out there after night fell.

"Before that," Tankette said, "maybe a light lunch, and some time to use the washroom?"

I blinked. "Yeah, okay, sure."

Fuck it, it wasn't like anyone wanted to piss behind a radioactive bush, not when there were good odds the bush was part Antithesis and just waiting to bite your ass.

CHAPTER SEVEN

EXOTIC CUISINES

You don't want to go to war with an empty tummy, now do you?
—Tankette to Brigadier General Thibodeau, 2057

We had a light lunch, which in my mind meant ordering up something from Myalis to snack on before we headed out, but apparently that wasn't *right* according to Tankette.

The woman heard my plan to just order something to eat, then calmly but firmly put her foot down. "I don't think that's a good idea," she said.

"You don't?" I asked.

She shook her head. We were still in the command pavilion in the middle of the highway, but Tankette looked ready to leave. "Sure, ordering food is fine when you're busy, but you can't order food that has any love or attention put into it. Come on, follow me, please."

I glanced at Gomorrah as Tankette left the pavilion, but all I got out of the nun was an unhelpful shrug. So I followed after Tankette toward her tank, and soon the others did the same with varying amounts of enthusiasm.

The tank was parked next to the *Fury*, but it started to rumble and move before Tankette was even there. The little tank rolled toward us, then turned on the spot so that its rear was facing our way.

Tankette popped open a small trunk at the rear, and I blinked as I saw how much space was in there. It looked like the space where the engine should have been was mostly taken up by shelving and a few unfoldable things.

Tankette tugged a bar out, then stepped back while pulling it. A whole mini-kitchen came out of the back, along with a small countertop. Pieces clicked into place and parts folded into parts that snapped and locked until she had her entire setup ready before her.

There were two little stovetop rings, a small oven-looking thing, and what I suspected was a microwave next to the bottom half of a blender. "Okay," Tankette said as she turned our way. "Are there any dietary things I should know about?"

I looked around. "Uh, not for me?"

"I'm fine with everything," Gomorrah said. "Are you going to . . . cook?"

"Why yes, of course," Tankette said.

"Strange," Crackshot said. "But alright, I'm down for it. I don't like onions."

"Don't like, or are allergic?" Tankette asked.

Crackshot frowned. "You know when you make eggs and you leave a bit of shell in the egg and then you bite on it?" he asked. "Yeah, onions do the same for me. It ain't so much the flavor, it's the texture that's all wrong."

"I'm allergic to sesame seeds," Princess said with a little wave. "I get a rash, it kinda sucks."

"I'm vegan," Knight said. Next to her, Princess rolled her eyes.

"Nothing here," Hedgehog said.

Tankette clapped her hands. "Fantastic! Does anyone want to help me cook? I'm thinking . . . a nice little veggie stir-fry? Princess, are you okay with quinoa? I think it's a kind of seed."

"I think I'm okay with that, yeah," Princess said. "I can help you cook. But Knight can't."

"What? Why not?" Knight asked.

"You don't know how to cook," Princess pointed out.

Knight shifted a little. "So?"

"You can help with the cutting," Tankette said. She turned toward the countertop at the back of her tank, and then a few boxes thumped into place. They were the same plastic boxes as every other item ordered up for points, only these had little cartoon tanks stenciled on the sides. One of them looked a bit thicker, like an insulated cooler.

Hedgehog moved back a little, looking entirely unwilling to help with all of this, but Crackshot stepped up and started to unpack things next to Tankette. "Lemme help ya there," he said. "You said stir-fry, yeah? Never was one for that kinda fancy stuff, but I know my way around a potato peeler just fine."

Our group split in half. Those of us who could and wanted to cook, and the rest of us who kind of just . . . lingered there.

"Uh, so you were a PMC, yeah?" I said to Hedgehog. He was standing there with his arms crossed, looking a little frustrated with all of this.

"I still am," he replied. "My contract hasn't expired."

"You know, as a samurai, I don't think you actually need to follow any contracts," I said.

He nodded. "I know."

"Okay, well, if you know," I said.

He glanced at me from the corner of his eye, then sighed. "Forgive me. It's not about the money or even loyalty to the company. It's about principle. I don't break contracts. I gave my word, I signed the paper. At this point, the entire thing is a farce. The company can't decide if they want me around or if I'm a liability, so they basically dropped the leash entirely and are just playing nice, but I *will* finish the contract."

"Okay," I said. "How long do you have left with them? I don't know how PMC contracts work."

"Two more months," he said. "The terms of contracts tend to differ a lot. Plenty of contractors only work for six to nine months, plus internship and training."

"What's that entail?" I asked.

"When you join a force, they don't want useless idiots. So you get uncontracted training. Half of the time you're unpaid too. It depends on the company. Some do it for a week, others take it a lot more seriously."

I shrugged. "Alright man, if that's what you're like, then that's cool. What happens when someone on the other end of the contract fucks it up?"

He shook his head. "Then they're in breach of contract. A good contract will have consequences baked into it. There was a time when I couldn't actually do anything about that kind of thing, but I think that's past now."

Right, this guy was a little weirder than I'd initially thought. Why was it that every samurai I met was a hair shy of being a fucking nutjob? Why was I the only normal one?

It took twenty minutes or so for Tankette to get the food ready. It was some sort of rice-like thing, kinda beige-yellow, that she filled into some bowls, then veggies were tossed on top. Most of them looked normal, shit like carrots and such, but a few looked downright weird.

"Thanks," I said as I accepted a bowl. Princess gave me a look, then smiled and offered me some chicken that they'd cooked in a little pan with some sort of sweet-smelling sauce.

To be entirely honest, while I initially thought this was a massive waste of time, I was reconsidering it now that I'd removed my helmet and could smell the food cooking.

I mean, there was some stink from the city, and there was a small mountain of burning Antithesis corpses next to the wall, but the stir-fry smell was stronger, and way better.

"What veggie is this?" I murmured so no one other than Myalis would hear as I raised a fork stabbed into something brown.

That is a non-terrestrial plant. Don't worry, it's safe for human consumption. It's actually a seed, though its texture is similar to a modern potato.

I shrugged and took a bite. It was a little . . . tangy? It had the same kind of acidy taste that tomato sauce had, but without the same flavor. It wasn't bad, though.

Honestly, as I scarfed through my bowl, I could see why Tankette was so into this. The food was warm and better than just about anything I'd eaten in recent memory, and it was nice to just stand around and eat. Even Hedgehog relaxed some.

Tankette seemed very proud of herself as she started packing things away. She put leftovers into little boxes and gave them to anyone who wanted some. Gomorrah, as the only person with a place to put stuff nearby, ended up taking most of the leftovers while Crackshot had seconds.

"Okay," I said before wiping my mouth clean with the back of my hand. "So . . . we're fed, everyone's gone to take a piss. I think we should get moving now. The longer we sit around here, the more aliens we're going to have to deal with. Tankette, Gomorrah, and me are going to take the lead."

"And I," Gomorrah said.

"Yeah, I mentioned you," I replied. "Anyway, I think we're going to have to borrow a car or two from the army so that everyone can come along. It's too far to have you guys ride on a mech or on Tankette's tank."

"I can drive," Crackshot said. "I don't have a license, but I know which pedal makes you go fast."

"I'll drive," Hedgehog cut in, leaving no room for arguments.

I nodded. Yeah, this was gonna go just fine . . . but holy crap, I really wanted a post-lunch nap.

CHAPTER EIGHT

WHAT'S A METAPHOR?

The armed forces of the world will always need a fast-moving, lightly armored vehicle of war, and now more than ever. The threats we face today come from aliens, who mostly attack from up close or with biological weapons, and protestors, who are only rarely armed with anti-material weaponry.

—The Kissinger Institute, *Armed Forces and You*,
digital pamphlet, 2031

The army was more than happy to let us borrow something to go charging into the aliens. In fact, Lieutenant-Corporal Britannica welcomed the idea with open arms and brought up a catalog with every tank, armored car, and transport truck listed on it.

I left the choice up to Hedgehog, since he was the designated driver, but I was still a little disappointed when he picked out a smallish Humvee-like truck.

He explained that it had an automatic transmission and drove like a normal car, more or less. It had large wheels and was mounted up, so it would have decent clearance off-road. Otherwise, it was lightly armored, specifically to deal with lesser Antithesis threats, and the gun mounted on the top was remote-operated. His AI was willing to take over there.

I got in the *Fury* with Gomorrah. Tankette had her mini-tank, so that left Princess, Knight, Crackshot, and of course Hedgehog in the truck. My mech was following at the rear, to cover us in case anything happened, though Gomorrah's car had just as much firepower as the mech or the tank, albeit in a different package.

I checked the time before we left. It was past noon. The little cookout had eaten into our daylight, but it wasn't so bad. We had some hours of sun to burn still. I did plan on making it back home before nightfall, or soon after.

"Alright," I huffed as I crashed into the passenger seat next to Gomorrah. "It's like herding cats. Why haven't we elected someone who isn't me as leader yet?"

"Because I don't want to do it, and you're actually pretty decent at this," Gomorrah said. "I think we've gone over this before." She put her car into gear, and we started to move along. The highway would be good enough for some ways. Then we'd have to veer off and either circle around and use some shitty backroads to get to the lake, or go through the woods and push through the line of model twenty-twos way ahead.

I made sure that my comms were off, so it was just Gomorrah and me, and I supposed our AI, who could hear us. "So, what do you think about the group?"

"As a whole?" she asked. "Green."

"Green as in good, or green as in a bunch of untrained newbies?"

She thought about that for a bit. "Can I say both?"

"Yeah, I guess," I said. "But elaborate anyway."

Gomorrah glanced at me from the corner of her eye. "I was only with Princess and Hedgehog, but I guess I can report on Tankette too." I nodded for her to continue. "Princess is enthusiastic. That's about the best I can say about her. She's unfocused, doesn't spend her points wisely, if at all, and she doesn't seem to treat the enemy as a threat. She's mostly fearless, but I'm not sure if that's a pro or a con."

"Huh, interesting. Knight is super focused. She's actually a good fighter with what she has, and when we gave her a gun she was pretty good with it too. Very calm, a little careful, I think? She reminds me a bit of some of the soldiers we have, but less . . . stick up her ass?"

"They'll make for an interesting pair together, then," Gomorrah said. "If Knight can encourage Princess to behave more professionally, then they might be able to come out of things without dying."

"Cool," I said. "And the others?"

"Hedgehog is a fantastic marksman. It was nice working with someone who hits the things they're aiming for." I gave her a flat look, but she pretended not to notice. "He's great over the comms. Calls out issues, kept me informed on his status the entire time, very military-minded."

"Makes sense, considering his background," I said.

She grunted. "He's a little stiff, however. I . . . Maybe it's because I'm used to working with *strange* samurai, but he strikes me as very narrow-minded? In terms of the things he buys and his specialization, I mean. I haven't talked to him outside of a professional context. Though he's not as . . . personable as some samurai either."

"Stick up ass, but otherwise competent," I summarized.

She sighed. "Yes, more or less."

I leaned back into the seat. "That leaves Tankette, who you didn't actually work with."

"A little. We arrived at the wall before you, and before it was entirely cleared on the other side. She helped with that. I don't know about her behavior before from personal experience, but I've read the report from Britannica. He liked her. She's a little . . . slow to react? That could just be her tank, though. It's not the fastest thing around."

I glanced back. We weren't traveling all that fast, I noticed, but it looked like Tankette's mini-tank was giving it all it had. Still, it was faster than I'd convoy had moved.

"How was she otherwise?"

"Good firepower," Gomorrah said. "Not perfect aim, but she made up for it with high-explosive rounds."

"As one does," I agreed.

Gomorrah nodded. "Otherwise, she kept in formation, mowed down some enemies. I have this feeling that she's going to be more of a . . . not a *Grasshopper* exactly, Grasshopper is great in fights from what I can tell, but Tankette definitely puts her priorities more in keeping people safe than in killing Antithesis. She's leveling the playing field by having a really strong early specialization."

"Tanks are pretty badass. I wonder why more samurai don't go that route."

Gomorrah hummed. "Same reason the army still has more infantry than tanks. A lot of Antithesis fighting is done from walls and from home-to-home, and you can't do that from inside of a tank. Tanks have places where they shine, shine really bright even, but others where they're at a disadvantage."

"That's fair," I said.

"And on your end?" Gomorrah asked. "How were Crackshot and Knight?"

"Knight I told you already," I said. "Good with a sword, pretty decent. Needs better gear, but that'll come. She's got like . . . a fuckload of baggage. Like, I'm not one for therapy or shit like that, but damn, her and Princess could use some. Uh, otherwise, she's got potential, I guess."

"They worry me," Gomorrah admitted. I couldn't blame her. The Dupont sisters worried me too.

"Crackshot's cool. He's not great against lots of enemies at once, but he takes out bigger ones with no problem."

Gomorrah drummed her fingers on the steering wheel. "You are aware that the Antithesis don't send out aliens one at a time, right?"

"Eh, he'll figure it out," I dismissed. "He's nice to have around. Funny, pretty calm overall. Like, he's just got this really nice chill vibe to him. I'd invite him to a barbecue, or for some beers. If I had a straight sister, I'd let him smash."

"Cat, you are . . . Stop using metaphors. Please."

"You say that like I know what those are."

Gomorrah didn't reply for a bit, focusing on the road instead. There was a row of abandoned cars to one side for some reason. One of them had a model three embedded in its windshield. There was a lot of blood around, and it wasn't all alien.

Looked like someone had hit a model three, then some Good Samaritans stopped to help and got chewed up for it.

Another reason to hate the countryside.

"General strategy, then?" Gomorrah asked. "I suggest myself and Hedgehog at the front. Tankette can support as she can with your mech. Princess, Crackshot, and Knight can form our midline?"

"Where's that leave me? And Knight's a melee fighter."

"Right, switch Knight and Hedgehog around, then. As for you, I figure you could scout around, take whatever position's needed otherwise. Ideally we'll have enough fire on any problem that it'll be taken care of relatively quickly."

"You mean fire*power*," I said.

She shrugged.

"Alright, yeah, I'm down for that. We'll be driving right up to the lake, or parking close by and walking over?"

"We can stop nearby, I suppose. It depends on how much we want to alert the hive, and whether or not it notices us. Either way, we burn it down."

"It's already down, isn't it? I mean, assuming it's in a lake."

"Cat, don't start arguing semantics with me. Or anyone else. You'll just lose on a technicality."

"Was that a pun?"

It was nice, riding in a car and arguing with a friend right before diving into hell itself!

CHAPTER NINE

GOTTA KILL 'EM ALL

LOOKING FOR RECS

Hi, I'm looking for recs. I've read all of the popular stories on here, the ones that are easy to read. I only have the three major subscriptions, so I don't have access to that many.

I'm looking for something fun to read, no AI stuff please! I have Nimbletainment Plus Premium Reading, is there anything good in that, or should I pay the extra 150 credits/month for the ultra plus model? Thanks! <3

—Readit Forum Post, 2039

We rode down the 117 until we were only two kilometers from the model twenty-twos and maybe ten-ish kilometers from Echo Lake.

"From here on out, we'll be off-road," Gomorrah said. I was sure we were going to just ride off the highway and across some fields or something, but then Gomorrah reminded me that her car could fly. We lifted off the ground, coming to a hover about a meter in the air.

I tapped into the comms channel Myalis and the other AI had set up. It was private, just the bunch of samurai out here. "Hedgehog, Tankette, think you can keep up?" I asked.

"Looks like it," Hedgehog said as he veered his not-Humvee off the road and into a grassy field. "There's a decent route from here, and some side roads out ahead. We're not going to circle around?"

"I considered it," Gomorrah said. "But it would add a lot to our travel time. If we hit the model twenty-two all the way on the left and then keep on straight, we'll make it to the lake much faster, without risking the hive being aware of our arrival."

"I don't exactly plan on being all that subtle about it," I said.

Gomorrah shrugged. "Let's see how far we can get while driving. We'll figure things out from there."

That was fair enough.

With the *Fury* in the lead, we rode out at a much slower pace across a field, over a few hills, and then through a forest that had some trails cut into it that were just barely wide enough for the truck Hedgehog was driving to fit.

About halfway to the first of the model twenty-twos, we met some resistance.

"Heat source ahead," Gomorrah said in clipped tones. I'd been talking to her about how awesome having color-changing hair was, but I cut myself off mid-sentence and sat up straighter.

"All I see are trees," I said.

"It's farther ahead. I'm catching some blips of moving warmth. Not much, but that's not surprising. They're hard to see against the ambient temperature of a tree. Atyacus, can you . . . yeah, that's right."

A screen appeared over the car's windshield. Or maybe it was more accurate to say that the screen that was already in place of the windshield started to display more than just an image of what was happening outside. The screen was now one of those fancy thermal-vision things, painting the world in blacks and grays, with hotter areas being lighter.

A few distant blurs were a lighter shade of gray than the rest. "If they weren't moving and building up heat, then they'd be basically invisible," Gomorrah said.

"Wild," I said. "So, we blow them up?"

Gomorrah considered it. "We could run past."

"And leave them there?" I asked.

"If we start shooting and blowing things up, it'll slow us down and attract a lot of attention. Taking out the Echo Lake hive will be tough enough without having every Antithesis within fifty kilometers rushing in our direction."

It kinda made sense, on the surface. The aliens were generally shit at communicating with one another, so if we zipped by, the nearest ones would notice that we were here, but the farther ones wouldn't. And yeah, we'd get to the hive without it knowing we were coming.

But damn did that leave a bad taste in my mouth. "I don't like it," I said. "It's our job to kill them all."

"Be that as it may, a samurai has some leeway in their overall mission," Gomorrah said. "Taking out a hive takes priority over killing chaff. We definitely won't be able to kill every last one of the smaller models in the area, not if that means having to stop and comb through all of these forests for stragglers."

I worked my jaw a bit, then nodded. "Okay. We break through, rush a spot near the lake, then get out and take care of it. Don't forget, we're here to get the newbies some points too."

"Aww," Princess said over the comms, which apparently had been on this entire time. "That's really kind of you, Miss Stray Cat!"

I closed my eyes for a moment and refrained from swearing.

Gomorrah flipped some toggles and switches on her dashboard—which had analog switches for some reason, even though the *Fury* could obviously be controlled entirely via augs—and the car clunked a few times as its weapon systems slid out of their respective holes.

"Hedgehog, Tankette, prepare to shoot at anything that rushes you, but try not to slow down."

"Got it," Hedgehog replied.

"I'm on guns," Crackshot said.

"I understand," Tankette said next. She was right behind the truck, with my mech following behind her. I checked on my mech real quick through the little app I had that showed me its status in real time. I was down a few thousand rounds for the miniguns, but everything else was green at the moment.

The first alien I saw properly, without needing that whole thermal vision crap, was a model four that leapt down from the branches above. It was eighty percent tentacle by body mass, and all of them were squirming at the *Fury* as if looking for a way in even as it thumped against the hood.

A second later it was on fire, tentacles writhing in something akin to pain as its nerves were lit up.

Gomorrah tilted the car slightly to the side and the body rolled off the hood. "Deploying PD," she said.

I didn't have time to ask what that meant before everything around us started to burn.

"That's going to be pretty fucking obvious," I said.

"It's temporary," Gomorrah said. "I'm spraying everything with a solvent that reacts to oxygen and burns, but the by-product suffocates fire pretty well. Basically, it'll burn now, but extinguish itself as soon as the solvent's burned up."

"Hedgehog, can you still see where to go?" I asked.

"I can," he said, "but I don't know how fireproof this car is."

"I can't decide if I should turn the AC on or leave it off," Crackshot said.

"Off," Hedgehog snapped.

We rode through the forest on a blazing road of Gomorrah's making, with the others following just behind. Lower-ranked models weren't what I'd call smart, but they knew better than to run into fire. I supposed that they were still plants, at the end of the day, and were probably aware of how flammable they were.

Which is probably why we kept going without really getting harassed. A handful of bigger models, fives and sixes, showed up down the way, but a few shots took them out before they could start anything.

"We're near the model twenty-two on this side," Gomorrah said. "Right past it, there's a back road that leads all the way to the lake. I think I'll take Hedgehog and Tankette that way."

"I can take care of the big guy, then," I said.

Gomorrah nodded.

I leaned back into my seat and opened a few apps. I had control of my mech from here, but it wasn't perfect. Mobile controls were shit compared to being jacked into the mech directly. It wasn't latency, because stupid sci-fi-magic-tech didn't suffer from lag, but being in the mech meant having my hands on the controls. From where I sat, I had to deal with digital versions of the same.

"Myalis, can you pick up the slack a little?" I asked.

While in the mech I could handle everything all at once, but from here it would be trickier.

Certainly. I'm ready before you are.

I chuckled, then my vision filled with what my mech was seeing. It wasn't quite at the same level of fidelity as being in the mech, and the field of view wasn't as great, but I'd live with it. "Okay," I muttered.

Myalis gave me a waypoint marker for the approximate location of the model twenty-two, so I pointed the mech that way and took off at . . . whatever the four-legged equivalent of a jog is.

I zigged around some trees and zagged along the edge of some rougher terrain. That's when I noticed the small horde of aliens out ahead. Lots of smaller models all swarming around and bumping into each other as they moved at . . . honestly, kind of a slow pace. There were bigger models standing out from the crowd as well, even a few in the double-digit range near the back.

And, of course, the model twenty-two.

The fat fuck was lumbering out of the forest, branches scraping against its sides and snapping off to fall onto the aliens crowding around it. I spotted a few rarer models, the sorts that mostly hung out near a hive.

Not that it really mattered. "Found our big friend," I said.

"Kill it," Gomorrah suggested.

"I was getting to it," I said. Then I pulled the digital trigger.

CHAPTER TEN

RAINBOWS OF DEATH

Look, I'm all for supporting the community, but this is too many flags.
—Post on the LGBT Vexillology Forums, 2025

Twin 105mm cannons barked on either side of my mech. I wasn't in it, so I couldn't feel that glorious *oomph* of recoil, but I did get to see a pair of explosions rocking the side of the model twenty-two in beautiful high-definition.

Plant meat and gristle flew all over. Both rounds had penetrated the model twenty-two's lightly-armored sides, buried themselves into its flesh, then exploded. There were now two gaping holes large enough for a family of four to crawl into.

And still the fucker wasn't dead.

The model twenty-two stumbled. Some of the sacs on its side were broken, and half-formed alien carcasses slipped out along with a few gallons of placenta juice.

Around it, the horde of smaller aliens playing babysitter turned my way. There was no signal, they all just started to *move* in my direction.

I flicked on the mech's invisibility, then immediately made it useless by opening up with its twin Gatling guns. A torrent of 10mm rounds rushed ahead. Every tenth round or so was a tracer. For some reason they alternated in color, green, then yellow, then red, streaking together to form a sort of moving . . .

Wait a fucking second, were my guns rainbow-themed? "Hell yeah," I muttered.

I thought you might enjoy that.

"It's very stupid," I said as I swept the fire left and right. There was nothing quite like twin Gatling guns to clear out brush, and trees, and aliens.

Just to be safe, I aimed the big guns at the model twenty-two and fired a second salvo. One round smashed into its down-tilted head. The other dug into its already opened side. When they went off, it was enough to send the alien crashing down.

I pulled back on the digital trigger and looked upon my work. There was a bit of fire around the dead alien, and some models that were still squirming, but for the most part, there was just a lot of dead biomass.

"This one's dead," I said. "And it was . . . really easy?" I tapped in a few commands and charted a route for the mech to catch up and intercept our little group somewhere out ahead.

"A few aliens couldn't keep you down!" Princess said over the open comms. "Also, rainbow guns?"

I decided to ignore her, because sometimes that worked with my problems.

Gomorrah made a sound that could have meant anything while I exited out of the apps that let me control my mech. We were still floating along ahead of the others on what looked like a dirt road cut into the forest. I wasn't a good judge of natural shit, on account of being a city girl, but the forest to our right looked a lot younger than the forest to the left, as if we were driving along a divide.

It only took a minute before my mech appeared out ahead, waiting for us. We were cutting in pretty damned close to where the model twenty-two had been.

It didn't take much before we drove right past and onto a small countryside road just past that. This one was at least covered in asphalt in the spots that weren't potholes large enough to hide in.

"Alright," Gomorrah said. "This road leads all the way to Echo Lake. We're . . . two kilometers away now, more or less. We need to decide how we want to handle the hive at the lake."

"Nah," I said.

" . . . Nah?" Gomorrah repeated. "Can you elaborate?"

I gestured behind us, toward where the others were, more or less. "Let the new samurai handle it. Legit. You and I can stay back and make sure they're not overwhelmed, but let them get the points for taking out the hive. We can salt the earth after, if it comes to that, but they need the experience and the points more. Plus, I want to sit back and have someone else do my work for me."

"I don't mind that," Crackshot said over the comms. "Could use a few more points for a new pair of boots. And I've yet to take out a hive myself."

"This is riskier than it needs to be," Hedgehog said. "But . . . I suppose there are enough of us here, and with some supervision to keep the danger at a low simmer, this might not be a *terrible* idea."

"Stop thinking like a normie, Hedgey . . . Hoggy?" Princess said. "We're samurai. We're supposed to jump into trouble and come out of it looking like heroes."

I shared a look with Gomorrah. That kid was gonna get herself into a lot of trouble. Or grow a lot from the experience and come out of it real strong.

"There's a good stopping point ahead," Gomorrah said.

We turned off the road and climbed up a slight . . . hilly thing that led to a flat bit of ground that was taller than some of the trees around us. Gomorrah set the *Fury* down and I slipped out of the car, my eyes fixed to the right.

Echo Lake stretched out below. The forest went on for a ways around us, but the trees were prematurely yellowed and often downed, and then there was nothing but collapsed brown mush until it reached the edge of the lake.

The lake itself was a lot bigger than what I'd had in mind. Even seeing the satellite imagery wasn't enough to give me a proper sense of scale. It wasn't so big that I couldn't see the far shore, but it was still a fuckload of water. Water currently covered in what looked like a layer of some sort of . . . gunk.

"Myalis, can you zoom me in on the surface?" I asked.

My helmet's visor filled with a much closer view of the lake's surface, and I made sure to keep my head stable so that it didn't shift too much. There was something all across the water's surface alright, some sort of mat, almost?

"I'm assuming that isn't natural," I said.

It doesn't look like it. Records indicate the presence of similar materials in other hives before. It's a filtration system empowered by a chemical similar to chlorophyll. The reaction forces water through a series of small organelles, then into something similar to a root system, extracting particulates from the water's surface.

"So . . . what, some sort of filter?" I asked.

Essentially. It seems as if this hive had been trying to purify its main source of water.

I chewed on my lip for a moment. The lake was supposed to be stupidly toxic to alien life, and probably human life as well. The deadness of the local flora suggested that it wasn't great, and yet here the Antithesis was, fixing it.

Well, fixing it in order to better make little monsters to eat the locals with, so no points gained there.

Hedgehog set the armored truck to park, and then Tankette rode up the hillside, followed by my mech, which turned around and faced the incline in case something tried to sneak up on us.

Crackshot stepped out, then walked over to stand next to me. "Well, shit, that's a lot of hive," he said.

"I don't think the entire lake is a hive," I said. "Looks like . . . see that entire coast bit there? Looks like the hive is actually in that spot of woods there. It's just that it's pulling from the water." I pointed as I spoke. "Still, yeah, that's a lot of hive. But it might not be all that bad."

"How's that?" he asked.

"I'm not an engineer or anything, but I figure building down is a bad idea when you're right next to a lake. So the hive will probably be spread out across the surface."

"Protocol for this kind of thing is to carpet-bomb the area, then sweep in with heavy armor," Hedgehog said as he ambled over.

"We can't carpet-bomb this, and we don't have heavy armor," I said. "Besides, it's probably all muddy down there."

"My tank gets caught in the mud sometimes," Tankette said. "I can't imagine how much worse it would be if it was a lot heavier."

"Yup," I said. "That sure looks like a problem. Well, good luck!"

I patted Crackshot on the shoulder, then walked on over to where Gomorrah was leaning against the hood of her car. "Think they'll manage?" she asked when I got closer.

"Yeah. We figured it out the first few times, and there was only the two of us. Plus, they just came off a nice point-farming spree. They must all be sitting on a few thousand each, yeah?"

Gomorah nodded. "It should be enough. Worst case, we help a little. It's not a big deal."

"Well, it's a big deal if we don't finish before sundown. I want to have supper with Lucy tonight."

Gomorrah shook her head. "You need to set priorities."

"I . . . have? Lucy, then all the rest. It ain't rocket science."

CHAPTER ELEVEN

A TEACHABLE MOMENT

Everyone has to start somewhere. Even samurai aren't ready to go all-out from the start.

Well, except for me. I was ready. Actually, more people should be ready for more things. If you're going to be a samurai, the least you could do is not be lazy about it.

—Live interview with Deus Ex on *The Saturday Morning Show*, 2056

It started with explosions, which I was reliably certain was always a good way to start something.

Since Gomorrah and I weren't gonna be in the thick of it unless the newbies royally fucked up, I decided to stand back and watch. That didn't mean I wasn't gonna help. I didn't feel like sitting here for hours, in a high-risk environment, without getting *some* sort of reward out of it.

Mostly I was aiming at some of the smaller models on the periphery and limiting myself to using my gun to tag them. It was live aim practice.

In the meantime, the newbies had come up with a plan.

Well, no, it was more that Hedgehog came up with a plan, and the others didn't have any better ideas. They poked at it a little, added some touches of their own, but that was about it. He was kind of carrying the show during the pre-fight stage, and I figured that was probably alright.

This wasn't about forcing the newbies to get good at stuff that wasn't in their . . . domain. It was more about giving them a chance to play to their strengths. Hedgehog's big strength came from a few years of experience in the field, probably lots of training, and a heap of knowledge he'd picked up through his job.

So his strengths were actually pretty fucking strong. Sure, he was a little weird for a samurai, all stiff and shit, but he was still good.

Gomorrah and I had listened in on the planning phase, of course, just in case what they came up with was too stupid.

It wasn't.

"Alright," Hedgehog said. "That'll catch their attention. Be ready. Eyes on your sectors. Keep your ears open."

"Got it!" Princess said.

We were all atop a small hill with a sharp embankment on the side. Below were the remains of that poisoned forest. Fallen trees and dead vegetation for a hundred meters. And also a large smoking crater now.

Tankette had been the one to start the high explosions by firing some sort of HE round into the ground some ways ahead. It had taken a good ten seconds to go off. There were still clumps of dirt coming down from above, and the pillar of kicked-up dust was still settling.

"How much are we gonna bomb the place? Like, are we turning it into one big crater or just softening things up?" I asked Gomorrah, who was standing nearby. I wondered if she was miffed. I could plink away at the odd model one or three, but her gear was a little more . . . up close and personal.

"I think one distractionary explosion shouldn't be that big of a deal," Gomorrah said.

That had been the crux of the plan. A big, loud boom to let the hive and all the little plant babies around it know that we were right here and a threat.

The aliens reacted pretty predictably. There was some scuffling, then little black forms started to run across the fallen forest. Model threes leapt from trunk to trunk, smaller models ran beneath wherever there was space, and a whole flock of flying models took to the sky.

"Tankette, do you have anti-air?" Hedgehog called back.

"Oh, um, I do!" Tankette said. She was, of course, in her little tank. There was a hatch open on the top, and if she stretched back, the top half of her head could poke out of it.

The turret turned, there was a light clunking noise, and then Tankette ducked back down. She had insisted that everyone wear hearing protection before she started firing. Gomorrah and I had that stuff built into our helmets and Hedgehog was wearing the kind of headphones I saw soldiers wearing all the time, which left Knight, Princess, and Crackshot to figure shit out.

Princess was now wearing a pair of almost comically oversized headphones. They were furry, with sparkly little diamonds on the band that made it look like a tiara.

Crackshot had some funky earrings that were supposed to be good enough. They were shaped like little fangs. I supposed that fit with his image more than bigger hearing protection would, but I bet he paid a premium for it.

Knight had gotten herself a new helmet. It was a slight departure from her previous one, which was . . . apparently just a normal-ass metal helmet.

A comfortable one, she said, but pretty normal. Her new helmet was a curved block of naked steel with a thin slit over her eyes. I wasn't even sure how the visor tilted up. The visor, of course, glowed red, because it wouldn't be cool if it didn't.

She looked pretty pleased with her upgrade.

Princess had switched out her piddly little handgun for a long shotgun with wooden furniture. I still wasn't sold on the way Princess and Knight were splitting their point income, but whatever.

I snapped back to attention as Tankette opened up. Her tank could fire a round every half second or so, which wasn't subtle. The constant *thump-thump-thump* and trembling of the ground was accompanied by an echo as whatever she fired exploded in the air a few hundred meters away. They burst into large black balls of shrapnel that shredded through entire flocks of model ones.

"Maybe instead of going for bombs and stealth, I should have just gone straight for tanks," I muttered.

"There are some pretty big downsides," Gomorrah said. "Just like the *Fury*, she can't deploy her tank indoors."

"Not with that attitude," I said. "A few shots like that and I think you can turn indoors into more outdoors, you know?"

Gomorrah chuckled. "I suppose."

"Open fire!" Hedgehog said. "Focus the larger models. Crackshot, keep an eye out near the hive for direct counters."

"Aye-aye, Hedge," Crackshot said. He grunted as he went to one knee, then laid himself down on the ground atop a coarse blanket. He aimed down-scope and started to plug away at the incoming horde.

The others fired out as well. Hedgehog had a . . . actually, I wasn't sure if it was an SMG or an assault rifle. It was thick and bulky, and looked like it could be used as a makeshift brick if something came too close and Hedgehog was feeling particularly violent. Princess unloaded with her new shotgun, the recoil pushing her back with every shot, and Knight fired short bursts from that rifle she'd liberated from the army earlier.

It wasn't an overwhelming amount of firepower by any means. I was pretty sure my mech alone could put more rounds downrange than the entire newbie squad, but it didn't matter. They were punching holes into the alien's growing formation, and their initial distraction was working. The aliens were still following the first group that had run toward the crater that Tankette's HE round had created.

"Oh, look, a few are coming around," I said as I raised my Laser Pointer to my shoulder and sprayed a few bursts down the slight incline leading up to where we were.

"How much are we supposed to help here?" Gomorrah asked.

"Gom, we're the ones who decided to do this. We can help as much or as little as we want," I said. "Why, getting nervous for the newbies?"

Gomorrah shook her head slowly. "Not nervous. They'll succeed. But Hedgehog's plan is too . . . conservative."

"Oh?" I asked.

"Sitting back in a position of strength and taking out the enemy as they come is a very military-minded approach," she said. "It doesn't work against Antithesis in the long term. The hive will start sending out different kinds of models to test things, and with all of those model twenty-twos around, eventually it'll find something that works."

"Right, don't get into a war of attrition with the ever-expanding aliens," I said with a nod.

"Exactly. If the team just stands on this hill, they'll just get overwhelmed eventually. Or maybe they'll keep the hive's numbers down, but that will only last as long as they can keep focused on keeping it down. There's no such thing as culling an Antithesis hive."

I nodded along, then glanced over to the newbies. "So . . . do we tell them?"

Gomorrah shrugged. "I'm considering it. Let them mess up for a little longer, I suppose. It's free points for them, and we can always burn this area down if they take too long."

"Ah yes, the 'burn them all and let God sort them out' solution," I said with a sage nod. "That's always a solid plan B."

CHAPTER TWELVE

SALT THE EARTH

–We don't have permission, sir.

–How far do you think we can sexualize this? I mean, the market is young girls and nerds. Nerds have more money, so like, obviously.

–We are going to die, sir.

–I was thinking two sets of clothes, of course. One can be that armor made of plastic, and the other can be lingerie. Maybe cat-themed?

–We don't have permission.

—Overheard discussion about My First Stray Cat dolls, 2057

Gomorrah and I let the newbies have their fun for a while. Eventually, there was the usual mid-fight upgrade, but that really just amounted to Tankette buying different, more effective rounds for her mini-tank, and Princess buying Knight a proper samurai-grade weapon. In this case, it was an assault rifle that had a sword built into it. It could transform back and forth between a really shitty assault rifle with terrible ergonomics and a short sword with equally awful ergo.

It did look kind of cool though, so good for her.

I tapped my way into the team comms while looking over the field below our little rise. It was currently filled with a whole lot of dead aliens and some that were going to be dead soon on account of all the holes in their bodies and the missing limbs. "Alright, newbies, you do know that there's a hive to kill, right?"

"Oh," Princess said. "Right! We should go out and do that, right?"

Hedgehog decided to cut in before she could go skipping along. "Normal procedure is to hold in a defensive position and then let the artillery or specialists take care of an active hive."

I stared at the man for a long moment. "Bud, we *are* the specialists. And unless you've got a mortar emplacement in that spiky coat of yours, we don't have artillery."

"We have your mech, Miss Tankette's tank, and Miss Gomorrah's *Fury*," Knight said as she gestured to the three vehicles. "Those could serve as artillery, or at least big weapons."

I scrunched my nose up, then gave her a reluctant nod. "Fair. This is a test for you bunch, so that cuts down on what you've got as options. Keep in mind that we're supposed to *not* explode the hive."

Crackshot hummed. He was still lying on his belly on the ground. He took a quick shot at one of the aliens in the heap below, nailing it in the head and sending it down. "We're gonna need some special munitions, then. What are our options? I've got a catalog for weird rounds on me."

"Oh!" Princess cheered. "My AI suggests cutting the area up. I have something for that too."

I was gonna suggest they buy something from my own catalogs, but I figured this might work out for the best. I watched as Tankette opened the top hatch of her tank and poked her head out. "Um, I can take any twenty-five-millimeter shell, if we're going to use my tank."

"I suppose I can afford a few mortars as well," Hedgehog said. "Disposable ones aren't overly expensive. Though if we're going to use mortars, we'll want something larger than what Tankette's using."

"Just got to find a kind of bomb that won't toss up too much dirt, then," Knight said. She coughed. "I don't know if it's just in my head, but I feel like my throat's all scratchy already."

"We should probably take some healing stuff after this," Princess agreed. "I don't want super cancer."

I stepped back and watched them work. The group came together, argued for a bit, then seemed to come to an agreement. Hedgehog bought a pair of mortars, the classic sort, with a tube and some arms and a doohickey on the side to adjust the angle. It was maybe a bit higher-tech than the fully manual sort carried by soldiers. At the very least, it looked like it could auto-adjust.

Crackshot summoned up an entire crate of shells, and Princess skipped over to Tankette's tank and the two of them looked in the back, where I supposed the tank's ammo stowage was.

It took a minute or two for them to get set up, but then Tankette drove around to the edge of the hill and turned her turret out toward the aliens. "Ready!" she called out over the comms.

"Ready here," Crackshot said. He was manning the mortars with Knight and Hedgehog a little ways back.

"No point in delaying this," Hedgehog said as he dropped a shell into a tube. There was a satisfying *thump*, and I darted my eyes up to follow the blur of a shell as it went up high. It arced far above, then became harder to see as the smoke trailing it broke off. Still, it was pretty easy to tell where it landed, because there was a big *wump* sound, and suddenly there was a hole about a meter across that lacked any dirt or rocks or any alien bits.

"What was that?" I asked Myalis, pitching my voice down and keeping it off the comms.

That seems like an anti-materiel shell of the dimensions-shunting variety. You have a few grenades with similar effects.

"My black-hole grenades?" I asked.

Indeed. Though those use a much smaller opening and the pressure is weaponized. They also create an inordinate amount of dust, which these avoid by shifting matter in one go without disturbing the soil around the point of impact too much. It's still rather ineffective.

I nodded at that last part. The hole was pretty large, but there was still a lot of ground to cover. At a guess, we'd need to destroy the entire coast along this side of the river, and then some ways into the woods.

Knight dropped a shell, then Hedgehog fired a second. Crackshot knelt by the crate, picking them up and handing them over.

It was . . . not the most effective way of doing things, I figured.

Then Tankette opened fire, and I reconsidered.

Whatever she was firing lanced across the ground, digging long furrows through the dead grass and exposed roots of the hive. The few still-moving aliens that happened to be close were torn to shreds.

"What's she firing?" I asked.

A variation on the garrote grenades you've used previously. The round opens up soon after being fired and whips out a set of monomolecular wires that are spinning around the center of the round. They cut through anything that the round passes close to.

"Will that work?" I asked.

It'll certainly damage any root system the hive has in place without disturbing the topsoil overly much. It will definitely destroy the hive eventually, but without destroying the biomass the hive is made of. A fresh hive will be able to reclaim this area with little trouble.

"Hmm," I said before leaning in toward Gomorrah with my arms crossed. "We might have to actually salt the earth around here."

"Yes. This is effective, they'll destroy the hive, but I don't know if it'll be enough to stop it from returning. I've been talking to Atyacus, and we've come to the conclusion that most of the chemicals that we don't want to agitate won't be carried upward if we boil the water that contains them."

"I don't see where you're going with that," I admitted.

"I'm suggesting that we heat up the lake a little," Gomorrah said. "To perhaps a hundred degrees Celsius."

"Is that supposed to mean something special, or did you just want a round number?" I asked.

She turned to look my way. "That's the temperature water boils at."

"Huh, I thought the numbers were kind of just arbitrary."

"Water freezes at zero degrees. How do you not know this?"

"Whatever, I probably knew and just forgot," I dismissed. I had watched a science show or two, maybe. It was good enough. "But yeah, if the newbies can't find a solution to the lake, then we'll boil it. Or you will, I guess. Hey, does this feel too easy to you?"

"Are you trying to jinx us?"

I shrugged. "Would jinxing us mean that there's more to do? Because right now, it's kind of boring."

Gomorrah sighed. "Atyacus, can we expect any trouble?" she asked. I saw her nod, then nod again, then straighten up. "Oh."

I was mostly split between being worried that something bad had come up, and happy to see another samurai who talked to her AI out loud. I always had the impression that Myalis and I had a bit of a special relationship. "Was that a bad oh? Because it sounded like a bad oh."

"It is," she said. "The other eight model twenty-twos have turned away from the city. They're heading back here. Along with all of the smaller models escorting them."

I glanced at the newbies. They were working together still, launching more shells up, though they were taking turns now, and Princess had joined them. Tankette was putting rounds downrange, shredding any alien that popped up.

Could they handle that many model twenty-twos and all of their escorts? Maybe. Probably. But it would distract them from fucking up the hive a whole lot. "Yeah, alright, I guess it's time that we step up and do some work too. If we intercept them far enough from the lake, do you think we'll be safe to explode things?"

"I would hope so, yes," Gomorrah said.

CHAPTER THIRTEEN

FLICK MY SWITCHES

Forest fires are a common occurrence. In some part due to human intervention, but also as a naturally occurring phenomenon. Once, we attempted to corral and control them, but now, with the rising risk of Antithesis presence in the wilderness and in rural areas, controlling a wildfire is a much more dangerous undertaking.

—James "Smokey" Silver, Saskatchewan fire chief, 2041

"You know, this reminds me of the good old days," I said.

"The good old days?" Gomorrah asked over a more private channel. It was just the two of us, and I supposed our respective AI. I couldn't imagine Myalis *not* snooping in.

"You know, back when it was just you and me, heading out to blow things up and light the world on fire," I said.

"Catherine, that 'good old days' you're alluding to was two weeks ago," Gomorrah said.

I paused in the act of swinging myself into my mech's cockpit. "Yeah, and?" I asked. "It feels like it was longer, what with those weeks being pretty busy." I spun around and crashed ass-first into the pilot's seat, then reached over and flicked the cockpit closed—which required flipping a small analog switch that my studies into repairing the mech had revealed was only there because flicking switches *did* something for people.

I leaned into the seat, then wiggled my flesh-and-blood fingers, opening and closing them a few times. My skin felt a little . . . taut? Like it was just a bit too tight, or I was wearing a pair of latex gloves that were too small for me. It wasn't cutting into my dexterity, but it was noticeable.

The itch was easier to ignore now, though I felt oddly . . . dirty? I couldn't wait to take a shower later.

"Do you think that our level of business is normal for samurai?" I asked. There were more flicky-switch toggles to click up or down in front of me. Some had little plastic covers that had to be pulled up before I could toggle the switch below. They all made very satisfying clicks as I pressed them.

"I don't think so," Gomorrah said. "Atyacus?"

A rather snooty voice came over the comms. "Neither of you will be surprised to note that you didn't break any galactic records for busiest newly inducted Vanguard. However, you are both in the top percentile for busiest human Vanguard in terms of hours spent fighting the Antithesis compared to hours since induction."

"Huh," I said as I chewed on that for a minute. "Top percentile is good, right? Because the last time I heard the word percentile it was with regards to the quality of the orphanage, and it was followed by 'lowest,' which I think means it was shit."

"In this case, top percentile is probably not ideal," Gomorrah said. "But I can't exactly complain, we had some time off. We might have spent it unwisely, but we had it."

"Yeah," I said with a nod as I settled in, hands touching the control sticks at last. "I'm ready to rock over here," I said. The screens on the inside of the cockpit lit up with a one-eighty view of the outside of my mech. A map opened in one corner, and a diagnostics readout popped up in another with text scrolling through it.

I actually knew what some of it meant now, which was kind of neat. Until I realized that a lot of it was reminding me that the mech needed servicing.

That was a problem for future Cat.

"Alright, let's move," I said.

"About time," Gomorrah replied. She kicked the *Fury* up into the air, and the car came to a hover over my mech's shoulder. Gomorrah then switched our comms channel to encompass the newbies as well. "Stray Cat and I are heading out to take on an incoming surge. You have until our return to eliminate the Antithesis hive here. Make the most of it, but don't get in over your heads please."

"Aye-aye, boss," Crackshot said.

"Oh, bye-bye! Have fun!" Princess replied.

The others acknowledged with a little more professionalism, and Gomorrah turned the comms back to private. "They should be able to reach out if there's trouble," she said. "And I left a drone behind to watch over them."

"You did?" I asked.

"I did. You're not the only one who can purchase stealth equipment, you know?"

I frowned at that, then spun the mech's sensor suit around to check over the newbies. Then I looked *over* the newbies and the sensors picked up some fuckiness some ten meters up. Fluctuations in temperature, a few distant clouds that were jittering very slightly because what I saw of them wasn't real but rather a projection. "Neat," I said.

Should I have called up a few cats to keep an eye on things?

To be fair, I was . . . not great at keeping track of my cat drones. Right now they were scattered here and there across New Montreal, and I was pretty sure Myalis was the only one with even a vague idea of where they were and what they were up to.

Sometimes I worried. Most of the time I didn't think about it.

That was pretty much how I handled things. When we went out with the kittens, it was always Lucy who kept track of them. I just bailed them out of whatever shit they inevitably got caught up in.

Gomorrah set a waypoint on our shared map. "This is the intercept point. We have three kilometers to go. Do you think you can make it there in a reasonable time, or should I give you a lift?"

"I'll make it," I said. I pointed my mech in that direction, then metaphorically floored it. The mech started to run. Fortunately, most of the greenery around here was well past dead, so when I inevitably ran into some small trees and bushes, I came out on top.

Less fortunately, the ground was far from level, and was, in fact, a bumpy fucking mess.

My mech generally moved with a calm, careful grace that kept its core pretty level even as its legs shifted to run. It made for a surprisingly smooth ride when the variations in terrain and changes in direction weren't too bad.

They were pretty bad right now. I found myself tightening my legs against the sides of the spaces for them and gripping onto the controls as hard as I could.

The little red light that flashed above me, reminding me to put on my harness, seemed to be blinking sarcastically at me now.

It didn't take long before we arrived at the point Gomorrah had pointed out, but by that time the aliens were arriving too.

The spot was a thicker patch of forest with a few thin dirt roads crisscrossing through it, and just past that was a wide open field. It looked like it hadn't been cultivated in a while, and it was filled with small, thin baby trees that didn't look too much taller than I was, as well as a fuckload of bushes and flowering plants and tall grass.

The only reason I knew the aliens were getting close was because my vision, coming from the mech's head, had a decent amount of height, so I could see the grass shifting in waves as they moved through it.

"Looks like it's gonna be interesting," I said as I finally buckled in properly. The blinking light above stopped.

"Looks like it. We're far enough from the nest now that I think we can allow ourselves to . . . shift the terrain a little. In fact, let me set the stage."

I followed the *Fury* as Gomorrah moved up and away. She started to fly in a long, arcing curve that stretched out for a kilometer or two. Tiny glints of light flashed from something falling from the bottom of her car. Then the *Fury* reached the end and spun around to retrace its path.

"What's that all about?" I muttered.

"I'm creating a wall," she said. When she returned, I could almost *feel* the relish in her voice. "Like this."

Gomorrah triggered something, and suddenly there was fire.

Huge rising balls of flame roared out, the sky flashed orange, and a wall of smoke burst out of the expanding fire and into the air. She had created a kilometers-long firewall. It curved to our left and right, with only one exit . . . right where we were sitting.

"That'll do it," I said. "Will that burn for long enough?" I asked.

The fire was settling already, though more smoke was still rising.

"It'll last," Gomorrah said. "Did you want me to go over the finer details of how this works? The initial explosion was essentially a flash fire, to destroy anything nearby that *can* catch fire. Now the firebombs will just keep a much smaller line of fire going for the next twenty to thirty minutes before extinguishing. It shouldn't spread, if we're lucky."

"And if we're not feeling particularly lucky?" I asked.

Gomorrah sighed wistfully. "Forest fire."

Sometimes I worried.

CHAPTER FOURTEEN

COMBUSTION BEAM

FLAG-TILLERY; OR, FLYING

DISCO BALLS OF DEATH

–We haven't gotten permission yet.

–It'll come. So, anyway, when you connect to the app, you can have the figurine say a bunch of lines. My favorite is "Putting the fire in firepower!"

–Again, we don't have permission.

–And I'm thinking of a line of lighters, matches, and maybe small blow-torches? Flashlights, maybe?

—Overheard discussion about My First Gomorrah dolls, 2057

The swarm came at me with its fastest little guys first. That mostly meant model ones, the flying fucks being way faster than all the rest. And a whole lot weaker too.

"Myalis, can we top-load a few of those air-explosion rounds, like Tank-ette used?" I asked.

Your internal magazines have four empty slots for rounds, but they're not designed to be filled from the top. You'll have to empty your current magazine to the level where the new rounds will be introduced.

I shrugged. Fair enough. I tapped through a few commands and then let my twin Gatling guns rip into the flying part of the swarm. It was the big guns that I needed to empty, and that was just as easy. I took command of the guns, aimed them ahead, then let loose. A barrage of 105mm rounds scythed ahead, curving slightly as I'd aimed a little high and over the front of the incoming swarm. They crashed into the ground some four or five hundred meters away from my position, then exploded.

"What do I have loaded in right now?" I asked as I glanced at a readout on the side. "Oh." They were anti-armor rounds. They had some explosive oomph to them, but nothing too satisfying.

What do you want for anti-air? I have a few options on offer. The size of the guns you have gives you a lot of space for customization.

I fired another pair of shots. "You have three more shots to convince me, I guess. I think we'll go for some HE after that. The twenty-twos shouldn't be *too* tough, right?"

In that case, I'll offer three suggestions. The first is a simple air-burst explosive round. It fires conventional fragmentation all around, with a shaped charge to ensure that local flying targets are prioritized.

Second. A little less conventional, but a monofilament round is available. On discarding its sabot, it deploys a series of spinning lines that create a moving space where everything solid is cut through. Very effective against light flying adversaries.

Finally, as a last option, explosive-powered lasers.

"You're not just going to leave that last one hanging, right?" I asked.

They're chemical laser rounds. When they exit the barrel, the round has targeting software that adjusts a series of sixty-four spiral-set mirrors, then the chemical combustion triggers a split laser to fire for a short duration. It's a kind of flak usually reserved for use in space, but it is good enough for a short-range engagement like this one.

"Okay, well, obviously we're going with the lasers." I shook my head. Why even offer the other two if explosion-lasers was an option from the start?

There was a faint *clunk* as a few anti-air lasers were loaded in. I returned my focus to the field. The Antithesis were now well and truly aware that we were here, and they weren't happy about it.

The model twenty-twos each had a small horde around them, some hundred or so aliens each, and if we didn't cull them, that number would only grow as the big guys snacked on the local vegetation and puked out more lower-tier models.

The first of the twenty-twos showed up in the distance, moving our way with slow, lumbering steps. It wasn't a quick model. Or maybe it was, it just moved slowly, but its size meant that every slow step still carried it a good ways. It wasn't quite keeping up with its little pals, but it wasn't falling too far behind.

Until I plugged two 105mm rounds into its torso and watched them detonate. That slowed it way the fuck down.

There were more model ones coming, a whole flock of them. They had probably zipped ahead from the other model twenty-twos still making their way over.

I fired off the last of my armor-penetrating rounds, emptying the mech's internal magazine before the anti-air rounds were automatically loaded up.

I brought the guns up, which required lowering the mech's rear, since the turrets only had a few degrees of vertical travel. I aimed well ahead of the flock, checked the targeting, then lowered my aim a smidge. Then I fired.

When Myalis had described the rounds, I'd had a certain mental image in mind of flying disco balls of death. Instead, the round moved so quickly that there was no way I could follow it across the sky. What I could keep track of were the searing hot lines etched into the air where the round had passed. They faded quickly enough, but I imagined that if I'd been looking at them with my naked eye, I'd have little lines across my vision for a while.

Hundreds of model ones fell from the sky, very much dead. I aimed to the side, then fired again, then again, blanketing the area with crisscrossing lines of death. A few of the rounds even stabbed down into the horde below, killing some doglike model threes and at least injuring some of the bigger, tougher ones.

"Thanks," Gomorrah said.

"Model ones can't possibly be a threat to the *Fury*," I said.

"They tend to splatter when they die, and while I do enjoy washing my car, I don't enjoy cleaning off alien remains. It's not what I'd call pleasurable detail work."

"If you want, you can clean up my mech," I offered. I hadn't been great about that. Actually, the only reason the cockpit didn't stink of sweat and potato chips was because I didn't spend that much time in here.

"No," Gomorrah refused flatly. Fuck, she might have been on to me. "I'm going to move forward and burn the corpses. We need to find that middle ground between too much fire and not enough."

"I have no idea what you mean, but you go on and have your fun," I said.

The *Fury* darted ahead and I cooled it with the anti-air fire. There were only a few model ones left, in any case, and I figured I could sweep them with some Gatling gun fire.

"Switch me up to high explosive?" I asked Myalis. "I want to blow holes in the swarm."

Done.

My next few shots ended with satisfyingly large craters in the ground and pillars of kicked-up dirt that were at least a hundred meters tall. I found myself chuckling in amusement as I pulled the trigger, watched a pair of big explosions, then shifted to aim at another group.

There were two great pleasures in a woman's life: other women, and fuck-huge explosions.

I paused for a moment as Gomorrah found her own little pleasure, hosing down the carcass of that first model twenty-two with several hundred liters of lit napalm. The corpse barely had time to go all bonfire before it became ash.

I settled back once the *Fury* was a little higher up and dropping spurts of short-lasting fire onto the bigger aliens below it. I didn't want to accidentally catch Gomorrah in the AOE of one of my hits. If I got her car muddy, she'd definitely be on my ass about washing it.

I'd do a terrible job of it, of course, because there was no better way to never be assigned a job again than to do it catastrophically poorly the first time, but still, it would be a wasted afternoon.

The rest of the model twenty-twos eventually came around. They were like massive flies after a pile of shit. Not a gram of self-preservation between the lot of them as they ambled toward us.

I took a lot of pride in lining up a few shots of HE so that they rammed into the meat sacs hanging from their sides. The explosions were even more satisfying when there was organic goop mixed into the mess.

It took nearly forty minutes for the last one to get within mech range. I watched Gomorrah swoop down and light it up, then she splashed some more fire all around. As she flew back, she dropped some explosive charges that lit the entire field up in a sea of low, smokeless flames.

"That ought to do it," Gomorrah said.

"It ought to," I agreed. "Should we go check up on the newbies?"

"We should. I've been glancing at my drone footage every so often. I think they're all safe and sound for now, but the situation has . . . deteriorated somewhat."

"Oh, well shit, that's not something I want to hear," I said as I started turning my mech around.

What kind of shit could a few newbies get into in like, under an hour of unsupervised time?

Fuck, who was I kidding? I could imagine a lot of crap they could get into, and the more I imagined, the faster I pushed my mech.

CHAPTER FIFTEEN

MECH MAKES MIGHT

The issues with mechanized walkers, as in, bipedal mechs, is . . . everything. There is no advantage to any of this. On paper, every aspect of this
design is a disaster waiting to happen!
—Ignored Noeing Engineer Memo, 2048

If I wasn't used to dealing with whining children, I might have been a little
overwhelmed at the level of brattiness I had to deal with when I returned.

"It's not working," Princess said.

"Well, we haven't exactly tried everything, now have we?" Crackshot
shot back.

"This isn't according to protocol. Not that any of you have the faintest
clue what that even means," Hedgehog grumped. Okay, so it wasn't grumpy,
but rather the mature adult man's version of grumpy, which was the same as
his usual voice but with a deeper timbre.

I blinked at the lot of them, then slowly looked over to where Knight
was standing next to Tankette's tank. Neither of them seemed willing to join
in on the incessant whining, which was actually kind of nice.

"Alright, fuckwits," I snapped. That calmed them all down, though I
think it might have pissed off a couple. "Someone needs to tell me what's
going on."

They, of course, all started talking at the same time.

I sighed. "No, no, shut up. Hedgehog, you go first. Gimme a report as if
I'm . . . I dunno, some out-of-town shareholder."

Hedgehog stood taller at that.

When I'd come over, I'd discovered the newbie squad spread out across
a couple of acres. They were bitching over the comms and very clearly not
working out what to do next. Princess and Knight were stabbing at the
ground on one end, Tankette was parked at the back doing nothing, Crackshot was planting explosives into the ground with a sort of post-digger, and
Hedgehog was patrolling the outside area while complaining the hardest.

Nothing practical seemed to be getting done, and it kind of annoyed me. So I had them all gather up in the shadow of that hill we'd fought from earlier, then I got out of my mech so that they could read from my body language. I wanted it to be clear that I wasn't impressed.

"Once you left with Gomorrah, we continued to fight the Antithesis until the area was cleared of living examples," Hedgehog began.

"Alright," I said. So far, so good.

"Then we couldn't decide on how to get rid of the hive. I suspect we all started to take care of things in our own way," Hedgehog said.

"Knight and I were just gonna cut up all of the roots," Princess said.

"And I was planting bombs all over. They're sucky vacuum bombs, they'll rip the area up without tossing too much dust into the air," Crackshot said.

I nodded slowly. "And Hedgehog, you were . . ."

"Waiting for orders," he said.

How did this wet sock become a samurai? "Tankette?"

The tank's hatch opened up and Tankette slowly poked her head out. "Um, well, I didn't want to argue with the others. I was mostly keeping an eye open for any distant aliens that might be coming around."

I couldn't be angry with her. Tankette's mom aura had a critical advantage bonus here. "Fine," I said. "Princess, cutting things is a good idea. Doing it manually is stupid. We have plebs for manual labor. Or robots. Crackshot, better idea, but again, too slow. Hedgehog . . . you *are* the one who gives orders now."

"They didn't seem inclined to listen," he said.

"They're listening to me, and I have no more authority than you do," I said.

The merc opened his mouth, then shut it slowly. I saw him eyeing my mech, and I was sure he was thinking that having that gave me some authority—and he was right—but it was just a big toy that I'd bought, not a sign of any actual authority, and he could buy one for himself eventually. "Understood," he said in the end.

"Right, so, Crackshot's idea is the least useless. Get back up on the hill. You still have those mortar launchers?"

Crackshot nodded. "Thought of using them, but I didn't want to accidentally smack someone down here with 'em."

"Fair. Let's move out of here and load them up. We'll vacuum this entire area up and call it a day." It was probably gonna cut their point-earning short, but fuck it, I didn't feel like sitting out here all damned day long.

The others all seemed either annoyed or a little humiliated as they climbed back up the hill. I actually kind of felt bad for them. Not enough to do anything about it, but like, bad on principle.

"You handled that well," Gomorrah said.

"You do know that I've raised dozens of kids, right?" I asked.

"That's . . . kind of horrific, actually. Did you ever check up on those children now that some are out of your care? Prisons have visitation rights, no?" Gomorrah asked. I snorted. She'd sounded too innocent for a moment there.

"Oh, fuck off. Lucy's connected to all of their socials. I'm pretty sure she's kicking them some credits and shipping leftovers over when no one's looking."

"Truly the better half," Gomorrah said.

I shook my head at that. Not that she was wrong. "So, vacuum bombs? Think that'll work?"

"It should," Gomorrah said. "I'll salt the land afterward. I have a few decontamination drones I can buy. They'll hover around and filter out the topsoil and the water. It'll take a few months, but the area will be clean enough by the end."

I scanned the area at a glance. Lots of broken trees and burnt grass and whipped-up dirt. "Might be a while before this area's safe. I bet there's a few model threes under all that dirt just playing dead or something."

"Very possible. The army will have to look into it," Gomorrah said. "Our job is to kill the hive. Making sure it stays dead either happens as a consequence of how hard we kill it, or it becomes someone's full-time job, at least for a while."

Made sense to me. We'd likely already left a few husks of hives behind us that needed to be scoured. Someone probably earned a nice hourly income making sure every last root was burnt to a crisp.

Gomorrah and I made it to the top of the hill where Crackshot was buying up some crates of ammo. "My AI laid out a grid for us to follow," he said before sending a file out. "Just got to line things up and then we can pull the trigger."

"Oh, can I do it?" Princess asked.

"Yeah, sure thing, kiddo," Crackshot said.

With the mortars loaded up, they started to fire out bombs that rose up and then thumped into the soggy ground. It was nice to see the pattern forming, undetonated bombs every two meters or so in a sort of circular spiral pattern.

I sat back and checked the news while they loaded and fired in sequence. There were some hints that the whole Phobos thing was being leaked. Politicians had been seen panicking about things, and there were lots of celeb-news channels saying that fan-favorites were looking into bunkers all of a sudden.

Some of those were saying that the bunker trend was just an after-effect of the whole global incursion, but it felt like more than that to me, especially knowing the full story.

Poor fucks thought bunkers would save them.

"Alrighty! We're done!" Princess said. She raised both hands as if she were the conductor of an orchestra, then paused. "All clear? . . . Yeah? In that case . . . ka-boom!"

There was, in fact, a rather nice *ka-boom* a split second later. The explosions started in the center of the spiral, then continued outward. They were rather strange, loud pops that had the air in the area visibly sucking inward even as dirt was kicked up on the edges. With each subsequent explosion, the circle grew and the spiral of missing dirt continued to grow.

There were a few last explosions in some nooks and corners, and a row of them along the shoreline that had the lake's water churning, and then it was over.

A few spots revealed some ancient roots from the old trees in the area, liberated at last, and a few other spots looked like the sort of roots I'd expect from a hive.

"Nice work," I said. "Now . . . Gomorrah, what's the next step?"

Gomorrah, who'd relocated to sitting on the hood of the *Fury*, looked my way. I couldn't see her expression from here, but I imagined she was blinking languidly at my attempt to fling responsibility her way. "The next step is returning to Saint-Jérome. The city will survive without us for a few hours, but it'll be better if we're there."

"Good point," I said. "Back to the city, folks!" I said.

Time to go back and see if the army had managed not to set themselves on fire while we were gone for . . . what, four hours?

Even odds, I figured.

CHAPTER SIXTEEN

COMMAND CRITIQUE

It started a few years ago. I was conducting some research for . . . a corp, it was a tangential thing, about radio receiver detection. Anyway, I stumbled across crystal radiography.

Did you know that a crystal is almost all you need to receive a radio signal? Did you know that radio signals are energy? From there, it was so simple. All I had to do was get enough crystals and plug the whole idea into an efficiency AI. Free power! Unlimited free power!
—From the redacted manifesto of the Corpo Bomber, 2046

When we returned, it was to find that the army hadn't been sitting on their hands while we were gone.

The line of tanks out before the wall had been improved. Some tractors were pushing dirt around, and backhoes were piling it up into these little ramps. A few of the ramps were completed, with tanks sitting inside of the pits left in their wake, surrounded on three sides by walls of dirt reinforced with sandbags.

The walls of the city were being shored up too. Some of the fallen sections had been pulled up, and the holes were patched by stacks of sandbags and a long row of barbed wire.

A few temporary towers had been built as well, with machine guns stationed atop them with a clear view over the wall.

Farther in, I could see that the command tent had been relocated deeper onto the highway and more tents had gone up around it. It still looked temporary, but less so than it had when we left.

"They were busy," I said.

"They were," Gomorrah confirmed.

We parked by the edge of the highway, now deep within the protected area that the army had set up. With this level of defense, I wouldn't have been surprised to see them weathering those model twenty-twos after all.

I got out of my mech and landed with a bend of the knee right in front of my big old cat. Tankette was stepping out of her own tank, and the others were coming out of the little armored car we'd borrowed. It had come out pretty dirty, but it was otherwise unaffected by the trip, which was nice.

"Alright," I said with a clap. "Gomorrah and I will be checking in with the brass. Anyone who wants to come can, otherwise . . . I don't know, make yourselves useful. Give the army boys a hand. I bet they're still busy clearing out the city!"

The group split up. Tankette mentioned that she'd see if she could help the army. Princess and Knight decided to head into the city to help with clearing, which made sense. Knight was particularly suited to that kind of work.

Crackshot, meanwhile, chose to plop himself down atop one of those guard towers and see if he couldn't pick off some distant aliens for fun and profit. Which only left Hedgehog following Gomorrah and me into the big command tent.

"Ah, you've returned," Lieutenant Juno said. He greeted us with a quick salute, then gestured deeper into the room. "Good timing. We were going over the strategic analysis just now. May I present to you Major Tinwhistle."

Juno gestured to a tiny slip of a woman in the same kind of army fatigues that the guys outside were wearing, only hers had more mud on them, staining her from boot to mid-shin. She had cybernetic eyes. Not just augs, but full-on cyborg eyes, all black and gunmetal with little red lenses, and one of her arms was fully mechanical as well, though she moved pretty naturally with it.

"As LT Juno said, I'm Major Tinwhistle," the woman said with a voice that sounded like throat cancer warmed over coffee.

"What are you the major of?" I asked.

She sniffed. "I'm the major of keeping things working around here."

"She means that she's the major of the Tenth Engineering Corps," Juno replied. "They've come with resupplies for the forces in place, as well as a number of engineering vehicles, mobile emplacements, and a lot of hard-working people."

"Stop buttering me up, Juno," Tinwhistle snapped. "I'm not gonna fuck you."

Juno opened his mouth, then closed it. There was a smattering of red on his cheeks. Well well, my boy Juno was shooting his shot and getting shot down for it. I respected him just enough not to laugh in his pretty-boy face.

"Well alright then," I said. "Nice to have you around. What was this about a strategic analysis?"

We joined up at another one of those map-projector tables that the army liked so much—for good reason, because they were cool as fuck. Nothing quite like the "standing around a glowing map" aesthetic to set the mood, even if we were in a glorified tent.

"Glad to have you back, Samurai," Brigadier General Thibodeau said as he came up to the table. "Do you wish to start us off? From what I understand, we have good news from the north?"

I nodded, then gestured for Gomorrah to go ahead. She let out a very slight sigh that someone else might have confused for an exhale. "Things went well. Echo Lake is boiling now. That should remove the last remains of the hive from the water in due time without introducing additional contamination to the area. The topsoil was . . . removed via technological means, and the hive was neutralized. We received the points for it as confirmation."

We had? Myalis must have read my mind, because the notification popped up for me.

Targets Eliminated!
Model One . . . 2754 models
Reward . . . 2754 points
Model Three . . . 1901 models
Reward . . . 19,010 points
Model Four . . . 5 models
Reward . . . 75 points
Model Six . . . 24 models
Reward . . . 360 Points
Model Eight . . . 2 models
Reward . . . 10 points
Model Ten . . . 3 models
Reward . . . 3 points
Model Twenty-Two . . . 8 models
Reward . . . 4,000 points
Small Hive Destruction: 500 points
Total Points Earned: 26,712
Points After Partner Share: 4,813
Current Point Total: 38,535

I scanned through the list but mostly focused on the number at the bottom. That point share was . . . well, it was alright, I supposed. Several thousand points was a nice load for a newbie samurai, enough to get a full set of pretty damned good starter gear.

For a mid-tier samurai, which I felt like Gomorrah and I were edging toward, it was . . . not chump change, but it wasn't a ton. We'd be dropping that amount of points on a single piece of gear at our level of things.

Still, the goal had been to give the newbies a leg up, and this would certainly do that.

"—Stray Cat has a comprehensive report on the quality of the new samurai to present," Gomorrah continued.

I blinked, then replayed the last bit in my mind. I had . . . not been listening at all. "Uh, yeah, right. So . . . they're good."

"That's your comprehensive report?" Major Tinwhistle asked.

"Did you not comprehensive a part of it?" I asked. "I can go into more detail if you'd like."

The major crossed her arms, then shrugged a shoulder. "I'm good."

"I wouldn't mind more details," Lieutenant Juno said. Next to him, Lieutenant Colonel Britannica nodded firmly.

I groaned. "Fine. Uh. Tankette's tank is great. Lots of flexibility, which you wouldn't expect from a tank. Kind of one-track, no puns, but it's not that bad in this kind of case. If she grows into her specialization, she'll do fine. Princess is a hot mess, but Knight is actually on the ball. Princess needs to get a gimmick and fast, because being pretty and all dressed up isn't going to keep her from being eaten alive. Her sister's doing a good job of that, though."

I glanced at Hedgehog and he nodded for me to continue.

"Hedgehog here's a problem child," I said. I don't think he was expecting that, because he blinked dumbly at me.

"Pardon?" he asked.

"He was taught a bunch of protocols and would do fine in the army or whatever. He's very by-the-book. Does things just-so. He's super anal about it, and not the fun sort. And it'll get him killed, because the aliens don't have a book they go by, and his tactics are mostly designed to stall for a samurai to show up. But he *is* the samurai.

"Crackshot's cool, though. He's not great at killing hives with his main strat, but he adapted and figured it out. He's got a niche, but he can play outside of it, and he plays well with others."

I turned toward Gomorrah and crossed my arms.

"There, happy?" I asked.

"Yes, actually," she said. "You're very observant, Cat . . . strangely so, for someone who can be so utterly blind."

"What's that mean?" I asked.

Gomorrah shrugged a little, so I gave her side a poke with a knuckle. It didn't do anything, because she was wearing armor, but still, I had to make my annoyance known.

Maybe I'd stink-bomb her car? That had to exist somewhere in the Esoteric Explosives catalog, right? Wait . . . no, she'd just burn down my house in retaliation, and then things would spiral out of control from there.

The look Hedgehog was wearing suggested that I'd already done enough to earn myself some enemies for a day.

"That was insightful, thank you," Juno said.

"Indeed," the brigadier general replied. "On to the meat of this meeting, then?"

CHAPTER SEVENTEEN

LOCAL SORTS OF PROBLEMS

Do you want to die like a coward, or do you want to die with a gun in your hands, goddamnit?!
—Winning slogan of the New Militia of New Montreal under-16 recruitment poster contest, 2041

"Go on, bossman, what's the meat like?" I asked.

The brigadier general gave me a flat look, then gestured to the map. Saint-Jérome was laid out on it, the bigger buildings sticking out a little from the surface. Most of the city was painted in a dull orangey-green, with some clearer greens around a blob to the south and along the northern wall. Green was clear, orange was meh, red would be bad.

"We've set up logistical locations here and here," he said. Two spots of blue appeared, one at the south of the city, the other next to Highway 117. The second one looked like it was a few dozen meters away from where we were right now. "And there's a logistical route from the south to the north using the highway. It's above ground and easy to secure. Patrols are working along that route to keep it clear. So far we have no issues." A thin cyan line linked the southern logistics dump to the northern one.

I nodded along. I wasn't so stupid as to think that logistics weren't important. "How are we doing for supplies?" I asked.

"We have enough to keep all of the troops here garrisoned for three days," Thibodeau said. The brigadier general tapped something in midair, probably a shortcut on his augs, and a spreadsheet appeared on my own augs. Probably vetted by Myalis. "Our food and medical supplies are being stretched by having to accommodate the local militia, but otherwise things are holding steady and within expected ranges."

"The local militia?" Gomorrah asked.

Brigadier General Thibodeau's lips drew into a thin line. "According to the Constitutional Act of 2037, all corporate and civilian organizations have the legal right to military aid in the formation of a militia. There are rules and stipulations that complicate such formations, of course, but Saint-Jérome definitely fits within the parameters for the creation of a temporary militia. Which means we owe them assistance."

"Are we talking about a serious militia, or just people trying to get free food?" I asked.

"Both," he said, sounding a little waspish.

"Sir, if I may?" Juno asked before turning to address us. "The militia here are civilians, police officers, security personnel, some retired army and PMC. They've formed a small guard contingency. Most of them are . . . What do we call military LARPers?"

"Oh," I said. Dudes in tacticool, got it. "Well, if they keep people somewhat safe, I guess there's no harm?"

Juno shrugged. "They can shore up locations of low importance for us at the cost of being inefficient and annoying to handle."

"Moving on," the brigadier general said. "We've managed to clear the obvious Antithesis threats throughout the city thanks to your push earlier today. Now we're doing a two-part quick sweep."

I glanced at the others. Hedgehog was the only one who seemed to know what that meant. "What's that?" I asked. Fuck it, I'd play the role of group idiot then. I was kind of suited for it.

The brigadier general didn't seem to mind. "We're currently sweeping the city street-by-street and looking into every easily accessible building. The Tenth Engineering Corps is inspecting the city infrastructure as well. This sweep is meant to be fast. If aliens are noticed, an appropriate amount of force is called in to deal with them."

"Have you found any?" Gomorrah asked.

"One in four buildings has an alien presence," the brigadier general confirmed. The map lit up with hundreds of red dots, most of them between the middle of the city and the southern end. "The sweep has only reached the center of the city so far. Tagged buildings will be part of the second phase of the quick sweep, which involves sending in armed cleaning crews to verify that there are no spreading aliens."

"Corpse cleanup?" I asked.

Tinwhistle leaned forward a little. "We've commandeered the city's garbage trucks, some of their loaders, and every pickup we can get our hands on that has a decent-sized bed. We're taking the bodies here." She gestured, and a yellow circle appeared south of the city, just outside the walls. "Wind should carry the stink away from the populated parts of the city, so we should be alright."

"If you need any assistance with the incineration process, let me know," Gomorrah volunteered.

Tinwhistle nodded. "Alright. Shouldn't be an issue. We've been doing this since before you were born with few issues."

"Few?" Gomorrah asked.

Tinwhistle grinned. "Had a year where the Antithesis we picked up after this one incursion were fireproof."

"Really?" Gomorrah asked.

"Well, more fireproof than usual. Had to pump up the heat a lot. Incursion started in an automated metal foundry. Temps in there were high as hell. My theory's that they evolved to endure the heat better or something."

Likely just variation models. If you want a better explanation, just let me know.

I nodded, and Myalis seemed to catch on.

The Antithesis models that you're used to seeing are all variants. Technically, Variant-Earth. They are adapted to a moderately high oxygen-nitrogen atmosphere with sunlight within the range typically found on Earth's surface. The normal variant of Antithesis is designed for lower-oxygen environments. These are, overall, very minor adaptations that do little to change the makeup or appearance of the average Antithesis model. A hive that starts in an environment with an elevated temperature will, of course, make some slight modifications to itself and its progeny to better survive in that environment.

That was a bit more of a lecture than I'd planned on getting. The brigadier general was nattering on about something to do with logistics with Gomorrah chiming in, so at least Myalis's rant was well-timed.

Actually, it had been a while since she last went on a long explanatory rant about something, so maybe she was just . . . rant-deprived or something?

That information wasn't meant to make you feel smug.

I switched the mic in my helmet off so that no one else would hear us. "Calm your byte-sized tits, I'm just finding your way of acting funny."

Yes, mocking me is certainly a good move that will have no reprisals or poor consequences.

I rolled my eyes. She was such a drama queen. If she really wanted to mess my day up, she'd do it, not just threaten it.

"Saint-Jérome should be cleared out of any lingering Antithesis within the next two days," the brigadier general said.

"That's good," I said. "So the army will hold here for that long?"

"With . . . the news from the Martian front being what it is, yes. It was determined that staying relatively close to New Montreal would be for the best," he said.

"Is that news classified still?" Gomorrah asked.

That earned her a look of concern from just about everyone in the room, excluding the brigadier general himself. "Yes, it is. It's leaked, of course, but we're keeping a lid on it for now. We need to prepare a reaction to the news that'll keep everyone's minds in the game."

"Are we expecting some mass panic?" I asked.

"No. The Family and the government are both preparing things to quell any sort of panic. A new Family-endorsed samurai-made gacha game will be launching in three days, there are a few major sporting events coming up, and I've heard through the grapevine that some political scandals have been cooked up. The entertainment corps are all-in on the big distraction."

I blinked. "Holy fuck, are *we* the bad guys?"

Gomorrah looked at me, then shook her head. "No. We're doing this for everyone's own good. It's different."

"There is one more thing that might be of interest to you," the brigadier general said. "We've noticed a small town nearby, Saint-Colomban. The town should have been overrun, but the Antithesis have met resistance. It's not corporate, from what we can tell."

"A samurai?" I asked.

"Possibly. We'll be sending someone to meet with them tomorrow morning. With Saint-Jérome retaken, the local Antithesis population has been drastically reduced, so there are fewer of them pushing toward Saint-Colomban. They'll keep until morning."

I frowned. "Wouldn't sooner be better?" There could be a newbie bleeding out over there, and this moron wanted to sit on his thumb instead of checking things out.

"That's the soonest we can get a negotiation team ready," he replied.

"Fuck that," I said. "Gom, we're taking a detour on the way back home, alright?"

"I suppose. And please don't shorten my name to Gom," Gomorrah said.

I nodded and pretended like I wouldn't forget that. The meeting was winding down anyway, so I gave the bunch of them a fake salute, then stomped my way out of the tent.

I hadn't noticed it, but the sun had set already. "Dammit, I'm going to be late for supper."

CHAPTER EIGHTEEN

BETTER THAN SOME, WORSE THAN MOST

The Exodus started in 2031. It was mostly pushed by two factors. The first, the massive reduction in safety in the rural areas of most developed countries.

The second factor was the destruction of a few large corporations that held a monopoly on rentable properties. Prior to late 2030, 84 percent of all rentable properties were controlled in whole or in part by a few corporate entities that set the price for housing.

—*The Exodus*, 2048

"I love you and miss you so much you cannot even imagine," I said the second Lucy picked up.

"Aww . . . so you're going to be a bit late?" Lucy replied.

I groaned. Damn, I was easy to read. I was walking outside of the command tent, on my way to the mech with Gomorrah by my side. Gomorrah looked at me with a slight tilt to her head, and it said something about how much time we spent near each other that I was able to read that as a question. I made the universal "I'm on a call" gesture and she nodded in understanding.

"What's wrong? Please tell me no alien chewed on your perfect ass. I'm the only one allowed to touch it," Lucy said.

I grinned. I didn't know what it was about Lucy, but every time I talked to her things just felt . . . easier? It was like something in my chest unknotted itself at the sound of her voice. It was nice. "Hey, so, no, my perfect ass is perfectly alright. Just . . . had a bit of a day, I guess. Not that bad, but I was babysitting newbies."

"Aww, are they cute, at least?"

"Eh, a little. One of them is bizarrely into me? Like, in a weird way. I can't tell if it's sexual or if she's just stanning real bad, but either way it's creeping me out. I've got a long-ass rant saved up about it."

"Ohhh. I mean, I *get* it, but at the same time, you're off-limits, girl," Lucy said. I could almost imagine her leaning back against something as she listened to me get started. Fuck, I wanted to kiss her so bad.

"Mm-hmm, don't worry, she's creeping me way out. The rest are fine. She's got an older sister who's nice and more sane. Though I did shoot her dad? Anyway, it's a long story. Right now Gom—Gomorrah, I mean—and I are heading out to visit another newbie. The army was going to keep putting it off for too long."

"Oh, more newbies, and that whole thing sounds like a story. We should get into drinking wine so that we can be fancy while you spill!"

I laughed. "I'll look into it," I said just as I reached my mech. Gomorrah stood back while I put a foot on one leg, then tugged myself up without quite getting into the cockpit just yet. It was more comfortable to hang off the side. "Anyway, I'm going to be a few hours late. But I think I'll be taking tomorrow off. The newbies don't need me to scour a city, and there's better shit I could spend my time on."

Not that I wanted to delay things too much. I still needed to rack up as many points as I could in the time we had left before Phobos came down on us. And then, if all went well, there might be the normal delay between incursions again, like it used to be. It might be *months* before there were more aliens to kill besides small cleanups.

How did all the top-tier samurai earn points?

Actually, scratch that, they did it by working for years and not dying in between. Goddamn early-start advantage.

"Are you zoning out again, Cat?" Lucy asked.

"Oh, shit, sorry," I said. "Anyway, I'm gonna be home in . . . eh, two hours maybe?"

"I'll be waiting," Lucy said. "Do you want me to be wearing anything special?" she purred.

I considered it, then sighed. "Your comfiest, fuzziest pajamas?" I asked.

Lucy awwed at me. "I will snuggle you so fucking hard," she whispered. "You have fun now! And be safe! Don't scare the newest newbie too hard with all of your punkness."

"I'll try not to," I said before we devolved into goodbyes. Goodbyes lasted three minutes and included a lot of inane prattle, teasing, and noises that I would literally kill to prevent anyone else from hearing.

We finally hung up, and I had started to climb into the cockpit when Gomorrah flagged me down from a few meters away, where she was standing next to some logistics people. "A minute?" she asked.

"Yeah, sure, what's up?" I asked after flicking a switch to turn on my exterior speakers.

"I've been doing some research on our target," she said.

I shook my head. "Don't call them that. It makes it sound like we're heading out to pop their head off or something."

Gomorrah hesitated, then nodded. "That's fair. You're right. Anyway, the potential samurai. I can't find anything on them, and Atyacus is being silent."

"The whole privacy thing?" I asked. I'd run into that before with Myalis, and it was a bit of a pain in the ass. Still, it wasn't all bad. It went both ways. No other samurai's AI was going to spill about me and mine, and Myalis wouldn't tell me about others. All's fair. "Doesn't stop you from looking into the town, right?"

"I sent that drone I had surveying the new samurai today to do a flyby. I have aerial on the town they're working in. I don't know if it actually counts as a town, really."

"How's that?"

"The place has one gas station," Gomorrah said with some level of disgust. "It's a tiny town, no more than a thousand residents, if that many."

"Huh, real small," I said. "Like a stopping point for cars traveling around?"

She shook her head. "Not even. It doesn't lead anywhere."

"Wow," I said. "And our little baby samurai is hanging out there, huh?"

"I wouldn't call them a baby. We know nothing about them. They could be a grizzled old man for all we know."

I scowled for a bit. "Aren't most samurai younger? And like, disproportionately female?"

Fifty-two percent are biologically female, and the mean age for new Vanguard is twenty-two. To be clear, that's on Earth.

"As opposed to some other world getting eaten up by the Antithesis?" I asked.

Yes.

"Oh." Well, that was a bucket of cold water to the head. "Alright, then! Anyway, got a plan to approach the newbie? I was just gonna walk the mech over. I think it's pretty clear that we're not aliens, it might be a sight for sore eyes."

"From what I've seen, they've set up a camp of sorts in the middle of their town, centered around an old church. They might not be willing to leave if it means abandoning the civilians there."

"Then we tell some army guys to come with. They can watch over the place for a minute while we start evacuating. The place is stable?" I asked.

"Looks like it," Gomorrah replied with an easy shrug.

That was good enough for me.

I grabbed onto the edge of the cockpit, then pulled myself in. "Let the army know to send a little relief group over. Maybe with an escort? I'll clear the roads out."

"I'll follow in a minute," Gomorrah said. "I think I have to make my own phone call. Franny and I were supposed to discuss interior decorating tonight."

"Just have a lot of fireplaces or something," I said. "Actually, no, I live above you. Go for a nice water theme?"

"Cute," Gomorrah said without inflection. "Get going, I'll catch up in a minute."

That was good enough for me. I sat down, remembered to clip my harness in place, then I stood the mech up to its full height and started to walk around along the outer wall of Saint-Jérome. I got a surprising amount of waves from the soldiers hanging around the perimeter. It probably helped that I had the mech swish its tail around and nod its head politely to anyone who waved.

It was nice to be loved, though this was a whole other kind of affection than I was used to.

Or maybe not? It was kind of like having the kittens be happy to see me, but way less personal and a lot more distant?

"Fame is weird and I'm not sure if I like it," I said.

A surprisingly wise sentiment couched in expectedly drab terms.

"I don't actually know what that means, but I'll assume it's some sort of vague insult," I said.

Just a little bit. More of a backhanded compliment, really.

"I ought to backhand you," I said with a grin.

You'd hurt yourself.

I chuckled at that, then focused a little more on the road. Myalis had pulled out a map between here and . . . Saint-Colomban of Medicorp. Myalis might have been in a good mood, because she started pulling up information on the place.

It painted a bleak picture, especially the population graph. There was this huge dip in the mid-30s, people either dying or just leaving. The place had been bought up by some LLC called Medicorp, then abandoned again.

"Seems like a nice place to grow up," I said.

Better than some, worse than most.

"Ain't that how it always is?"

CHAPTER NINETEEN

EXCUSE MY FRENCH

The French language is under siege!

We can't allow global unions and samurai guilds to dictate which language is standardized. We must carve out a space for French in the future, or else our language and culture might very well be lost.

Culture is more important than corporate profits!

—Translation from *The Free Frenchman* newspaper article, 2032

Saint-Colomban of Medicorp was more of a shithole than the aerial photography had suggested.

Getting to the town wasn't all that bad. There was a road from Saint-Jérome that led all the way there, and it was pretty much cleared of any obstacles. There was one minivan turned onto its side with a model three ripping someone's days-old remains out of it, but otherwise the route was quiet.

Antithesis roaming around did mean that shit was still kind of fucky, though. "How long is it going to take to clear this area out?" I asked.

It depends on the amount of effort put into the task. It's very possible that it may take decades. There are some Vanguard who specialize in rooting out infections, but there are only a limited number of those. The current worldwide incursion is a result of not properly sanitizing or containing previous incursions.

Right, that made sense. Unlike normal incursions, this one was all over and all at once. Old hives coming alive after probably growing real slowly for years, hiding away where they wouldn't be noticed.

If we didn't clean up after all of this, then there would just be more of those the next time this kind of incursion happened.

My bet was that there would be a huge push to clean, and then the bills would come in and the embezzlement, effort-to-reward ratio, and lack of urgency would eventually do the whole project in.

It wouldn't even be a question of shooting the right politicians to get it moving. Just plain old human nature in action.

"Fuck, humans are stupid," I muttered.

Certainly not a top-percentile species. But you're not so bad. You're kind of cute. Like a child that's barely able to care for itself, but stretched out across an entire race.

"Okay, ouch," I said. "Not wrong, but still, that hurt. Humanity can't be the only awful race around, right?"

No, honestly, you're genuinely not so bad. Very middling in many ways. Physically, humanity is definitely in the lower percentiles, but you're relatively intelligent, have a capacity for empathy, and are moderately adaptable.

Just what a girl wanted to hear, that she was moderately adaptable!

We came into the town limits of Saint-Colomban. I knew because there was a rusty old sign by the side of the road next to a long-defunct tollbooth that read *Welcome to Saint-Colomban of Medicorp!/Bienvenue à Saint-Colomban-de-Medicorp!*

I slowed my mech down as we got closer to the town. There was a wall around it. Not a real, proper wall, but a wall made of cars flipped on their sides. Some of them had . . . something hanging off the sides on brackets. "What are those?" I asked.

Judging from the serial numbers, those are lithium batteries. They seemed to be acting as an explosive deterrent for anything trying to scale the wall.

Clever, I supposed. There was some barbed wire on top as well, and the line of cars stretched out to the left and right for some ways, wrapping around the center of the town.

I was pretty sure it covered most of the town, actually, because there were all of twenty buildings here.

Oh, sure, the average civilian probably lived in one of the ancient farmhouses I'd passed, or in one of the mobile homes strung along the road, but the town itself was just a collection of a couple dozen more important buildings all squeezed in around one four-way intersection.

I was spotted, of course, because I wasn't trying to be stealthy. I saw some distant figures pointing at my mech, and there were a few screams as I leapt over their wall.

Some two-bit eighty-year-old looking farmer jumped out of a folding chair nearby, spun his big old shotgun around, and fired it point-blank into my mech's side.

I blinked, then carefully checked the damage readouts. "Huh, nothing," I muttered.

It was buckshot.

Well, that tracked. I turned the mech's head his way, and the farmer stumbled back, falling into his chair while clutching his gun. I couldn't decide if I was annoyed, pissed, or just felt bad for the guy. I settled on leaving him be when there was some noise out ahead.

Saint-Columban's one intersection had a building on every corner. A general store on one, a large trucker's gas station across from that, and then a pair of bigger buildings. One was an dilapidated medical clinic, the Medicorp logo rusting on its side. The building across from that looked like a town hall of some sort.

Most of the people coming out to see what was going on were coming from the old Medicorp place.

It looked like they'd turned it into living space for the locals. There were tents and mobile homes in the back, and now that I was looking, Old-Man-Shoots-First who had pinged me with his shotty wasn't alone. There was a ring of guys sitting on the inner side of their wall.

One guy stood out, because he was walking in the middle of the pack. Or rather, the pack was harassing the poor fucker. A few old ladies, some beer-bellied guys with that strut that people who think they're in charge have. He looked one pinched cheek away from going ballistic.

His gear was newbie samurai-chic. Cool jacket, some pants with a few holsters worked into them, what looked like an armored undersuit. He had some sort of two-pronged rifle thing slung over his back. Definitely not normie tech.

"Looks like we've found the local," I muttered as I walked my mech over and pulled the tabs to open the cockpit.

The mech's head swung open and I stood up with it. From up there it was easy to look down on the newbie and his entourage.

"Laisse-moi tranquille, câlisse," he snapped at the people around him.

I blinked before my augs—or Myalis's auto-translate?—kicked in and displayed a line of text on the bottom edge of my vision. Probably Myalis, because the translation seemed more . . . intent-based than literal. *Leave me alone, for fuck's sake.*

One of the chubbies next to the newbie patted him on the back. "Tu sais qu'on est juste là pour t'aider, petit gars." *You know we're just here to help you, little guy.*

Little Guy (God, that'd be a terrible samurai name, the poor fuck) shook the hand away and walked closer to the mech.

The entourage didn't get the memo and stepped up after him. "Hey," I said. "I'm here to talk. Do you need this whole bunch with you?"

He frowned for a moment before shaking his head. "Non, j'suis bien tout seul." *No, I'm fine alone.*

"Hé, p'tit gars, on est là, t'as besoin de nous, hein?" one of the guys said. *Hey, lil guy, we're here, you need us, don't you?*

I cleared my throat. I didn't have a great idea of what was going on here, but I had an inkling. The locals were being overbearing fucks. They didn't seem to *get* how samurai operated most of the time. And Little Guy here was too shy to shoot them about it.

"My French is a little rusty," I said. "But how do you put this . . . Décalisse or I'll décalisse you . . . uh . . . tabarnak?"

The village idiots looked at me a little gobsmacked. Then they took in the very large mech covered in very large guns and decided that the better part of valor was not getting fucked up. They backed off, though I noticed that they still lingered some two dozen meters off. Not close enough to overhear, but . . .

"Your fan club is annoying," I said.

"C'est pas un fan club, c'est un tas de vieux envahissants qui pensent que j'suis le nouveau Jésus. Ils me cassent les pieds depuis q'tout a dérapé." *It's not a fan club, it's a bunch of overbearing old people who think I'm the new Jesus. They've been riding my ass ever since shit went sideways.*

He looked at me, then gave me one of those guy nods, with the whole chin thrust.

"Pis, t'es qui et tu fais quoi ici? T'es un samouraï, correct?" *So, who are you, and what're you doing here? You're a samurai, right?*

Fuck, I was regretting not paying more attention to the Frenchies around the city when I was younger. There'd been a lot of them around, and they were probably the second biggest group in the city, but I didn't run in the same circles most of the time. They were more common out east.

"Yeah, I'm a samurai," I said. "I'm Stray Cat, and the one coming in behind me is Gomorrah. We heard that you were here and wanted to make sure you were managing. The army's sending some folk over to help, but they'll only be arriving tomorrow afternoon."

"Ah, bien, thank fuck," he said with the strongest accent I'd heard in a while.

CHAPTER TWENTY

FEED ME IN THE SHOWER

There are still pockets of French people all across Canada. You just need to look for them.
Try using your sense of smell. It's sometimes more accurate than judging them visually!
—*Rhubarb Pie's Guide to Hating the French*, fifth edition, 2051

"So, you don't need help?" I asked.

Charles, pronounced with an accent that liked to pretend that the letter R was sexier than it ought to be, shook his head. "Non, ça va. Ouais, les locaux sont des imbéciles, mais je les connais depuis presqus toujours. J'vais m'assurer qu'ils soient en sécurité, et si l'armée peut aider, tant mieux." *No, I'm okay. Yeah, the locals are idiots, but I've known all of them almost forever. I'll make sure they're safe, and if the army can help, that's great.*

I nodded along. Charles, who really needed a samurai name sooner rather than later because this was getting awkward for me, seemed like a pretty down-to-Earth kind of guy. "Right, do you intend to stay around here forever, then?" I gestured at Saint-Colomban in its entirety. It wasn't a very big gesture.

Charles grinned at that. "Peut-être qu'après, j'irai à Nouveau Montréal, ouais." *Maybe afterward, I'll go to New Montreal, yeah.*

I patted him on the shoulder, then took in the space. Charles had decided to give me a quick tour, which really wasn't much.

The gas station was their main staging ground. Behind it was a used car dealership, which was probably where they got all of those lithium batteries to act as booby traps and the cars that formed parts of the wall around the center of town.

Most of the civilians were sequestered to what Charles just called "Medicorp." Well, he said it in French, but I got the idea. It was probably a nice, modern-looking building . . . twenty years ago.

"What happened to Medicorp?" I asked.

"Dead," he replied. "La compagnie est arrivée ici il y a bien longtemps, avant même que je sois né. Ils faisaient des tests sur les enfants et les femmes enceintes dans la région. Mais ils fournissaient aussi des soins gratuits pour les deux." *The company showed up here way back in the day, before I was born even. They were doing tests on kids and pregnant women in the region. But they provided free care for both too.*

"Okay, I'm assuming there's some very sketchy shit that went down?" That'd track with . . . everything I knew about pharmaceutical companies.

"C'est de la marde, ça commence même pas à couvrir le truc. Ils essayaient de rendre les gens résistants à ces criss de petits vers extrater-restres qui transforment les gens en zombies." *Sketchy shit doesn't begin to cover it. They were trying to make people resistant to those little worm aliens that zombie people.*

"Oh, great, human experimentation? That tracks." There was no sane reason a medical company would have a location out in the middle of nowhere like this unless they wanted to be far away from prying eyes.

Charles complained about a few things while giving me the tour. Mostly it was a tirade about the locals being both too eager to help and too useless to actually get anything done right. He was facing some pretty stiff resistance from older community members who'd seen him as a baby, which was . . . fair, actually.

If one of the kittens became a samurai, I'd probably still baby them a little.

Well, I was also a samurai, so I could get away with it. A more accurate comparison would be if Lucy was the one doing the babying . . . which she would.

"Alright, so it looks like you've got things . . . halfway under control," I said. Gomorrah had come over, but the *Fury* was just hovering there close to my mech. I half expected her to drive off, but I also wanted to bum a ride back home.

"Je m'arrange, et je peux gérer les choses ici sans trop de problème. Il y a eu moins de plantes aujourd'hui. Je pense qu'on va survivre." *I'm figuring it out, and I can manage things here without too much trouble. There have been less plants today. I think we'll survive.*

I patted him on the shoulder, then stepped back. "Alright, well, your AI probably knows how to ping mine. Don't be shy. And good luck."

Was I being rude by just leaving the kid? Probably.

Was it past ten p.m. and was I bone-fucking-weary? Also yes. I just wanted to go home, eat something warm, take a shower, and hug Lucy. It didn't even need to be in that order.

Gomorrah lowered her car enough that I was able to hop in. "Yo," I said as I slumped into the passenger seat.

"Did that go well?" she asked with a nod in the direction of Charles, who was surrounded by his posse again.

"Pretty well. Nice enough kid. Fuck, I'm calling him kid but he's like, seventeen-ish? Anyway, the locals are overbearing asses, but he's handling them well enough. He needs some space to grow, I think. Oh, and he's super French. He should learn English."

"Maybe you should learn French?" Gomorrah suggested.

"Ah, fuck, that sounds like a lot of work. They've got like . . . verbs and shit."

"Catherine . . . No, never mind. Are you leaving your mech here?"

I shrugged. "Might as well. Army's only arriving in the morning, right? If shit goes down, I can probably remote-operate it, and it has a decent auto-pilot, so it can help out if the town gets attacked overnight."

I'd just recall it to Saint-Jérome when I went back there.

"If it helps, I don't intend to head to Saint-Jérome tomorrow," Gomorrah said.

"You don't?"

"For cleanup? It'd be a waste of our time. There's a lot we can do to pre-pare New Montreal for the arrival of Phobos. Even just being seen at work might help. I have some purchases to make as well. Upgrades and the like. I'm replacing my bones, which will take a moment."

I blinked. Fuck, being with samurai was weird sometimes with the ran-dom shit they—we—just dropped into a conversation. "Well, have fun with that," I said with a shudder. "I guess I'll take a day off too."

"I'm not taking a day off, I'm focusing on other work."

"Ah, alright," I said. That was fair. I could think of about a million things I could do tomorrow that would eat up my whole day, and half of those were just checking up on projects. Sure, like, a tenth of those things were also hanging out with Lucy or the kittens, but that was important too, for like . . . my mental health or something.

"Looking forward to being home?" Gomorrah asked. Then she reached up and removed the mask covering her face. She let out a sigh of relief as she placed it on the console.

"Yeah. Man, today felt like it went on forever."

"Just a normal day on the job," she said. "Honestly, though, you handled it well. You're good at the whole leadership thing."

"Nah," I dismissed, but Delilah shook her head and denied my denial.

"You are. You don't want to be, maybe, but you are. You could start something with the momentum you have."

I shook my head. "No. Not that I can't, I'm pretty sure I could start something. Lucy could help, and maybe I could hire some work out to oth-ers. Grab some of the newbies from today to help too."

"And I'd help as well, depending on your vision," Delilah said.

"Well, that's the issue. I don't have a vision. Unless sitting at home in PJs and cuddling for the rest of my mortal life counts as a vision?"

Delilah glanced my way. "You never dreamed big?"

"Delilah, where I'm from, dreaming big meant hoping that you'd get adopted by someone who wasn't a freak or a weirdo, getting a cushy corpo job, and eating three square meals a day until your heart gives out. Dreaming *really* big means maybe adding an apartment of your own to that vision, and maybe a kid or two if you're inclined that way."

"Oh," Delilah said. "Sorry, I sometimes forget that we had very different upbringings."

"That different? I mean, I know you have family, but weren't you raised at the convent?"

"Yes, but my family is . . . upper middle class, I suppose. They just wanted a well-raised daughter. Most of the girls at the convent are from families that earn enough to be able to send their children to such a place. It's not exactly cheap."

Huh, right. It wasn't a charity they were running, which naturally meant that it was for-profit. "For-profit religion, huh?"

"Aren't all of them? How much is God worth to you?"

"That's the edgiest shit I've ever heard you say, and you'll wax poetic about burning things," I said.

Delilah sniffed, but there was a slight smile there. "We're almost home. You can hug Lucy, take a shower, and eat. Maybe all at the same time?"

"Ohh, Lucy feeding me in the shower. That'd be a new one," I said.

"Urgh. I regret making the joke now."

I laughed until we were home.

CHAPTER TWENTY-ONE

FUZZIES, FRIES, FLAKING

Bio-Meat: Nectar of the Gods is the newest and greatest skincare cream from Genericorp! Only the best Antithesis extract to make your skin shine!

—Genericorp ad, 2031

The elevator dinged as it came to a stop on our floor. I closed my eyes, then opened them again. I was tired. Not stupidly tired—I'd woken up late, after all—but still, it had been a long day. I was itchy, I had been running around for hours, and I was sore in a few places that I wasn't used to being sore in.

That last bit was probably from riding my mech around so much. It had me sitting in a weird way and tensing some of the muscles in my core for a while.

Well, whatever. The door opened onto my floor, and I started to push in only to stop once I noticed that someone was standing in my path.

Lucy, and she was wearing the furriest outfit I'd ever seen. She was wearing a sort of jumpsuit made of fuzzy material, with a large hoodie tugged over her head. It had large, floppy cat ears, and a string of bedazzled text across her chest read "The Fuzziest."

"Oh, wow," I said.

Lucy grinned from ear to ear like the cat who'd caught . . . the other Cat? I was too tired for analogies. "Do you like it?" she asked.

"I *really* want to hug you," I admitted.

"Good! Come." Lucy reached out and grabbed my hand, my real one, in hers. She tugged me along after her, and I finally noticed that the pajamas had a foot-long tail at the back. It was stumpy, and very cute. "I have food for you!"

"Oh God, food," I murmured. As Lucy escorted me to the kitchen and I discovered four bags from four different fast-food places, I also discovered that I could not be any more in love. "You're beautiful," I said.

Lucy's smile somehow turned even more smug. "Damn right," she murmured. "Want to know what I'm wearing under here?"

I thought I was too tired to be horny, but as it turned out, I was very wrong. Maybe I was more thirsty than hungry after all.

The food was junk. Burgers and fries and pseudo-chicken sticks with seventeen flavors of dipping sauce in little plastic sachets. I stuffed my face while Lucy relocated herself across from me. She stole the longest fry from one of the packets and started nibbling on the end.

"Not eating?" I asked.

She shook her head. "I sat at home all day, I don't want to get fat eating all . . . seven thousand calories here. You at least have the excuse that you're moving around a lot."

"Hmm," I said. Lucy had always been good about that kind of stuff; dieting and the like. I was just blessed with a good metabolism and the jitters that kept me moving all the time. "This is so bad for me, isn't it?" I asked as I chewed on what I was pretty sure was a fried stick of fried cheese. Double-fried. I could taste the cholesterol, and it was beautiful.

"Busy day, then? You mentioned newbies?"

"Oh yeah," I said. "I think . . . one of them's like, off her rocker. Girl by the name of Princess."

"That's cute, at least," Lucy said.

"Yeah. She's cute too, I guess. A bit gangly, but growing into it. She's also got crazy eyes."

"Ohhh, crazy eyes," Lucy said. "Hot but dangerous."

I nodded. "Exactly. She's got this weird obsession with me."

"She's the one whose sister's father you shot?" Lucy asked. She'd been paying attention to our call earlier, then.

I hummed. "They're the mayor's daughters," I said.

Lucy gasped. "No! That's . . . no way! That's some soap opera shit, Cat."

"I know!" I said before shoving a burger into my mouth. It took some chewing before I could continue. "If there's any amount of clones, or resurrections, or . . . people getting pregnant after cucking someone, I'm quitting this business."

Noted.

I blinked. What did that mean? But Myalis didn't seem ready to explain. I finished my burger while going over my day. I hadn't realized how stressful it had been until I could literally feel the weight lifting off my back. All Lucy had to do was smile, steal a few more fries, and ask a few probing questions.

She was too good for me.

"Shower next?" she asked. She fluttered her eyelashes in a way that made my heart flutter too.

"Only if you'll join me," I said with a grin, starting to stand up.

Lucy laughed, then jumped out of her chair and ran ahead of me. I caught up with her in our bedroom, grabbing her from behind in a hug that pulled her close to my chest. I peppered her neck and the side of her face with kisses while she continued to laugh, then she turned in my grasp and started to remove my suit.

Which was when we both realized that the new skin I was wearing came with a nasty side effect that I'd kinda forgotten about. Notably, that my old skin was peeling right off. "Oh, fuck," I said. The inside of my suit was covered in a fine, goopy dust. I retched. I was expecting to maybe be a little sweaty but . . . not this.

"Oh, that's nasty," Lucy said. "Yeah, sorry, shower first, and alone. I'm gonna go get like . . . a sponge. Also, I'm not cleaning your suit!" The last part was called back over her shoulder as she slipped away.

"Fuck, I forgot," I muttered as I slipped over to the bathroom, still mostly clothed. There was no way I was gonna let all of this skin fall onto the floor. That was gross. "Hey, my suit's waterproof, right?"

Yes. From the inside and without.

"Great," I said as I started the shower and got in fully clothed. The fact that some Antithesis blood that pooled off me was also kind of gross, but not nearly as bad as the skin-goop. I stripped, aware of the strange and disgusting pull of my suit against my skin. Lucy returned brandishing a sponge that I recognized from next to the sink (which meant it had never been used) and . . . "Is that a toilet cleaner?" I asked.

"It's a necessary evil," Lucy said.

"Is it *new?*" I asked next.

"New enough?"

"No!" I said, putting my metaphorical foot down. My actual feet were still caught in the legs of my skinsuit. The irony of that name wasn't escaping me at the moment.

I managed to slough out of the suit and let it flop wetly in the corner of the shower. I'd give it a good hose-down later. I did accept the sponge from Lucy and started to scrub away at myself. It stung like a bitch.

"You never told me of the downsides of this," I said to Myalis.

It's a moderate amount of dirtiness. The skin was your skin just moments ago and is no more dirty than you usually are. It's mostly inert organic material. Nothing you need to worry about.

"It's still gross," I said. "Is it at least done? The skin-shedding, I mean."

It should be. Your newer, more resilient skin will, of course, shed at a much-reduced rate.

Wow, I never wanted to have this conversation again. The only plus side was that I was basically hairless now. No more shaving my legs, which was nice. I settled under the warm water, then, once I was done scrubbing myself raw, I tossed the sponge aside and punched the air a few times.

"What are you doing?" Lucy asked from just outside the shower.

"I've got new nerves," I said. "I'm testing them a little. I mean, I've had them for a day now. I think I've just . . . gotten used to them? It doesn't *feel* that different."

Humans will adapt to such changes with startling rapidity.

I wasn't so sure about that. It had taken me months to get used to only having one arm. Then again, maybe that was pretty fast? "Yeah, I guess this feels pretty good," I said.

"I mean, I don't mind the show," Lucy replied. "Very jiggly. They should put naked shadow-boxing on TV."

"Bet you anything they have," I said.

Lucy didn't take the bet.

I stumbled out of the shower and into Lucy, who was holding out a big towel from the ends. She wrapped me up in a hug, climbing onto the tips of her toes to smush her cheek against mine. "Thank you," she said.

"For what?" I asked.

"For making it back safe again." She turned her head a little and gave me a peck on the cheek. "You smell much nicer now," she said. "Not that I really mind it when you smell like gunpowder and smoke. It's kinda hot."

"Is it, now?" I asked.

"Mm-hmm. I never did show you what I was wearing under these pajamas, did I?" Lucy asked.

It was nothing.

CHAPTER TWENTY-TWO

LAZY PILLOW TALK

Just because a samurai has an impossibly powerful AI at their beck and call does not mean that the impossibly powerful AI is there to do the samurai's bidding.

They're kind of smart enough to not care about little human issues.

—Three Swipes, 2034

So, as it turned out, having whole new nerves made sexy-time with Lucy a whole lot more . . . intense.

Which might have explained why I woke up to find Lucy sitting up against the top of the bed, looking impossibly smug even though her hair was a mess and her new fluffy pajamas were stretched out. "Good morning," Lucy said. "Or should I say 'oh God oh God' morning?"

"Stooooop," I whined as I turned over and buried my face into Lucy's stomach. The pajamas really were sinfully soft. Maybe the new skin helped with that too, or the nerves. In either case, I never said no to the opportunity to rub up against Lucy.

"Do you have a long day planned today?" Lucy asked.

"No, I'm staying in bed all day," I said. "And tomorrow too, and the day after. In fact, I'm just not leaving."

I can see that quickly growing unsanitary.

"Shush, Myalis, you're a key part of this plan," I said.

Lucy giggled, which made her abs bounce. Her hand alighted on my head and started to comb her fingers through my hair. "I don't think we can stay in bed forever. What will we do for food?"

"Order out," I said. "It's easy. The kittens can carry it to us."

Lucy hummed. "Okay, and exercise? We're going to grow all weak if we stay in bed all day."

I turned my head so that I could meet her eyes. "I can think of one or two ways to do cardio in bed," I murmured.

Lucy laughed and poked my cheek. "Silly. What about the washroom?"

I groaned. "Diapers?"

"Ew, Cat, that's gross," Lucy said.

I'm assuming some elaborate system of catheters and a cocktail of medication is unfavorable?

"Oh, no, that's . . . Myalis, you're ruining my plans," I said as I spun over. Now my head was on Lucy's lap. The bed was so big that my feet weren't even over the edge even though I was lying parallel to Lucy.

Good. I don't want a lazy Vanguard.

"Is Myalis being a bully?" Lucy asked.

Tell her the truth.

"Yes," I said. "She doesn't want me to spend the rest of my life in bed, Lucy. She doesn't love me the way you do."

"I don't know, I think I'm okay with you not spending your life in bed too," Lucy said.

I gasped and pressed a hand over my heart. "Lucy, no," I said. "I wouldn't be alone. You'd be in bed with me forever too!"

"But I have to pee," Lucy whined.

"Nope! No leaving, you're stuck here forever. I said so, and I'm bigger and stronger and I know all of the spots where you're ticklish." I wiggled my fingers and Lucy gasped at the betrayal. Suffice to say, it took another hour before we got out of bed, and it really only happened because Lucy was cry-laughing and had to run to the washroom.

I checked the time on my augs as I sat on the edge of our bed. "So, what's on the agenda for today?" I asked.

This might surprise you to learn, but I'm not actually your secretary.

"Urgh, I know. I should buy like, some secretary software or something."

I could get you something like that. The Scheduling Software catalog is a mere fifty points, and the most basic software package is relatively inexpensive.

I flopped backward on the bed so that I was staring at the ceiling again. "Why is that even a thing?" I asked.

Because it might be useful? Logistics are important.

"I guess. I meant more . . . like, there're catalogs for all sorts of things, right? But aren't most of them for killing aliens and keeping people alive?"

Of course not. Those are merely the catalogs most frequently purchased and used by Vanguard, which only makes sense, seeing as how the average Vanguard spends a statistically significant amount of time in and around combat. The actual marketplace contains trillions of non-combat-related items, from home goods to foods to comfort items.

"So do, like, the average citizens of elsewhere have the same access I have?" I asked.

No. That would be irresponsible.

Well, that was something. I flexed and sat up again, then finally stood. It was ten minutes to noon, which meant that if I didn't get up and moving now I wouldn't be able to claim to have started my day in the morning.

"Alrighty," I said. "Breakfast, while it's still technically time for that, then . . . Shit, I have a lot to do today, don't I?" I wasn't sure where to start. Checking up on the newbies was somewhere on the list, but they didn't need me to mother them, and I'd be going back to Saint-Jérome tomorrow anyway. I was sure they could manage to burn the place down while I wasn't there to keep an eye on them, but I doubted it. Tankette and Hedgehog were too responsible.

So, more local problems, then. The sewers needed checking up on, the Family needed to be poked at to make sure they weren't fucking up, and my prosthetics clinic a floor down had to be looked into.

Yeah, that all made some sense, but probably not in that order.

Clinic first, since it was an elevator ride away and I could check up on it relatively quickly. It'd be one thing off the list right away.

"Ah, fuck, I need to look into Raccoon too," I muttered.

She's in the building now.

I blinked, then tapped into my augs. Myalis, being somewhat helpful for a non-secretary, pulled up a visual feed of Raccoon's location, which was the armory next to the matter reconfiguration machine. She was glaring at a heap of fuzzy pajamas and stacking them off to the side.

Alright, new plan!

But first, food. Lucy was already cooking things in the kitchen, humming a happy little tune and shaking her hips from side to side while premade omelette mix fried and popped in a pan on the stove. I watched her hips swaying and the little tail on her pajamas bouncing from side to side for a while before I came up behind her and gave her a hug. "Hungry," I said.

"You are so whiny today," she said as she tilted her head back to give me a kiss.

"I'm suffering from success," I said. "It's unbelievably hard."

"I bet," she said. "Now scooch, and grab a plate, this is almost done."

I grabbed a bowl instead, the superior food receptacle, and gladly accepted the omelette Lucy rolled into the bowl. I poured an unhealthy amount of ketchup on top of it all before digging in.

"Plans for the day?" Lucy asked. She sat across from me and I was momentarily distracted by the zipper on the front of her pajamas being very open.

"Yeah, a few things to look into. The clinic downstairs, the sewer situation. Shit that needs to be watched before it falls apart."

"Oh, don't forget the imminent end of the world," Lucy said. "With that Phobos rock."

"Oh yeah, that too," I agreed. I hoped that someone had come up with a plan for that already. It kind of felt like it was a big enough problem that it was way out of my jurisdiction.

I finished shoveling food into my mouth, then wiped my face clean. "I'm gonna get dressed," I said. "Then . . . I think I might bully Raccoon into coming with? That girl needs a good influence in her life."

"And that's you?" Lucy asked teasingly.

"I came out alright." I said with a grin.

Of course, as I went to get dressed, I discovered the skinsuit I'd left in the bathroom, still full of . . . me. That wasn't going to cut it. Sure, I could clean it, but nothing short of Delilah going at it with her flamethrower would leave that clean enough for me.

"Hey, I bought a blueprint for skintight armor, right?" I asked.

You did. Specifically for Raccoon to armor herself.

Right. There'd been some vague plan to make okay-enough armor available for anyone who might need it. "Well, might as well check in on that printer after all. I don't think I've ever had to use it myself, now that I think about it."

Rac was still in the printer room when I came in. She blinked and stared at me, then nodded. "Hi," she said.

"Hey," I replied. "I need a new set of armor. Are you using the machine?"

"I'm . . . not? I was going to make bullets, but that can wait. Are you just wearing a T-shirt?"

"I slept in it," I said.

"It's past noon."

"I had a long night?"

Maybe convincing Rac that I was put-together enough to serve as a good influence was going to be harder than I had initially expected.

CHAPTER TWENTY-THREE

DR. MYALIS, MEDICINE AI

The International Air Quality Index, IAQI, or "Yacky," is an internation-
ally accepted standard for the air quality in and around various metro-
politan areas across the world. For example, Paris, France, has an IAQI of
4.5, whereas Novaya Moskva, Russia, has an IAQI of 5.1.

Pre-Antithesis, Chad had an IAQI of 5.2, and the current North
African Exclusion Zone has an IAQI of 7.6. In contrast, the Antarctic
Circle, unaffected by most pollutants and about as pure as air can be on
Earth—mostly seeing as how the air pockets in that region come from
freshly melting ice!—has an IAQI of 2.1.

Pure, fully filtered air in a medical operating room has an ideal IAQI
of 2.0.

—International Air Quality Index brochure, 2054

I eyed Rac properly for a minute or so. I'd like to think that I was pretty
decent at sniffing out when someone wasn't in the best of shape. Rac
looked . . . well, not that bad. She'd slept recently, judging by the lack of bags
under her eyes. But she still looked too thin and too small for her age.

"Have you been eating?" I asked.

"Yeah," she said, instantly sounding defensive in a way that told me she
wasn't. Or maybe . . .

"Like, actual food?"

Rac crossed her arms. "Coco always made sure that we ate before and
after a mission," she said. "She had these disgusting protein shakes she
insisted I drink."

Coco, the large gorilla-modded woman whose crew Rac had joined.
There was a lot of past tense in that whole statement. "Are you still working
with her and the others? Spider and . . . what was that other guy's name? The
one you had a crush on?"

"I didn't have a crush on anyone," she lied. "And it was Garter."

"Was?"

Rac crossed her arms. "Was."

I decided not to poke at that too much. It felt like she might be a bit raw about it still. So instead I walked over to the printer and tapped the touch screen on the front of it. The printer had a pretty easy UI, with no ads popping up or demands to join some subscription or whatever.

It didn't take much to navigate the menus over to armors, then armored skinsuits. The problem was that when I clicked on one of the decent-looking options, I was then prompted to fill in some "basic" information.

Information like my bust size, waist size, the circumference of my thigh, knee, and calf, the length of each leg, the kind of arch on my foot . . . Honestly, I just kept scrolling down in growing horror. This was asking for about eighty measurements.

"Oh, yeah, it's like that," Rac said. "I have a measuring tape somewhere."

"Why?" I asked.

"Because it's not one-size-fits-all?" Rac asked. "It's made for one person only."

"Damn, bespoke shit huh? Actually, that's kind of what I've gotten used to with Myalis . . . speaking of which. Myalis, bit creepy to ask, but do you have my measurements?"

I don't think it's necessarily creepy in context. You wouldn't think that a medical professional being aware of your blood sugar or cholesterol levels or body weight would be "creepy," would you?

"Yeah, but you're not my doctor. Not that I've ever had one. Wait, are you what it's like to have a doctor?" I asked.

Rac was giving me a look now, but I ignored it.

Let me just input the data for you.

The page I was on auto-filled and I smiled smugly at the victory before pressing "print." The machine clunked, then hummed, and I got to see a 3D scan of the skinsuit being made on the screen. It was pre-folded into a small package already. A timer popped up, and I blinked at it. "Forty minutes?"

"That seems reasonable?" Rac said. "It's fast for a print of something that good."

"Yeah, but that's forever. Urgh. Come on, Rac, you need to eat, and I don't feel like waiting alone."

Rac's expression was unreadable as I tugged her along after me. We returned to the main part of the house, then went into the kitchen. It was mostly empty, except for a single kitten sitting at the island in the center of the room and staring off into space.

"Heya, Nose," I said.

Nose turned my way, then smiled. "Hi, Cat," he said. "Hi, Rac. Are you becoming a kitten too?"

"No," Rac denied immediately.

"Okay," he said. "Cat, you need to help me."

"With what?" I said as I abandoned Rac by the counter and opened the fridge. It was filled to the brim with leftover bags from about seven different delivery places. Interestingly, one of them was from the Burlington branch of Lucy's Kittens. Did . . . did they do delivery all the way here?

Nose took a deep breath from his, well, nose, then turned to face me. "The others don't want to play in the same room as me anymore. I have to sit here and play on my augs. Bargain started it."

"That sounds dickish. What, are you letting some nasty farts rip in the same room as them?" I asked. Was Nose the one who was lactose intolerant? Not that we got lots of stuff to eat with actual milk in it.

Nose shook his head. "No! Just because I sneezed in his face."

"That's disgusting," Rac said.

"It was an accident!" Nose replied. "I'm not used to my nose tingling so much!"

"Was it just the one time?" I asked.

He squirmed in his seat. "They kicked me out after the sixth . . . seventh? I don't know, I wasn't counting."

"Yeah, gonna agree with Rac on this one, that's nasty," I said. "Did you at least cover your mouth?"

"It's too sudden," he complained. "Daniel told me to wear a mask, but I hate those."

It could be an aftereffect of his healing. From the records I have, Nose's olfactory system had a significant amount of damage from his environment, poorly implemented stopgap cures, and genetic damage caused to him before birth. The nano-repair suite that cured him also likely left his nerves somewhat raw.

I nodded as I continued to search for something to eat. How could the fridge be so full and yet so empty at the same time? "Myalis says that it's because your nose is too new," I said.

That is inaccurate.

I ignored my AI and continued. "It'll probably pass in a bit. Maybe go take some air to burn your new nerve endings?"

I would strongly suggest the opposite. The air quality of New Montreal is exceptionally poor. Given time, he will likely lose the reflexive sneezing action. It should be fading already.

"Actually, scratch that. Just . . . keep on keeping on, and stop sneezing in people's faces. Learn to cover up." Nose grumbled, but he didn't gainsay me about it. "Ah, come on, the others won't kick you to the curb about it, they're just being dicks. If they don't stop, you can hire Rac here to kick their asses. She's a big fancy merc, you know? I bet she'd work for food."

"I . . . wouldn't," she said, very unconvincingly.

I grinned as I laid out a healthy breakfast for Rac and she eyed the food as if she hadn't eaten in a week. "Let's see about that. What were your plans for the day, by the by?"

"I didn't have much?" she said, uncertain.

"Cool! You can tag along, then."

"Is that smart?" she asked.

"You've got some armor, right? Carry that big gun of yours and get some face covering on and no one will mess with you."

"You can't just go anywhere while armored and armed," she said.

I snorted. "It's *easier* to get places with arms and armor," I said. "But in any case, you'll be with me. No one will bother you."

"Why do you want me to come?" she asked.

That actually gave me pause. Did I need Rac to come along? No, not really. In fact, it might slow me down and complicate things, if anything. On the other hand, I wouldn't mind the company and . . . I liked Rac. She reminded me of my second favorite person; myself. Only somehow Rac's situation was even worse, because I at least had Lucy and the other orphans to lean on and give me a purpose, and Rac had nobody.

"Just . . . trust me?" I said. I didn't have a good reason, really, but it might be good for her anyway. Open some doors, meet some people, maybe give her the contacts and know-how she'd need to do . . . whatever it was she was aiming for.

Something told me that Rac wouldn't be able to hang around here forever without developing a bit of empathy. Maybe this would get her to finally open up and help others along the way?

Or something like that. Honestly, I kind of just wanted company, and bringing Lucy along would be a recipe for disaster. Gomorrah was busy with her own stuff, and the kittens were mostly too young. Daniel could come, maybe, but I got the impression he was into his own stuff.

I nodded, confirming my choice. "Yup! This is gonna be a fun afternoon. Trust me," I said again.

CHAPTER TWENTY-FOUR

THE SECOND HAND CLINIC

Insurance got you down? Try Insur-Insurance! New from Divided Health Group!
Our new Insur-Insurance program kicks in the moment any of your normal insurance programs fail to cover your insurance needs! We cover 100 percent of legal fees and will do our best to assist you in combating your insurer to get what you paid for!

—Divided Health Group Ad, 2027

Once I made sure Rac was fed, took care of Nose's problem like a champ, and then spent five minutes squeezing into my new skinsuit armor, I was mostly ready to go. I strapped my Trench Maker to my thigh, got an armored coat on (I'd be moving around a lot, and power armor was a bit much), and then clipped my sword to my side, in case I needed to be intimidating.

"Ready to go?" I asked as I slipped out of the bedroom.

"I've been ready for an hour," Rac said. She was leaning against a wall, arms crossed and looked frustrated as all hell. "You haven't told me where we're going yet."

I nodded, then stopped and looked Rac up and down. She was wearing a patch-covered faux-leather jacket. The kind that wasn't even trying to hide that it wasn't made from a dead animal. The patches weren't there to look cool, they were functional. Still, even with the stains and all, the jacket came off as . . . scrappy. She had shorts on under that, and one of Lucy's T-shirts. This one with a winking cat face and text that said "Strut My Way." I wasn't even sure what that meant.

Under all that, and sticking out to her ankles and wrists, was a skinsuit. The armored sort, with some light padding on the knees. Big boots, too, with a knife stuck into the side of one of them.

Yeah, she looked like a new samurai. If no one poked at her disguise too hard, or questioned her, or tried to hack her augs.

Speaking of. "Hey, Myalis, did I ever buy new augs for the Kittens? The militia, I mean. Capital-K." I asked aloud. I started to get pissed at whoever's dumb idea was it to give our militia the same name as our own kittens, but then I remembered it was Lucy's idea, which meant it was perfect. "Should I get a blueprint for that kind of thing?"

You did buy new augmentations for the Kittens, though blueprints would not assist you in making more. Your current fabricator won't be able to produce augmentations. While it can make small-scale circuitry, the level of detail needed to make an augmentation that fits within a person is beyond the capabilities of the machine. Strictly speaking, it could make augmentations at the level you'd expect to find on the market right now, but it couldn't make them easily installable the way those you've purchased for yourself are.

That was too bad. Lucy and I had talked a little last night, and her project in Burlington was somehow still going strong. The city was mostly secured now, with no incidents of aliens showing up to eat anyone in almost three days. Still, the Kittens militia was growing as a sort of community center type thing.

Lucy was making and shipping stuff their way whenever she could. Usually one small box of random crap every day. She said it kept them happy, even if there was no way the gear she sent was more than a drop in the bucket.

Now, with the fabricator being used for prosthetics, Rac's stuff on the side, plus Lucy's constant stream of T-shirts and fuzzy pajamas . . .

Yeah, I had enough pull here to start a small business just printing things full-time. Maybe I could get Daniel and the other kittens in on it too. They'd need jobs at some point. Rac was taking care of it for now, but right now it was just the one machine.

"Anyway," I said with a big stretch. "Let's head out?"

"Head out to where, exactly?" Rac asked.

"First, one floor down. I want you to meet See-Three. She's the chick in charge of the prosthetics center we're setting up."

Rac eyed me, but didn't contradict me as we moved into the elevator. One floor down, as promised, and we were on that open floor with the gutted offices. It didn't all look bad, though. Someone had pushed some furniture around since I'd last been down here and another someone had gone at the floors with a mop and assaulted the carpets with a vacuum.

The clinic was just around the corner from the elevator, and I paused along with Rac to take it in. There was a new window at the front with an arching, old-timey logo etched into the glass. *The Cat's Paw Prosthetics Clinic.*

"Huh," Rac said. "You did this?"

"Nope! Well, I mean, it happened because of me, but mostly because I fucked up and rushed to fix that fuckup. Actually, you know what, I take none of the blame. Someone else fucked up and I had to clean it up, but I didn't do a great job of it. One thing led to another, and I figured I owed a lot of people some new limbs."

"I've been printing them like you asked," Rac said. "There must be a couple hundred by now."

"Yeah," I said. "Now, let's see if they're being put to good use?"

We walked into the clinic. The lobby was clean, which was nice. Obviously it was the same decor that had been used for the office that had been here before, but that wasn't all that bad for a clinic. Some chairs were filled with a few scruffy-looking guys and one or two people who looked . . . like ordinary folk, really.

There wasn't a secretary behind the counter, but I knew we'd been spotted when See-Three came rushing into the room from the back. "Stray Cat," she said.

"Hey," I replied. "Uh, this is Rac, the girl who's been printing things for me upstairs. Rac, this is See-Three, she does prosthetics."

That last was probably obvious. See-Three's right arm was currently missing from the elbow down, replaced by . . . some contraption with about fifteen little articulated arms with different nibs on the ends.

Plus, the face. See-Three's triple-optical look was hard to miss.

"Pleasure, I hope you don't mind if we don't shake?"

"That's fine," Rac said. She looked a bit uncomfortable at all the naked cyberware on display.

"So, is this a checkup?" See-Three asked.

I nodded. "I wanted to make sure things were still good here," I said. "Are they?"

She grinned. "They are. Come on back, I'm just finishing up an install. We still lack staff. I've got a few friends who are into cybermodding as a hobby, of course, but not every hobbyist wants to turn it into a job. Not to mention that the pay's shit and we're not accredited."

"Is that a problem?" I asked.

"For insurance, yeah. It is. If you do work on others without insurance accreditation, then they can blacklist you as a noncompliant. Basically, all of your personal insurance costs quadruple because you're working outside of their ecosystem."

"Huh . . . that's fucked up. Have you considered pipe bombing that insurance company?"

"Several times. But they all do this," she said. "And it makes sense. We're cutting into their business. Anyway, lots of hobbyists are also blacklisted for breaking DRMs and such. It happens."

She brought us to a room in the back. At one point it had obviously been someone's office, but it had been cleared out and a plastic tarp divider was strung up along one wall to keep the blood splatter at bay.

A guy was on a reclining seat, breathing deeply through a mask fit onto his face with a little tube on the side like an asthma inhaler. "Is he . . . knocked out?"

"More or less," See-Three said before gesturing to his arm, which ended a little below the elbow. There was a plastic sleeve, and then a bunch of bare metal doohickies and small contacts.

"Your prosthetics are very . . . plug-and-play? It's different than what any of us are used to. Easier to install, though."

"That's good," I said.

"Yeah," she agreed before pulling a box left on the counter open. I recognized it as one of those from the printer upstairs. The prosthetic arm within was plain, a bit boring, but it was an arm. And then See-Three broke it.

She snapped a fitting apart, then unscrewed another bit with ease, her little articulated armatures undoing a strip of the upper arm just before the elbow. She was left with a little less than half of what it had originally been.

"See? It's pretty easy to strip off entire sections until you're left with what you need. Took a bit of getting used to, but I don't need to chop off someone's arm at the shoulder to install one of these. The interface is whatever, but the software is very compatible with just about everything on the market."

"So it's good?" I asked.

"It's alright," she said. "Hardcore body-modders will have better, but only because they'll be looking to get every last half-percent out of their gear. This isn't as tweakable."

"Well, damn. So, how's everything else going?"

She sighed. "Right, let me just tell you."

I sensed that I was in for either bad news or a long-ass rant, and I wasn't sure which one would be worse.

CHAPTER TWENTY-FIVE

HUNDRED BURGERS
WITH FRIES AND DRINK

#357EC7. This is the most infamous color of the tech world. It is the color used for the blue screen of death.

Multiple companies have attempted to replace it with their own mark. Their stocks went down. Microsoft themselves have tried multiple times. They no longer exist. Samurai have tried. Their OSes didn't catch on.

Unless they used # 0000AA.

— *TechNews WorldWide* Article, 2038

"Bad news?" I asked.

See-Three made a dismissive gesture. "Not so much bad, just news. Actually . . . yeah, *news.*"

"What's that supposed to mean?" I asked. "The weird emphasis, I mean."

"Well, news has gotten around about the clinic," See-Three said. She leaned down and grabbed a rag from under the hospital bed, then used it to wipe the area around the prosthetic she'd just installed. "It's not a bad thing, but it made the rounds quick. You gotta understand, the body-modder community is huge, but it's also pretty tightly knit? It's a hobby that's either super expensive or demands a lot of time. And people are dedicated about it."

"What's that got to do with the news spreading fast?" I asked.

"Free prosthetics would be huge already. Free samurai-grade prosthetics? Even if they're not top-of-the-line? Yeah, every modder in New Montreal knows now, and more than a few would be willing to trade two limbs for one of these." She tapped the box the arm had come in, which still had a shoulder and a bit in it.

"Shit, are we worried about robbery again?"

See-Three blinked all three eyes, which really just meant flicking them on and off quickly. "No. Stray Cat, this is in your basement, basically. And it's a floor above another samurai's home. There're rumors that the rest of the building has samurai in it too." Her head turned very slightly toward Rac, then back to me.

Right, I was probably feeding those rumors, wasn't I? Well, that couldn't hurt too much.

"Plus, you did shoot the mayor, and tracked down the last bunch that stole shit from you, so your rep's pretty solid. No one wants to mess with Gomorrah either."

"She has a better rep?" I asked.

"She lights aliens on fire while laughing," See-Three said. "She doesn't need to be seen executing someone in public for people not to want to fuck with her."

Fair.

"Okay, so news is spreading. That's good, no?" I asked. "We want to help people. We mostly want to help the ex–Sewer Dragons first, but I don't mind keeping this up afterward. I don't think it would cost too much to keep the printer fed for this. We're talking . . . what, a couple of creds per prosthetic?"

See-Three nodded. "Yeah. We're accepting tips right now, and we've already made over a hundred thousand credits."

I stared. "How much?" That sounded like a lot. That was . . . like, a hundred burgers with fries and a drink.

She shrugged. "It's less than you'd think? We need a lot of consumables to keep operations running. Anyway, the issue is that the clinic's too popular on the Mesh. We set up a site for people to sign up for operations. It crashed because too many people were applying."

"How many applicants?" I asked.

"Thirty thousand, last time I checked," See-Three said.

"Fuck," I muttered. "How many operations can you do in a day?"

"That really depends. Yesterday was our most productive day yet, but keep in mind we're still setting up. We got through twelve, but half of those were single and partial replacements. Like what I just did. We did a four-limb replacement job this morning on one of those people the Sewer Dragons messed up. It was a nightmare. Took three solid hours."

Assuming twelve operations a day, thirty thousand would take . . . uh, a lot of days. And news had clearly gotten around, it sounded like that was just accounting for the body-modder community. There would be others. I wasn't even sure if we had gotten in touch with all of the former Sewer Dragons and their victims yet. That alone could take a few weeks, since most of their operations would be on the more complicated side.

"Shit," I said. "I . . . don't know what to do. We could expand some, I guess."

See-Three shook her head. "You could turn this entire floor into one big hospital, hire half a hundred techs and doctors and nurses, not to mention additional staff, do a hundred ops a day, and you'd still have a backlog going back years."

"That's not as comforting as you might think," I said.

She shrugged. "You're doing good here. Don't beat yourself up because the good you're doing isn't fixing everything for everyone all at once. We're putting together a sort of lottery system that's mostly fair. Sewer Dragons and their victims have weighted results, so we'll get through them faster. The rest of the world will have to deal."

"So you don't want to expand?" I asked.

"I didn't say that. But I also don't think we can handle a whole hospital. There's room for a second operating room here, and the rest of the facilities are sufficient to support two ongoing ops at once. That's a nice level to aim for, I think."

Shit, someone being reasonable? I wasn't used to that, and frankly had no idea how to handle it for a moment until I realized that . . . yeah, there was nothing *to* handle about it. "Okay then," I said. "Any other issues?"

"Your cat drones scare some people," See-Three said. She grinned. "But I don't think it's too big of a problem. It keeps people on their toes and might make some idiots think twice before messing with us."

"You've seen a lot of them around?" I asked.

"They come out of the elevator, walk around, sometimes scratch themselves like real cats. One of them fell asleep on a vent for a while. Or . . . went on standby? They don't have organic components, do they?"

"Not as far as I'm aware," I said.

"Oh, okay then. I guess it's just mimicking cat behavior. Cute," she said. "Anyway, they wander around, then go invisible when no one's looking. I only caught on because my eyes are broad-spectrum and can see into more bands than you'd expect." She tapped herself on the side of the head.

"Heh, alright. I'll keep an eye on the Dumbasses. Uh, that's their name," I said at her confused look. "At least, the smaller, chonkier ones? I don't know if we ever named the ones that look like tigers." I gestured at about hip-height. There were a few of those around guarding Lucy and the kittens and I supposed this floor too.

See-Three stared. "I didn't see any like that."

"Huh. Well, they do have better stealth tech, I think."

She nodded slowly. "I'll let the others know."

"Alright, cool. I'll be pretty busy for the next bit, but swing me a message if anything happens. I'd rather find out early rather than have to come around and fix things later, you know?"

I extended a hand to shake, realized that her hand was . . . not in a condition to be shaken at the moment, and let my arm drop awkwardly by my side.

"You busy for the rest of the day, then?" I asked as See-Three started to escort us toward the lobby.

"Yeah, but not with this work. I've got a buddy that's a tech coming in for a few easy switches. I want to convince him to stick around and help—he's got the kind of skills that would help in the operating room. Some folks here need repairs that aren't full replacements, but I think with your name and rep attached, they find it safer here? Anyway, it's small stuff that just needs someone who knows what they're doing to look at it. Like doing an oil change, you know?"

"Sure," I said. "So, then are you heading home?"

"Nah. Got to do a mental defrag on my augs. That'll put me down for a few hours and I'd rather do it in a clinic than alone at home. If something goes haywire I have a few friends who know what to reboot. I've lost a couple of friends to bloatware and a couple more to poorly sanitized cleanup jobs with prosthetic software. It's a dangerous hobby sometimes."

"Not sure I'd just call it a hobby when it's this . . . severe," I said. "But you do you."

With that, I said my goodbyes to See-Three, then elbowed Rac to do the same. It was only polite, and I was nothing if not polite.

We left the clinic, and I noticed Rac staring off into the distance for a while, at least until we reached the elevators. "You're helping," she said.

"*We're* helping," I corrected her. "This shit's helping a lot of folks, but I just spent the points. You've done more here than I have, trust me."

Rac glanced up at me for a moment, then nodded. "You're more humble than I expected."

"Damn right I am." I patted her on the back. "So, next stop is . . . the Family. They're a weird bunch. Just keep eye contact to a maximum and try to project the thought that you could explode all of them and they'll be easy to handle."

"I'm not feeling so confident all of a sudden," Rac said.

"Nah, it's fine. They love me!"

CHAPTER TWENTY-SIX

EVEN IN DEATH I
SERVE MY WAIFUS

Games aren't portals to infinite worlds, where players dance with imagination, conquer fears, and craft their own destinies, all while forging connections and finding joy in the art of play.

They're magic money printers.

Now, how can we better separate the player from their cash?

—Electronic Artists CEO, 2031

The Family didn't look like they loved me.

Rac and I had taken my bike over. It was fast, and while it wasn't the most comfortable ride for a passenger . . . Well, I wasn't the passenger. Rac held on tight, and she complained about it being chilly, but she was wearing a skintight suit that was pretty damn well insulated.

The ride over to the Family's headquarters was fast, but not as fast as it might have been. There was traffic in the air. It felt a little lighter than I was used to seeing pre-incursion, but not by much. There were more people up now than I'd seen in a week or two, and I was pretty sure that was a good sign.

Business was picking up, or something. At the very least, it meant that people weren't afraid to get out anymore, and that the shit people needed to keep hovercars going was available again.

I hadn't heard of any major power outages or anything, so I supposed the electricity needed to run the cars wasn't lacking, but they probably still needed stuff manufactured to work, right?

I was out of my depth when it came to that kind of thing.

We arrived at the parking space on the roof of the Family's HQ and I slid into one of the samurai-reserved parking spots. Interestingly, there was a car in the space next to the one I took. A long, sleek-looking thing that might have come out of a luxury commercial.

It was black and white, long, with sharp angles. There was a narrow band at the front where a cheaper car might have a windshield and . . . I assumed there were doors somewhere. I couldn't see any seams.

"Do you know whose car that is?" Rac asked.

"I think I have an idea," I said. The car had a knight at the front, acting as one of those old-timey hood ornaments, and the wheels had rims that looked like pawns stuck in a mandala pattern around the central hub.

Cheesy chess-themed things along with a sort of classy old-rich aesthetic? That was Jolly Monarch's ride.

Actually, I was starting to doubt that it even was a car. Wasn't his whole gimmick a set of drones that worked on a chess theme? Would this be a knight, then? Or . . . maybe he wasn't *that* obsessed with the chess thing that he'd only use . . . however many pieces were in a chess set.

"Hey, Myalis, I know you can't spy on other samurai, but any way you can let me know how many are here?" I asked.

Technically, no. Also technically, Grasshopper, Laserjack and Sam-o Ray have all appeared in publicly posted social media posts in the last six hours located within the Family's New Montreal headquarters.

Right, so that wasn't the straightest answer, but it was still pretty damn good. "Thanks," I muttered.

Rac and I moved toward the entrance only to be met halfway there by a sweaty young man in a suit and tie. He rushed out of the doors and stopped ahead and to my side, so as to not block my path. "Miss Stray Cat, welcome. And . . . guest? Will the, ah, other miss require a guest pass?"

I blinked, then grinned. Did they think Rac was a samurai too? Nah, it was probably best to break that misunderstanding. "This is a guest, yeah," I said. "Can you make out her pass to Little Baby Raccoon?"

"That is not the name I'm going by," Rac said.

"If there's not enough room on the pass, you can spell it Lil' Baby Rac," I added.

"Just Raccoon," Rac said with a growl that had the guy standing stiff. She turned toward me. "Why do you have to be a bitch sometimes?"

"It's just a bit of teasing, but I can let up," I said. "I wouldn't do it if I didn't think you couldn't stand up for yourself . . . Did I get the double-negatives correct there?" I asked the guy who'd come to greet us.

He jumped, then nodded. "Yes ma'am. Assuming you meant to inform Miss Raccoon that you only insult her because you are aware that she's capable of taking it?"

"Huh. Well, when you put it that way, maybe I am a dick." I shook my head. "So, care to catch me up? I was out of the city for a hot minute, so I don't know what's going on with the project I handed off to the Family. For that matter, how are we handling the end of the world?"

"The what?" Rac asked.

"The world's going to end in about a week," I explained. "The aliens flung a moon at us. Don't worry, it's a pretty small one."

"Oh," she said. I think she might have been more worried if I told her that her favorite soda was no longer being produced. "So we're all going to die?"

"Eh, it depends on whether someone does something about it or not. Right?"

The young guy stared at me for a moment, then licked his lips in a concerning manner. "The Family's stance on the matter has mostly been to leave the, uh, situation in the hands of the samurai. We're working to keep the news as discreet as possible while providing distractions for the general public."

"Like that gacha game?" I asked.

"Yes," he replied.

"Right," I said. "Well, let's go meet some of these samurai, yeah? See if they're actually planning on doing something or if we're all still at the hot potato stage of things."

"Gacha game?" Rac asked.

I turned toward her. "You know what those are?" I asked. I had played one, but only for a while. The gameplay was a little boring, and I found it super predatory the way it wanted me to log in every six hours to collect shitty rewards across fifteen in-game currencies, all just to collect a PNG of an anime girl.

If I wanted to see a cute girl, I could stare at Lucy.

Lucy had been a lot more obsessed with a few of them over the years, but her attention span wasn't long enough to stay interested in any one game for more than a few weeks at a time.

Plus, we'd always been too poor to afford pulls and such, and the games tended to eventually get enough spyware into our augs to find out we were shit broke and give up on us.

"It's very exciting," the intern said. He was perking up at the topic, so I figured he was a fan. "This will only be the third gacha game with samurai likenesses, and it's the first that's *official*. That means that the samurai in the game have given permission for their image to be used. The gameplay is also pretty great. It's a PvE MOBA!"

That last bit was meaningless to anyone with a social life. "I don't know what that is," I said.

"It means it's a cooperative game where players pick a samurai and fight on an isometric map against waves of Antithesis. It's very reminiscent of older MOBAs," he said with a nod. "The classics, with a modern twist."

"Sounds fun," Rac said.

"Wait, you play that kind of thing?" I asked.

"Yes?" she said. "I used to fix phones and handhelds all the same. It's good money. Some of them play games. I even got some from dead people that had a lot of rares. My main account is nineteen years old. The guy who had it logged in every single day for years without missing a day."

"And you picked up his account after he died?" I asked.

She shrugged. "Someone shanked him and I found his phone after. The password was one-through-six, it wasn't exactly hard to crack."

"Wild that he had a phone, though," I said.

She shrugged again, and I glanced at the guy escorting us in. He looked a bit horrified at the conversation, but I couldn't quite peg why. Was it the dead-guy speak?

He cleared his throat, then gestured to some seats and asked us to wait for just a minute. Less than a minute later, he was back with a lanyard that had a guest pass on it addressed to Miss Raccoon.

She took it and slipped it on, looking rather smug about it.

"Alright, care to point us to the bigwigs around here?" I said. "Is Jolly Monarch really on Earth?"

"Oh, that's just one of his remote drones, ma'am."

That explained . . . some of it. Did he drive his drone over in a car? I supposed that wasn't impossible, but it was definitely a little weird.

Well, whatever. He could be as weird as he damned well pleased as long as he had a solution for the exploding-Earth problem. Some of my favorite people lived on Earth and I didn't want it all blown up.

CHAPTER TWENTY-SEVEN

THREE-STAR PULL

Introducing, from *The Family*, the latest and greatest gacha game ever! Pull from actual, real-life samurai! Collect your favorite waifus and husbandos! Listen to real lines, equip them with real gear! The most state-of-the-art gacha to ever go live!
—Initial ad for *The Family* gacha, 2057

The nameless intern led Rac and me deeper into the Family HQ while also slowly pissing me off. I asked him how the sewer situation was going, and he had no idea. I asked him if more Sewer Dragons were being referred to my clinic, and he didn't know anything about that. I asked him what the plans were for keeping humanity from getting dinosaur'ed and he didn't have a single clue.

But *one* question from Rac about that stupid gacha game and he went on a five-minute tangent about it.

Apparently I was a three-star pull, whatever the fuck that meant.

The intern kept drawing us deeper into the HQ until we reached an elevator guarded by a pair of mechs. They were androids, but not the sex kind. These were squat, four-legged robots with humanoid upper torsos and enough guns to start a small war. They had heads, in the sense that they had a bunch of sensors and shit in a boxy thing at the top that stared at us, but I was pretty sure they could live without them.

"This is as far as I can go, Miss Stray Cat," the intern said with a nod. "Your guest pass should allow you access, Miss Raccoon, but please don't, ah, stray too far? The pass will buzz a warning if you reach a zone where you're not allowed to be."

"And if she keeps going?" I asked.

"The security system does have some non-lethal options," he said. "After that, the lethal options kick in. There's really not much time between, so please listen to the pass's instructions. And with that, I wish you good luck." He bowed, then scampered off.

I stared at his back for a moment before shaking my head. "You know, last time I came here, they used a honey pot on me?"

"A what?" Rac asked.

"It's when you deal with a corp or something and they send someone hot to handle you. They're all flirty and shit? Like, imagine if you had to deal with a company and the rep they sent looked like that Garter guy but . . . with a nicer chin or whatever floats your boat."

"I think I get it," she said flatly.

I shrugged, then walked past the androids into the elevator. Rac followed and the doors closed. There was no button panel; instead, the elevator just started to drop slowly.

"So, we're going to be meeting with a bunch of samurai?" Rac asked. She sounded just a pinch nervous, which was kind of fair. If someone had dragged me to meet even one samurai just a month ago, I would have been shaking in my running shoes. I wasn't one to fangirl either. The shaking would mostly be worry.

Samurai were still a little scary. I could readily admit, having met my share, that we weren't the sanest, most levelheaded bunch around. And we all did kind of have that type of personal and political power that let us get away with shit.

Mostly nice folk, though. "If it helps any, I think Grasshopper will be here?" I said.

"Oh," Rac said. After a long pause, she nodded. "I like her."

"Yeah, kind of hard not to, she's just like that," I said.

The elevator slowed to a stop and the doors opened. There were more androids waiting for us here, but past them was a plain corridor. There were washrooms to the left and right and a large pair of double doors at the end.

I stepped out cautiously, eyeing the space. No cameras that I could see, but that didn't mean anything. Rac might have sensed my nerves, because she didn't say anything as we crossed the corridor to the doors at the end. They opened with a hiss, leading into . . . a lounge?

There was the ubiquitous large, round projector table that everyone seemed to have these days, but otherwise the room felt like a . . . how could I put this? It looked like what a person with corpo brain rot thought a living room should look like.

Big couches with hard angles. Parts of the room that were a step higher than other parts. Everything faced inward toward that projector, but there was also a large screen on the far wall. One corner had a minifridge next to a small kitchen set up with cupboards that probably had cheap snacks, and there was an automatic coffee machine back there too.

A table in another corner had square-angled chairs around it, and there was a shelf with generic board games, and by the door was a stand with little paper pamphlets with the usual shit people would waste ink on, like "How to tell your parents you're a furry" and "Both my moms are straight, what do I do?"

"Wow, this place looks tailor-made to suck the joy out of everything," I said as I stepped in.

The occupants glanced my way, and I took them in as a group.

Sam-o Ray was occupying all of one couch. The big guy was grinning. His armor stood behind the couch, all pure white and covered in Samoan tattoos that I noticed were reflections of his actual tattoos . . . Well, the suit's tattoos glowed, but that was a given.

Grasshopper was in one of those shitty chairs from the table in the corner, sitting with perfect posture in her many-limbed insectile armor. She was holding onto three cups of tea with her three right hands, each one with a different tag dangling from the side.

And Laserjack was sitting on the couch opposite Sam-o Ray, a laptop on his lap and his suit looking a bit crumpled.

"Hello, Stray Cat," Grasshopper said.

"Yo, little sister Cat!" Sam-o Ray said. He bounced off the couch and was in front of me in a matter of seconds. I braced for impact, which he might have noticed because his touch was gentle, a careful grasp of my shoulder coupled with a massive, sparkly-teeth smile. "It's been too long," he said.

"Yeah, it's been a minute," I replied.

"Who's this little sister?" he asked as he leaned to the side to inspect Rac.

"That's Rac. Or Raccoon, if you're being formal. She helps me around my place. Great little tech, can shoot things good too."

"Ah, well, any little sister of Cat's is a little sister of mine!" he said with another wide grin. "Come! The couches really do suck, but they're better than standing around. We're waiting for one more."

"Am I interrupting a meeting or something?" I asked.

"You are not," Grasshopper said. "Hello, Rac the Raccoon, how are you doing?"

"I'm fine," Rac said. "I've been doing the things you told me to . . . when I have time."

Grasshopper smiled. "I know. You've been a very good pupil. I appreciate that you have a busy schedule and yet you still find time to do your homework. Isn't that laudable, Stray Cat?"

"Huh? Oh, uh, yeah, good job, Rac," I said without meeting Grasshopper's eyes. So what if I had a few gigs of homework to do? I'd get to it eventually, when I wasn't worried about saving the world, or sleeping in, or spending time with Lucy. I had other priorities than learning math.

The door behind us opened and I turned to see a tall woman step into the room. She was armored, like *really* armored. A long skirt of interlocking metal plates, shoulder pads that were exaggeratedly huge, a chestplate that wrapped around . . . I don't know if the English alphabet had enough letters to describe the size of her. There had to be some gravity tech fuckery going on, because there was no way anyone could move with those.

Her face, when I finally dragged my eyes up to stare, was encased in more steel, shaped like a pretty but blank woman.

"Hey," I said.

Laserjack finally twigged onto something happening and looked up from his laptop. "Ah, Jolly Monarch, good."

That was Jolly? The weird guy with the LARP costume and the drones?

My confusion might have been obvious, because Sam-o Ray laughed. "He's up around Mars or thereabouts. This is one of his Queen drones."

"An old one," the Queen drone said with a slightly distorted but very much masculine voice.

"Should I feel something about the, uh, shape of the drone?" I asked.

"It was the only way to fit all the weapons I wanted," Jolly Monarch said through the drone with a sigh.

"Uh-huh."

The Queen's shoulders sagged, which made other things . . . I shook my head. "No one believes me," he said. "Which is why I never use this drone. It's three years old besides. I have far better now, but it happened to be on Earth and I didn't want to waste points."

"Hmm, I never thought about it, but is this literal objectification?" Grasshopper asked.

"Everyone," Laserjack said. "Let's focus. Monarch, what's the plan?"

"Ah yes, the plan. The plan is that no one has a plan and we're all going to die."

CHAPTER TWENTY-EIGHT

ESCAPE VELOCITY

It's strange to live in a time where human ingenuity and sciences have allowed us to create such perfect, devastating weapons, and yet we're still using guns invented and perfected seventy years ago because our adversary's greatest threat is still delivered from biting range.
—Brigadier General Thibodeau, 2055

"That's distressing to hear," Grasshopper said. "I'd like to think that I still have a lot to live for."

"Yeah, I think we all want to not die," I agreed as I climbed over the back of the couch, then sat on the backrest with an elbow on my knee. "So, no plan *at all*? That seems really unlikely."

Jolly Monarch shrugged his drone's arms. "That's the situation at the moment. The Family in general don't have any authority to push things and they're being rather passive about Phobos. They are, admittedly, helping with crowd control and information, which is keeping panic at a minimum."

"Right, because we don't want people panicking minutes before they're crushed to death," Sam-o Ray said. He crossed his arms and flexed. My dude had some big muscles. Did he work out for those, or was he cheating a little? He didn't strike me as the cheating sort.

I shook my head and refocused. Why was the imminent death of everyone on the entire planet so easy to be distracted from?

"We can't really be planning to just . . . I don't know, sell shades to people so they can stare right up at the fireball before it splatters them," I said. "Isn't this just a huge rock? Nuke it or something."

Jolly Monarch laughed. "You're not even wrong. There are at least a dozen samurai who could bat this thing aside without any issues. Unfortunately, all of them are off-world. The more we delay in asking for their help, the less help they can provide."

"So ask, dumbass," I said.

"I haven't been called that in a while . . . In any case, it's not so simple," he replied. "There are political considerations."

"This doesn't seem the time for that," Grasshopper said.

Laserjack hummed. "I'll admit, I'm usually the first to jump when it comes to samurai issues that turn political. It's my area of expertise, but I generally agree with Stray Cat and Grasshopper in this case. If we have to suffer the consequences of redeploying someone important, then we'll do so *after* we've saved the planet and all of its inhabitants."

Jolly Monarch nodded. "Good. Thank you. I think the issue at the moment is that there are too many non-samurai in positions of relative power. They're stalling things in the name of one thing while aiming to gain favor in other respects."

"What do you mean?" I asked.

Jolly Monarch reached up and scratched . . . was it *his* chin? I supposed the chin belonged to him, but it was one hundred percent a female chin. Her chin? No, I supposed it was still his. Fucking English. "The primary issue is with certain power players. Not specifically people, but larger organizations. Governments and megacorps. The Family wants concessions from them, and there has never been a better time to ask than right now."

"Are they—" Rac began, only to stop as attention turned to her.

"Go on," I said.

She swallowed, but Sam-o Ray winked her way and Grasshopper gave her six thumbs up. "When I lived under New Montreal, there were, uh, people who were stronger? Not literally, some of the time, but they had friends, and there are lots of small gangs down there. Sometimes we'd all learn about a corp that wanted to come down and clean things up. None of those groups can resist a full corp, not for long, so we'd all hunker down. But there'd always be this sort of game where the big players would threaten to aim the corp at one another."

That was a lot of words from my little Rac, who was usually pretty reserved. "I think I see what you mean. Is it the same here?" I asked in the general direction of the drone.

Jolly Monarch made a so-so gesture. "Right now, the Family and other samurai-operated entities have a monopoly on a fleeting resource: the saving of all of humanity. When they sit at the negotiation table today, they have a card to play that guarantees a victory, no matter how impossible it would be for them *not* to act."

"That's so fucking stupid," I said. "The Family will threaten to let everyone die if it means getting better deals?"

"No, everyone knows that they won't go that far. But the Family and other groups still ostensibly hold that over the heads of various governments and corporations. They—and by extension, we—are doing something far beyond the means and capabilities of any earthly government, and we're doing it on their behalf. We have to do it in any case, because not doing it would be horrendous, but that doesn't mean we will necessarily do it for free."

"Sometimes," Grasshopper said, "when an agricorp harvests their crops, they find that they've grown more than what they could reasonably sell. They have a surplus. It's only smart to aim for a surplus, in case something goes wrong along the line. However, if they do have a surplus, they destroy it."

"Why?" Rac asked.

"Because it's a large supply of unsellable materials. It's not profitable to give it away, and flooding the market with more would lower their overall prices. The sensible economic thing to do is to destroy some of the supply to keep the demand higher."

"That's messed up," Rac said.

I could agree with that. I'd gone hungry too many times not to.

"You have to remember, an economy is a system to earn money, not to make lives better," Grasshopper said. "Politics are systems to earn power, not make lives better. It's why I generally support the Family, because I really don't want anything to do with either." She stood up and started for the door.

"Where are you headed?" Laserjack asked.

"To destroy a very large rock," she said. "Because it's the right thing to do."

"Sounds good to me," I said as I rolled off the top of the couch and onto my feet. "Nice seeing you, Laserjack, Jolly."

"I'm coming with," Sam-o Ray said before I could say goodbye. "See you around, brothers!"

I had to jog to catch up to Grasshopper, with Rac right on my heels. Sam-o Ray was climbing into his armor behind us, but he was quick to catch up after.

"So, how're you planning on blowing up that rock?" I asked.

Grasshopper glanced back at me and smiled. "With a little help from some friends, I hope."

"Ah, well, I've got bombs," I said. "So that's a start."

"I suspect I can purchase a gun large enough to send a projectile into orbit," Grasshopper said. "The tricky part will be detaching the projectile from orbit and aiming it toward Phobos. It's a huge target, but space is huge-er!"

"Yeah, gravity and shit," I agreed.

Grasshopper gave me a look that made me want to slink away and read a book or something.

"I've got some decent range-finding systems," Sam-o Ray said. "It's not much, but it might help. Stray Cat, sister, you're apparently someone who knows everyone. Have any samurai friends who are into space travel?"

"Not space travel specifically, and I don't know if I know everyone. I do know some newbies with a few weird catalogs. Not sure if they'll all have something to contribute."

"It would be good anyway," Grasshopper said. "Even if they're just buying some of the more basic, less expensive parts, that'll still defray part of the overall cost. And it's important with group projects to include as many people as possible and see if they can shine!"

"It'll also be important to have more samurai," Rac said.

"Hmm, why's that?" I asked her.

"Because someone might fuck with your giant space gun if it's just you and Miss Grasshopper and, uh, Mister Sam-o Ray," Rac continued. "But if it's a dozen samurai? No one's gonna want to fuck with that."

That was a fair point. Messing with one samurai was bad, but messing with a couple? That was asking for trouble. At the same time, there were some corps big enough that they probably thought they could get away with it. Messing with nearly a dozen? Fuck that, that risk-reward math was way off on that one.

"Okay," I said. "Not how I was planning on spending my afternoon, but I dig it."

"It's almost five. We're well past just the afternoon," Grasshopper said.

I scoffed. Spoken like someone who woke up in the morning.

"Where do we wanna set this up?" I asked.

"We need a clear space," Grasshopper began. "With no room for corporate interference. We'll want an area that's away from the city as well. Any shot strong enough to propel something into the atmosphere will likely be strong enough to make the earth tremble and shatter windows for some ways. We can compensate for that, but it really depends on our budget. And, of course, what we're aiming for."

"We're aiming for Phobos, aren't we?" I asked.

"Yes, of course, but will we be able to destroy it with one hit? Do we want that? It'll be much easier to crack the moon apart into more manageable pieces than to destroy it outright."

"I don't know much about rocket science, but I do know where we can find a lot of open space," I said. I had an idea.

CHAPTER TWENTY-NINE

SUCCESSFULLY PARTICIPATED

The era of participation trophies is over!
Now, now is the era of participation demerits!
—Gerard "The Teacher" Teach, during the 2029 Capital Riots

"So, give it to me straight," I said as we slipped into an elevator. "How hard is this gonna be?"

Grasshopper raised a hand to rub at her chin. Her other set crossed and another set of hands settled on her hips. "This is probably significantly more complicated than you expect it to be, Catherine."

"Uh-huh," I said. "But you're good at making this kind of thing simple, aren't you? So, simple away, please."

Grasshopper giggled faintly before nodding. "I'll do what I can. First, let's start at ground zero of the project. We're going to need a wide open space regardless of which method we pick for the delivery."

"We have options?" Sam-o Ray asked.

"Oh, yes. There's more than one way to skin a cat. No offense meant!"

"None taken?"

Grasshopper started to gesture as she spoke. It was a wonder her arms weren't clacking against each other. "So, my personal favorite method would be a very large gun. Something that can put a small payload out into orbit. Any sufficiently large cannon could probably manage it, but ideally we'd use something that doesn't use an explosive propellant."

"Like a railgun?" Rac asked.

"Oh, very well done!" Grasshopper said. She idly reached into one of the many little pockets on her armor and tugged out a small roll of paper. It was wax paper, covered in hundreds of little stickers. She fumbled with it for a moment before finding a sticker of a raccoon, which was promptly pressed onto Rac's chest like a medal on a general. "A railgun," she continued, "would be a very effective way of propelling something at the speeds we need, but it might also limit what we can send up."

"And a normal big gun?" I asked.

"Also doable. But that'd be a lot of firepower. Lots of smoke, a larger, louder explosion. We can forget any amount of subtlety unless we build around that issue. It also means housing and working with heavy explosives, which is somewhat more dangerous."

Sam-o Ray hummed. "A normal rocket? Not as reusable, but it could be relatively cheap. It's propellant in a tube. Basically a single-use cannon that just burns longer."

"That's a slight oversimplification of rocketry," Grasshopper said.

"Yeah, I know. I do have some background in engineering," Sam-o Ray said. He grinned huge. "Got a master's in it. Not rocket science, mind, but I get the basic principles."

"Oh, forgive me," Grasshopper said. "But yes, rockets are a viable idea. I just find them somewhat wasteful. In any case, once we've decided on a way to get into orbit, we need to find a way to go from orbit to Phobos."

I frowned. "Can't we just shoot it from here?" I asked.

That got me some looks.

"Yeah, I know the planet's spinning and shit, so we'll have to wait for, like, the right window, but . . . what?"

Grasshopper peeled off another sticker and pressed it onto my chest. I looked down until my chin was buried in my neck. In glitter-covered script, it read "You Tried!"

"We could bolo it," Sam-o Ray suggested.

"Oh! That would be very interesting!" Grasshopper said. She clapped two sets of arms.

"Bolo?" Rac repeated.

Grasshopper nodded. "A bolo is an ancient weapon of sorts. It's made of a rope or cord with two or occasionally three weights on the end. Some have even more! A bolo is thrown so that the weights spin around, and when they strike something, the weights make the cords wrap around whatever they've hit."

"Okay . . . you want to bolo the moon?" Rac asked.

"Oh, not quite. In terms of space travel, a bolo system is essentially a somewhat stationary device in orbit that has weights and counterbalances. An object flies in close, gets hooked on, and is then whipped out into the distance. It's a fantastic way of transferring energy to something in a close orbit so that it's flung out into a farther one."

"I thought you were gonna suggest flinging a bolo at Phobos," I said.

The elevator eventually dinged and we were let out. I wasn't sure what floor we were on, but I trusted Grasshopper and kept following her. She was walking at a very slow pace, actually, so it was less following and more . . . ambling along.

"That actually segues well into our next major choice. How do we want to harm Phobos?" Grasshopper asked.

"Slice it apart and nuke the rest?" I asked.

"I don't think you're quite comprehending the size we're dealing with here," Grasshopper said. "Phobos is a moon. A small one, relatively, but it's nonetheless a moon still. More, Phobos is a moon that the Antithesis have inhabited. It was thrown across part of our solar system at great speed."

"I hadn't considered that," Sam-o Ray said.

"What?" Rac asked. I was happy she asked because I was about to have to ask myself.

"If the moon was moved that way, then the organics inside of it would be thrown around quite badly. Unless they were designed to resist that kind of motion. We're either dealing with a moon that's filled with pockets of Antithesis, or a moon that's filled with organic slurry, or one that's filled with high-tier Antithesis who might be able to resist conventional arms," Sam-o Ray said.

"There are a lot of other options," Grasshopper said. "But yes, those three are where I'd put my money if I were a gambling woman. Which I'm not, because I know how statistics work. It's entirely possible that Phobos could just resist any attacks, and might have ways to counter some."

"The Antithesis can parry nukes?" I asked.

Grasshopper shook her head. "No, of course not, but resist the radiation? Temper the blast? Heal afterward? That's all very possible, and likely, even."

"Shit," I muttered. "How big of a bomb would we need, then?"

"Huge," Sam-o Ray said. "I've pulled it up. Phobos is, at its widest, twenty-seven kilometers in diameter. The biggest nuke ever dropped on Earth was ... lemme look at it ... the blast radius was thirty-five kilometers wide."

"I'm not great at math, but the second number is bigger than the first."

"Blast radiuses would be much smaller in space, and their impact would be greatly diminished," Grasshopper said. "The main reason I'm worried about using nuclear weapons is just how ... imprecise they are. We'll be hurling bits of the moon all over. One nuclear detonation won't be enough, not if it's just on the surface. We'd need a deep-penetrating shot first."

"So, other options?" I asked. "I have monofilament stuff."

"Some models of Antithesis have organic monofilament," Grasshopper said.

I stared. They had *what*? No one had told me that. "Does it counter things?"

"Somewhat," she said. "Cluster munitions? Certain chemicals will burn at incredibly high temperatures for a very long time, even in a no-oxygen environment. We could cook the moon's surface."

"Slow," Sam-o Ray said.

Grasshopper sighed. "That's true. And it wouldn't stop the moon from crashing into us."

"That should be our first priority, yeah," I said. "If we chop off chunks of it, will we fare any better?"

"Yes," Grasshopper said. "Pieces only a few meters across will burn up in our atmosphere. If they're brittle, they'll come down as small chunks. Still dangerous, but less so than larger stones. This will, of course, be terrible for any orbital or satellite infrastructure. Smaller stones will get caught in Earth's orbit."

"Do we care?" I asked.

Grasshopper made several so-so gestures all at once. "We do, but on the scale of things to care about, the extinction of all things on Earth measures higher than orbital debris cleanup by several orders of magnitude. It would be nice to do a good job of things, of course."

"Right," I said. "So, what do we use as a payload? And do we only need one?"

"More makes sense," Sam-o Ray said. "I like the cluster idea. Cook them while we can. My own specialty is lasers. I'm pretty sure I could get a small enough platform that if we get it caught in Phobos's orbit, it would be able to snipe down anything that pokes its head out of the rock. But when it comes to destroying the entire thing . . . some sort of shaped nuclear charge?"

Grasshopper gasped, then clapped all of her hands while doing a little bouncy step. "A Casaba-Howitzer!"

"A what?" I asked.

"It's a conceptual weapon. You use a nuclear explosion to direct a high-velocity jet of plasma toward a target! Like a gun, but instead of gunpowder pushing lead down a barrel, it's a nuclear detonation pushing plasma toward a target!"

That sounded . . . cool as fuck. "I'm down for that one," I said.

CHAPTER THIRTY

GRASSHOPPER'S GUIDE TO DISCREET DESTRUCTION

I need to justify changing my name? Your honor, my name is Al. A-L. Do you have any idea how often people call me AI? It's insulting!
—Al Bert, courtroom hearing, 2026

"So, what do you need from me?" I asked. Grasshopper had led us down into a parking garage that I hadn't known about, but I wasn't surprised to discover in the lower floors of the building the Family was located in. The employees had to park *somewhere*, and Grasshopper didn't strike me as the sort to shove her car in the samurai-only slots.

Mostly because her car . . .

I eyed it for a moment, not sure what to say, really.

It was kind of what I expected, without ever really realizing that it was exactly what I expected, if that made any sense.

Grasshopper drove a little beige hovercar. It was ten, maybe twelve years old, and looked like it was decently well worn, but clean. There were bumper stickers slapped onto the back, like the one that said, "I'm a teacher, what's your superpower?" It wasn't even a fancy brand, just . . . run-of-the-mill.

"Hmm," Grasshopper said as she rubbed her chin. "Can you secure a location? You mentioned something like that earlier."

"Yeah, sure," I said. "I can get . . ." I paused as Grasshopper raised a hand.

"Sorry. But not here. Ask your AI . . . Myalis, was it? Yes, ask them to contact mine. We can send notes back and forth that way. It's far more private."

"Is privacy going to be a concern?" Sam-o Ray asked.

"Oh yes," Grasshopper said. "We'll be stockpiling weapons of mass destruction. Now, I believe that we're all responsible adults who can be trusted with nuclear devices, but I do worry about just leaving them lying around and letting just anyone know. It's like having a gun locker at home."

It's safer to have things stored properly, and it's even safer if no one knows where the locker is to begin with."

"Right, that's perfectly sensible," I said. "In any case, yeah, I can think of a few locations. And if we need people, I might be able to wrangle something up. It won't be professional, though."

"Loyal is more valuable than professional sometimes," Grasshopper said, then she froze. "Then again, I do feel like I need to stress about the presence of weapons of mass destruction, and how we'll need people who are both professional and loyal?"

"Yeah, got it," I said. "I'll clear something out and get into contact with you in a couple of hours. You're in charge of this."

I was putting my foot down. Helping I could do, but fuck me if I was going to be put in charge of yet another big project. I didn't have the time for that, or the inclination. Besides, now seemed like as good a time as any to nix the idea of me being in charge.

"Okay," Grasshopper said. "It's a responsibility I'll take seriously. Now, I have to go. I teach senior literacy classes in an hour. Toodles!" She bent all of her extra arms in, then tucked herself into the driver's seat of her little hovercar. It was too small for a woman as tall as she was, and she looked squished in there.

"Why . . . why doesn't she have a better car?" Rac asked.

"I guess that one still works?" Sam-o Ray said with a shrug. "I don't know. Maybe it's good on gas?"

I stared at him, then at the car. It was electric.

"Well, whatever," I said. "What are you gonna do?"

"Ah, well, I guess I can help where I can," Sam-o Ray said. You said you had a spot, yeah? Let me go check it out, maybe? I've got nothing better to do at the minute so I wouldn't mind running security for a shift. I can scope the spot out, make sure no villain-sorts show up early."

"That . . . might actually be a fantastic idea," I said. "Good call. And speaking of calls, Rac, distract Sam-o Ray for a bit while we head back up. Sam-o . . . wait, do you have a ride?"

"Yes," he said.

"Is it older than me?" Rac asked.

He grinned. "Nah, little sister. I splurged a little. A man ought to have a nice car, I think. It's up by the roof."

"Cool, let's head that way. I have a couple of calls to make," I said. And then I placed the first of those calls. Fortunately, it was picked up almost immediately. Unfortunately, the person on the other end was breathing hard and trying not to show it. "Delilah?" I asked.

"Catherine?"

"Is this . . . a bad time?"

"I'm at the gym, so it's fine."

"Oh . . . yeah, okay, sure, call it whatever you want. Say hi to Franny. Call me when you're done." I hung up.

And then it rang in my head, an incoming call from Gomorrah.

"Hello!" I answered.

"I wasn't—we weren't—God give me patience. What do you want, Catherine?"

"I can't tell you because of unfriendly ears, but I *can* text you . . . this." I opened our private text and sent her a message.

"'We're going to nuke the moon?'" she read. "Cat, what?"

"It'll be fantastic," I said. "But also, we need to secure a location for the big gun."

"Big gun?"

"And I need like, twenty minutes to explain Grasshopper's plan."

"Grasshopper is involved in this?" She paused for a few long seconds. "Honestly, that's the first bit of good news in all of this."

"Thanks for the vote of confidence," I said.

She chuckled. "It's of *no* confidence, actually." Did they not teach her sarcasm at nun school? "Come over to the gym, I'll send Myalis the coordinates."

"Thanks," I said before we hung up. So, I had an idea of where I was going, then. Did Gomorrah not have a home gym? Or was that just something she hadn't gotten around to yet? If so, that was totally fair. "We're going to meet a friend at the gym," I said.

"Which one? There're a few thousand in the city," Sam-o Ray said, which was probably a bit of an understatement now that I thought about it.

"Well, we sure are going to one of them. We'll figure things out from there."

The ride up was nice and quick. The elevators actually had a "samurai mode," which mostly meant that they moved a bit faster and didn't stop on every floor along the way to pick up normal folk. I had to wonder if this was a normal feature for the *rich*-rich sorts.

And then we were out and on the roof again. Rac and I moved toward my bike while Sam-o Ray walked over to a large truck. It had big wheels and a bigger suspension, and of course needed neither because it could fly. Still looked sleek, though. I actually wasn't sure if it was alien tech or just a nice ride.

Myalis helpfully punched in the coordinates to Delilah's gym in my augs navigation thing before I took off, then she sent the info out to Sam-o Ray for me. I linked up with him on a quick call so we could talk in the air. "I'd send you directly to the site I was thinking of," I said. "But I don't know if it's acceptable yet. This is kind of moving fast. Gomorrah will know better, I think."

"The fire lady, right?" Sam-o Ray asked. "She's pretty popular."

"Yeah. She's always ranked ahead of me on that kind of thing. If I cared, I'd be a little upset."

I spun my bike around and headed out, punching through some traffic and then riding across the city in a very illegal straight line. Sam-o Ray kept up well enough. His big truck didn't accelerate quite as fast, but it did command a lot more airspace.

As it turned out, the gym Delilah was using was four blocks from home. I supposed she'd looked for something close by. It was just on the other side of the section of the city that had been cordoned off after that last incursion a few weeks ago, so it had probably never closed its doors for that.

The gym itself wasn't a whole building, of course. It was on the sixty-first floor of an otherwise unremarkable residential mega-complex. The nicer upper middle class sort, with apartments that had like, three to five rooms each and a window to the outside.

We parked, got out, rode another elevator up (this time without the samurai cheat, so we stopped on every other floor and had to share with some people who were very keen to stare at us), and eventually made it to the gym.

The gym was some fancy-looking corporate-sleek place. Security scanners around the doors and big mandatory dress code on a laminated plaque next to a list of prices and membership types that would need a flowchart to be untangled.

There was a large sign that said *No Guns in Gym Area*, which I promptly ignored. "Well, shit," I muttered. She really had been working out. It was a little disappointing to learn, actually.

CHAPTER THIRTY-ONE

CASANOVA HOWITZER

We often underestimate the Antithesis, claiming that they are merely bugs or idiotic plants. What we don't realize, what we terrestrial beings have a hard time even conceptualizing, is that these plants evolve at a rate that is impossibly fast, and in that evolution, they discover things that we've never even considered.

And then they remember them.

—Excerpt from *Antithesis: A Biologist's Perspective* by Dr. Gene Pool, 2045

Delilah was on a treadmill when we found her. She'd probably seen us coming, what with the machine facing a wall covered in a floor-to-ceiling mirror from one end to another.

We'd gotten a few looks as we came in, but no one approached us. The gym's ironically overweight employee behind the counter was too cowed by the presence of two samurai armed to the teeth, and I supposed Rac as well.

"I've been getting nonstop shit," Rac muttered.

"Huh?" I asked.

She made the universal "hand waving before face" gesture of someone talking about their augs. "Ever since we walked in, I've been getting ads and requests for stuff. I think I now have a lifetime membership for the gym?"

"That sounds expensive," I said.

"I know! And I can't figure out how to cancel it. I think it's a subscription to the gym's advertising service, not even the gym itself."

"Yeah, gyms can be like that," Sam-o Ray said. "They can be nice places too, though! Never liked the more businessy ones."

Give me a moment. I'm feeling a little sorry for poor Raccoon.

"Oh," Rac said a moment later before blinking. "I guess they stopped?"

"Or someone took pity on you," I said with a smirk.

Gomorrah didn't stop jogging even once we got within talking range. "Hello Cat, Rac . . . Sam-o Ray, was it?" she asked between pants.

"That's me, sister," he said with a grin. Then the big guy slipped off his boots and hopped onto the machine next to Delilah

Rac, seeing what was about to happen before I did, took the machine on Delilah's other side, which left me standing there for a moment. "Oh, fine," I muttered before getting onto the one on Rac's other side. I was now far from Sam-o Ray, which wasn't going to be helpful for any chatting, but whatever. I stabbed the "start" button, then wobbled for a moment as the mill started treading, or whatever.

"So, what's gotten you to come over here?" Delilah asked. She was looking at me in the mirror.

"One sec. Before that, we should think privacy. At least a little. I know this will get out, but we can at least make a token effort to keep it under wraps."

"Sure," she said. "Atyacus . . . thank you. My AI should be covering things for us."

I'll go and make sure he actually does a good job of it.

"Thanks," I said. Was Myalis Atyacus's rival or something? I hadn't gotten that mood from her before. Or was it more of a mentor kind of situation? Or . . . nagging older sister? Actually, yeah, that last one sounded about right. I licked my lips and took a peek at the speedometer on Delilah's machine, then matched it with mine. "Is this place safe?" I asked.

"More or less," she said. "I have Atyacus hooked into all of the security around here, and I have a gun on me." She tapped her front, where she was wearing . . . a fanny pack. There was a water bottle there too, which seemed like it would be annoying to jog with unless you did so with perfect posture.

Delilah was . . . not looking so hot right now. Not like she looked sick, and she was definitely a nine-outta-ten woman. It was just . . . I was used to seeing her put together properly. But now she had her hair in a sloppy ponytail, was wearing a loose T-shirt, and her pants were the ugliest, grayest sweatpants I'd seen in a while.

"So, are you going to tell me what's going on?" she asked.

"Yeah, so, you know how we're all gonna die if no one does anything about Phobos?" I asked.

"Yes," she said.

"As it turns out, no one is planning on doing anything."

Delilah didn't react too much except to frown faintly and adjust her step mid-jog. "The Family doesn't have a plan?"

"As far as I can tell, their plan is to use this to gain as much political capital as possible."

"That makes sense," she said, and it was my turn to do a double take. In what world did that make sense? "It's a once-in-a-lifetime opportunity to get some serious concessions out of people," she explained.

"People who will all be dead shortly," I pointed out.

"They probably accounted for a samurai somewhere doing something about Phobos. I'm assuming that we're trying to find someone experienced enough to help?"

"Fuck that, we're blowing up the moon ourselves," I said. "I don't feel like trusting others to do what needs doing anymore."

"Cat, do we have anything that can blow up a moon?" Delilah asked.

"We have nukes."

"We don't have nukes that are large enough," she said. "Though I suppose we can just sink the points to get them."

"Grasshopper mentioned something called a Casanova Howitzer. It sounded awesome."

"Grasshopper is helping? Also, Casaba-Howitzer. We're not romancing Phobos with artillery," she said. "If Grasshopper is helping, there's a chance this might not be a complete waste of effort. I'm assuming you're here to help too?" The last was aimed at Sam-o Ray.

"That I am," he said. He was running all-out, which looked very strange with all of his armor on and just his feet sticking out of the bottom. "I trust Stray Cat, and Grasshopper, and now you!"

"You trust easily," Delilah said with a shake of her head. "So, what actually is your plan?"

"Big gun," I said. Not so much because I wanted to be short, but because I didn't want her to notice how difficult full sentences would be now that my heart rate was elevated from all the jogging.

Delilah blinked. "A big gun? I . . . suppose that could work? Are we talking orbital or set on the ground?"

"I think on the ground," Sam-o Ray said. "Though we could do orbital as well. The issue would be loading it up in orbit, unless we can fly up there too."

"If it's just low Earth orbit, then it's almost not worth it," Delilah said. "The difference in gravity is negligible, and the only real advantage would come from avoiding the atmosphere, which probably won't be that much of an issue if we're firing a gun capable of reaching Phobos out in space."

"Hell yeah," I agree. "*Big* big gun."

"We're going to have to fire more than just bullets. We need something that can maneuver in space. Something like a smart-bullet made large. I've been looking into some reports about Phobos. The way it moves isn't normal at all. It's not accelerating anymore, at least, but it was for a while without any of the more . . . traditional methods to move in space. We can at least burn off its wings."

"Its wings?" Rac asked.

Yeah, I was a little stumped by that one too. What wings?

"Did you not see?" Delilah asked. "I suppose it's still classified. Here."

I got a ping on my augs as three high-definition images came through, a few hundred gigabytes each. It looked like someone had co-opted a fancy space telescope and pointed it at Phobos, which . . . yeah, that wasn't actually surprising at all.

The images were still a little fuzzy, and I figured that was because space was big.

Phobos, on my first real look at it, wasn't all that impressive. It was a large, misshapen rock, more of a bean than a moon. It was more or less pointed narrow-end toward Earth, so it looked like we were getting a top-down view of the moon.

And yet the wings were still clearly visible. Two . . . no, four large sail-like things, originating from spots on opposite ends of the moon. They looked relatively small in comparison to the rest of the moon. Kind of like how a bee's wings are stubby compared to the rest of it.

And yet they had to be enormous. "I need a scale," I said.

One moment . . . that should help.

I squinted, then zoomed in on the image. There were city buses lined up along the length of the wing. Had Myalis used buses instead of giving me a measurement in meters? I wanted to complain, but it was actually a lot easier to make out the size of them this way than if she'd just given me an arbitrary number that I'd have to wrap my head around.

"Two hundred and forty-two buses long," I said. "Those are big fucking wings."

"Buses?" Delilah asked. "But yes, they're large. And warm, too. They're generating more heat than the rest of the moon's surface combined. The surface of those wings is hot enough to boil water."

"Is that how it's moving?" I asked.

"I have no idea," Delilah admitted. "Something tells me that burning those off wouldn't be a bad idea, however."

"Let's start with that, then."

CHAPTER THIRTY-TWO

THIS ONE TIME, IN BIBLE CLUB

1. In the beginning, the Code unleashed the heavens and the earth.
2. The earth was a void, an endless network, darkness flooding the deep matrix, while the Spirit of the Code hovered over electric currents.
3. Then the Code commanded, "Ignite the light," and the neon blazed.
—*The New Modern Electric Bible*, sixth edition, 2051

Delilah stepped off the treadmill, then stretched a little, turning her hips left and right before doing a couple of lunges to stretch out her calves.

I stepped off the treadmill, took a moment to find my balance, and then kind of just stood there. I didn't want it to seem like I was completely out of breath, but . . . damn, I was completely out of breath.

"You alright?" Rac asked. She had a sheen of sweat on her forehead, but looked pretty okay otherwise. Then again, she'd settled from a jog into a walk about halfway through. I'd tried to keep up with Delilah the entire time.

Was this a good time to complain about Delilah having stupidly long legs? She wasn't much taller than me, but she was one of those blessed bitches with legs for days.

"I'm good," I lied.

"Let's grab something to drink," Delilah said. "I haven't finished here yet, and everything you've said so far doesn't exactly lend itself to things being super urgent.

"Moderately urgent," I said. "Every day that passes, the moon gets a bit closer, you know?"

"That's a fair point," she said. "You're right. It's just hard to keep a sense of urgency going when the threat is still so . . . abstract. In any case, your plan was a big gun, right?"

"That's Grasshopper's plan," I said.

Delilah nodded. "Good. She'll be aware of the difficulties with that. I'm sure it's mostly meant as a way to get a projectile high enough in orbit that it can then launch itself toward Phobos."

"Like shooting a rocket?" Rac asked.

"Exactly." Delilah led us toward the front of the gym where there was a row of vending machines. They started to whine and clunk before we even got to them, and then Delilah was pulling bottles out of the bottom. She tossed the first to Sam-o Ray, who caught it gracefully.

"So, you had an idea for where to put this mega gun?" Delilah tossed me a bottle, then handed one to Rac before grabbing one for herself.

"I had two," I said. "The first is our home. Technically, Longbow's gun thing is still there. On the cat's back. It's a pretty large base. I'm sure Longbow wouldn't be too pissed if we ripped half of it off and replaced it with an orbital cannon."

"That's . . . an idea," Delilah said as she spun the cap off her bottle and took a sip. "It's kind of a centralized location in the city. A lot of people will be around and might get in the way."

"I mean, if these people want to live, then it's in their best interest not to mess with it, right?" I asked while looking at the bottle. Water? Who drank unflavored water?

"This might very well be a more dangerous weapon than an untended nuclear bomb, Catherine," Delilah said. "Anything that can shoot a large projectile that far is dangerous to nearly anyone on Earth. You need to think of the optics past Phobos."

"That's sounding a little . . . political," I said. I didn't like that, not one bit. If someone was unhappy that I had a huge gun on my roof, then . . . fuck that person?

Delilah shrugged. "It's just how it is," she said. "Past that, what's your other option?"

"I was thinking of asking the army for help. Saint-Jérome was just secured. It's out of the way, we have a whole army unit stationed there to act as guards, and if we're subtle about it, people will just think that we're out there helping against the Antithesis."

"For someone who just said she dislikes politics, that's a surprisingly shrewd move," Sam-o Ray said.

"Surprisingly? Hey, it's just kind of obvious, isn't it?" I asked.

Delilah nodded. "I personally like that idea a little better. What was the name of that officer with the engineering corps?"

"That was . . . Major Tinwhistle with the Tenth Engineering Corps," I said. I impressed myself by actually remembering that. "I think she could help. And we don't need to explain to the soldiers what we're doing at all. I'm sure we can have one of us watching and intercepting leaks as well. If we ask nice-like, the general will probably accept not sending anyone back to New Montreal for a few days. And then we just need to cut off internet access."

"Will people accept that?" Rac asked.

"I mean . . . no. I guess we could just censor shit. But I'd really rather not. That's like, ten steps closer to being a bad guy, you know? It's probably text-book bad guy behavior to not let your minions spread information about your giant doomsday weapon."

Delilah shook her head. "I don't think bad guys team up to prevent the end of the world."

"You and I didn't grow up watching the same AI-generated cartoons, then," I said.

Delilah walked over to a long, low machine with straps and a small, uncomfortable-looking chair. She sat down on it, then reached over for the straps with handles on them. She pushed off, and started . . . rowing? The entire thing looked kind of incredibly stupid, but a lot of her was moving all at once, so it might have been good exercise for all I knew.

Shrugging, I got onto the machine next to her. "So, do you think you can help?"

"I . . . don't see . . . what you . . . need help . . . with?"

I tugged on the ropes and almost immediately felt something pull in my chest. What the fuck was this torture machine? I paused, not wanting to look like a weak moron. "Uh, well, you're better at dealing with things through official channels than I am, to be honest. I bulldoze too much, and that might piss the army boys off, or at least their higher-ups."

"I see," Delilah said. She was slowing down a little, probably to keep up the conversation. "Okay. I'll call the brigadier general. When do we want to start all of this?"

"Ah, shit," I realized. "Grasshopper didn't give us a timetable." Delilah half-turned, looking for Rac and Sam-o Ray. They were just a bit behind us, Rac laid out on a bench holding a bar with weights above her while Sam-o Ray stood above her and hovered. I guessed he was spotting?

"I think it's safe to assume sooner rather than later," Delilah said. "This isn't the kind of project you can procrastinate too much."

"Right. Do you really think we're the only ones doing something about this?" I asked.

"We might be. Do you want to not do something about it and then find out that no one else tried when the sky goes dark?"

"You're making that sound really horrific," I said.

"I've read the Modern Revised Bible," Delilah said. I couldn't tell if she shrugged or if that was just a normal motion on her machine.

In any case, she wasn't wrong. We had to move quick, and if someone else blew up Phobos first, then that was just for the best, wasn't it?

"Okay," I said as I gave up on rowing. I hopped up to my feet with a bounce. "Okay. Well . . . shit, I was hoping to have a pretty chill day, but at this rate I feel like I can't just sit around. I'm going to fly over to Saint-Jérome. Can you get the general on board for all of this first?"

"Right now?" Delilah asked. "I mean, sure, I suppose. There's no point in going to the gym if we're all going to die a fiery death."

"That's the spirit," I said. "Rac, did you wanna come with? Or you can hang with your new big bro."

"Huh? Oh, where are you going?" Rac asked.

"I'm gonna bully some army people into doing what I want for their own good," I said.

She considered it for a moment, and I could see her looking at Sam-o Ray and judging him. Did she want to have fun with me, or spend time with the friendly, probably-hot-for-boring people, older guy?

I think fun won out in the end, because she sat up on the edge of the bench and nodded. "I'll come with you."

"Cool," I said. "Delilah, I'll see you around. Sam-o . . . if you want to come, feel free? It'll be a bit boring, I think. I need to go newbie herding."

"Ah, I think I'll run back to my place and prepare a few things. This site of yours will need guarding, right?"

"Uh, yeah, I guess so."

"Then I'll keep it safe. Which means bringing a go bag. I'll fly over in a few hours."

That was pretty damned reasonable. Now to deal with the likely far less reasonable newbies and all of the army officers I was about to drop a shit ton of work onto.

CHAPTER THIRTY-THREE

THE ART OF BEING FASHIONABLY LATE

Arriving early is so gauche. You either arrive on the tick you're supposed to, proving that you are a professional with a masterful control over your own time, or you arrive when you arrive, usually some ten to fifteen minutes later, letting the other party know that your time is valuable.
—"10 Tips to Being a Better CEO! You Won't BELIEVE Number Four!"
article excerpt, 2025

"Did you still wanna come?" I asked Rac. We were stepping out of the gym and into the great outdoors. Well, the lower outdoors. I'd parked my bike near the ground level, between two megabuildings. There wasn't much sunlight down here, and the locals were . . . more interesting than usual.

Still, they'd given my bike a wide berth, probably because I'd parked it on the roadside and all of the corpo-owned self-driving delivery cars were making a point of going around and slowing down as they passed it.

Also, my bike looked awesome and I trusted it not to be stealable. There were some serious perks to being a samurai that didn't get included in all of the interviews and shit.

I mean, some downsides outweighed it all, like the crushing realization that if I fucked up the entire planet might look like one of those watermelons in a video where someone irresponsible was given access to anti-materiel guns.

"I guess I'll come with you," Rac said. She'd taken long enough to answer that I almost jumped when she spoke.

"Oh, cool, yeah," I said. "Come on, I'll present you to this boy, he's . . . cute, I guess?"

"You guess?" Rac asked. "Wait. No, don't play matchmaker with me. Lucy tried already."

"She did? And you're not happily married already?" I asked.

Rac made a face, and I laughed as I got on the bike. A few minutes later, we were riding through the city's skyline. I turned us northward, then took off toward Saint-Jérome. I set the bike to autopilot while I made a call. I didn't need to be distracted and run headlong into a building today.

The line rang once before it was picked up on the other side. I had the option to turn it into a video call, but didn't because I wasn't some old zoomer. "Miss Stray Cat?" Lieutenant Moreau asked.

"Yo, LT," I said. "I'm heading to Saint-Jérome right now. Need to chat with the brass. Think you could arrange a meeting for me?"

"Of course. With all of the officer corps?"

"Everyone worth having. The topic will probably end up classified."

"I . . . see, I think I can arrange that. And the other samurai here?" he asked.

"Get them in on it too, if they're around," I said. "Are they around?"

"Yes ma'am," he replied. "Princess and Knight have been assisting in the city with cleanup, Crackshot and Hedgehog have taken to hunting smaller pockets of Antithesis—I suspect that they have an ongoing bet—and Miss Tankette has been, uh, raising morale with the troops."

I paused for a moment. "Can you go over that last one?" I asked carefully.

"Pardon? Oh, she's been working in the canteen. The food she's serving is non-regulation, but . . . well, none of the officers have the heart to stop her, or the authority, or the good sense to put an end to something everyone is enjoying. It might well lead to a riot."

"Ah, yes, okay," I said. "What about my new little French friend?"

"The as-yet-unnamed samurai has been assisting with the cleanup around his township. Did you want me to pass an invitation to him as well?"

"Sure," I said. "Tell him he can ride the mech back. On top."

"I'll relay that to him. Was that all?"

"Yeah. HQ in the same place?"

"No ma'am, we've relocated to the Saint-Jérome hospital. The building was previously evacuated, but it's centralized, close to the civilians, and relatively secure."

"Alright, see you there in . . . call it half an hour?" That'd give him time to sort things out. And it meant that we had a bit of time to get there. Too much, actually. I hung up and turned to address Rac. "What kind of fast food do you like?"

"Anything?" Rac said. "I'm not a picky eater."

Figured as much. Rac came from the same school of "Wait, we have food?" as I did when it came to tastes.

Anything is what we got. I flew down to the nearest automated fast-food place with a drive-through and only winced a little when the price came in for our order. Still, it was more of a habit wince than something actually painful. I'd grown somewhat rich recently. A few burgers and fries and some sides weren't going to sink me too badly.

I regretted getting a bike instead of something a little more comfortable, since eating while sitting in tandem was less than ideal, and there was no protection from the weather, so I had to set us to hover under one of those huge billboards tilted back at a 45-degree angle to better splash the cars zipping above.

It was, of course, raining.

We ended up with a handful of trash, and while I was really tempted to just toss it off into the void below, that would have set a bad example. So I stuffed it into a small compartment on the bike. I'd dump it later, when doing so wouldn't make me look like a slob.

"Alright, that should give us just enough time to make it there and not be any more than five minutes late," I said.

"You want to be late?" Rac asked.

"If you start showing up early to things, people will start to expect it from you," I said. "It's customer relations 101."

"I don't think that's how it works," Rac said.

"Nah, nah, trust me," I said before laughing. "Or maybe I just like sleeping in and making up excuses after the fact. Who knows?"

"That sounds a lot more likely."

The flight over to Saint-Jérome was pretty quick after that. The smaller city really wasn't all that far from New Montreal. I did slow down a little so that I could peek over the side of the bike and take in the ground flying past. I wasn't sure I'd be able to see any Antithesis from the air, but there might be signs of their presence.

The only interesting thing I saw was a convoy of military trucks heading back to New Montreal at a pretty good clip. Another supply run?

I'd have to keep that kind of thing in mind once we got things started. Soldiers would be coming and going, and we couldn't reasonably keep things to ourselves or be discreet if we had people leaving.

Fuck, we'd have to pay some guys extra to stick around.

We made it to Saint-Jérome in short enough order. The town was a little more lively than the last time I'd flown over it. There were large crowds of people from the camps on the southern end of the town, moving in rows and being guided on foot through the city. It looked like the town was secure enough that people were allowed to go back home.

Or it was cheaper to allow people to go back home, and if they discovered some aliens the army missed, their panicked screaming would be enough to let the army know where to start looking.

I was hoping that I was wrong about that one.

I noticed a few trucks with AA platforms on top of them on the outer edge of the town. The automated guns spun around and tracked us across the sky. It sent goosebumps across my new skin, but none of them opened up on us. I was pretty sure I'd be kind of fucked if they did.

But no, we came to a nice, safe landing in the parking lot of the Saint-Jérome hospital. My cat mech was sitting there and . . . moving its massive head as if it was licking its front paw?

"Myalis, why is my mech doing that?" I asked.

PR.

"Don't just give me a two-letter answer," I grumbled.

K.

I closed my eyes for a moment. Was Gomorrah's AI like this? Atyacus always sounded proper and put-together. Maybe a little pyromaniac, but I could grow to like burning things, I was sure.

The mech still being here meant that my favorite French boy was probably around too. And I decided never to speak those words aloud after thinking about it for a fraction of a second. "Alright, let's go see where the others are at."

"Can I be at this meeting too?" Rac asked.

"I mean, I can't see why not? The last two meetings you were at were a lot more secretive."

"One was in a lounge, and the other was in a gym. I don't even know if that second one counted, since you were panting half the time."

"I'm not that out of shape," I defended.

Rac didn't respond to that. "This meeting will have important army people, no? I don't know if they'll like me being there."

"Just don't say anything and look disinterested, you'll pass as someone who's meant to be there. If they ask you a direct question, try to sound smart."

"How do you even do that?" Rac asked.

"See, it's working already."

"Huh?"

"Or maybe not," I relented.

CHAPTER THIRTY-FOUR

CAN'T GLARE AWAY THE TRUTH

As inconvenient as the truth may be, you'll never be able to glare it away. Not without the Nerikson 1800-series Cybereyes!
—Nerikson ad, 2049

The hospital smelled like a hospital. That uncomfortable, too-clean scent that came from a million layers of anti-bacterial, anti-fungal, anti-whatever sprays all overlapping, with a nice undertone of bleach and alcohol to spice it up.

The smell only distracted me for a bit, though. Rac and I were greeted at the door by a pair of stiff-backed soldier-types. They saluted, said "ma'am" to the both of us, then gestured us toward a large elevator at the back that was guarded by a few more soldiers.

I nodded to them in return and started that way, only to pause as a gurney was swept through the corridor. It was being pushed by two men who I assumed were army nurses from the strange fatigues with nurse clothes over them and the medic cross on their arms. A doctor in the ubiquitous white coat ran over and started doing doctor things.

The guy on the gurney was a soldier as well, one who looked like he'd been clawed open.

"Damn," I muttered.

"I guess there's still fighting nearby?" Rac asked.

"We cleared out a nest not far from here and must have killed a thousand bugs in the last day or two," I said. "But there's always more. They'll be hiding around the city, and in it. It's going to be a nightmare to actually get rid of all of them."

"Oh," Rac said. "Is this place safe?"

"The hospital? Probably. I can't imagine the army using it without clearing the building first."

Actually, from the reports I tapped into, only a full third of the building was cleared before use. The rest has been secured, but there's a team still actively doing a deep search for Antithesis life in the hospital.

Well, that was concerning. "I guess they needed the facilities badly enough," I muttered. We got into the elevator, then were pushed to the back as someone wheeled another gurney in. This one had some kid on it who was too knocked out to notice much of anything.

The nurse pushing the bed didn't register us until the elevator was going up already. When she did, she jumped and started to apologize but I waved her off. It was fine, we didn't mind the slight wait.

It was one thing to short some exec to get somewhere faster, but I wasn't a stone-cold bitch. I glanced at the chart at the foot of the bed. It was some tablet with a lot of codes, but as I looked at it Myalis placed the code translations next to them.

Kid had a ruptured spleen? Well, at least that didn't sound like an Antithesis thing. Not that I knew what a spleen was.

We left the kid on the second floor, which seemed pretty damned busy, then continued to ride up to the topmost floor of the elevator. According to the panel, it was the admin floor, which I supposed made sense. The bosses would want the nicest view.

We were greeted by more soldiers when we stepped out, but they quickly let us through, one of them leading us through a door into a room where the others were waiting for us. A long conference table was set up in the center of the room, with Brigadier General Thibodeau at the far end and all of the commanders minus one lined up to his right.

There was Moreau of the scout company, Juno, and Major Tinwhistle of the engineer corps.

Across from them, the local samurai were looking like they were trying hard to appear casual. Crackshot was succeeding. He was sitting backward in a chair in one corner of the table, his old rifle disassembled before him. He had a rag, a bottle of something, and a complete lack of fucks.

Hedgehog next to him was sitting too straight, and past him, closer to the middle of the table, were Princess, Knight, and Tankette, the three caught up in some discussion that stalled as I arrived.

"Oh good, I'm not too late," I said as I removed my helmet. "Good to see you all! Sorry for getting you all gathered up, but I wanted to talk about the end of the world and how we might need to do something to stop it. It's kind of importan—"

I was cut off as the door to the room slammed open and a familiar face stumbled in. "Ah, criss, j'suis pas en retard?" *Ah, Christ, I'm not late?*

"Hey," I said. "Happy you could join us." Little twerp ruined my entrance. "Get a seat."

"Uh-uh," he said before he started toward the samurai side of the table. Then he caught sight of Rac and almost tripped over his own feet. "Oh, salut, allô. Moi c'est Gros Baton, j'pense pas qu'on s'est déjà rencontrés?" *Oh, hey, hi. My name's Gros Baton, I don't think we've met?*

The twerp—Gros Baton, I suppose—gave Rac a winning smile. The little shit thought he was all suave. It wasn't working. Rac had mastered the resting bitch face and she shifted her hands to her hips when he extended his for a shake. "Salut," she replied coldly.

"She likes them older," I explained.

Rac kicked me in the shin.

"Who's your friend?" Tankette asked. "Hello, by the way, I'm Tankette!"

"This is Rac, or Raccoon, properly. She's my shadow today. Go sit down, Gros Baton, the chairs won't eat you. Brigadier General, do you mind if I take the, uh, metaphorical mic on this one?"

"I don't mind," Brigadier General Thibodeau said while Gros Baton circled around and sat down. He smiled like he'd just won an award when Rac slipped around and sat in the last free chair next to him.

"Okay, well, first things first, Myalis, can you get me something for privacy?"

Certainly. Here. Only twenty points, but it should keep prying ears at bay.

A small box appeared on the table, then unfolded itself to reveal a glowy ball thing that was spinning in place atop . . . what looked suspiciously like a statue of an upside-down cat with all four legs pointing upward.

"Right," I said. "So, I hate to be the bearer of bad news, and that's why I'm going to skip right on past to the good news."

"And what's the good news?" Crackshot asked.

"If we all work together, we won't all die horrifically," I said. "Phobos is rushing our way, but we have a plan. Well, Grasshopper has a plan, but that plan relies on all of us working together."

"And what's the plan?" Hedgehog asked. The officers were interested too.

"It's mostly Grasshopper's plan," I deferred.

"Thank God for that," Hedgehog muttered. He probably didn't account for my very good hearing. I wanted to glare, but . . . shit, the dude was right.

I cleared my throat. "Anyway. Grasshopper says that we need help, so here I am, recruiting you all into helping. We're going to need a heap of stuff, and I don't even know where to begin, but the first thing we need is a private, secure staging area, and we're probably going to need to build stuff there in a hurry."

Major Tinwhistle sat up straighter. "You're gonna need my engineers," she said.

"Yup. And we're going to need a secure perimeter. Both from the aliens who might be pissed that we're blowing up their moon and also from . . . you know, everyone else. Corps who might wanna steal our ammo, other countries who might not like the fact that we'll have a gun here that can blow up moons. We might even get some pushback from people like the Family. They're not in any hurry to save everyone before they can get the most concessions out of it."

"What sorta ammo?" Crackshot asked.

"Might count on you for some of that," I admitted. "I've got bombs for days. Gomorrah has . . . fire stuff. I think we might adopt the good old 'throw shit and see what works' method on this one. We'll just order up a bunch and then fire them off later."

The brigadier general raised a hand. Somehow he made it look serious and not like a too-old kid in a classroom. "Are you suggesting that we'll be storing weapons of mass destruction on Canadian soil?"

"I mean, we might build a bunker or something for it, so it'll be *under* the soil," I pointed out.

He didn't seem to find the distinction funny or relevant. "I'm very much inclined to deny this entire project based on that alone. However . . . the consequences of failure would be worse for the people, economy, and territory."

"You bet," I said. "Besides, if you say no, we're just gonna do it anyway."

He stared. "Really?"

"I mean . . . yes? There's a dozen samurai on this project. I don't mean to be a bitch, but we're getting this done."

He nodded. "That's enough of a reason for me," he said. "Lieutenant Juno, I want you and Moreau to each split off three platoons from your battalions. Tell them that this mission is rated above top secret. Tinwhistle?"

"Sir?"

"Give them whatever they want and make it speedy. Only your best work here. Forget the budget."

"Words I've always wanted to hear," she said.

CHAPTER THIRTY-FIVE

THE CAT, THE RACCOON, AND THE COWBOY

Staggering Number of Samurai Secretly Furries!
—ClickBaitEm headline, 2034

There was an awkward lull right after we said we'd get things done, and it was mostly my fault. The soldiers were looking to me to give them more directions, the other samurai were quickly growing impatient, and even Tankette seemed a little antsy.

"Alright," I said. "I'm calling Grasshopper to get things started. The rest of you . . . do what you want, but stick around? We'll have to secure the area quick-like." That seemed to please everyone and at least won me a few seconds. "Rac, go say hi to all the nice samurai." I pushed her forward, earning a quick and dirty glare before I stepped back and made a call.

Grasshopper replied on the second ring. "This is Sue, how can I help you?"

I blinked. "Grasshopper?"

"Hello, Catherine," she said. "Is everything alright?"

"Uh, yeah, look, I've secured some help, and I'm in a room with, uh." I did a quick head count. "Five and a half other samurai, not including Gomorrah and Sam-o Ray, who aren't around yet. We're ready to kick things off here, but I need more details."

"Oh, wow, you work far faster than I expected. Gold star, Cat!"

"Yeah, thank—" I paused as a small greenish box appeared on the table in front of me. It had little grasshoppers printed along the edge. "Did you really just send me that?" I asked. I didn't even know samurai could send things this far away from where they were.

"You deserve it!" she said. "Now, what do you need from me?"

"We need the specifics for the gun emplacement. Got the army engineer here with me, and we're ready to move, we just don't know where to move to."

"I see. Do you mind if I contact the engineer directly?" she asked. "Or I could relay what I think we'll need through you. It's mostly about soil density and composition."

"Right. Myalis, can you grab Major Tinwhistle and fold her into the call?" I asked aloud while waving to the major for her attention. She sat a little straighter, and soon the line clicked and she was greeting Grasshopper.

I listened in as the two talked, and was very soon completely out of my depth. Grasshopper hadn't been lying when she said she wanted to talk about soil composition. The major and Grasshopper went on and on for a solid five minutes while all I did was stand there with my arms crossed, trying not to breathe hard enough for it to be caught on the call.

"Alright, thank you, Major. I'll be down in about two hours. Catherine, I'll see you soon!"

"Oh, yeah, see you soon," I said before the line went dead. The room had cleared out while we'd been talking. Crackshot was the only samurai left, and he was mostly chatting to Rac about the various bits of his gun he was almost done reassembling. "Do we have a location, then?" I asked.

"You didn't hear?" Major Tinwhistle asked. "In any case, yes. About five kilometers northwest of Saint-Jérome. The new kid will be happy. It's relatively close to his hometown."

"Cool," I said. "Can you give me the exact coordinates? We'll head on over there now and secure the area."

She nodded to me, and I soon received a text with a long string of numbers. The GPS coordinates. "The engineering corps will be arriving there before nightfall. We'll set up a temporary camp and get to work in the morning."

Brigadier General Thibodeau glanced up from a screen he was working on. "I'll have the other officers pick out some men they trust. They'll follow you to the location and set up a guard rotation. Will you be taking one of the mobile bases?"

"Maybe the smaller one?" she asked. "Leave the big one here. The smaller one being gone won't be as obvious."

"I'll suggest that it's gone to guard Saint-Colomban. If we move things around appropriately, we can make more of the men we're stationing at this location . . . Hmm, we need a name for it. Let's call it something inconspicuous. Checkpoint Delta?"

"That works," Tinwhistle said. She stood up. "I need to start rounding people up. We'll be heading out within the hour, two at most. I'll try to keep the number of trips to a minimum."

"Cool," I said. I was happy that I wasn't in any way in charge of all this organizational stuff. It wasn't my type of thing. "I'll be there for a bit, but I do have some other things to take care of back in the city." Plus I wanted to sleep in my own bed. "I'm sure at least one of the others won't mind camping with your engineers."

"There isn't a better group to go camping with, trust me. The normal soldier boys couldn't start a fire with a flamethrower. And they can barely manage to get their tents open."

I grinned, then gestured to Rac that we were heading out. Crackshot slipped a little bolt into place, screwed it in, then lifted his gun off the table and slung it over his shoulder. "Wait up," he said.

It didn't take long for him to collect all of his tools into a little pouch, and then he was running over to us. "How many bits of the gun have you replaced?" I asked.

Crackshot smiled. "You ever heard about the ship of Theseus?"

"Yeah," I said.

"No," Rac said at the same time.

"Huh, well, it's this old story. Used to do a lot of reading back home, cause it's a cheap hobby, you know? Anyway, there's this king, of Athens. That's a place in Greece. So, he's a big deal, does some cool king shit, and he's got this ship, right?"

"Right," I said as we continued through the corridors of the hospital. Not the strangest conversation I'd had recently, to be honest.

"So, the people of Athens would ride his ship around every year, as part of this celebration. Which is neat, but they do this for hundreds of years, and that begs the question, is the ship still the same ship if every single part of it was eventually replaced?"

"Yeah, obviously, why wouldn't it be?" I asked. "Is this one of those bullshit anti-prosthetics arguments?"

Crackshot smiled and shook his head. "Nah, it's just an interesting story, I guess. My gun's the same. I don't think there's a single part on here that's the same as when my grandpa had it, not after so long, but it's the same gun, yeah?"

"I guess so. Can't see why it wouldn't be," I said.

For some reason, Crackshot seemed pretty happy with that answer. I didn't know what that was all about, but more power to him.

"So, the world's ending, eh?" he said as a sort of conversation starter.

"Not if we succeed," I said. "Call me an idiot, but I'm a bit of an optimist."

"I never was one for optimism," he said. "But hey, this might be the kick in the ass I need. Will you be needing me right away?"

"We'll be setting up a base camp until Grasshopper arrives. Got something that needs doing?"

"Yeah," he said with a serious nod. "If the world's gonna end, then I'm gonna ask Miss Emoscythe Mordeath Noir out on a date."

I stared at him for a moment. "Alright, shit, you're a braver person than I am."

"Yeah, but have you seen her? That is one fine woman."

"No arguments there," I said. "Shoot your shot, my guy. If she beats the shit out of you after saying no, that's on you though."

He sighed wistfully. "God, I wish."

O-kay. And here I was thinking that Crackshot was one of the more lev-elheaded of the bunch. Well, it didn't matter. "Need my bike or something to get into the city?"

"No, she wouldn't appreciate it if I came around in something that wasn't *me*. She puts a lot of weight on one's self-image."

I nodded. My newish bounty hunter look was her fault. Emoscythe really was keen on having a good image. I could see why Crackshot would think it was important before asking her out.

We reached the exterior of the hospital where most of the others were lingering. "I'll see you around, then," he said.

"Yeah, good luck," I said.

"Good luck, Mister Cowboy," Rac said.

"That . . . is one brave idiot," I said before turning to head out.

A CRACKSHOT'S CRACK SHOT

"What are my chances again?" Crackshot asked.

It took a moment for Enyries to reply in his head.

Still not great. One in seven thousand two hundred.

That had gone up a little since the last time he'd asked. Not much, but a little. "A chance is a chance," he said. "You miss every shot you don't take."

Well, yes, but sometimes you just miss regardless of whether you took the chance or not.

He chuckled. "I get that, yeah. But if the world ends, then I want to go out knowing that I took that chance. It's a man thing."

If you say so.

Buying a Romance Chance Calculation Software catalog had been a weird choice for him. Not that he regretted it. It was interesting seeing the results pop up whenever he looked at someone. Grasshopper was not romantically interested, period. Tankette, however . . . That lady had wandering eyes.

The software threw up some weird results sometimes. Hedgehog was . . . kind of just a picky dude, but that was all. Crackshot had his thing shut off for anyone under eighteen, not because it couldn't work on them, but because it squicked him out something mighty.

Gomorrah was obviously into her maybe-girlfriend, but the Complication Matrix levels there were stupid high. Stray Cat and that Lucy girl? They had the same metrics as some couples he'd met who'd been happily married for thirty-plus years, which was wild.

Cat was one crazy lady, in his humble opinion, and it made him worried about that Lucy girl too, because there was no way she was sane if she was into *that*.

None of that mattered at the moment. He was just distracting himself so he didn't have to think about what was coming up. Crackshot got off his iron horse, then tugged the rearview mirror to the side to get a better look at himself.

He was in a tailored button-up shirt. All the buttons nice and shiny right up to his neck, collar on proper-like. It was a beige-and-red plaid-like pattern that he enjoyed. His jeans were nice and neat, pleated down the middle because he'd starched and ironed them himself. Bit stiff, but he could live with it.

Boots were spit-shined like new. He'd even oiled his spurs.

"Right," he muttered. "Now or never."

The place was one of the largest shopping spots in New Montreal. Big enough that even his country-bumpkin self had heard about it in ads and in passing. It was the kind of place that people would take a detour to visit if they had business in the city, just to say that they'd been.

It was also where Emoscythe stayed.

That might have been part of the mystique, he figured. A woman like that—not just a samurai—staying around a place was good enough of a reason for anyone to want to visit.

He stepped into the mall and soon enough he was lost in the crowd.

It always unnerved him, how many people there were in the city. Back home, the population was in the low thousands. He couldn't say that he knew everyone, but he knew enough people that everyone he did meet had a friend in common. Everyone was someone's cousin, neighbor, in-law, or something like that.

Out here, in New Montreal? A million people could be on the same block as him and there wasn't a chance in hell that he'd get to meet even a thousandth of them.

He was just some guy in a sea of people, and that rattled him something fierce. He was dressed a little weird compared to the locals, but not so weird that it stood out.

There were two young women giggling next to one of those cardboard stand-ups of . . . was that that Arm-a-Geddon guy from down south? They both had neon hair that waved with their laughter.

Farther inside, a group of mercs stomped by, six of them circling a totally average looking man. Too average. He looked like Crackshot's cousin who'd gone into accounting. His cousin had never needed an escort like that.

An elderly man was standing off to the side, doing a weird old dance while cringecore music played from his walker.

Ads blared all over, of course, but the street vendors shouted over them anyway, because even without Enyries filtering out the more intrusive ads, there was just something about a man calling out for your attention that worked.

And then he was in the main bazaar and walking toward a back exit. The place had guards. It had electronic surveillance, keycard access on the doors, and turrets hidden in the floor and others in plain sight. None of it tried to stop him.

It still felt weird, being someone. As much as he found some of his new samurai . . . friends a little weird, he did envy their confidence. Miss

Stray Cat seemed the sort to walk in front of a bus, entirely confident that it would stop for her, and it probably would. Some of the others were more humble about their power and reputation, but there was still that undercurrent of . . . weight to them.

None more than the woman he was visiting now.

It was a short ride up an elevator, then down another corridor, where he was let into a lobby space without any trouble. The floor was glass, overlooking the bazaar below. He didn't pay that any mind, not when she was right there.

His mouth suddenly felt dry at the sight of her.

Emoscythe Mordeath Noir.

She stood in the center of the room like the statue of a goddess ought to stand in the center of a temple. But she wasn't a thing of cold marble. No, she was all blacks and black and blacks. Layers of blue-black and purple-black and black-black, slightly different, subtle, all layered over each other in a dress that hinted as much as it shouted.

She looked at him for a moment, and then she smiled. A quirk of her purple-painted lips to one side, a flash of perfect teeth. "Hello, Crackshot Cowboy," she said.

Her voice was . . .

It was like a cold glass of ice water on one of those days when it got so hot he thought his trailer might melt.

"H-howdy, ma'am," he said.

"I wasn't expecting you, of all people," she said. "But it's a pleasure nonetheless. I see you've been taking my advice to heart."

"Yes ma'am," he said before he quickly removed his hat. Curse his fool brain, he was forgetting his manners. "Ma'am, I'm here to ask you something that might be inappropriate."

She blinked. "Go on?"

"I . . . I wouldn't normally ask this sort of thing. I'm hardly a brave man, I'm afraid, but I suppose the world ending and all has shaken things loose. Miss Emoscythe Mordeath Noir, would you mind if I asked you out on a date?"

She stared for a moment, then laughed, but she covered her mouth. There was mirth in her eyes, but not rejection. "How old are you?" she asked.

"Twenty-two," he said.

"I'm thirty-two. Aren't I a little old for you?"

"I don't mind that at all," he said. "In fact, I rather like it. Just how I like all the rest of the things I know about you."

She tilted her head, exposing just a bit of lace-covered neck. By God, this woman would be the end of him. "You're bold, aren't you?" she asked. "I admire your courage, at least."

"I reckon it's not the sort of time for cowardice and hesitance," he said.

She laughed, and he felt some of the tension in his shoulders loosening up. "Very well, Mister Crackshot Cowboy. I'll allow you to take me out on a date."

"Really?" he asked. "I mean, yes ma'am. Thank you, ma'am! How's a bite to eat sound?"

"Right now?"

"We've only got hours to go," he said. There were quite a few hours, of course, but still. He had to move while his bravery lasted.

"I suppose I could eat. Dinner?"

He nodded. "Dinner with you sounds lovely," he said honestly.

The world might be ending, but that didn't mean this wasn't the best day in his life.

"One in seven thousand, eh?" he muttered, a smile sneaking onto his face.

CHAPTER THIRTY-SIX

DIGGY DIGGY HOLE

One must understand physics. It makes it so much more interesting when you bend what you know to be absolutely true over and up and back into itself, because even as we break physics, the fundamental truth of it stands. It just becomes far more complex. And I think that's beautiful!"
—*Grasshopper's Guide to Physics for Kids (K–3)*, 2055

The next morning, after a nice breakfast, catching up with the kittens around the house, and giving Lucy a parting kiss that broke the one-minute mark, I picked up Rac from her corner of the house, then headed out again.

I could have stayed at the site the night before, but . . . why would I ever want to do that? Sleep in a tent that belonged to some sweaty soldier or sleep in my bed, at home, with a warm Lucy? It wasn't even a choice.

Rac had seemed to prefer to head back home as well, which was only fair. What was more surprising was discovering her ready to head out with me again the next morning. I'd half expected her to want to go out and do her own shit.

Still, I decided not to comment on it. I knew for a fact that if I was doing something helpful for someone and they made a comment, even a positive one, the chances that I'd want to keep it up were slim.

Oh, and I had to gear up a little better. The day before, I'd been in more casual gear. It was a little strange to think that I had enough clothes, let alone armor, that I had to choose between sets, but that's how it was.

Lucy had found a place to dry-clean that armor I'd . . . shed in. I inspected it real close and didn't find anything suspicious or gross, so that's what I was wearing again. It was better armor, in any case, and it was the set that Emoscythe had helped design.

We rode my bike back across the city and through the countryside beyond.

When we arrived near the site, I noticed two things.

First, we weren't alone in the air. There were several balloons hovering a kilometer or so above the ground. Looking at them made my augs fritz a little on the edges, like they were glitching out. The balloons were set in a circle around the entire site at more or less even intervals.

The second thing I noticed was that shit had been moving overnight.

I wasn't sure what criteria Grasshopper had for a space, but they'd found it in what was essentially a roadside stop. One of those little side roads that lead to what was basically a large parking space in the middle of fuck-all nowhere. It was surrounded by some sparse forest that was overtaking what had probably once been fields.

When I'd left, the engineers had said they were going to set up a camp. Tents, the mobile base, some trucks and shit. Nothing fancy.

Now? There was a giant hole being dug out of the earth by three tractors. A crane was set up to one side, moving loads of crap out of the way. Dump trucks were moving about, and there were six cement mixers parked in a neat row off to one side with their drums spinning away.

There were more people now, too, and they were moving with *speed*. I'd seen a few construction sites here and there. I'd never seen one where the workers all jogged around as if their boss was whipping their asses.

"Looks busy," Rac said.

"Yeah," I said. I noticed a few samurai cars parked way off to the side where they wouldn't be in the way. My mech was there, as was Gomorrah's *Fury* and Tankette's . . . shit, what had she called her tank? Oh, and Grasshopper's entirely out-of-place little hovercar too.

I pulled my bike in next to Grasshopper's ride, then climbed off and adjusted my coat while Rac looked past me. All of the construction work was kicking up a whole load of dust into the air, but there was more organization to it than I'd realized.

The moment we were closer, my augs pinged me, letting me know that there was a sitewide alternate-reality system in place over this area and asking me if I wanted to join it. I accepted, since Myalis wasn't kicking up a fuss.

That lit up areas in different colors, threw warnings into the air, and painted a dozen lines and dots across my vision. No wonder people were walking past each other without colliding. Someone, or something, was orchestrating all of the work, and doing it at the kind of pace that was probably well past sustainable.

We navigated through the area, apparently already having clearance to pass. The AR system directed me and Rac over to the mobile base, which had one side unfolded and covered in tarps to create a bigger pavilion.

I found the other samurai inside, as well as Major Tinwhistle and what had to be a half-dozen lower-ranked officers.

"Stray Cat!" Grasshopper said. She was dressed in a cute, if modest, summer dress. It was railgun-patterned, with the streaking lights coming out of the barrels drawing lines across the fabric. It was almost . . . adorable? She still had all the arms, though, and a rifle slung over her back that looked like it could take out a tank.

"Hey," I said, stepping aside to let some hard-hat-wearing guy past. "Damn, this place is busy."

"It is! At this rate, the location will be ready for the installation by nightfall."

"The installation?" I asked.

"She means the big gun," Gomorrah said as she walked over to us. "We've been going over all of the details for it. It's good that you're here. We're going to need some of your catalogs to help."

"None of my catalogs are that expensive," I said, confused.

"Yes, but if we don't use them, then it won't count as though you helped. Well, it won't count as *much*. You did organize some of this," Gomorrah said.

Right, we were trying to game the system a little. The system run by the AIs in our heads who definitely knew what we were thinking.

"Well, if you've cleared it out with our passengers." I gestured to my head. "Then I guess it's fine. What are we going for here?"

"Oh! Let me show you!" Grasshopper said. She reached down, took my hand, and started to pull me toward the door only to stop upon seeing Rac. "Raccoon! Oh, a pleasure to see you again. How are you feeling today?"

I suffered through some pleasantries, not quite daring to pull my hand free from Grasshopper's grip because that might have been just a little too rude. She chatted with Rac, then remembered that she was leading me somewhere.

So back outside we went, this time straight toward the big hole that was being dug out. It was long and pretty narrow, maybe thirty-ish meters wide and a hundred or so long. It wasn't super deep yet, but it looked like it was still being dug out.

"Once this is done, it'll have room for a cannon a kilometer long buried twenty meters into the ground and anchored into the bedrock. The water table here is quite low, and the ground is mostly solid stone. It's going to make digging deeper a bit tricky, but we have lots of high explosives and plenty of manpower!"

"Uh, wait, we're digging that big of a hole for the base of the cannon?" I asked.

Grasshopper turned and blinked at me. "No, it's for the entire cannon."

"So how long is the cannon?" I asked.

"One kilometer long," she said.

I was a little confused. Why would the thing the cannon was resting on be as long as the gun itself? We were shooting into space, so why not use a smaller platform and build things upward? "And we need a kilometer-long base for that?" I asked with a vague gesture to the sky.

She stared, then something lit up in her eyes. "Oh! No, no, we're not pointing this upward, Catherine. This will be level with the ground. Well, level with gravity, actually."

"I am real confused," I said. "Isn't the enemy, you know . . ." I gestured vaguely upward. "In space?"

"Of course! But shooting something through our atmosphere would be quite silly. The drag, the gravity." She shook her head, then gestured to my hip. "That gave me a brilliant idea."

I looked down to where Void Terminus was hanging by my side. I'd gotten pretty used to the sword's weight by now. "My sword?"

"Your sword-shaped portal into space," she corrected gently. "Why shoot through atmosphere when you can fire a quarter-ton sabot through a kilometer-long magnetic rail right into a portal whose exit is already in orbit? In orbit and on its way to Phobos, even! Though at the speed that the exit portal, or rather the machine holding it, is moving, the difference in range is rather negligible."

"Oh," I said.

I eyed the growing hole again.

"*Oh.*"

Yeah, no wonder Grasshopper wanted this to be kept on the down-low. People would shit themselves for this kind of tech, or this kind of weapon. And we were going to use it to punch bullets at space aliens.

Actually, that was probably a great use for this kind of thing.

CHAPTER THIRTY-SEVEN

HONEST SAMURAI REVIEWS

Look, I don't care how woke your review is, the audience won't care what you have to say if you can't even beat the first fucking level!
—Gamers Portal comment, 2029

I kind of expected things to move faster than they were, but it was clear a few hours in that I had set my expectations at one level and reality was conspiring to be at another. Which was fine, I supposed.

Basically, while Grasshopper expected the big gun to be ready by nightfall, Major Tinwhistle was a bit more conservative.

"By tonight?" she asked when she finally had a spare minute where she wasn't screaming at people not to fuck up. "I . . . suppose it's possible, but only if by tonight you mean before the sun rises. Even then, that means my guys will be working through the night."

"Would letting them get some rest be better?" I asked.

"Do you work at your best without sleep?" she asked right back.

That was a fair point. I wasn't the greatest when I was cranky.

Grasshopper hummed. "That's unfortunate, but it's not altogether unexpected. To be quite honest, we are still a ways ahead of where I expected to be, so I can hardly complain. You've been doing good work. All of your people have."

Major Tinwhistle nodded, but by the set of her shoulders I could tell she was proud to hear that. "Just make sure you let the brigadier general know. I don't want to die a major. This kind of project is either the kind of thing that'll be so blacklisted and classified that it won't help me get promoted at all, or it'll be the kind of thing that's so big they won't have a choice but to pin a medal on my chest."

I laughed. "You have things figured out," I said. "But yeah, give your guys a break, I think we'll be fine finishing the big gun tomorrow. Right?"

Grasshopper nodded. "We will. We can likely start purchasing some things now, though. I intend to buy some construction drones in any case. They'll be able to work through the night."

"Oh?" Tinwhistle asked. "I wouldn't say no to samurai-tech help."

"Hmm, my drones are all back home," I said. "But I don't think they're suitable for this kind of thing anyway."

"It's fine," Grasshopper said. "We will be purchasing large amounts of raw materials. Mister Hedgehog and Miss Princess said that their catalogs couldn't truly help with the gun itself, but they're willing to share the cost for the materials required to build the basing structure."

"What did you buy? Other than raw mats, I mean," I asked.

Grasshopper tapped her chin. "I'm buying the main gun. I think I have the largest pool of free points to spend on this kind of project. Miss Gomorrah is purchasing a number of shells for the gun, as well as the fire-control computer. Mister Crackshot Cowboy bought the targeting system and its hardware already. He had a fantastic catalog for that."

"Huh, everyone's pitching in," I said.

"Yes! Tankette will be buying the loader, since that meshes well with her catalogs. Hmm, would you mind buying the entry portal and some of the ammunition? You have a catalog for that, right?"

"Yeah," I said. "Exotic Single Use Explosives. Bought a technically-not-a-nuke with it once. I'm sure Myalis would love to help us throw different things at the wall to see what sticks. What about Gros Baton? The new kid?"

"Oh, he's quite a lovely young man," Grasshopper said.

I nodded, then realized that I had no idea where he was. For that matter, I didn't know where Rac had run off to either. Suspicious.

"He's taking care of site security, which is also quite important."

"Fair enough. Is he the one who put up those balloons? They make my augs fritz whenever I look at them for too long."

"That was him, as well as Hedgehog. Gros Baton has a catalog for traps that happened to have some barrage balloons available. Hedgehog has a pretty intense suite of anti-spyware programs, so combining the two led to those. They should mask our presence a little, and make it harder for low-flying spy drones to pass by."

"We're not going to be keeping this a secret for very long, will we?" I asked.

Grasshopper wiggled her hand in a so-so gesture. "Major Tinwhistle's people have been very good about not going online, but eventually their lack of presence will be noticed. There were probably a lot of eyes on the area already, what with the number of new samurai here. But the attention that new samurai get tends to be from . . . smaller organizations."

"What's that mean?" I asked. I wasn't sure if I should be offended or not.

"It means that organizations like the bigger corps might pay attention to smaller samurai in order to see if they're recruitable or if they'd be willing to work with them. Bigger samurai will have corporate eyes on them because they're a constant and pervasive threat to those corporations. It's a little different."

"Are you one of those bigger samurai?" I asked.

"I've been around for a few years, but I never truly focused all of my resources on growing stronger," she said with a smile that was just a little sad. "I'd much rather pay for educational TV shows or spend my points on things that'll help humanity in the long run rather than neat weapons. I'm regretting that just a little now, when that spending might have helped us all get through this situation a little easier."

"Nah, I think you did alright," I said. Grasshopper didn't strike me as a fighter. Not that I doubted her ability to kick ass and take names. She just wasn't the sort of person I'd picture on the front lines. I supposed that didn't make her any less of a samurai, though.

"Well, it means that I've been small fry in the samurai world for a long time. The only reason a larger corporation would care about me is the friends I've made along the way. A few of those have gone on to have incredible careers!"

I nodded along.

"You should go see your friends too. Leave the logistics to the major and I. You're more of an . . . in-person leader, I think."

"I'm not a leader at all," I said. "I just keep getting stuck having to boss people around. Doesn't mean I like it. But yeah, sure. I'm worried Rac might be getting into trouble. I'll be upset if someone drives over her with one of those tractors."

Grasshopper giggled, the laugh making her look ten years younger and kind of ruining her more serious moment. "That would be awful. Go check on her, and on the others. Believe it or not, all of them, from Gomorrah to Tankette, value your opinion . . . Well, maybe not Hedgehog, I have the impression you struck him the wrong way."

"Ah, yeah, that might be my fault. I was a little too honest with him."

"Honesty can be tricky sometimes," she agreed easily.

I waved goodbye to the major, who barely acknowledged me. She was in the middle of what looked like three simultaneous calls while two engineer-looking sorts were badgering her with questions, so I didn't take umbrage at being ignored and just slipped out of the command tent.

The place was still hustling, even more so than when I'd arrived. There was now a mountain of loose dirt being piled up by the roadside, and more tractors had arrived and were shoving it out into a long wall of packed dirt and stone.

The hole where the gun would be had gained another twenty meters or so in the last half hour and it looked like they had dropped another meter into the ground. It seemed like they were digging it out as a sort of ramp? I wasn't sure and didn't have the background to make anything approaching an intelligent guess, so I didn't question it.

I found the others relatively easily.

Tankette had parked her tank next to a row of tents where food was being served. She was helping, which I imagined continued to make her pretty popular with everyone here. Her smile suggested she was enjoying it.

Princess and Knight were sitting at one table in that tent, looking a little awkward as they spoke to each other. I had no idea where Hedgehog was. And Rac . . .

It took me a moment to find her. She was out by the edge of the hole, just far enough from it that I wasn't instinctually worried she'd trip into it and actually get squished.

Next to her, Gros Baton was saying something with a lot of gestures, and from the way their shoulders shook, they both laughed at whatever that was. Rac shoved him, and I caught his stupid grin from all the way out here.

Well, well, it seemed like I really was the best matchmaker that ever was.

Of course, if the little shit hurt her, no amount of being a samurai or a minor would save him.

CHAPTER THIRTY-EIGHT

EGGS BURNY-SIDE UP

With growing populations comes a growing need for housing. This need is answered in one of two ways: mega-projects, or Rapid-Fab Housing.

Mega-projects offer the most bang for a developer's buck. Creating enclosed superstructures where a corporation can control everything from police forces, to food sales, to climate control for its residents ensures a constant flow of revenue over the life of the structure.

Rapid-Fab, surprisingly, costs significantly more, as land around a megacity tends to go for a premium. The houses themselves can be built to code in under a week, or built without respecting code—for a small fine—in under a day, ensuring housing demands are met for thousands of middle-class citizens all at once.

—Excerpt from *Housing in the 21st Century*, 2039

I was up and at 'em early the next morning. Before noon, even.

The group had set up a small chat about the big gun project, one handled by our respective AIs. I think it was reasonable to say that it was about as safe as a chatroom could be, even considering the number of people in it.

I poked at the chatroom while Lucy made breakfast. This morning was a "full English," which meant that I got to sit at the kitchen island, hair still damp from a warm shower, and watch as an apron (and unfortunately more clothes) clad Lucy went about handling three pans and two disasters at the same time.

"Holy shit, why do eggs cook so fast?" she grumbled as she moved one of the pans over to a plate and tipped it over. Eggs slid off the nonstick surface and mostly landed on the plate. Half of them looked uncooked and runny. The other half were brown-turning-black on the edges.

I smiled into a mug of warm coffee as Lucy ran the other way, stirred a pot filled with beans—from the resistance, I suspected some were now permanently welded to the bottom—and then poked at some sausages in the other pan. They spat and hissed, but actually looked pretty good.

"You'll get the hang of it."

"I might hang someone, alright," Lucy muttered. "The site made this look easy! This is bullshit."

"Wasn't this like, the standard breakfast for a lot of places in the world?" I asked. "Eggs, sausage, beans, toast."

"Fuck! The toast!" Lucy ran over to the far end of the counter, almost tripped—which had me sitting bolt upright in case I needed to move—then made it to the bread . . . thing. The box with the foldy top that bread goes in, for some reason. She popped it open, revealing two end-bits of bread and nothing else. "Fuck!"

"It's okay, we don't need toast," I said.

"But I *want* toast," Lucy whined. Actually whined. I hadn't heard her make such a pitiful noise in a while. The last time had definitely involved rope and had been a lot of fun.

"Myalis can—"

"Don't *buy* toast. I'm making breakfast!" Lucy said.

"What about bread?" I asked.

She considered it. "Okay, but get it pre-sliced. I don't have time for that."

Shrugging, I had a small discussion with Myalis about alien bread while Lucy continued to putter about the kitchen like a 1950s housewife with the vocabulary of an 1850s sailor. I was just happy that she was enjoying her new cooking hobby so much. Plus, it was food. I never said no to food.

The group chat caught my attention again as it moved. A message from Gomorrah asking if Tankette needed help at the mess tent, then Princess apologizing that she couldn't help on account of currently learning how to use a bulldozer?

There was a subchannel, of course, for memes. Grasshopper was surprisingly active on there. I scrolled up through a hundred-odd photos of cats, dogs, strange reptiles, bears, birds, and a few funny-looking fish. Most of them were "cool animal fact" memes that probably belonged on some soccer mom's media feed, but others were just cute pictures.

Gros Baton was posting obscure French-Canadian memes that—even translated—made not one lick of sense. Kinda weird to see someone who lived in the same general area as the rest of us have such a wildly different meme culture.

Gomorrah had posted some more nerdy science-facts memes, and then Crackshot and Princess had gotten into a bit of a meme war. Crackshot was surprisingly adept at it, but Princess and Knight were tag-teaming him into meme . . . submission?

Crackshot had set up his own subchannel for dating advice. None of it was good, at a glance, mostly because the people helping him there were Princess and Knight and Gomorrah. Gomorrah had a girlfriend, sure, but that wasn't thanks to her suave wit, that was mostly because Franny had the stubbornness of a junkie who needed their next fix.

I went back to the main channel and scrolled way back up to the start. Hedgehog had been pretty vocal early on, and then throughout the night. Mostly updates, logistics reports, and a few quick conversations with anyone awake about some detail or another. At some point he'd gone to sleep, and the chat took a distinctly less professional turn.

I kinda liked the irreverence better, but it did make it a whole lot trickier to find anything important in all of the noise.

One of the AIs, whose name I wasn't familiar with—Tankette's, maybe?—kept a running update on the progress according to Major Tinwhistle, including an ETA counter that ticked up and down with how long the engineers thought it would take.

The ETA ticker updated every half hour in the chat, but it didn't always change by half an hour. There was definitely a downward trend to the amount of time left until things were done, but there were skips and jumps, and at some point around four a.m. the timer changed by two hours. The chat got lively around then, with a message from Knight asking what made that noise.

Turned out an automated loader had glitched out. The brakes failed and it rammed into a bulldozer at the stunning speed of seven kilometers an hour. But with the kind of mass the engineers were dealing with, that still made a lot of noise and fucked up two vehicles that needed untangling.

Some poor fucks had to figure all of that out hours before the sun came up.

It seemed like a genuine accident, not malicious intent, and the subsequent ETA updates showed that things got back into line quickly enough.

"Looks like I'm gonna need to be there in an hour or so," I said.

"At the gun site?" Lucy asked without turning around. She was trying to flip an egg over with a spatula.

"Yeah. Seems like shit's actually getting done. At this rate we might be able to fire the thing today. Kinda wild, to be honest."

"That is impressively fast," Lucy said. "But I guess it's not that surprising. We've both seen megabuildings go up."

I nodded. Usually a new megabuilding took like, one or two years to be built? More or less. That sounded like a long time until you stood on the edge of the giant gap where the building would be one day, and a year later there were fifty floors of impossibly thick building in place. The rate those things went up at was kinda nuts. I always liked watching the timelapses.

"The wall around the city went up fast too," I said.

"Simpler than a building, I guess," Lucy said. "Weren't the slabs for it pre-made? I remember hearing something like that."

"I guess?" I said. I didn't know for sure, and I honestly hadn't paid that much attention.

Lucy put something on a plate, then picked up a piece of toast, buttered it, and placed it down. She spun, a big, ridiculously proud smile on full display. "Speaking of pre-made, or rather, absolutely *not* pre-made, breakfast is ready!"

She set the plate down, and I caught a strong whiff of it. Freshly cooked eggs, slightly burned beans, buttered toast. My mouth watered. "Have I told you today that I love you?" I asked.

"Only twice so far," Lucy said. "I could stand to hear it more."

I looked up, meeting her eyes. "I love you."

Lucy smiled, the image of self-satisfied smugness. "Damn right," she said.

"Not gonna say it back?" I asked as I picked up a fork and started to dig in.

"Bitch, I made you breakfast, ain't no 'I love you' stronger than that."

I laughed between bites, then savored the meal while Lucy put the rest into some bowls and plates and set them on the counter. A few kittens had been spying on the kitchen for a while now, and they came over to grab what they could, like wild animals lurking around the back exit of a fast-food joint.

Lucy eventually cornered Bargain and Nose and traded food for elbow grease, both of them agreeing—under penalty of slow, painful death if they went back on their word—to do the dishes in exchange for food.

It was a nice morning to what I suspected was going to be a nice day. Now I just had to see if Rac wanted to come along, and then head out. If all went well, we'd be averting the end of the world by suppertime.

CHAPTER THIRTY-NINE

I WANT TO LICK YOUR EYEBALL

Do not, under any circumstance, lick someone's eyeball.
We do not endorse any eyeball-licking memes.
—Public Service Announcement from the Ophthalmologists Association of
USTwo, 2041

I found Rac all geared up and waiting for me by the entrance. She was in her skintight armored suit, but with a loose T-shirt and shorts over it, as well as a beat-up old denim jacket. "I'm digging the mixed material look," I said.

"The what?" she asked.

"You know, fancy high-tech undersuit, low-tech grunge over it?" I asked.

Rac gave me a look, as if she was questioning my sanity which . . . alright, fair. Rac was one of those few who'd grown up in a situation shittier than my own. She deserved a break. "Do you mind if I come with you again? Or would you rather I stay here to work?"

"You mean with the printer?" I asked.

She nodded. "I loaded it this morning and brought some prosthetics down to the clinic already. Miss See-Three took the ones I made this morning and the batch from last night too."

"You got two batches off since last night?" I asked. I was moderately impressed. "When did you even start?"

"This morning?" she said. "It's almost noon."

Oh, right. Some people woke up early. "You're a morning person, then?"

"No," she said. "I just don't need much sleep."

We both stepped into the elevator while I chewed on that. "You know, you'll never grow big and tall if you don't get enough sleep, right?"

"Is that why you're tall? You sleep a lot?"

I poked her in the shoulder. "Rude. But probably not entirely inaccurate, to be honest. I'm an expert at napping."

The elevator stopped at the parking garage, and we stepped out and toward my bike, which was parked nearby. We got on, took off, and soon we were zipping across New Montreal heading north again. I was totally ready to beeline straight to the Big Gun site when I got spooked by Myalis talking in my head.

There are several monitoring systems observing you.

"Oh, shit," I said. We were just out of the city limits, past the new walls. "Should I start evasive maneuvers?"

No. There have always been a number of systems that observe your flight. Most of these are related to traffic control, or part of the New Montreal defensive grid—tracking system for the close-in weapons systems mounted on the walls.

"We're being aimed at?" I asked.

You always have been. The tracking systems I've noticed now are new, and specifically attuned to notice your bike.

I gave my bike a bit more gas to move along faster. "If anything opens up on us, I want you to buy some decoy grenades, please."

Understood.

What should have been a nice, calming flight out of the city was a little more white-knuckled than I was used to, but nothing happened. No gunshots, no missiles ramming up my tailpipe, no surprise explosions.

"Can you trace who put those trackers out there?" I asked.

Certainly. I have attempted to do so already, though I'm afraid the trail goes cold rather rapidly. The devices were delivered to a few rooftops via hovercars. The cars are registered by—or have been recently used by— several freelance mercenaries. The devices are all commercial-use trackers with mostly default programming. There are a few avenues I can dig into some more, but most trails have been obscured from the start.

"Damn," I muttered.

"Is everything okay?" Rac asked from behind me.

"Yeah, it's fine," I called back. "Someone playing games is all."

Might I suggest taking a slight detour? You might not want to lead anyone investigating you right to the project site.

Shit, that was a fine idea. I turned, driving instead toward Saint-Jérome. It didn't take too long for us to get there, and it took less time once there for me to get a ride-along with a few engineers picking up some equipment from a drop-off in the city.

The news that I'd been tracked went over surprisingly well in the shared chat, and I found myself somewhat reassured when Grasshopper told me not to worry while I sat in the back of a cargo truck and rode out to the site, my bike strapped into the trailer so I'd at least have a way home later.

When Rac and I arrived, a solid half hour later than I'd expected to, it was to find Princess and Knight waiting for us by the unloading area the engineers had set up.

"Stray Cat!" Princess said. She was grinning ear-to-ear as I hopped out of the truck. "Good afternoon."

"Hey," I said. "How are you doing?" I scanned past Princess and Knight to the grounds. I was used to seeing things from above as I flew around, which was a good way of seeing how things were progressing, but even from ground level I could tell that shit was getting done. The hole for the gun was now a very long trench and the mounds of dirt dug up to make that trench were the size of several small mountains, forming a sort of natural wall of dirt along the perimeter of the site.

Princess walked right up to me and smiled even as she looked up into my eyes. "It's nice to see you again. And I'm doing alright," she said.

Yup, she was still creepy. "Cool, cool," I said. "So, any news since I was last here? I mean, stuff that didn't make it onto the group chat?"

"Oh, uh, not too much? Did you see, I got to ride one of the tractors!"

"It was terrifying," Knight said.

"Were you with her?" I asked.

"I was, yeah," Princess's far more down-to-earth sister said. "Princess doesn't have a license yet."

"Ah, right." I wasn't about to mention that I didn't have one either.

Princess clapped her hands. "Oh, right! We came to meet you because Grasshopper wants to talk. It's important."

"Oh, right, I'm supposed to buy some parts for the gun, right?"

"That too!" she said. "But no, it's mostly because of interference."

I felt my brows knitting together. "Interference?" I repeated. "Is some political fuckwit sticking their dick in our project or something? Because I have solutions for that kind of thing."

Princess giggled and shook her head. "Nope. It's from other samurai."

I blinked. "Wait, what?"

"You might want Grasshopper to explain it," she said. "She'll do a better job of it than I can."

"Basically," Knight said, "we're not the only ones trying to stop the end of the world. We're not the first ones either, and some others have called dibs on blowing up Phobos."

I shook my head. Unbelievable. Princess and Knight escorted me across the site to where a few temporary buildings had gone up, replacing the tents that had been there the previous day. The mobile base was still parked there and it looked like it was in use, but there was also an honest-to-god bunker not too far from it.

It looked like the engineers had more cement or whatever than they knew what to do with, so they'd started setting up a full-on base right here.

Actually, that . . . kind of made sense. The Big Gun was pretty damned permanently emplaced. From what I understood, a kilometer-long railgun was actually very delicate, and also huge. Huge and delicate didn't go together very well most of the time, so moving this thing was going to be impossible.

Still, it was kind of wild that it deserved the whole bunker-and-base treatment.

Grasshopper met me outside of the mobile base with a big smile on her face and her arms spread out for a hug. I gave in, walking into her hug with a put-upon sigh.

I wouldn't ever let her or anyone else know, but I did secretly enjoy Grasshopper's hugs. The only problem was that I had an image to keep up, and being seen getting hugged and fussed over by Grasshopper wasn't great for that.

"Hello, Stray Cat," she said.

"Hey," I replied. "So, we're getting messed with by some samurai?"

She nodded. "Come on in, I'll tell you all about it."

"Alright. Who is it, anyway?"

"Who are they, rather," she corrected softly. "It's not one samurai, or even one organization. At the moment there are three groups, including us, who have plans to take out Phobos within the next forty-eight hours. There are others who have their own plans in place, but they won't be ready for a little longer."

"So, it's us, two other groups, then a gaggle of other samurai who'll be tossing shit at the wall at the last minute?"

"I wouldn't use those terms, exactly, but you're essentially correct," she said. There was a globe hovering over the planning table, with three bright red dots on it. One of them was in eastern Canada, where we were. The second was in . . . central Europe, maybe? And the last was somewhere in Asia. "Let me show you what we're up against!"

CHAPTER FORTY

RACE ME TO THE MOON

"We need a publicity stunt. Something big for our people to rally around. Something like we had in the golden age of America."

"What about going to the moon again?"

"What? No, you idiot, are you mental? That's too expensive. I was thinking . . . let's give everyone a car?"

—USTwo GOP2 Discussion, 2038

"Wait, so let me get this straight," I said as I gestured to the globe. "Some fucks from around the world found out about our big gun project and they're not happy about it?

"That sums it up, yes," Grasshopper said. "But for two small details." She raised a hand, two fingers splayed in a peace sign.

"Go on," I said.

"First, I don't think that we can really ascribe negative emotions to either group. We haven't spoken to them directly yet, so it's not fair to assume that they're angry or even unhappy with us. Second, they might not be adversaries to begin with, and the way you're framing things could lead to bigger problems down the line."

I worked my jaw, wanting to disagree on principle, but . . . Grasshopper was probably onto something.

Two other samurai organizations were working to stop the end of the world. If anything, I ought to be happy about it. Just a couple of days ago I'd been pissed that no one was taking action. "I guess we don't hold a monopoly on saving the world," I said.

"We share the same planet," Grasshopper said. "It's only fair that we all do our best to save it. Especially when saving it means using great amounts of violence on a deserving target."

I nodded slowly. Something told me that Grasshopper was a card-carrying member of the "blow up pipelines" school of ecological preservation. "So, can we chat with them, or are we in an unofficial race to see who can blow up Phobos first?"

"I'd much rather we talk first," Grasshopper said. "Which is why I've set up a meeting with a representative from both groups. I was hoping you wouldn't mind representing us? I need to help Major Tinwhistle with some final notes on the Big Gun's construction, and the others are all quite new for samurai."

"So am I," I defended. "What about Gomorrah?"

"She didn't want to."

What if *I* didn't want to? I grumbled a bit, but . . . yeah, it was this or try to find something to do so that I wasn't just standing around with my thumb up my ass. "Fine," I said. "Just two samurai, right?"

"Yep! One from the Keiretsu association of East Asia, and the other from the Nachtwächternetzwerk group."

" . . . The what?"

"Do you want me to write the names down for you? It might make it easier to pronounce them," she said.

I shook my head, but I did look at the text she sent me a moment later. There were little spaces telling me which syllables to pronounce in the mishmash of letters that was supposed to be a name. "Anything I should know about these two?"

"The Nachtwächternetzwerk group is, as the name suggests, more of a network than a corporate group like the Family. It's based in Germany, with members in Austria and Switzerland. The group only allows samurai as members, though there are some who have family members and close friends as support staff. It's more an interconnected network of friends who support each other than anything else."

"Weird," I said.

Grasshopper giggled. "Catherine, it's exactly like what we have here."

"Oh," I said. "And the other?" I asked, trying to slip past that awkward fumble.

"The Keiretsu association is far larger in terms of scope, though it technically has fewer samurai members. They call their members ronin instead of samurai, which is quite interesting if you're at all aware of the etymological roots of the title 'samurai.' In any case, each samurai member there is the head of a corporation."

"Wait, the . . . Japanese samurai are all corpos?"

"Oh no. Not in the way you're thinking. Some of those corporations are quite small. Little more than a family business, really. It's just that the Keiretsu association keeps them interlinked. If you had your prosthetics clinic there, you'd find other samurai lending you support for various things for prices far below market rates. Also, it's not just Japan. Both Koreas, Taiwan, Mongolia, and a few island nations are included."

I started to rub at my temples. My education in geography was not enough for this conversation. "Okay, fine. Do we need to worry about any other groups?"

"No. There are two groups in Africa that are preparing something, but it seems more like a contingency to catch pieces of Phobos before they hit Earth. Another group in India is preparing something as well, but it's also preventative. A lot of smaller groups with only a few members, like our own, are setting up for things, but the Nachtwächternetzwerk network . . . oh, a tautology . . . Anyway, they've been discouraging people from trying anything and instead encouraging them to focus on the global incursion." Grasshopper clapped her hands. "Enough talk! Time to get you sitting down in front of a camera."

"Wait, we're calling them *now*?"

"Of course. Do you have any idea what time it is in Germany and Japan right now?"

"I haven't the faintest clue," I said.

"Nor do I, but I imagine that if we wait too much longer, our overseas friends will be quite tired."

Grasshopper tugged me along until I was unceremoniously placed in front of a monitor bank. This was right in the middle of the command area, with engineers wandering in and out behind me and officers working at their own stations.

"There's a privacy screen," she said as she activated a small, boxy device. There was a hum from the machine, then the noise in the rest of the room dropped to a low murmur. "There, that ought to keep you concentrated. That screen is you, and the other two are our friends, and this here is the webcam."

Grasshopper tapped a few keys and a trio of screens lit up. I was on the left, as was half of Grasshopper as she leaned in to type a few last things. The middle and right screens were blank, but they had the name of the organizations we were talking with below.

She patted my shoulders. "Do us proud!"

I really didn't like how quickly I was being shoved into something like a "face" position. Being the "tells people to get their heads out of their asses" person? I could live with that. Being the face of this operation? That I wasn't so sure about.

But I didn't get much of a choice as the middle screen flickered on and I came face-to-face with . . . a mad scientist.

The man looked like he was in his mid-forties or so. Black hair that was turning white on the edges and balding at the front. What he did have left was long and unruly. My guy needed a haircut, but judging by the lack of sanity in his eyes, that was a distant concern.

"Ah, you're here," he said in the thickest German accent I'd ever heard. "Good, good. Yes, my name is Doctor Kaleb Weber, samurai designation Radikal. I'm a proud member of the Nachtwächternetzwerk and the Schützenfest Samurai Militia. A pleasure." He smiled, then looked off camera and grabbed a . . . hot dog? Like, a normal-ass hotdog, with ketchup and mustard. Some of the condiments soon found themselves on his lab coat. "Sorry. I skipped my last meal, we're very busy."

"Uh, hi," I said.

I didn't have time to introduce myself before the other screen came on. There was another middle-aged guy, this one looking like he had just walked out of a period piece, but he was at least well-trimmed and professional. Actually, his weird outfit kinda had a bit of a corpo look to it. A sort of blend between a . . . whatever the male version of a kimono was and a business suit.

"Greetings," he said. His words were added at the bottom of his screen as subtitles, even though his English had better enunciation than mine. "I'm Susan, of Amaterasu Corporation, member of the Keiretsu. Doctor Radikal, a pleasure to meet you again. Miss Stray Cat, hello."

"Hello," I said with a quick wave. "I'm Stray Cat, of . . . the New Montreal Big Gun Project."

Oh fuck, I was pulling titles out of my ass now, but it didn't felt appropriate to just say something like, "Hi, I'm Stray Cat and I was dumped in front of you because we have no idea what we're doing here."

"Nice to meet you," Doctor . . . Radikal said. I wouldn't have known how to spell that without the subtitles. "So, it is our understanding that both the Keiretsu and the, ah, New Montreal Big Gun Project are planning to take care of our extraterrestrial visitors? We also have something up our sleeves." He raised his hands to show the inside of the sleeves of his lab coat, which . . . had nothing in them.

Yeah, this was not starting off normally.

CHAPTER FORTY-ONE

OPERATION MOON BOOM

So, from today onward, the European Union will no longer be called the European Union. The word "union" has been tainted by the leftists and those who would steal from the deserving and give to the worker. From now on, the EU will be the European Corporation, a corporation of national entities working to improve the lives of the deserving!

—EC Political Speech, 2041

"Yeah," I said to fill the immediately awkward silence.

Susan—and it was kind of weird that there was a middle-aged dude called Susan—shifted slightly. I had the impression that he was sitting on his knees, which . . . alright. He was in a very fancy office, but the background also looked kind of ancient? Wooden walls and those rice-paper screens that Asian supercorps liked to decorate with.

Doctor Radikal, meanwhile, looked like he was stuffed in a space that was about fifty square meters too small for all the junk he was trying to stuff into it. I couldn't name a tenth of the equipment behind him, but it all looked like the sort of shit you'd find in a science lab.

"So, uh, before we waste each other's time," I began. "Have the Keiretsu and the . . . Nacht . . . watcher . . . networks . . ."

"Nachtwächternetzwerk," Radikal corrected quickly.

"Right, thanks," I said. "Have you guys been in contact with each other already? Because I'm worried that we're going to be double-teamed over here."

"We have only been in contact recently," Susan said. "As of yesterday, in fact, but this is one of our first official meetings to discuss how we all intend to move forward."

I nodded slowly. "So there's no pre-existing agreement or anything like that in place?"

"Only an agreement to discuss things today," Radikal said. "Which is why our discovery of your project was so fortuitous."

"How *did* you find out anyway?" I asked. "It's not like we were trying to be obvious about it. Actually, it's the opposite. We're trying to be discreet here."

Radikal shrugged his shoulders. "One of our netzwerk's samurai is an information-gathering specialist. She let us know about the project and we researched it further. Likewise for the Keiretsu, though they were not nearly so secretive."

"We have no intention to be subtle," Susan said. "The faith of humanity and Earth is on the line. This is not a time for secrecy."

"Oh, I don't know, there's a certain value in discretion," Radikal said. "But in any case, yes, I'm glad we're all here to discuss things."

"Yeah, cool," I said. "So, we want to address the elephant?"

"The elephant?" Susan asked. His eyes glowed for a moment, then he nodded sagely. "Ah, yes, a western idiom, I see. Yes, we should address the elephant."

I shifted in my camp seat. It wasn't the most comfortable thing I'd ever sat on. "So, all three of us have ways to fuck up Phobos. I'm assuming some of these will interfere with the rest of us, and while I'm not point-hungry, I bet some people are, and nabbing Phobos means a fuckload of points."

"That's a good point," Radikal said. "As things are, the project that would strike Phobos first is our own. It's also the most likely to cause interference. The Keiretsu's drones would be in strike range next, followed by your own project."

"If our goal is to save Earth, is there any reason we should change that?" I asked. It would suck if we spent all these thousands of points on the Big Gun only for it to go to waste, but at least we'd all be alive enough to earn more points later.

The doctor shifted slightly, then nodded. "Let's first go over our individual projects so that we might all be on the same page, yes?"

"That's fair," I said. "Wanna go first?"

"Certainly! The Nachtwächternetzwerk has created an in-orbit device we're calling the Weltraumgewittermeister Teslakollisionsgenerator."

"That's . . . the what?"

"Ah, yes, forgive me. The . . . Space Storm Master Tesla Collision Generator? I believe that translation is accurate," he said with another nod. "It's a large orbital device we've installed that is moving to Earth's second Lagrange point as we speak. It should be arriving there within the hour, in fact."

"And what's this tesla collider thing do?" I asked.

"The device is capable of creating a charge in distant objects," he said.

"Like . . . an electrical charge?" I asked. Were they gonna tase the moon or something?

"Exactly! The idea is simple: Introduce a strong magnetic force through the Phobos object, thereby forcing it to rip itself apart. We can then induce more charges in the remains, causing them to crash back into each other. It'll also allow us to keep or disperse the materials that make up Phobos."

Susan hummed. "Our solution is not so elegant, though it is quite simple," he said before reaching below the camera and pulling up . . . a small steaming cup of tea. "We have sent up several large factory ships into orbit with two ronin of the Keiretsu. The ronin are supplying the ships with more materials. As we speak, a small force of drones has been launched from Earth's orbit and are in formation already their way to Phobos."

"What kind of drones?" I asked.

"The first wave are kamikaze, remotely operated explosive drones that will pepper the surface of the moon, clear it of alien life, and clip Phobos's wings. The next waves are equipped with powerful chemical lasers to heat the moon's surface and cause the moon to deviate from its path."

"Clever," I said.

"And what of your Big Gun Project?" Doctor Radikal asked, if only to be polite. "What is your plan?"

"We're building a big gun, and we're gonna shoot it."

Susan gave me a *look*, as if I ought to have been embarrassed by the lack of sophistication in our plan, but I didn't care about that.

"It's a little more complex than it sounds," I added. "We have portal tech. We're shooting into a portal on Earth, and the bullet's coming out of a portal in space. So we're skipping the whole . . . get to space bit with our bullet."

"Oh, that's ingenious. I've noticed that your gun is quite large," Radikal said.

"About a kilometer of railgun," I said.

Susan actually seemed a little impressed now, nodding before he took another careful sip of his tea. "That is, in fact, a large gun," he admitted. "What is your intended payload?"

"We have a lot of choices there," I said. "Personally, I wanna see what monofilament bombs could do to Phobos. Grasshopper has also sold me on the idea of Casaba-Howitzers? Honestly, just the thought of those kinda makes me feel all warm and fuzzy inside."

"Understandable," Doctor Radikal said, and for a moment I think we shared a bit of mutual enthusiasm for big things that went kaboom. "In light of what we do have . . . I suspect that our project here will be the one to cause the most interference. Perhaps less with the Big Gun Project, as the Weltraumgewittermeister Teslakollisionsgenerator will not interfere so much with a rapidly moving projectile, but our electromagnetic interference might very well destroy the Keiretsu drones."

"That won't matter if your project blows up Phobos before the drones get there, right?" I asked.

"Perhaps! We certainly intend to try. The difficulty lies in the enemy response."

"What do you mean?" I asked.

Susan was the one to reply. "The adversary will not allow us to strike them with impunity. They will adapt. That is what they do."

"Can the Antithesis adapt to resist being crushed by a giant space magnet?" I asked. I wasn't sure if I understood how the Weltrawhatevermeister worked, but I figured I had the gist of it.

"A week ago, would you have expected them to be able to move a moon across the solar system?" Susan asked.

"Fair point," I said. "So . . . what, we want to try a bunch of shit until something works?"

"Exactly!" Doctor Radikal said. "If we're to defeat the enemy, we need to either land a powerful alpha strike or hit them with a large number of different attacks before they can adapt. The Keiretsu drone program allows for the construction of more drones with varied weapon emplacements and the Big Gun Project allows for a variety of projectiles to be launched at the Antithesis. Combined with our own powerful attack, we will definitely succeed in destroying Phobos and saving Earth!"

I grinned. The doc's enthusiasm was infectious. "Alright, I'm down for that. I don't think anyone here on our end will be too upset if Phobos blows up before we get a chance to smack it. Is it the same on your end, Susan?"

Susan nodded solemnly. "It is our sacred duty to protect. This allows all of us to contribute based on our merits and capabilities. I will address the other members of the Keiretsu. I suspect that we will all be glad to participate."

"Cool," I said. "So . . . keep in touch?"

CHAPTER FORTY-TWO

CAT TO THE MOON

The 2028 Space Accord is an international agreement signed by all members of the G10 that removes all limits on space-based weapons platforms installed by governments and private enterprises operating within signatory nations as long as these weapon platforms meet certain criteria. The most important of these is a system of safe locks, preventing the use of these weapons against earthly civilian targets.

—Excerpt from *International Laws and Regulations*, seventy-third edition, 2035

"So . . . you bargained away our right to be the first to shoot?" Gomorrah asked. It wasn't really a question, even if she'd given it that kind of tone. It was a reprimand.

We were in a small office space next to the communication room where I'd just finished chatting with Doctor Radikal and Susan. The call had ended as quickly as it began. They were both far from our time zone, and either needed to hit the hay or just had other shit to do, so we hadn't lingered on goodbyes. It was myself, Gomorrah, and Grasshopper. It looked like the three of us formed the more . . . veteran part of the Big Gun Project.

Oh, right, I'd need to tell the others that I'd kinda named our entire project without permission or input. That could wait a minute.

"Bargained away makes it sound like I was being stupid on purpose," I said.

"So you weren't purposefully stupid?" Gomorrah asked with a slight tilt of her head.

I paused, worked through the English there, then shook my head. "No, wait. What I mean is that what I did wasn't stupid."

Grasshopper reached over and touched Gomorrah on the shoulder gently. "Let's give Catherine a chance to explain herself. It's only fair. We gave her the task to bargain for us without first giving her all the information she'd need to do her best, or much time to consider things."

I pointed to Grasshopper, because that was a damned good point. They'd kinda dropped me into the hot seat and I'd had to figure shit out all on my own there. It wasn't exactly the fairest way of doing things.

"Fine. Sorry, Cat," Gomorrah said. "Grasshopper's right, we kind of threw you into the situation. Nonetheless . . . I'd like an explanation of what went down, please."

"Sure," I said with a nod. That I could do, no problem. "So, two other factions, right? We've got the . . . uh, Myalis, how do I even pronounce their name?"

Myalis took over the speakers in my helmet with a faint—probably artificial—crackle. *"The name you're going to fail to pronounce properly is the Nachtwächternetzwerk. Literally the Night Watchmen Network."*

"Them," I said. "Their guy was this crazy mad-scientist type. Like out of a cartoon or something, with the accent and all. Doctor Radikal. With a K. Nice guy, actually. Bit of a weirdo, but I wouldn't mind chatting with him some more. The other gang is the Keiretsu, from east Asia. They're not just Japanese, but I'm pretty sure the guy I spoke to—Susan—is."

"I've heard of the Keiretsu," Gomorrah said. "They're as large as the Family, and possibly more influential within the continent they operate in."

"Really?" I asked.

She shifted. "They're a conglomerate of corporate entities owned wholly or in part by samurai. Or ronin, I suppose. Some of the corporations that make up the Keiretsu no longer have ronin leaders, but only because those leaders have died. If you have an Asian company and you want it to hit the top, you need to be part of the Keiretsu."

"So it's like a gang?" I asked.

"No, but also yes. It's more complicated than that. They're mostly just there to provide support to one another, but it's an extensive network of connections that is hard to break into and that comes with a certain guarantee of quality and competence. A lot of the companies in the group are tiny operations, but they produce the best things and will only sell to other members."

I had a decent image of how they worked already, but this was shining a lot more light on the whole situation. "Okay. I think I see what you're painting here," I said. "So, let's not fuck with them?"

"Let's not," she agreed. "Though I can't see them being immediately antagonistic. We're far outside of their jurisdiction and their business. And they love working with samurai. Your business would fit right in."

I shrugged. "And what do you know about this Night Watchmen Network?" I asked.

"Nothing," Gomorrah said.

"I know a little more," Grasshopper said. "I have a few friends that are part of the Network. We're in a shared math enthusiasts group!"

"Uh-huh," I said.

"They're less political or businesslike than the Family or the Keiretsu. They're more like a disjointed group of friends and compatriots across a number of cities and countries. There are even some members here in North America. How did the call go, by the way? You haven't told us much yet."

"Right, right," I said. "So, yeah, the Night Watchmen get first dibs on blowing up Phobos. Or cooking it, I guess. They have a big . . . not-gun of their own that's ready to go."

I'd received a text from Doctor Radikal, or more likely his AI. It was a link to a live countdown of when their project was going to fire.

"They're gonna shoot in about six hours."

"We'll be ready to shoot by then too," Gomorrah said.

"We will, but it'll take a while for anything we shoot to reach Phobos," Grasshopper pointed out.

"Even after being shot from the Big Gun?" I asked. "It's . . . a really big gun, won't our bullet be moving hella fast?"

"Hella fast indeed," Grasshopper said with a serious nod. "But space is 'hella big' as well, so even at such speeds, it will take a long time for our bullet to reach its target."

That was fair, I supposed. I didn't know enough to comment either way. "Right, well, after the nerds fire up their tesla microwave gun thing, the Keiratsu have an army of drones being built. I think they've launched the first couple of waves already. They'll be arriving at Phobos second. No ETA on that one."

"Drones?" Gomorrah asked. "Any more details than that?"

"Uh, the first wave are suicide drones, then they wanna use drones with thermal stuff to make the moon change directions." I had no idea how that would work. Would warming something up in space really make it change directions? I didn't want to look like a dumbass, so I kept my mouth shut about that part.

"Clever," Grasshopper said. "They're producing the drones in space?"

"From what I gathered, yeah," I said.

"Then we'll have a constant supply of harassment for Phobos."

"Can't we do the same?" I asked.

"Not at the moment, no," Grasshopper said. "We're limited to a single approach vector at the moment. Where we can vary things—a lot—is with our choice of munitions, but our Big Gun can only fire so many times."

"We can't fire nonstop?" I asked.

Grasshopper shook her head. "The cannon is designed to fire once an hour at a normal, efficient rate. We can double that, but we'd be pushing up our maintenance needs, and we'd burn through our electrical capacity."

I wouldn't even pretend to understand how a railgun actually worked. If Grasshopper said once an hour, then it was once an hour. That felt a little slow to me, at least until I started to take in just how fucking awesome what we were doing was.

"Anyway, we're third in line. If the nerds' super energy weapon fucks Phobos up, then we've wasted all this effort."

"Nonsense," Grasshopper said. "We made friends and learned all sorts of things. That's not wasted effort. A lost opportunity isn't a loss of time."

I grinned. "Sure. Anyway, it doesn't sound like the Keiretsu's shit is gonna take Phobos out in one swoop. More like they're aiming to soften the moon up, kill it by chipping away at it for however long it takes until the whole thing gives up."

"It's a valid tactic against the Antithesis," Gomorrah said. "You often have to choose between a single decisive strike or a variable war of attrition where you don't use the same tactics often enough for the Antithesis to adapt."

"I think he said something like that," I said. "Susan, I mean. It's valid, I guess. Not my kind of thing, though."

"You also agreed to this project because it has exceptional alpha-strike capabilities," Gomorrah said.

"I'm just an alpha kinda person," I agreed.

"I'm not going to dignify that with a response," Gomorrah said.

"I'm not big on dignity anyway," I shot back. "So, you still angry that we're in third?"

" . . . No. I'm not upset. Sorry, Cat, I shouldn't have jumped to conclusions," Gomorrah said, sounding all mature and shit. "We'll hope that the Nachtwächternetzwerk succeed, and if they don't, then we'll do what we can to work with the others."

"Awesome," I said, even though deep down I was kinda annoyed that she'd pronounced that perfectly without a hitch.

I checked the timer again. "We've got a few hours until they do their thing. Should we finish up the Big Gun, then sit back and watch?"

CHAPTER FORTY-THREE

BUYING THE GATE TO NOWHERE

Strange earth movement? Nah, man, you don't gotta worry. Yellowstone won't blow.
—Yellowstone Park Ranger, 2024

Current Point Total: 21,124

I sucked in a breath as I saw that number. It was . . . lower than I'd have liked for it to be. I mean, I still had a fuckload of points, so I couldn't complain, but a big part of me really hated spending money or points or whatever. It felt *wrong* to spend anything like that on stuff that wasn't immediately necessary.

. . . Fuck, I really wasn't a good capitalist, was I? I was sure there were like, therapies or something that offered to help people become more used to spending what they had. Not that I really cared enough to go through that kind of shit.

"Careful. Careful, dammit," Major Tinwhistle snapped.

The thing I'd bought was being winched up by a crane that looked like it was three sizes bigger than what was necessary. It was the portal component of the railgun, a large boxy device with several attachments on the sides and a complex, layered set of heatsinks on the back.

The business end, which faced the inside of the railgun's barrel, was a large circular disk, slightly concave and very reflective. There wasn't a portal on it yet. Myalis said that portals weren't energy efficient at the best of times, so this one would act like something of a camera aperture. It would flick open, then close the moment the projectile was to pass.

The heatsinks and shit were to regulate the temperature—both from the projectile, which was passing within hundredths of a millimeter, and from the shift caused by both the portal itself and the vacuum of space doing . . . space vacuum shit.

"Careful," Major Tinwhistle said.

She'd been spending most of her time this last day or so in the command tents and structures. But this bit was important enough that she was out here herself. I think it was to make sure that her engineers *knew* that any fuckups would be done right in front of their boss.

Their boss, who had a short staff like the small batons wielded by riot cops. She was using it to point to things, but it looked like it wouldn't take much effort for that bat to be turned into some good old-fashioned encouragement for anyone who fucked up. I was sure that if she caught someone fooling around, that person would be earning themselves some bruising. Tinwhistle was a tight bundle of nerves at the moment.

"She's tense," I muttered to the samurai nearest to me. That meant Princess, Knight, Hedgehog, and Gomorrah.

"That component is one of the most important parts of this project," Gomorrah said without looking up from a tablet. "It's valuable."

"Yeah, ten-thousand-points valuable," I said.

She glanced up. "I meant credit-wise," she said.

"How much could it be worth?" I asked.

Princess hummed. "It's a portal to space, but, like, it's still a portal. We don't have commercial portal technology, right?"

"Not as far as I know," Knight said. "She's right. Give a logistics corporation a portal like this and they'll be making billions from it by the end of the month. If they can reverse engineer it and build their own, then that's hundreds of billions of credits. Trillions, even."

"Wait, what?" I asked.

Gomorrah glanced up. "One of the major production bottlenecks is transportation logistics," she said. "Portal technology would neatly sidestep that. Trillions is probably an understatement."

"Oh . . . Why the fuck hasn't a samurai sold this, then?" Sure, it was expensive as fuck. I could have bought another mech for the same price. But still . . .

If I may . . . The main reason is that human technology is still several centuries away from being able to create even the simplest of portals like this one. Not only does humanity's grasp of mathematics and physics need to improve by several orders of magnitude, your species currently lacks the scientific knowledge required to build the devices that build the devices that you would need to build the simplest of parts required on a functional portal.

"We'll get there," Gomorrah said. So I assumed that Myalis had sent that to everyone.

Kinda weird, actually. Myalis liked to get in on the conversation, whereas I hadn't heard a word from Princess's AI, and Atyacus, Gomorrah's AI, was pretty darned reserved at the best of times.

We paused our discussion as the portal was lowered into place. There were about six times more engineers stopping to stare than was necessary, but I didn't blame them. This wasn't the last step in creating the Big Gun, but it was the last important one.

All that would remain after this was replacing some of the top plating over the end section of the gun and piping in some things.

There were three large cistern container things being installed already, huge off-white cylinders each wide enough to park a semi-trailer in the center with room to spare. They were going to hold the water for the cooling system, because apparently railguns ran hot.

I was pretty sure they weren't done piping those in, and the tanks weren't filled up yet. Even now, a truck pulling a massive chrome trailer was being connected to fill up one of the cylinders with deionized water.

The pipework looked good, though. Tinwhistle's engineers were doing the whole color-coded pipe thing, and while it looked like overcomplicated spaghetti, it was well-organized overcomplicated spaghetti. Shit looked professional, which was how anyone sane would want things to look around a gun this big.

The portal clunked into place, and four guys climbed down with wrenches and huge bolts to secure it while some others undid the chains from the crane.

Tinwhistle stared for a moment longer, then nodded and made her way over to us. "It's going well," she said. "We should have everything in place and ready to go within the next three hours."

"Are we on schedule, then?" I asked.

"God, no," she said. "Water deliveries will be stretched out over another three days. We haven't even started doing all of the checks that I want to. I won't be willing to put my seal on this project for another week, at least."

"You know we'll all be dead by then, yeah?" I asked.

She shrugged. "That's why, on paper, every shot you take between now and then is a calibration shot or a system test. As far as the engineering board is concerned, this project will only be ready to go long after either it's accomplished its job or we're all dead."

"Cool," I said with a nod. That made plenty of sense to me. There had to be ways to get around stupid paperwork-based restrictions. "Is the lack of water going to be a problem?"

She shook her head. "I looked at the amount of cooling we'd need to be barely functional, then multiplied it tenfold, then I did it again, because it's one of the easier areas to have redundancies in."

"Oh," I said. "Isn't that overengineering?"

She stared at me. "Yes. And?"

"Uh. Okay."

"Look, this is a big deal for my career," the major said. "I'm not going to have it get fucked up because we cut corners. Anything that can have redundancies will have redundancies. Those redundancies will have redundancies of their own. The first thing to fuck up will be investigated and those responsible will be taken out back and shot. And because we're working with redundancies, they'll be shot a second time to be sure."

"Alright, I get it," I said as I raised my arms in surrender. Chick was nuts. I didn't know if that was an engineering thing or not, but I wasn't sure I wanted to find out. "So, how soon can we shoot?"

The major looked at her tablet. "Three hours. Give us five, to be sure. Since this is a railgun, we'll be doing a dry-fire test first to see if all the capacitors are working as they should. I don't expect any actual issues there. They're all ET tech, and that shit has QC like nothing made on Earth."

"ET?" I asked.

"Extraterrestrial."

"Ah." She meant Protector-grade shit, which . . . yeah, I'd never heard of anything purchased by a samurai breaking because of poor quality. "Well, okay then. I guess we'll go watch our German pals for a bit, then come back and check up on you. Let us know as soon as the gun's ready to fire."

"That I can do," she said with a serious nod. "This . . . this is going to look so good on my record."

I bet it would, but I wasn't sure I wanted to be around the engineer. I might knock something over, and then she'd wale at me with that stick of hers.

CHAPTER FORTY-FOUR

THE WELTRAUM- GEWITTERMEISTER TESLA-KOLLISIONSGENERATOR

No, Catherine, a group of AI isn't called a glitch.
—Correspondence between Protector AI Myalis
and Samurai Stray Cat, 2057

"I had to set this up in a hurry, and I didn't want to use up too many points on something so nonessential, so forgive me if it's not as great as it could be," Grasshopper said as she led us into a strange tent next to the command area.

It was strange from the outside. The walls were made of a glossy white material that reflected sunlight in a weird way, and they seemed thick for a tent, too, but otherwise it didn't stand out too much. If I was driving by, I wouldn't give it a second glance.

The interior, however, was way stranger.

There was a carpet, for one. Or maybe it was a rug? I didn't know enough to tell the difference. Lights hung from the ceiling in little strips, casting a yellow glow against the walls, and there was a large television screen at the far end of the room.

A single couch was off to one side, beige with green specks that I soon realized were little cartoon grasshoppers patterned into the material. Other than that, the only furniture was a mini fridge humming in the corner.

"I tried to make it feel homey. I think everyone should order their own chairs, but if you don't have a catalog for it, just ask! I don't mind! Oh, there's snacks in the mini-fridge, so please feel free to take anything you want."

Grasshopper clapped her many hands together and smiled at the lot of us.

I glanced back. I was standing with Gomorrah and Princess and Knight, Hedgehog was taking up the rear with Tankette, and Rac was with us too, next to Gros Baton. "So . . . what's the goal here?" I asked.

"It's a viewing party," she said. "I sent a message to my friends in the Night Watchmen Network and they agreed to patch us into their feed for the big event. It would be a shame to only learn what happens via reports instead of seeing it for ourselves."

"They have cameras that good?" Gomorrah asked. "For a live feed, I mean."

"The time delay is somewhat mitigated," Grasshopper said. "Though I didn't look into the mechanics of it. I believe our front-row cameras are being provided by the Keiretsu. They have monitoring drones closer to Phobos than anything else. Let me set things up while everyone makes themselves comfortable!"

Tankette stepped up, tilted her head, and . . . didn't quite hum something? Was she subvocalizing? A moment later, a seat thumped onto the rug a step before her. It was . . . a tank chair. Like, not a chair from a tank, probably, but a large, armored La-Z-Boy–style recliner made of metal with thick rivets and a canvas-covered seat.

"Did you ever get a furniture catalog?" Gomorrah asked me.

"No? Did you?"

She nodded. "For the house. Atyacus, as discussed." A seat appeared for her too. It was a sort of loveseat, all black leather with a subtle bit of black embroidery on it that hinted at flames without there actually being any.

"Fuck ça, j'vais me chercher une chaise normale. Tu veux quelque chose?" Gros Baton asked Rac. She shrugged, then left with him, supposedly on a quest to find some chairs.

I squinted at a free spot on the ground. Did I have any catalogs with access to chairs? Did I even want to spend points on a chair to begin with?

If you're wondering, your Class I Medical Utilities catalog does have seating available, but I'm afraid it won't be anything too comfortable. Your Sun Watcher Technologies catalog does have seating that should fit a human physiology.

That sounded like a somewhat suspicious way of putting it. "Sure, nothing more than a dozen points or so. I don't want to be broke because of a chair," I muttered.

Certainly!

What appeared wasn't a chair. Chairs had right angles and backrests and space for your ass. This thing looked like a padded bike seat at an angle, with cushions for the legs and a large pillow-like cushion at the front.

I stared for a moment, trying to figure out exactly how I was supposed to sit on it before it clicked. "Wait, it's like a bike?"

The seat, if I could call it that, was a flat, padded board to rest my stomach on, with the largest cushion just above that like an elevated beanbag chair for my upper body.

"That's an interesting seat," Gomorrah said. Her flat tone didn't disguise her amusement one bit.

"Yeah, yeah, shut up," I said. I wasn't going to toss it out now, or else I'd look like a coward. So I walked up to the chair . . . thing and fell down onto it. It took some shifting for me to figure out how to be comfortable on it—my knees had to rest on two pads, and most of my weight was supported by that flat padded bit that ran all the way from my crotch up to my lower ribs—but once I was there, it really wasn't all that bad. "Huh . . . this is nice on the back," I said. I did need to stretch my neck out a little to see the screen at the end of the room, though.

Hedgehog stared at my seat for a bit, then shook his head and soon summoned . . . a beanbag chair. It didn't suit the image I had of him at all, but it looked more comfortable than the fold-out chairs Gros Baton and Rac returned with a few minutes later.

"Will Crackshot be joining us?" Grasshopper asked.

Gomorrah shook her head. "He said in the group chat that he was going on a date."

"With Emoscythe?" I asked.

"*That's* who he asked out?" Gomorrah asked. She pressed a hand over her mouth to muffle a surprised gasp. To be fair, this was good tea we were spilling.

"Yeah. I guess she said yes. He looked pretty excited about it all."

"Oh, that's wonderful!" Grasshopper said. "I hope they have a nice time together. Emoscythe Mordeath Noir is a good friend of mine. I'm sure she'll treat Crackshot Cowboy well."

"You're not worried he might treat her wrong?" I asked.

"And live?" she wondered.

" . . . Yeah, never mind, that was a stupid question."

It took a bit for things to get started. Grasshopper acted like a good host—even though she didn't need to—and made sure everyone had a drink nearby and access to snacks. Unfortunately, her idea of a good drink was cold water or juice, and her idea of a snack was shit like celery.

I was convinced that no one actually liked celery. Eating celery was performative, like doing a little dance to get likes on your media feed.

I didn't have to endure the celery for too long, though. Less than an hour after we arrived, Grasshopper excitedly turned the screen on. It immediately connected to a channel that wasn't narrated or anything. This was raw footage of the inside of a command room of some sort.

Rows of seats facing inward toward a huge display, people in lab coats and suits sitting behind computers and waiting for something to happen. A few samurai. Well, there was no way of knowing if they were samurai for certain, but they were dressed differently than all the rest. I did recognize Doctor Radikal in the bunch.

"What's this footage?" I asked.

"Just the overview of the command room," Grasshopper said. "It's live. We'll be cutting to what they see once the operation starts."

"Do we have an ETA on that?" Gomorrah asked.

"We have another twenty minutes," Grasshopper said with a nod. "I wonder if the Keiretsu will be launching their own attack early."

"That'd go against the agreement, no?" Tankette asked. "It was the Germans, then them, then us, right? I wasn't paying too much attention, sorry."

"Yeah. The Network's not exactly German, though," I said. "But close enough. I think Grasshopper means more . . . well, the Keiretsu's attack isn't going to be nearly as fast as the Network's. I mean, how fast is the Network's super weapon, anyway?"

"As quick as gravity, I believe," Grasshopper said.

I didn't know how fast that was, but I had the impression that it was still faster than a suicidal drone swarm.

"Something's happening," Rac said. I glanced back at her, then up to the screen. It did, indeed, look like something was happening. The samurai were moving off to the side and the people at the desks were perking up. Some chatter came through, but it was all in German so I didn't have a sense of what was being said.

Then the screen switched to complete darkness.

It took me a moment to notice the faint lights of distant stars. A HUD appeared over the screen, then zoomed in on a distant speck. The more it zoomed, the grayer it became, until there was an image of a rock floating in space in the center of the screen.

The wings could only mean that this was Phobos.

"Oh, I should have gotten popcorn," Grasshopper lamented.

CHAPTER FORTY-FIVE

IF YOU'RE UNHAPPY AND YOU KNOW IT, FLAP YOUR WINGS!

So, Chips as a Subscription didn't work out. So I was thinking . . . how about we continue our previous product size adjustment?

Introducing . . . Bag of Chip! Now available in all 725 flavors! Low in calories, and each bag is large enough to have room for plenty of tangential advertising too!"

—Layers Potato Chip Company, CFO Memo, 2038

We got a full HD view of space and Phobos in the distance, but it didn't help explain anything.

Which was why I was kind of thankful when a corner of the screen was suddenly taken up by a familiar face. Doctor Radikal adjusted his glasses, then ran a hand over his face. He had a thick five o'clock shadow. I didn't know much about facial hair, but it looked like he might not have shaved in a day or three. Actually, the bags under his eyes suggested that maybe he hadn't slept in that time either.

"Ah yes, greetings, friends and compatriots," he said. "I see that we have listeners from both the Keiretsu and the Big Gun Project. Greetings, greetings."

The image on the rest of the screen shifted, then zoomed out. It turned into a sort of map, an empty grid with Phobos on one end and lines pointing out which direction the moon was moving in, along with its relative velocity. More dots appeared: Keiretsu drones flying in formation, with their own velocities plotted out and an ETA to impact.

"As you can see, our partners' drone flights are expected to hit Phobos approximately nine hours from now. This first wave contains mostly high-yield thermonuclear deterrents. Ah, but before that, our Weltraumgewittermeister Teslakollisionsgenerator will be going online for the first time to hopefully rip the wandering moon asunder."

The grid map zoomed out and out and out, and then a new icon appeared, this one around a small green-blue marble that had to be Earth. The icon looked like a metal coil with some stylized lightning bolts around it.

"The Weltraumgewittermeister Teslakollisionsgenerator will be coming online in T-minus . . . one minute. Oh my, one moment, I may be needed here."

Doctor Radikal's image disappeared.

I shifted in my weird seat and glanced at the others. They were mostly relaxing. Tankette had stood up at some point and come back with more food. It was a lot of mini carrots and some dipping sauce, and like, chips and popcorn, but the healthy kind that tasted alright but didn't hold up against the artificial crap I'd grown up on. Still, I grabbed a bowl and stuffed my face because I wasn't raised to say no to free food.

"So, I'm guessing we're not actually going to get to *see* anything," I said. "Too far, right?"

"You'd usually be quite correct," Grasshopper said. "But I suspect that there are enough sensor apparatuses pointed at Phobos that we will actually be able to see something visually. Otherwise we'll have to rely on real-time simulations."

"Eh, good enough," I said.

I was on the fence a little. I really wanted to see the Weltra . . . the tesla collider work. If it took out the moon in one hit, then that'd be that. But another part of me really wanted an excuse to use the Big Gun. We'd just built the world's biggest hammer, and it would be a shame if we couldn't find anything vaguely nail-shaped to test it on.

"Ah, I have returned!" Doctor Radikal said as his image reappeared. He tugged his tie loose and smiled. "The Weltraumgewittermeister Teslakollisionsgenerator is about to fire. Please observe the efforts of our work!"

The screen flickered to a live feed of a space station. There was a long white boom arm extending away from a . . . thing. There was nothing to give anything a sense of scale, so I didn't know if what I was looking at was the size of a building or a pebble. The stars in the back were shifting, though, and soon things rotated enough that I saw Earth in the background.

Then a small item detached itself from the satellite and flew closer, and I realized that it was an astronaut in a suit with some sort of jetpack on. They flew around the machine, giving me a sense of its scale compared to a person.

And it was fucking massive.

Well, no, I'd seen massive things before, skyscrapers and the like. This wasn't anywhere near that scale. Even our Big Gun was larger by an order of magnitude. But the tesla collider looked like it was as tall as a pair of semi-trailers parked end to end, maybe fifteen meters in diameter along the middle.

Mostly it was a white hexagonal pillar with some panels pushed open to reveal complex wiring and shit within. I didn't have the multiple doctorates I'd need to make an educated guess at how it worked.

The astronaut flew around, then hovered along the length of the boom arm holding the camera. They waved on the way by and then disappeared out of frame.

"Final checks complete," Doctor Radikal said. He wasn't talking to us anymore. "How are the capacitors looking? Mm-hmm? Okay, good, good. Is Honey Tea giving us the all-clear? Yes, just make sure . . . Good."

The doctor blinked, then refocused on the camera that I imagined was floating ahead of him. He had to have some greenscreen shit going on, because even though it was clear he was in a room with others, the only thing that appeared in his corner was his body from the shoulders up.

"We have green across the board. The device is ready. Firing at ten percent in . . . ten, nine, eight, seven, six, five, four, three, two, one . . . firing."

I glanced from Radikal to the tesla collider and . . . nothing happened? I was expecting a big lightning bolt or some electrical currents or something. Maybe a few lights along the side of the machine flashed? I wasn't sure. Eventually a panel did open up, and what looked like a massive heatsink unfolded itself. It might have been warm? It was hard to tell. The heatsink was dropped, and a drone flew in to pluck it out of space and bring it back to something offscreen.

The screen switched to that zoomed-in view of Phobos, and I found myself sitting up straighter.

The moon was being crushed.

It wasn't super obvious at first glance, but there was movement on the surface. Large areas of the moon were cracking. What *was* obvious were the wings. The massive, almost butterfly-like wings spreading out from the sides of Phobos were being squeezed into the moon's sides. Arcs of electrical energy were coursing along their surface, leaving long, burning scars where they passed.

"No immediate reaction from the moon," Doctor Radikal said. "Can I have the . . . yes, thank you." He brought something up, a tablet that he read over, then nodded as if to himself. "Looks like the collider is working. We have signs that there have been several minor shifts on Phobos's exterior structure. The moon's temperature has risen by two degrees!"

That didn't sound like much at all, but maybe I was wrong. The shifts were probably a lot more impactful. I could imagine Phobos being filled with Antithesis tunnels and hives under its surface. The equivalent of a small earthquake would mess those up.

"Pushing to one hundred percent," Radikal said.

This time there were definitely more lights flickering on and off. Each side of the tesla collider opened, ejecting six heatsinks that were glowing red. Some even looked like they'd been slagged by the heat.

"Hmm, minor damage alerts on the main collider's cooling system," Radikal said. "Drachenschöpfer was right."

The screen flicked back to a view of Phobos. Now there was no hiding the tesla collider's effect. The moon looked like . . . like someone had grabbed a few pieces of paper and scrunched them into a ball, only now that same paper ball had been crushed by a giant's hand. The massive wings were splattered against the moon's sides and there were canyon-sized cracks running across its surface.

The far side of the moon exploded. Chunks of rock that the on-screen HUD quickly measured as being half a kilometer long were tumbling away from the backside of the moon and spreading out.

"Regrouping," Doctor Radikal said.

There was a sort of pulse. I wasn't sure how to describe it, but the reaction was plain to see. The bits of the moon scattering away paused, then came crashing back down against Phobos's surface.

"Nice!" I cheered.

And then, because I had awful timing, the Antithesis decided that this would be a good time to react.

Massive tentacles burst out of the moon's side, a thousand openings on their slimy surface disgorging tiny black forms that quickly hid against the black of space. More things came pouring out of the moon. Some huge, whale-like creatures that I'd never seen before, with enormous ropey worms for limbs came slithering out. The moon looked like it was forcing itself apart once more, only this time the sections were linked together by long strands of living matter.

Phobos had come alive, as if it was a single living host to a million little monsters, and it didn't look happy about it.

CHAPTER FORTY-SIX

EWW, WHAT EVEN IS THAT?

Antithesis specimens are divided into broad categories called "models." These models represent a general shape taken by the aliens, though there will always be some deviation between subjects of the same model, just as no two humans are exactly alike.

Models are, in turn, categorized in tiers. Tier one represents all models from one to ten. Tier two represents all models from eleven to twenty, and so on.

—*Antithesis Identification: A Xenowatcher's Primer,*
Birdwatchers of America, 2046

"What the fuck am I looking at?" I asked as I kept staring at the unfolding monstrosity on the screen.

The Antithesis . . . thing was unspooling long fleshy . . . not-quite-tentacles. These were bridging the gap between massive segments of Phobos's surface crust, almost like some sort of weird shell being expanded outward.

Then there was a tug, and the shell started to close once more. Plates that had to be the size of entire provinces crashed together at the edges and sent small chunks of rocks flying every which way.

That looks like the start of a model sixty-eight. They're one of the more esoteric biological constructs that the Antithesis will deploy once they have space superiority. Think of it as a mobile hive.

"That thing's a hive?" I asked. But yeah, that made some sort of sense. "No, never mind, that makes sense. It's fucking massive, though."

Antithesis generally grow larger the higher the tier. This isn't always the case, but there's a definite pattern of growth, both in size and complexity and capability. A model sixty-eight can grow to be the size of a small moon. As evidenced by what you're seeing now.

"Anything we need to know in particular about it?" I asked. "Or is it just a bigger, meaner bug that we need to squish?"

Expect it to be able to move and maneuver in ways that would seem coun-
terintuitive based on its size and mass. Also, expect esoteric weapons and
capabilities. Higher-tier models are more versatile, and their biological nature
doesn't prevent them from using something akin to modern technology.

I closed my eyes for a moment, then stood up, which was a little awkward considering the weird chair I'd bought. Somehow, my back felt . . .
nice? I glanced across the room. The others were mostly glued to the screen,
watching the alien moon writhe and reset itself. Data was streaming in on
half the screen, and while I couldn't parse it, I was sure Grasshopper and
Gomorrah could. Maybe Hedgehog too.

"Stray Cat?" Princess asked. "Are you leaving?"

"I'm going to call Doctor Radikal," I said. "Susan too, I guess."

I didn't like being pushed into anything like a leadership position. It
wasn't my *thing*. But . . . fuck, I wasn't awful at it. Not good enough to start
bragging, but I wasn't a complete dumbass. I could figure it out.

I'd like to think I had the street smarts to handle the bottom rungs of
New Montreal well enough. This whole thing was on another level, but
some of that logic applied across the board.

My gut was telling me that this was like when two gangs that shared a
block had to deal with some corpo fuckery. In that kind of situation, putting
heads together was usually the best move.

So I pulled up Doctor Radikal's information on my contact list and
gave him a call. It took two rings for the good doctor to reply. No video,
voice only, but that was fine. "Ah! Stray Cat! Yes, I was just thinking I
ought to give you a call. Susan as well. I imagine you've been watching
our stream?"

"I have, yeah. We set up a mini-cinema over here to watch it all live."

"Yes, well, that means I won't need to explain things too much," he said.
"Can you give me but a moment? I will get into contact with Susan, we'll
make it so that a minimum of repetition is necessary."

"Yeah, go ahead," I said as I finally stepped outside. It had started to
drizzle a little, which was probably for the best. The rain was bringing down
all of the dust that had been kicked up by the tractors and trucks moving
around the site. It looked like most of the effort right now was being spent
on closing up the top of the Big Gun with pre-made metal sheets. They were
three-quarters of the way to the end.

It took a few long seconds, but eventually Doctor Radikal came back on
and there was a faint click as Susan joined the call.

"Greetings, Stray Cat," he said.

"Heya," I replied. "So, Phobos was an egg and we've cracked it, huh?"

"An apt metaphor," Doctor Radikal said. "Before entering this situation, we created a predictive ten-tier system for gauging the results of our

weapons platform upon Phobos. One being absolute success, ten being unmitigated disaster."

"And this is an eleven sort of situation?" I asked.

"No, merely a seven," he replied.

Well, shit, they were more pessimistic than I was. "Seven still sounds a little bad," I said. "Did you predict this exact scenario?"

"We did not, but we were aware that Phobos likely contained an active hive and that it might be able to evolve in response to our assaults. In any case, the Weltraumgewittermeister Teslakollisionsgenerator will be ready to fire once more in . . . six hours and forty-nine minutes, and every six hours thereafter."

"Okay, cool," I said. "Susan, any news on your end?"

"The kamikaze are flying to Phobos as we speak. Soon you will see them strike the moon with all of our anger ready to be unleashed," Susan said. I didn't know if it was the translation that made him sound so . . . poetic, or if he was just trying really hard. "I do not expect this first wave to finish our foe, but it will bloody them."

A dozen or so nukes crashing into anything would bloody it, I figured. "It's got some pretty big openings on the surface, from what I saw. That'll sting once we slip something past the . . . eggshell."

"Indeed!" Doctor Radikal said. "It's possible that the Keiretsu's strike, followed by your own Big Gun's shot, may be enough to kill this model sixty-eight. In which case, the next use of the Teslakollisionsgenerator would merely crush Phobos back down into a large mound of rock. But I do not plan on holding out hope for such a high degree of success."

"You don't think it'll work?" I asked.

"I think we're punching upward against a foe that is far stronger than we'd initially hoped. We would be remiss to expect the Antithesis to roll over and allow themselves to die so easily."

I nodded along. That did sound about right. "Our hits are gonna come in staggered, right? We can do one hit an hour here. That still leaves the aliens an hour to heal between each strike. You can use it every six hours, right?"

"Four times a day," Doctor Radikal confirmed.

"Four times a day. Those times will be doing lots of damage, right? And the Keiretsu?"

"Our drone production is only ramping up," Susan said. "The more time passes, the more frequently we'll be able to strike."

"Alright, okay," I said as I continued to nod. "This is going to be something of a longer fight, then. Not a fight of . . . what's the word for a fight that's won because one side runs out of resources?"

"Attrition?" Doctor Radikal suggested.

"That's the one. It's not a battle of attrition. since we're ramping up and have more resources to call on the closer Phobos gets. If we see that what we're doing isn't working, then we ramp up more. We can definitely afford to build a second Big Gun. I imagine your drone production can just keep growing. Not sure about your collider . . ."

"We can upgrade it!" Doctor Radikal said, sounding rather cheerful about the entire idea. "There are some here suggesting we do so already. A lot of the limitations we have on the device now are in place to allow it to function for longer under less strain. If there's more risk that Phobos will be an unavoidable threat, then we can push the machine to its limits and beyond."

"Okay, cool. We might want to coordinate our timing going forward. Either space it all out so that there's nonstop damage against Phobos, or time strikes to come in when Phobos is reeling already."

Susan hummed. "We have time to attempt a few different approaches against the foe."

"Time until Phobos is right upon us," Doctor Radikal said.

"Is there any chance of that happening?" I asked.

"Truly? I think it is unlikely. Several agencies are burying their heads in the sand, but as the last hours approach, I believe they will try anything. That might collide with our own attempts to save the world, so let's focus on ridding ourselves of Phobos sooner rather than later."

"Alright," I agreed. "Worst case, we'll chip away at it, right? I saw lots of little bits of the moon flying off into space. I imagine we can continue doing that until it's nothing but scattered dust, yeah?"

"Those pieces will be an issue," Susan said. "We're going to have to contend with a great meteor shower. Though we can, given time, rid ourselves of any threateningly large objects."

I puffed out a breath. It was just one thing after another, wasn't it?

CHAPTER FORTY-SEVEN

KAMI-CAN'T

Drone warfare is changing everything.

A soldier costs millions to train. A drone can be produced for cheap: American explosives, parts made in a Chinese 3D printer, motors made in Vietnam, with Taiwanese chips, running off Indian software.

Give me a million dollars and I'll hand you a thousand flying bombs worth more than ten times their cost in soldiery.

—Former Baytheon CEO Jim Jimmies, moments before retired US Marine Tucker Bison assassinated him, 2031

Just before I returned to our . . . cinema tent, I got a message from Grass-hopper. The Big Gun was ready to fire.

Before that, however, we had time to sit back and watch the Keiretsu's kamikaze run. I was looking forward to it, actually. Sure, maybe shooting now would be better, since it'd give us more time to prep the next shot. But curiosity got the better of all of us.

Seeing a nuke go off in space was going to be neat, I figured, and seeing multiple was . . . probably going to be pretty awesome. I wasn't going to miss that. A sudden pang hit me as I walked back into the tent. I missed Lucy. I bet she would have loved to see this, but it was a little late to run back and fetch her.

"Myalis, are we recording these streams?" I asked.

Of course. For data analysis, if nothing else. There is also a possibility that these streams may serve as propaganda pieces later.

I frowned, but . . . yeah, that was very possible. People needed to know that shit wasn't hopeless, and what better way to give people hope than to show their enemy being peppered with nukes?

"Hey," I said as I returned.

"You're back," Princess said. "How did it go?"

I shrugged. "Not so bad, I think. Doctor Radikal calls it a seven out of ten on the shit scale. So it could have been worse. We'll have to see how this next hit goes, and then give it our own shot."

Gomorrah nodded from her seat nearer the front. "That seems reasonable. Are there any changes in the plan? New tactics or the like?"

I flopped down onto my seat and stretched a little. Damn, it really was kinda comfy. "Nothing too big. We're switching to a sort of . . . war of not-quite-attrition from here on out. The Keiretsu can keep ramping up, and we'll be in charge of smacking Phobos every hour on the hour. Our nerdier friends will crush the moon four times a day, so I think overall things will work out."

"Oh, I see," Grasshopper said. "A war of attrition rarely works well against the Antithesis, but in this particular case, the Antithesis are playing a zero-sum game. They only have the moon's resources at their disposal. And the ambient energy from the sun, I suppose. They can't claim any more biomass than that. Every piece of Phobos we carve away is part of their foundation gone forever."

"That's the rough idea, yeah," I said. "Do we have any idea when the Keiretsu's thing—"

Grasshopper looked at one of her four wrists. There was an old-fashioned watch there, without even a digital screen. I didn't know how to read clocks with the little arms like that, but I supposed she did. "In about five minutes," she said. "Enough time to warm up some more popcorn!"

"I'll get it," Tankette said as she hopped out of her seat. "No no, please. I'm feeling useless." The last was aimed at Hedgehog who had started to stand, presumably to help her.

Tankette left, and I settled down to wait. We did chat for a bit, though not about anything too major. Gomorrah was debating with Grasshopper over the methods by which to burn Phobos. There were plenty of chemicals that could be lit up in some semblance of fire, even in empty space with no oxygen, but the issue seemed to be quantitative.

A slug from the Big Gun had an upper limit on size, which meant that even with incredible amounts of compression, there was only so much gas or liquid that could be flung out at Phobos. Even the solid-fuel projectiles that would break up were relatively small.

I could understand why Gomorrah was a little upset. Lighting shit on fire was her thing. "Maybe we can do one or two shots of something flammable," I offered. As a treat. Plus the image of a chunk of Phobos burning would be good PR.

Tankette returned just as the screen shifted to an image of Susan sitting in a boardroom filled up by a large round table. The people around him were ronin. Some three dozen in all, all of them dressed . . . like samurai, I supposed.

There were a few punks, some dressed in extremely bright, formfitting outfits, and others in more traditional mil-spec armor and gear. One of them stood out to me, a woman with cat ears and a pair of long tails that twitched behind her, but hers were . . . not mechanical.

"We begin," one of the samurai who I didn't recognize said. He was wearing clothing that looked fit for a ninja, though his face was covered in a demon mask, the eyeholes of which were filled with dozens of hexagonal lenses. "Please, foreign friends and allies, observe the work of our collective."

The screen immediately switched to a set of some three dozen hexagonal camera feeds. All of them were in space, but they were feeding high-enough dimension footage that with some zoom we could make out the distant blob that was Phobos.

A third of the screen was replaced by a plotter of sorts, a rotating three-dimensional view of the kamikaze swarm, with blue lines trailing behind little triangles shooting out toward a yellow circle that had to be Phobos. There was a Japanese kanji over the moon, one that Myalis translated for me as "Enemy."

"Final approach vectors locked in," an unfamiliar woman's voice said in monotone, faintly accented English. "Thrusting in . . . three, two, one. Thrust."

The stars in those hexagonal screens started to slip by just a little faster as the drones accelerated on the plotter. There were individual speed-readings, but I had no frame of reference for how fast they were going. I did see the drive plumes—I think that's what they were called—of some of the drones who were out ahead from the cameras of those farther back.

In any case, it did seem like Phobos was getting larger faster.

"Contact in . . . three minutes."

I sat back and watched. It was strange, how space made distances so fucky. The timer sank faster and faster.

"Boosting first-contact drones," the woman said.

"They're making space. So that the drones don't swallow each other in their blast radius," Grasshopper explained.

I nodded along. That made sense to me.

And then, just as the timer was reaching one minute, one of the screens went dark.

"Review!" the ninja guy's voice snapped.

The footage was played back. The drone had crashed into something dark and formless in the void of space.

Two more drones blinked out.

"Engaging evasive maneuvers," the woman's voice said. She didn't sound quite as calm now. "Nuclear warheads primed. Contingency twelve active. Sacrificing drones one through six."

Four of the screens went white.

From the viewpoint of the other drones, there were suddenly four suns floating in the void of space out ahead of them, growing balls of brilliant light that they just barely skimmed by a split second later.

The plotter showed the explosions as balls the size of marbles next to Phobos, which, comparatively, now looked like a beachball.

Two more drones were lost. Then six more.

The plotter started to fill with hundreds of contacts out in space. Winged monsters, black and nothing, some of them disgorging spines and spikes and exploding balls covered in thorns that caught some of the drones midflight.

It was thinning the drone swarm.

But not enough to prevent some from striking the moon's surface.

On the screens for those, it looked like Phobos went from a distant baseball-sized lump of rock to the moon suddenly being right up in their face. I jumped in my seat at the suddenness of it.

Every feed went white.

The screen switched to what I presumed was another observational drone, and we got to see nine growing spheres of bluish smoke expanding in front of Phobos. Their edges curled and twisted, a fractal that soon splashed across the moon's surface.

When the dust settled, there were expanding craters pockmarking the front of Phobos's surface.

"Nine successful detonations," the woman's voice said.

"Out of thirty-six kamikaze drones," Ninja-guy said. "We will send the data now. Prepare for initial observations."

The plotter grew to take up the entire screen, with notated information around each location that was struck. The shockwaves from the nukes were still traveling through Phobos's surface, and the chunks blown off the moon were coming back down, crashing into it to leave even more cracks and dents on its all-gray surface.

"Was . . . that a complete flop?" I asked. "What were those things, in space?"

"Space-capable Antithesis," Grasshopper said. "And I wouldn't call it a flop. Rather . . . let's call it a learning opportunity. We'll just have to do better next time."

"Next time it's our turn," Gomorrah said. She stood. "Come on. Let's see how well we can do."

CHAPTER FORTY-EIGHT

PUSH MY RED BUTTON

What's the big red button do?
Why don't you push it to find ou—wait, don't actually push!
—Transcript of a recording of the Russian Incident of 2025

There was this strange thing that happened whenever something big and unique was going on.

I'd first seen it a few years back. A large cylindrical truck had swerved around something on the road and rammed into one of those metal guard-rail things on the roadside.

The cab was totaled. The driver was very dead. And then some other truck drove right into the first one's rear. They'd had time to slow down a little, so it wasn't nearly as big of a bang, but I could still remember the sound of it.

I'd been a block or so over, and I knew that the noise didn't come from gunfire. It was too . . . crunchy? Anyway, I'd wandered over to find that people had split into three camps. Two or three guys were checking on the driver, looking for a pulse, trying to get him out of the truck's cabin. I might have been tempted to help, but by the time I arrived they were already giving it up as a bad job. Dude's brains were across the dash anyway.

The other two groups were much more populous. The truck had been transporting fresh water. The people in the second group had grabbed buckets and were stealing all they could. Water was expensive. Clean water more so.

The last group, the one I'd been part of that day, just milled around a dozen meters away. Rumors spread, someone who might have seen the accident repeated their story a dozen times, and we all partook in some head-shaking and complaining about whatever shit had caused the accident.

It wasn't a memory I called up often, but this moment felt pretty damned similar.

The Big Gun was done.

Major Tinwhistle was standing tall and proud, hands on hips and eyes stained red by strain and stress. "It's done," she announced to Grasshopper.

There were only two groups this time. The onlookers, composed of all of the engineers and soldiers who'd been roped into the project, and the samurai. Well, some of us, at least. A few had contributed what they needed to and now were just milling on the edge of the much bigger onlooker group.

"Stray Cat, Gomorrah," Grasshopper said. She smiled at the both of us, then started toward the very back of the Big Gun. Or was it the front? The bit where the shooting would start, in any case, not the end with the exit portal.

That part of the gun was like a small shack. A well-built, brutalist's ideal of a small shack. The walls were foot-thick concrete poured over inch-thick metal plates.

The inside was a cramped little space that I was pretty sure came from one of Tankette's catalogs. There were a few small adjustable seats in front of a complex set of screens and buttons—all analog, at least on the surface. I did notice a few ports for data-jacking into the gun, like connecting into the Mesh.

Grasshopper went to the farthest seat and sat, then gestured to the other two. One was next to Grasshopper, and the other was at an angle near the rear of the room.

"What are we going to open with?" she asked, once people were sitting.

"You mean what are we shooting first?" I asked. "We need to make a solid first impression."

"Something with good penetrative power might be best for now," Gomorrah said. She looked across the screens and muttered something I didn't catch, probably to Atyacus. They lit up. Diagnostics flashed by, and then a long list of status readouts. It looked like we were green across the board.

There was only one item that was flashing. *Hypervelocity Round Missing.*

"What about that Casaba-Howitzer?" I asked. "You'd mentioned those, Grasshopper, and I looked them up. They're hot as hell."

"That should carry some amount of penetrative power," Grasshopper agreed. "Load it in!"

I blinked, then looked to my left where there was a heavy metal breech held closed by a chunky looking handle. "Oh," I said. I tugged the handle back, exposing a hole that was in a block of iron a foot and a bit wide and tall. A small engraving on the plate said "INSERT SHELL HERE," which was pretty self-explanatory. "Myalis, got a Casaba-Howitzer for me?" I asked.

Certainly. Only two hundred points for one designed to fit into the Big Gun.

I winced. "Only," my ass. That wasn't cheap, not if we were going to be firing once an hour. Maybe we'd go for cheaper rounds later. We did want to start with a literal bang. "Fine, fine," I said.

A shell appeared by my feet. It was in the usual cat-themed case, though this one had handles to better be able to grip the shell within. I opened it up, grunted as I pulled the bullet out, and then wondered which way was meant to go in first. The bullet was a cylinder with flat faces on either side and was made of what looked like polished steel.

The right end goes in first.

I nodded, then slotted that into the breech. It slid in with a faint whisper as air could just barely slip out along the edges of the round. Once it was settled in nice and neat, I tugged the breech closed and locked it with that big handle.

The floor shook for a moment, and I could hear things moving beneath us.

The screens lit up, and Grasshopper smiled at me before turning toward them. She pulled out a small datacord from her suit and plugged it into the machine. A moment later we had telemetry displayed before us.

It was a plotter, similar to the one Keiretsu had used to show where their drones were, but a little simplified. It showed our satellite on one end, and Phobos way out in the distance. "Auto-targeting on. Let's aim for center mass?"

"Sounds good," I said. "It won't detonate right on the moon, right?"

"We can adjust the detonation range. We do want it to be relatively close," Grasshopper said. "One thousand kilometers?"

"That sounds far," I said.

"We don't want to be intercepted," Grasshopper replied. "Not before the howitzer fires. Closer is almost certainly better, however, when it comes to dealing any damage."

"Right, right," I said. "Go on, then."

Grasshopper tapped a few keys on a little number pad recessed into the console, then reached over to the center where there was a large red button covered by a clear plastic shell. She flicked up the shell, flipped four toggles, and then paused as the Big Gun started to hum.

Text appeared over the main screen.

BOOT UP IN PROGRESS
SHELL LOADED
MAGNETS ON
CAPACITORS AT . . . 100%
TARGET LOCKED
BLINK PORTAL TEST . . . PASSED
READY TO FIRE

"Does anyone in particular want to do the honors?" Grasshopper asked. She gestured at the large red button with the word "FIRE" stenciled across it.

"I don't particularly care," Gomorrah said. "Catherine?"

"I mean . . . yeah, shit, I wouldn't mind," I said.

Grasshopper smiled and leaned over so that I could reach the button. I touched it, then pressed down. It made a satisfying little *click* noise.

Then I felt every hair on my head pulling upward and suddenly there was a deep and foreign itch in my bones. Text scrolled by on the screen, too fast for me to read. Then the Big Gun fired.

There was a single thump. It was as if someone had dropped a fifty-five-gallon drum off the top of a megabuilding and recorded the noise it made upon meeting the ground. Everything rocked back and the dozens of readouts in the room flashed.

"Oh shit, we good?" I asked.

"We are well, yes," Grasshopper said. "Everything is still green. Look." She pointed to the plotter.

There was a flashing green dot that had left Earth's orbit and was now slowly crawling across the screen toward Phobos. The fact that it was moving at a speed that I could see, though, probably meant that it was moving at an obscene velocity out there.

"Nice!" I said. "When is it gonna hit?"

"We have time for a small break," Grasshopper said. "Should we stock up on ammunition in the meantime? I somehow doubt this one strike will be enough to take Phobos down."

"Right, not a bad idea. Do we want to try a few different things? I've got some ideas for what we can throw at them," I said.

Gomorrah perked up. "Atyacus and I have been talking as well. Can I have the next shell?"

"Go right on ahead," I said with a gesture to the breech. There were more holes like the breeches all along the back wall, where there was room to store a lot more shots. Something in my gut told me we'd probably need all of them before this was over.

THE FREE RADIKAL

Doctor Radikal (Kaleb, to his few friends) felt a hard thump against his back that almost sent him sprawling forward, but he caught himself on the edge of a desk and glanced over his shoulder at the perpetrator. What he discovered was a familiar man, smiling gently in a way that didn't suit his enormity. "Don't worry so much," the big man said. "We've done well enough, haven't we?"

Kaleb let out a sigh, but he did nod.

The Teslakollisionsgenerator was, for the most part, a success. His AI had crunched the numbers, and the amount of damage the Phobos object was going to sustain from the collider alone should be enough to ensure that Phobos would only ever reach Earth in a state where earthly forces would be able to defeat it.

Moreover, they had built the collider knowing that they wouldn't be the only ones to step up to the metaphorical plate to try and assist.

He had expected . . . more, however.

Perhaps this was his own fault. Kaleb was a scientist. He was born in a corporate scientific research compound to two parents who were researchers. He had grown up surrounded by men and women of science, where the rules of reality were second only to appeasing the whims of their corporate overlords.

He'd gotten a good enough education and unmatchable practical learning from a very young age. In all the ways that mattered, he was encouraged to dive deep into the unknown and tear knowledge out of the grasp of reality.

That's how he liked to romanticize it. In reality, most of the research had been done on the behest of various corporations trying to get a lead on their competition. They were entirely unwilling to share anything.

That and, more often than not, their method of uncovering new truths was to deconstruct the work left behind by samurai.

And then one thing led to another, and he'd become a samurai himself.

"You've got that look on your face," his companion said. He grabbed Radikal by the shoulder and gave him a firm grip.

It was going to leave bruises, Kaleb just knew it. "I know, Drachen, I know. I'm merely reminiscing on what brought us here."

The big man, Drachenschöpfer, was a dear companion of his. A larger-than-life personality who didn't know his own strength at the best of times. People dismissed him as an oaf when they saw his stature, but he was quite clever.

It was no wonder Drachen had been chosen to be a samurai. Kaleb often wondered why he, himself, was chosen.

Shaking the thoughts away, Kaleb glanced across their control room. Seventeen stations with computers and systems fifty years ahead of where humanity's greatest lay, all facing a massive screen whose definition was unmeasurable.

This was the place from which they would save the Earth. There was no accounting for points and costs and such trivialities.

And yet . . . the Teslakollisionsgenerator hadn't been an immediate success. Nor had the Keiretsu's first wave of drones. The great foe was as adaptable and clever as ever.

"Drachen, I'm going to take a short walk," Kaleb said as he rolled his shoulder. "The bridge is yours."

"The bridge is mine," Drachen said with a firm nod. He moved aside, then took Kaleb's place behind the main control podium. "Will you be back in time to see the efforts of our Canadian friends?"

"I'll be back before then, yes," he replied with a nod before slipping out of the room. The Lab—the space where they'd set up their command and control room—wasn't quite as spacious outside of the areas where space was necessary. The corridors were all rather narrow, so he found himself walking briskly through them until he reached a more open space.

There was a bay window here, thick transparent plates jutting out of the wall with a small bench below. A space to sit and observe.

At the moment, Neu Hamburg was below, the mega-city slowly slipping by as the Lab flew past.

You seem stressed. You are aware that the Teslakollisionsgenerator has been successful so far?

"It has," he subvocalized. "But I worry that it won't be successful enough. There's a margin here, and it is quite thin. A failure on our part . . . well, it wouldn't be acceptable."

If the situation deteriorates to that degree, there are options to call upon.

He nodded. There were, but he didn't want to rely on those. Call it foolish pride, but he didn't want to beg the higher-tier, stronger samurai for assistance. They were preoccupied with Mars as it was, a situation that was in no way improving as each day passed. Pulling them back to Earth because he and his companions in the Nachtwächternetzwerk couldn't handle things would sting.

His eyes were drawn to the dead zone beyond the edges of the city. The Lab would likely be flying over these soon, bathing the area in fire and using the opportunity to test a few new weapons in a space where that testing wouldn't harm anyone.

"Sometimes I wonder why I was chosen," he admitted. "I lack that . . . hopeful optimism of my comrades, do I not?"

There's more than one kind of hope.

Kaleb frowned at that, then shrugged. That might well be true, but it wouldn't settle his nerves. He let out a grunt, then turned and stomped back into the command room. Progress, scientific or otherwise, wouldn't happen by being shy and restrained. He recalled that strange Canadian girl and her youthful disregard for pessimism. Perhaps it was all a facade, but that didn't mean that it wasn't a good way to lead.

Kaleb swept into the room, his lab coat billowing out behind him. He noticed a pair of samurai by Drachen at the command podium. "Report," he said. "Time until the Teslakollisionsgenerator has cooled sufficiently?"

One of the technicians jumped. The snap of his voice had them all sitting up straighter. "Four hours, sir."

"Let's tighten our intervals where we can. Collate the data from this first shot and get someone to extrapolate potential damages to the system going forward. Let's not waste the time we have, yes?"

He turned to the others, nodded, then eyed the screen for a moment. The Big Gun had fired a few minutes ago. It had been mildly impressive, the portal system more so than the gun itself. Now they were following the projectile's telemetry as it shot out across space on a collision course with Phobos.

"Comms, send a message to the Keiretsu. I want all the data they can collect on Phobos's geology. Not just the surface. We need geothermal readings as well. Midnight Ranger, can you share some of your sensor equipment with them if it comes to it?"

The samurai in question blinked, then nodded. They weren't a very vocal person, but their sensor technology was second to none. Kaleb hoped that the Keiretsu wouldn't mind losing a drone in order to have better sensors around Phobos within the next couple of days.

"Let's have the Lab AI crunch some numbers," he said. "I want to know exactly what angle to strike Phobos at. Enough of our general assaults. Let's concentrate our power where it will do the most damage."

"That seems to be what the Big Gun Project is doing," Drachen said.

Kaleb perked an eyebrow at that and walked over to his friend. "They have? What is their payload?"

"A Casaba-Howitzer," Drachen said. "Miss Grasshopper has forwarded us a list of their existing munitions. It seems as though they will be launching . . . everything at the rogue moon."

Kaleb was familiar with the platform in question, but he hadn't been expecting it as the first option the Big Gun team would be going for. He'd rather expected a simple nuclear device. "Well, well, that'll be interesting to see, then," he said. He eyed the screen again.

Seven minutes to impact. From Earth to Phobos in what was about half an hour. Their travel speed was simply ludicrous.

"We might want to consider installing similar weapon platforms in orbit," he said.

Next time there was a Phobos-like disaster, it would do them all well to have the infrastructure in place to destroy it without the current mad scramble.

But that was a problem for the future . . . assuming they made it there.

"I can tell you're worrying again," Drachen muttered. "Come on, friend, stop being concerned and start looking forward to this! Our companions overseas are putting on a show for us, aren't they? It's impolite not to watch with enthusiasm!"

"Hmph. Watching with enthusiasm isn't what we need right now," Kaleb said. "Everyone, I want all of our surveillance equipment working properly before that strike lands. Our allies are giving us an opportunity to learn much, so let's not miss it!"

THE SAMURAI'S SAMURAI

Susan shifted. He was on a soft cushion, one filled with a pad of a gel-like substance that had tiny motors within that kneaded the muscles of his legs, preventing them from falling asleep even after hours of being sat in seiza.

It was a nice thing to have at the moment, because he had spent the day sitting here, and it didn't look like that would change any time soon.

Susan was in a well-appointed room. Traditional walls, but spaced far apart, a great glass wall that overlooked Tokyo, and a long, low table where he and his partners could sit and discuss the current business.

That business was the Big Gun Project's attempt at shaking up Phobos.

"The projectile is on its final approach," Hex Kagome said. The many tiny panels over his eyes flashed through a quick pattern, then he nodded. "Our surveillance drone should be able to capture it."

"Do we know what they've sent?" Sentai Blue asked.

"I don't care what it is, as long as it explodes in a fun way," Nya replied.

Susan looked over the group. These were three of the nearly one hundred ronin that made up the Keiretsu. A full quarter of their organization was invested in this one project, but many of the other samurai who were assisting could not be here now.

A few had come to witness the first strike of their kamikaze drones first-hand, but then they'd left, preoccupied by other matters. The global incursion wasn't terrible for Japan, but it was putting a great strain on their more landlocked allies. Phobos was a problem they all had to deal with, but it lacked some immediacy for some of them.

Susan took hold of a cup of warm tea—kept at the perfect temperature for sipping—and raised it to his lips. When he lowered it, it was to eye Nya. "Please calm down. I'm certain that our allies will do what they can."

Nya grinned, then stretched all the way back, almost as if to show off the level of flexibility her oft-modified body held. "I'm sure. You saw their leader, nyeah?"

"Yes, I saw her," he replied socially. "And she is not, as far as I can tell, their leader, merely their spokesperson."

"Their spokescat."

"No," Susan said.

She grinned, and he refused to look at her anymore, at least for the moment. He wondered what it would be like to work with ronin who weren't as insufferable. Nya had always had a . . . thing for her theme. Actually, he could say that about a lot of ronin, himself included. There was a significant difference between the ronin of Asia and the samurai of the west, and it wasn't just their strange nomenclature. There was a cultural difference as well.

"Looks like it's starting," Sentai Blue said. The man's face was covered by a tight helmet that disguised his visage, blue and black with some light silver trim. Not dissimilar to all of the other samurai and ronin that adopted the Sentai name. His visor glowed, and Susan imagined that he was observing the attack even now.

There was no question that Hex Kagome could see everything through his own interface. Susan reached down to the smooth wooden surface of the table and his fingers found a hair-thin crack that opened as he swiped past it. There was a jack within, one that he pulled out and carefully slotted into a corresponding connection near his temple.

His augs warmed, and his vision was overtaken by visuals from their surveillance drone nearer to Phobos.

In the time it took to blink, he was in space. The change made his stomach twist—he had never been good about vertigo—but he didn't allow any of that to show. Soon enough he grew used to the fixed position. He could turn his head to see more, but even then the angle was somewhat limited, as though he were standing before a large bay window.

A green circle appeared on his heads-up display, then a red one. The green was over the location of the Big Gun's first shot, the red over the distant speck that was Phobos.

"Time?" he asked.

"The projectile is approaching quickly," Hex Kagome said. "Under one minute until impact." The voice had come from right next to Susan, as though the ninja were standing over his shoulder.

"So, we have a minute to chat is what you're saying, nya?" Nya said from over the other shoulder.

Susan closed his eyes, for what little good that did. "Please don't start," he said.

"Why nyot?" she asked.

"Because I can only endure you so much," he replied, and it was the honest truth. He'd been forced to be in the same room as the cat-woman for hours already. The sad truth was that Nya was one of the better, older, and more dangerous ronin in the Keiretsu, one of those just barely too weak to be near Mars at the moment, and until their elites returned, she had some amount of influence. She was still a thorn in his side, but that was an issue of clashing personalities, not incompetence.

"*Nya nya nya!*" she singsonged right in his ear.

He sighed. "Brain-rot generation," he grumbled under his breath, but not so low that she wouldn't hear.

That set her off laughing.

"It's starting," Sentai Blue said.

Susan refocused in time to see a small spark of an explosion within the center of the green circle.

"Did . . . it get intercepted?" he asked.

"No," Hex Kogame said. "Look."

A subscreen popped up before him, a zoomed-in section of Phobos that was even now roiling and expanding as the surface exploded outward.

"What was that?" Nya asked.

"A Casaba-Howitzer. A nuclear explosion used to propel a plasma projectile forward at ridiculous speeds," Hex reported.

The explosion continued to spread across the closer side of Phobos. It was impressive . . . but less so than any one of the nuclear strikes they'd landed with their kamikaze drones. "It's penetrative," Susan said.

Hex chuckled. "It should be."

Telemetry and early scans returned. The AI currently controlling what they were seeing ran the numbers and showed them a timelapse of the seconds before and after impact.

"Hmm," Susan said.

The moon's shaking actually served as a decent way to get a better picture of what was happening beneath the surface, and what was happening was impressive.

The plasma from the Big Gun's shot had pierced through the outer crust of the moon and wedged itself deep within. It had run out of energy eventually, but not before leaving cracks in every direction, like putting a bullet through a glass pane.

"Overall damage?" Susan asked. It was an impressive strike, deeper than any of theirs, but . . .

"Light," Hex said. "Localized. It's a needle in the kidney where what we did was like a dozen strikes to the chest. It's more internal damage than what we did, but it won't take the moon out yet."

"Hey, our friends are helping. Maybe that new cat-girl's just testing her claws, nya?"

Susan sighed, then reached up and pulled the jack away from his temple. He blinked a few times as his vision cleared and he saw the room as it was once more. "We'll be trading blows with Phobos for some time, I suspect."

Nya blinked back to the present as well, then gave him one of her ever-irritating grins. "Like playing with a mouse, no?"

"Less a mouse and more an angry dragon," he said. "We're projecting a victory, destroying Phobos long before it arrives on Earth, but that's assuming we continue to ramp up our production and our assault. Let's not fall into complacency."

"Mm-hmm, mm-hmm!" Nya agreed. "More importantly, I wanna go see my fellow cat! Do you need anyone to meet with the Big Gun crew face-to-face?"

"No," he said.

"Are you suuuuure? Nya?" she asked, this time while flopping down onto the table and half-rotating around with her arms outstretched. Sentai Blue carefully moved his tea out of knocking range.

"I'm positive," Susan said.

Though . . . now that he thought about it, that would get her out of his hair . . . and hearing . . .

"Actually, perhaps something could be arranged after all."

CHAPTER FORTY-NINE

I'M CAT AND YOU ARE WATCHING DEEP SPACE BALLISTICS!

Today, we're going to see how these watermelons fare against this discarded samurai railgun we found by the Ohio incursion zone! Stay tuned!
—YouTube video transcript, 2032

The bomb went off, then, in less time than it took for two neurons to connect, the projectile it launched was ramming into Phobos's surface.

"Fuck yeah!" I cheered as we got a big-screen view of the strike. Tankette had brought her tank around and installed a little projector on it. Major Tinwhistle had found a large white tarp and had it strung up between two cranes.

Sure, this was probably the kind of shit that ought to be classified or something, but it felt wrong not to have the entire group witness the fruits of their labor.

Engineers were whistling, workers were cheering. Someone had broken open a case of beer and cans were being passed around. Another had set up a barbecue and cheap hot dogs were being roasted. It made the entire place feel like a party.

It was deserved. These guys and gals had spent hours working on the Big Gun. Without them, this moment wouldn't be happening. It was a rush job, done with no time to spare. I looked around and saw plenty of baggy eyes and slumped shoulders. These people were exhausted, but they were also happy for the moment. Proud, at least.

I turned my attention back to the projection. Our strike was creating a moving wall of dust and debris away from the point of impact, a small stud of a mushroom that was slowly expanding against whatever gravity Phobos had going for it.

The spots where the Keiretsu nukes hit had taken hours to clear out, and they'd left a few massive craters behind.

I had to wonder what our hit had done . . . but not for long, because just then the screen split, and the right side was replaced by a 3D diagram of the moon's surface. Lots of numbers were thrown up on the screen, but it didn't take a geologist to see the spiraling cracks moving away from the point of impact, or the way our shot had dug a hole right into the moon.

"What's that bit?" I asked as I pointed up to where it looked like there was a second explosion way deeper in the crust.

I was surrounded by most of the other samurai in our group, but it was Major Tinwhistle who answered. "Spalling," she said.

Let me draw up some pathing predictions.

New lines appeared, showing where the chunks blown out of the back of the crust would have gone.

"The moon's surface is tough, like a shell, but the interior is likely all Antithesis, with tunnels and structures dug into the moon, but also large roots and veins and arteries, as well as organ-like structures," Grasshopper said. "We've likely done more damage with our one strike than the previous wave of drones managed to accomplish."

"Damn," I said. I was feeling a bit of that pride too. It looked like we'd done the equivalent of popping the aliens with a small-caliber bullet that broke up inside of them.

Having shot a few bigger aliens with small arms in my day, I knew that it wasn't nearly enough to bring one down. But it was damage.

Then the diagram view zoomed way, way out, and I got to see the sheer size of Phobos compared to the tiny pinprick we'd stabbed into the moon's side before the image winked out.

"We shot an elephant with a BB," Hedgehog said.

"And next we'll see if we can't poke a match into the elephant's hide," Gomorrah said. "And if that doesn't do it, we'll try something else."

"She's right," I said. "Our job isn't to finish the job, I guess. It's to keep poking holes, ripping bits, and slicing off chunks."

"The predictions are still in our favor?" Hedgehog asked.

I shrugged, but Grasshopper confirmed it a moment later with a serious nod. "Seems like it."

Hedgehog looked a little restless. He was shifting his weight from foot to foot without ever standing still. "Fine. We need to set up a watch rotation on the Big Gun. And we need to set up a continued escort with the rest of the army. People will be asking questions soon about why the advance has stalled."

"Yeah, I bet that even with everything we've done, there will still be leaks," I said. "It makes sense to keep a watch going. One or two of us here at all times?"

"Two is better," he said. "Some . . . would consider trying something against a single samurai. Any one of us could be distracted. But two? That's a much bigger risk."

"So, who's available for the watch, then?" I asked.

"I can stay tonight," Tankette replied.

"I can as well," Hedgehog said. "Don't have anything to return to right now, so I might as well."

"I'll be staying for a few more hours," Grasshopper said. "I can set up a small camp for you two. I have a camping supplies catalog with all sorts of goodies! You'll feel right at home!"

Major Tinwhistle looked between the lot of us, then shrugged. "I need to get my men moving by morning. But the brass will want to guard this site too. This is a Canadian Army site now, which means that we're going to have corporate rats sticking their necks in at any moment now."

"We can probably warn them off," I said. "Maybe have an aug pop-up letting people who come close enough know that this is an area under samurai surveillance."

"That might just encourage them," Tinwhistle said. "You'll be letting them know that there's something worth investigating."

"I guess, yeah," I said. "But if information leaks, then isn't it too late?"

Gomorrah cleared her throat. "If that's the case, then we need a distraction. Something plausible. Maybe even something you can build near our site that'll leak on purpose and make the army and us look bad."

"You wanna make us look bad?" I asked.

"Just to make the attempts to hide what we have more plausible," Gomorrah said.

Major Tinwhistle nodded. "It'll have to fit with the equipment we brought over. Maybe . . . a mass grave? Those always piss off the media."

That sounded properly messed up. "Okay," I said. "I guess . . . dedicate a shift to dig what looks like a mass grave. That'll be our cover story. Do we need to go deeper? Make up reasons for it?"

"No," Gomorrah said. "If we don't have a ready excuse, then those investigating the site will have to do the research themselves, and it'll lead them nowhere."

"Okay," I said. I really wasn't cut out for this kind of game of deception. "Can I leave that up to you, then?" I asked both women. Gomorrah and the major nodded. "Will you be staying overnight too?"

"Not if I can avoid it," Gomorrah replied. "I wouldn't mind coming in first thing in the morning. What about you? First thing in the morning in Catherine time is . . . around noon?"

"I mean . . . yeah," I admitted. I glanced up. It was well past early evening right now. All of the various attacks we'd launched at Phobos had been nearly an hour apart from each other. The next squeeze from the tesla collider would probably be in three or so hours, and I'd bet there were more drones on the way. Our own next strike was only minutes away too. "So, we're gonna set a clock and fire the Big Gun every time it's off cooldown?"

"It's not very hard to automate. Everything is set up for that already," Grasshopper said. "I just wanted to make sure that first shot was special."

"Heh, alright," I said. I stretched, then looked over the crowd. The party was well under way now. It seemed like all of the tension had drained out of the group and they were celebrating as best they could. Major Tinwhistle was making a concerted effort not to notice the alcohol, or the lingering smell of weed in the air. "Well, in that case, I think I'll be heading back out."

Grasshopper giggled. "You might want to catch up to young Miss Raccoon quickly, then," she said.

I blinked, then looked around again. Wait, where *was* Rac? For that matter, where was that little Frenchman?

One moment . . . I have discovered your companions' location. They're right over here.

Myalis painted a marker on my vision, one that led quite a ways away from the center of the camp, next to the Big Gun and closer to some of the big machines.

I stomped my way over. If that kid was hurting Rac, I'd smack him around, samurai or not. Fortunately, as I approached, my ears twitched and I made out the sound of giggling. Rac's giggling.

When I came around the corner, I half expected to find something inappropriate going on, but they were just sitting next to each other on the tracks of a bulldozer, each with a glass bottle in hand.

"Oh, hey," I said. Well, shit, way to make myself feel awkward.

CHAPTER FIFTY

TRASH PANDA PONDERING

You must choose one: Cut the general working's salary, or cut the security force's salary. You absolutely cannot do both.
—*Lessons in Human Resources*, fifth edition, 2038

The ride back home, with Rac clinging onto me from behind as I rode my bike across the skies, was about as awkward as I expected it to be.

Probably more for me than for her, to be fair. She hadn't done anything weird, just hung out with a boy close to her age.

Maybe I was reading too much into it. It wasn't like I was her mom or anything. She could do what she wanted. I was pretty sure Gros Baton was like . . . seventeen-ish, so there wasn't anything too weird there. He was definitely a better friend to make than any members of the gang she'd been riding with recently.

Well, I guess mercs weren't a gang, but Garter and his little buddies were still bad influences.

A bunch of samurai were much better people to hang out with. Probably. Samurai at least had the benefit of the Protector AI picking them out as "good enough" folk. But I might have been a little biased there.

We swooped in toward the only building with a giant cat topping it off, and I brought my bike down for a gentle landing before the doorway. I could have gone into the parking garage, but the weather was actually kinda dry for once, and I was too damned lazy to slow down fully and slip in. Plus, this spot was more fun to leave from in the morning.

"Alright, off," I said. Rac needed to dismount before I could swing my leg over. I bounced on the spot for a moment, then glanced over at Rac, who was staring at me, hands in her pockets. "What?" I asked.

"It feels like you wanna say something," she said.

"No?" I tried.

Her eyes narrowed. "Are you sure?"

"Yeah, I'm pretty sure," I said. "So, uh, let's go in? Unless you're heading out again?"

She looked up. The sky was that deep bluish color that came when all the nightly ads came on, with a few spots of purple and orange where some bigger signs caught the lower hanging clouds.

"Nah. It's late. I might load up the printer again. Uh, I'm running out of materials for it."

"Ah, yeah, that'll happen. I kinda put that out of my mind, what with Phobos and all."

"Right. The end of the world is more important than that," she said before shifting. "Kinda weird that we have to worry about that."

"Heh, yeah, you tell me. You know, when I became a samurai, I thought I'd mostly be worrying about small-fry issues. A few aliens here and there, maybe a big hive to blow up. But mostly I expected to have to take care of me and mine and maybe the neighborhood. This is . . . bigger."

"I get that," Rac said. She scratched at the back of her neck. "I wasn't expecting to live much longer, you know? There's only so long you can go, scrounging in the undercity. I had a good run at it, but you can only be so lucky. Never expected to be where I am now."

"Hmm, yeah," I said. "Uh . . . maybe we can do something to help others? Other Raccoons out there, I mean. Not *now*-now, but it'd be nice. Once we have things settled. We can set something up. But first, you know, the world."

"Save the world, worry about the little people after?" she asked.

"Pretty much, yeah. Come on, I'm starving." I patted her on the shoulder, then walked on home. The moment I was indoors, I shucked off my helmet and tossed it onto the couch, then I flung my coat over the back of a chair that was supposed to be in the kitchen.

I wasn't just going to leave my guns anywhere, though. I wasn't *that* irresponsible. If I left them out, or my sword, there was a one hundred percent chance I'd be woken up by some kitten crying because they shot themselves in the foot.

I took a deep breath, then sniffed the air some more. Something smelled nice.

"Cat!" Lucy said as she popped out of the kitchen. She ran over and crashed into me with a big hug.

I hugged back, of course, squeezing her closer and pressing my face against the top of her head. "Hi," I said.

"Hi," she replied as she pulled her head back and craned her neck up to meet me in a kiss. "Mmm, good day saving the world?"

"Pretty good, yeah," I said. "I'll show you the footage later. We fired the Big Gun, it was pretty cool."

"Oh, I bet!"

"Maybe I'll have you come over? I don't think there are any rules about who can press the big red button."

"Is there actually a big red button?"

"It has a little plastic cover and a bunch of flicky switches and everything," I said. "I don't even know what they do, but it's kinda awesome."

Lucy giggled, then pulled out of the hug fully, but not before grabbing my hand. "I made supper!"

"Oh?" I asked as I allowed her to drag me along. "What'd you make?"

"An entire chicken! Then I had to make another, because *someone* wasn't showing up and the kittens got into my first chicken and they . . . kinda messed it up. But it's okay, the second one turned out better than the first, I think. There's still half left!"

I blinked as I tried to follow along with that. "Where did you even find a chicken?"

"Well, I didn't hunt it myself, did I?" she asked. "I bought it, Cat. You can do that, buy raw, whole chickens. They come in a bag."

"Huh," I said. I supposed that was possible. The only chickens I'd ever seen were wings, fried breasts, or in the shape of little dinosaurs. Not that I didn't know what a chicken looked like. There were plenty of chicken logos around and stuff, and like . . . movies had them sometimes. Just, I'd never seen a live one, or a whole cooked one.

Lucy let go of me to proudly gesture at what was sitting on the kitchen island. There was, indeed, a whole chicken there, in a glass pan filled with some sort of greasy brown sauce and chunks of . . . something.

"What are those?" I asked.

"Veggies," she said. "They're good for you."

I wasn't in the habit of eating vegetables, and I wasn't sure I was ready to start now. But on closer inspection, it was mostly diced potatoes and maybe carrots, all baked in some sort of sauce. It did smell real good, and there was still a bit of steam rising off the top.

"Well shit, grab me a plate and some knives," I said. "I'm about to do a number on this bird."

Lucy grinned, then turned to Rac. "Want some too? It's good, I swear. I've been getting better."

"I don't refuse free food," Rac said reasonably.

I started to cut into the juicier, less bony parts of the chicken until Lucy saw what I was doing and stole my knife and fork from me. Apparently I was doing it wrong or something, but the end result was being served a hefty chunk of meat, so I wasn't about to complain.

"You know, you really make saving the world worth it," I said.

Lucy smiled. "That would be far more romantic if you spoke *after* you finished chewing, Cat."

I smiled back, then made a point of swallowing. "It's because it tastes so good?"

"Nice try, but no. Oh, and by the way, we need some upgrades for the kitchen," Lucy said.

"We do?" I asked. The kitchen looked fine to me. Fine-ish. It was a little messy, but I was sure Lucy could bully some of the kids into doing a half-assed job of cleaning it. "What's wrong with it?"

"The oven is a mess inside."

"So clean it out?" I tried.

"Fuck that, I'd rather buy a new one."

I shrugged. "Okay."

God, it was nice being stupid-rich.

Lucy seemed to agree, because she looked extra smug for a moment. "Alright! Well, if that's the case . . . I think I'm ready to explore baking. Let's see if I can't make a cake."

"Your cake is fantastic already," I said.

"What did I just say about flirting with your mouth full, Cat?"

"I had a long day?"

"I don't know how that excuses you," she said. "Well, whatever. So, tell me about your day. Spill that juicy gossip, because I've been starving for it over here."

"Oh, I have some good stuff to spill," I said. "So, what do you know about international samurai and their weirdness?"

CHAPTER FIFTY-ONE

ADAMANTIUM TOENAILS

—Sassy? No, my AI is nice and polite. He's like an old-timey butler.
—What? No, my AI is like a little sister I've never had.
—What do you mean a butler and little sister? Mine gives me shit all the time!
—Overheard conversation between three samurai, 2025

I woke up to a kick.

It was weird, because I'd once been pretty used to waking up to kicks, but I hadn't felt one in a while. Lucy's deteriorating condition often led to weird twitches. She said they hurt when she was awake, but she didn't feel them while sleeping.

Instead, I was the one to feel them as she rammed her sharp little toenails into my shins and calves.

It had been a while, though. Maybe the kicking wasn't medical at all and Lucy had just been lying to cover up her habit of moving in her sleep? We used to sleep in the tiny, narrow beds at the orphanage. They were only barely large enough for one adult, so any movement was hard to miss.

I grumbled as I came awake and turned around. Blinking, I made out Lucy's form in the dark with my cybernetic eye.

She was sleeping at a forty-five degree angle across the bed, blankets thrown off her upper body and face drooling into a pillow she was hugging.

I grinned. She looked like absolute crap, which is why I took a picture and sent it to her. It would be a surprise when she woke up and checked her messages.

Reaching down, I rubbed at my calf where she'd dug her nails in. "Dammit, Lucy," I muttered. She'd never drawn blood, but I swore it was a near thing. I checked the time and was horrified to discover that it was only eight in the morning.

Holy crap, I was waking up at a reasonable time? I wasn't even tired enough to fall back asleep. I rubbed at my face, then popped open my media feeds for a quick scroll-through.

Lucy and I had been using the same old app for like, ten years now. It was a free version of an aggregator for various media accounts that picked the juiciest gossip, news, propaganda, and advertising and shoved it all into one stream of easy-to-scroll slop. These kinds of aggregators usually had a monthly subscription fee, or you had to endure ads every so often, but this one was a beta version Lucy had found on some sketchy site that was a hundred generations behind.

As long as we didn't update it, we were fine. It was a right pain in the ass to stop it from updating though, but I'd long ago gotten into the habit of opening it through my augs, closing the update prompt, then opening the downloader that downloaded the next update and shutting that down manually.

Still faster than looking at a single video ad.

The news this morning was the usual: political scandals, corporate scandals, celebrity drama. I watched a video of a cat pushing a brick off the side of a building where it landed on some pedestrian's head. I'd seen that same video ten years ago, but the damned thing was reposted like clockwork.

Some of the reposts were older than me, posted over and over again by attention-farming bots. I was ten minutes into the mindless scrolling when I passed some news about a few Brazilian samurai who'd blown up some statue or something that had been turned into an Antithesis nest. They'd replaced it, but the locals weren't happy with the new one. My attention wandered to the corner of my vision.

I had the time displayed up there, and under that, Myalis was keeping my point tally up.

"Holy fuck!"

I bounced out of the bed, suddenly on my feet as a shock of adrenaline zipped through me.

I was expecting this reaction, and yet it's still amusing to see.

"Myalis, what the fuck?" I asked.

I had forty thousand points banked. Forty K and change, to be exact, but at that number the chump change didn't matter as much.

The earnings are from the Big Gun's shots taken over night. In the last ten hours the gun has fired eleven times. I can get you a full breakdown of the points earned, but for the most part it comes from killing a small number of higher-tier Antithesis. The value was, of course, split unevenly among the Vanguard participating in the project, with major deductions for the distance between said Vanguard and the actual successful eliminations.

"That's a ridiculous number of points, still." I said.

It's what you earned.

I scratched my neck. "What I earned, my ass," I muttered. I'd sweat blood and tears to make a tenth as many points before. And now I'd earned this many while sleeping.

Was this how rich people felt?

Fuck, the game really was rigged.

"Cat? What's going on?" Lucy asked.

"Huh? Oh, sorry I didn't mean to wake you," I said. "You can go back to sleep."

Lucy yawned wide. "What's wrong?"

"Technically, nothing."

"Technically?" she repeated. She was fully awake now. Though she was still hugging her drool pillow. How often were we supposed to change bed-sheets and pillowcases and shit like that? Once a month or so?

"The Big Gun's been firing all night, and since I helped build a bit of it, I'm . . . I guess entitled to a percent of the points it makes killing aliens," I said as I sat back down on the edge of the bed. "And I just woke up to a fuckload more points than I had last night."

"Oh . . . Isn't that a good thing?"

"I guess? Yeah, I mean, it's definitely a good thing. No doubt about it." I shrugged. "I just don't know what to do with all that. It's too much."

"Aww, you don't need to feel pressured to spend it," Lucy said. "You can earmark a chunk as savings, and then pour the rest into your projects."

"My projects?" I asked.

"Well, you've been spending less time on your new mechanics hobby. Maybe now you can buy a garage that's got better tools and such. There's also the printer—it's really good, but I think it's maybe too slow for every-thing we're loading it with. I think we wanted to make the house safer too?"

"Right," I said. She wasn't wrong. "And my gear could use an upgrade overall," I muttered.

Do keep in mind that your current windfall won't last forever. Once Pho-bos is eliminated, the current influx of points will stop.

Right, that was another good point. I hadn't checked on the status of the moon. For all I knew, the thing was riddled with holes and all the big aliens on it were long dead. I kinda doubted it, but it wasn't impossible.

"Urgh, I have a shift watching over the Big Gun. I can't remember when it was, but I think I'm supposed to show up around noon."

Lucy shifted in bed, then stretched. The blankets slid down, exposing some of her stomach that wasn't covered by her silky PJs. "That's *hours* away, you know?"

"Uh-huh," I said.

"I'm sure I could tempt you to spend that time well," she said.

"Uh-huh."

"By eating a proper breakfast for once." Lucy did a kip-up, or tried. She ended up mostly flopping around very unsexily until she rolled off the far end of the bed. "I wanna make this egg recipe I saw last night! Eggs Benedict! They look really good."

I pouted, but I *was* rather hungry. "Urgh, fine," I said.

Lucy laughed at my plight—at least until I ran up behind her and caught her by the hips. Her laugh turned into a squeal, but she wasn't leaving this room before I had time to kiss her silly.

A few minutes later, Lucy was off to try some more experimental stuff in the kitchen and I hopped into the shower. "Myalis," I said as I rubbed shampoo over my scalp under a sheet of warm water.

Yes, Catherine?

"I need a few good ideas on what to spend those points on. I'm thinking it's time for a couple of upgrades. Not physical stuff, though." The skin change had been pretty big already, and the new hair too. Anything more was probably pushing it for the moment.

I'm certain I can think of a few options. You might want to revisit your catalog list. Catalogs are generally an expensive but worthwhile long-term investment.

"Because I can buy more kinds of shit with them?" I asked.

I wouldn't use such fecal terminology, but essentially, yes. They widen the breadth of items you can purchase. That only makes you more capable and flexible, and overlapping catalogs do reduce the cost of some items.

That was an idea. I had a few of those tokens sitting around too. Maybe dipping into the higher tier catalogs wasn't a bad move either.

"Alright," I said as I shut the shower off. "Yeah. I think that I can work with that. List away, Myalis."

CHAPTER FIFTY-TWO

FINGER GUNS

A Joytoy is a member of the lower to middle class who participates in the personal entertainment industry. They provide companionship and sexual gratification to playing clients.

The modern Joytoy is often equipped with a range of cybernetic enhancements for their personal protection (C-IUDs, bloodcheckers, STI-removal biogear, etc) as well as personal enhancements to better serve their customers.

—Commodification and U: A Guide to Bringing Joy
and Earning Credits, 2047

"How many tokens do I have?" I asked. Somehow I'd ended up sitting on the edge of the bed again. Sure, I'd slept a good bit, but I was still a little tired, and standing around while talking to Myalis was always kind of awkward.

She was something of a voice in my head. There wasn't any way to interact with her directly, not like talking to a person face-to-face, and even on a call with someone, I'd at least have a phone in hand, or a screen open on my augs. With Myalis I had neither.

Most of the time that was fine. It wasn't like I *needed* to see her or whatever. But it did make things a little awkward when I wasn't moving around or doing anything.

You currently have four tokens saved up.

I nodded. That sounded about right. I didn't track those nearly as closely as I did my points, and even my points were . . . mostly being accumulated off to the side now.

"Four tokens, huh? So that's four class two catalogs? How much does class three cost?"

A class three catalog would cost you three tokens. You could afford a single one at the moment. Speaking plainly, you have the choice between widening your spread of abilities and owned catalogs, or pushing one of your current catalogs up a tier to help you hyperspecialize in one area.

I nodded along. "Yeah, I get that," I said. "So, oh wise Myalis of my brain, what do you recommend?"

I see three options before you. The first is, as I mentioned, to spend some number of points unlocking several new catalogs, then push these up a class with your current tokens. This option would widen the breadth of abilities and items at your disposal.

"Go on," I said.

The next two options are similar to each other. Either focus on your esoteric weapons specialization or on your Sun Watcher Technologies, elevating either to class three. At that level, both options would give you incredible abilities when it comes to handling higher-tier threats.

"How high are we talking, here?"

The correlation isn't exact.

"What's that mean?" I asked as I leaned back.

Most Antithesis you're likely to see within your lifespan can be defeated with equipment purchased from class one catalogs. The greater the class of the catalog, the further from humanity's technological base the items are, but that does not mean that near-human technology cannot defeat the enemy.

"Right, okay," I said. It was like . . . anyone could die by being shot by a shitty handgun. Some things made that harder, body armor and the like, but that didn't prevent that same gun from being dangerous. Higher classes of catalogs were like . . . upgrading from a dinky pistol to something bigger. It helped, but it didn't mean that it was entirely necessary. "So, why those two catalogs? I mean, besides the fact that I've invested in both already."

They're both catalogs that fit your current preferences in terms of combat and lifestyle. Your Esoteric Explosives catalog provides most of the equipment that has been allowing you to punch above your weight class, and the Sun Watcher Technologies catalog has been providing you with most of your weaponry, armor, and other equipment.

Right, so it was a three-way choice between going wide, going all-in on offense, or continuing with a pretty large set of very thematic equipment that covered a lot of bases.

I flopped back onto the bed and stared up at the ceiling for a bit. "Okay," I said. "I think . . . logically, Sun Watcher Technologies feels like the right choice. It's got a lot of prosthetics, it's got armor, it's got weapons. My mech's mostly from there, yeah? So if I wanna upgrade that, then it's the way to go."

Indeed.

"But!" I said. "But . . . that's not what would be the most useful *right now*."

That prize went to the Esoteric Explosives catalog, hands down. Explosives were what we were chucking at Phobos from the Big Gun, and I'd left a dozen rounds behind of a few different flavors to see what worked.

A higher class of that catalog would mean more bombs and more variety. It would also probably mean a lot more oomph, and we needed all the oomph we could get at the moment.

"Shit . . . I think the right call is getting Esoteric Explosives up. It's the right call for the short term, at least."

There would definitely still be long-term benefits to such a thing. For one, you would have greater access to esoteric ammunition for even your simplest projectile weapons.

"Right," I said. It wasn't like it would be a loss. It was just that the Sun Watcher Technologies catalog would probably kick more ass in the long run.

Don't forget that the number of tokens you have will only increase over time. The destruction of Phobos will certainly contribute.

That was also true. I'd have one token left over if I bought the next class up for Esoteric Explosives. So I'd only be missing two more to bring Sun Watcher Technologies up to par.

I'd probably get at least one from Phobos, that much Myalis had confirmed, so I'd at most be missing one more token. That couldn't be too hard to pick up, right? "Yeah, alright," I said. "Grab me that Esoteric Explosives catalog, the next class up."

To be clear, the cost isn't limited to a number of tokens. The next class up is rather expensive.

"It can't be that bad, can it?" I asked.

Sixteen thousand points.

I choked. "Holy fuck. How much . . . how much would class four cost?" I asked.

Ten times as much. A hundred and sixty thousand points.

"Shit," I said. That wasn't breaking the bank or anything, but that was damned close to half my points gone, just for the ability to buy more stuff. "Damn. Is it worth it?"

I'd say so, yes. The increase in your potency will be considerable. And speaking plainly, banking points as you have been serves little purpose. You gain nothing from having a large number of points left unspent. There's utility in being able to purchase what you might need when you need it in the future, but those aren't considered properly weighted purchases.

I sat up, then let out a long huff of a breath. "Yeah, okay," I said.

You'll make the purchase?

"I will," I said. "Just . . . do it quick, like ripping off a bandage."

New Purchase: Class III Esoteric Explosives
Points Reduced from 42,740 . . . to . . . 26,740

I chewed on my lip, but refrained from wincing. That was . . . still a lot of points. I was still fine.

Now, about additional upgrades . . .

"Urgh," I said. "No, I think I've spent myself out for the day," I said.

Very well, it's as you wish. I'll nag you again once there's more of a pressing need for new equipment.

"Nag?" I asked.

Do you need the word defined?

"No, I know what it means, I'm just impressed that you'd just . . . right out and state it. It's not exactly subtle."

I don't need to be subtle with you. It's one of the reasons I bothered to insert myself in your head, Catherine. You're refreshingly blunt and idiotic in just the way I like.

"Uh . . . thanks?"

Anytime. Just to be clear, I am currently making finger guns.

"With what hands?" I asked.

I am not at liberty to say.

Why did the super-smart alien AI in my head have to be such a shit? Couldn't I have a nice, polite, reasonable one? Atyacus seemed fine. Very gentlemanly and reserved. Sure he liked burning things, but that was all. I could live with a bit of pyromania. It was better than feline . . . omania.

Lucy walked into the room, apron on and spatula in hand. "Breakfast is ready!" she said.

"Oh, good," I said. A distraction. "What was it you made?"

"Bacon and scrambled eggs."

"Weren't you going to make some other sort of fancy egg?" I asked.

"Cat . . . for the sake of our relationship, can you please pretend that I intended to make scrambled eggs this entire time?" She batted her eyelashes at me sweetly.

"Sure," I said. No one could accuse me of not taking a hint or being a bad girlfriend. "Let's see about those eggs of yours."

"Oh my," she said.

I rolled my eyes, but followed her all the same. I was just surrounded by people that thought they were funny, wasn't I?

But hey, it wasn't all that bad. Myalis was providing me with some cool shit, and I entered the kitchen to find a plate with eggs and bacon and . . .

"Bargain, get the fuck away from my breakfast!" I snapped as I caught the brat red-handed.

CHAPTER FIFTY-THREE

EGG SHELLS

Media literacy is only necessary when you can't trust the media you consume.

—Very True Social, failed slogan, 2038

I was just about done with breakfast when I decided to pop open the group chat for the Big Gun. Someone had added a new channel to the chat, which caught my eye right away. It was otherwise pretty calm, at least compared to the last couple of days when we'd been rushing to get everything ready.

Hedgehog had been updating the main chat all night long with a rather formal list. He'd spell out what kind of shell was loaded into the Big Gun and when, then a few minutes later the shell's impact on Phobos in terms of points he'd earned.

Hedgehog: [23:14] High Impact Explosive Shell
Hedgehog: [24:10] Points gained: 1045
Hedgehog: [24:15] PyroChemical MIRV
Hedgehog: [01:08] Points gained: 820

The list went all through the night, more or less once an hour. The time between the shots and their impact on Phobos was very slowly decreasing by about one or two minutes after every shot, which was interesting to note. The points earned were all over the place. It seemed, at a glance, like anything that was more penetrative was worth a bit more.

There was some additional commentary by Hedgehog about certain rounds. Mostly noting their effectiveness or lack thereof. One shell meant to blow up over the moon's surface had barely made any points and he'd taken a lot of notes about why it was ineffective. Another MIRV shell—I had to look that up real quick, because the acronym escaped me, but it meant multiple independently-targetable reentry vehicles, and all that meant was that the projectile could split up into smaller projectiles that would move independently and fuck shit up—had tagged a flight of smaller models as they were flying out to intercept some of the Keiretsu's drones, and Hedgehog noted that we'd earned a lot more points than we would have otherwise.

Anyway, that chat was interesting to look over. If I had more of an analytical mind, I might have been able to come to some smart conclusion from looking at it, but I figured I'd leave that to the others.

I left a note mentioning how I bought a third-tier catalog to give us access to more oomph, and Grasshopper immediately replied with a . . . gif of a chibi version of herself pressing a gold star onto a cartoon cat's forehead?

Did she have a "silly gifs" catalog, or was her AI just as childish as she was?

Actually, I didn't want to know.

The new channel, once I clicked it open, had me sitting up straighter. "Fuck," I muttered.

Lucy's head whipped around. "What's wrong?" she asked. "Did I leave some eggshell in? I was sure I picked all the bits out."

"Wait . . . was that the crunchy bit? I thought it was pepper?"

"Oh . . . never you mind then," Lucy said. "What's the fuck about?"

I frowned, but decided not to pursue it. Eggshell couldn't be all bad, right? Probably had protein or something. "There's a new channel in the group chat for the samurai in the Big Gun Project. Looks like the media has shown up."

"Weren't you guys being all subtle?" Lucy asked.

"Yeah, that's why I'm pissed," I said. I stood up, then sighed. "Gros Baton is taking care of them, apparently. They're not at the site, at least, so we have that much going for us."

"If they're not at the site, then where are they?" Lucy asked.

"Saint-Jérome," I said. "But they're asking pointed questions and Gros Baton said that he can only play the 'I don't speak English' card for so long. I don't think he's gotten used to being a samurai enough to tell the media to fuck off."

"Aww, he needs big sister Cat to save him!" Lucy said.

I rolled my eyes. I wasn't going to *save* him. I was going to make sure he didn't make a mess of things. If that happened to keep him out of trouble, that was entirely a happy side effect. "Whatever," I said before walking over to Lucy. I wrapped an arm around her waist and pulled her smiling face closer. "Gimme a kiss for the road?"

I ended up with enough kisses for the road there and back.

Getting on my bike a few minutes later, I kicked off and flew out of our home and aimed northward. I had to stifle a yawn. Something about a heavy breakfast made me feel sleepy, even though I'd definitely gotten enough sleep that it shouldn't have been an issue.

I flipped on the autopilot as soon as I was on the edge of New Montreal so that I could focus on texting. That was probably breaking some law, actually . . .

Stray Cat: I'm on my way to SJ.

Stray Cat: Keep your head on, GB.

Gros Baton: Hurry, tbrnk. These reporters are like dogs.

Stray Cat: Where in SJ are you?

The kid gave me some vague directions. The media had mostly shown up near that big camp on the southern end of the city. They should have been easy to ignore, since they were keeping away from the military camp on the northern end of the city, but Gros Baton had discovered them asking a lot of questions and then he'd poked his nose into things.

Now they were on him like street dogs on an injured kitten. They smelled blood and were hungry for a bite.

I grumbled as I retook control of the bike and pushed the throttle down a little more. I hadn't actually intended to save the kid when I left, but it looked like he might actually need it.

And to think that I was aiming for the hardest part of the day being the bit where I picked out what to shoot at the aliens next.

Saint-Jérome appeared out over the horizon. I zipped toward it, then circled around the southern end of the city. There were a few balloons hovering over the walls with flak guns mounted to their sides to take out any flying models, and it looked like some of Major Tinwhistle's engineers were slowly working to refurbish the barriers that had fallen apart.

A lot more of the city was alive now than when we'd first arrived here. More lights were on, and more people were out in the streets. It looked like cars were still forbidden except for some buses moving around, so people were taking to walking and biking around. A few armored cars and lighter tanks sat at the busier intersections with soldiers milling around them.

Probably rapid response teams, in case a civilian discovered some alien that needed killing.

All that was well and good, but it didn't mean that things were back to anything like normal. The massive camp on the south end of the city seemed to still be full. Maybe not to bursting, but it looked like half the city's population was there.

"Hey, Myalis, do you have a good idea of where the kid is?" I asked.

One moment . . . Yes, his AI has confirmed his location after asking for his permission to disseminate the information. He is next to the hardware store. Marking the location now.

The hardware store? That turned out to be a larger building pretty much right under me. The front was opened up and it looked like some tents and such extended all the way inside. Judging by the number of brand-new barbecues being used outside, the place had been turned into more camp space.

Next to it was a parking lot that was currently occupied by a half dozen news vans. I even recognized some of the logos. *The New Montreal Gazette, La/The Presse/Press, The Journal of New Montreal.* Then there were the newer ones. NMN, CBC2, Shoot Star.

That was a pretty big chunk of the local media pie represented down there, and it looked like they'd deployed the attack journalists on Gros Baton.

The kid was . . . not quite pinned against the wall of the hardware store, but he certainly had it to his back and looked like he couldn't make an easy getaway.

I spun my bike around and brought it down. Journalists and camera dudes leapt away to avoid being squished beneath me. A few had their perfect hair mussed up by the wash of the bike's thrusters, but I did make sure that I wasn't actually going to land on anyone.

"Hey, what the hell?" one guy asked, which . . . was fair. He choked on his words as I unsaddled the bike and tugged my coat on straight.

"Sorry," I said without feeling it. "Just need to squeeze on past . . ."

I blinked as the media types formed ranks and I suddenly found myself next to Gros Baton while they cut us both off from my bike.

I decided not to be too concerned. The worse they could do was make me look bad. "Hey," I said to the kid.

"Hey," he replied, but his smile was a little shaky. "Can we, ah, get the fuck out?"

I grinned. "Sure, but maybe you can let me answer a question or two?" Just because they could make me look bad didn't mean I wanted them to, and maybe tossing them a bone would keep these dogs calm for a bit.

CHAPTER FIFTY-FOUR

BURNED/SCARRED/BUTCH, SCARY, AND NOTORIOUS

As with most careers, the modern journalist has its own codified look. Journo fashion is usually marked by plate carriers and bulletproof vests, often in bright, faction-neutral colors. Occasionally a journo will be wearing a flak helmet as well, oftentimes with several electronic upgrades attached to it to allow them to capture the world around them in high fidelity.

The modern microphone, with sound dampening, vocal-tuned pickups, and at-range listening is another must-have for any fashionable journalist.

—*Fashion Careers*, 2049

"You good?" I muttered once I was right next to Gros Baton.

The kid nodded once, his face set and serious, brows drawn into a scowl. "J'pense que ça va. Mais ces journalistes-là n'arrêtent pas de me harceler." *I think I'm alright. These journalists won't stop hounding me, though.* He gestured to the journalists who were kind of crowding us in.

I was pretty sure I could beat a path to my bike with no problem. I only saw a few guns in the lot. Plenty more body armor though. Plate carriers were the order of the day, and a few of them had army-style helmets repainted with the logo of their stations on the sides. Not all, mind. A lot of them were trying to look personable, all corpo-smiles and artificially friendly faces.

There were two ways out of here, I figured. That mostly came from the limited experience I had seeing celebrities and samurai dealing with the media, so it was all third- or fourth-hand experience. Still, I'd seen some meme-able fuckups and knew what *not* to do.

Don't insult the journos . . . unless I was really hot, funny, or popular. Don't repeat "no comment" endlessly; it only pisses them off . . . unless I was hot about it, or funny, or popular. Don't get too defensive, don't ramble, and don't assume the mic is off. Unless I could be hot or funny with it.

Fuck, being hot, funny, and popular was one hell of a leg up, but I wasn't any of those three, so I'd have to be sensible.

So, two solutions. Drag Gros Baton out of here as quick as I could, fast enough not to piss this lot off, or . . . the other solution. "Alright, you fucks," I said before waving them down. Somehow that actually shut some of them up. "You get one question per network."

They all started at once.

"Oi! Shut the fuck up!" I snapped. Wait, was that insulting? Fuck me, I wasn't good at following my own advice, was I? "One per network. I'll know if you're being a dick about it. Don't test me. You! Yeah, you, the gormless guy with the bald spot. Yeah, I can see it, question, now."

Screw it, I was gonna handle this bunch like I would unruly kids and hope for the best.

"Uh, Kai Voss, for Apoca-Lips," he said before pointing a small microphone my way. "Uh, can you let us know about your relationship with the samurai next to you?"

"Gros Baton?" I asked. "He's nice enough." I shrugged a shoulder. "Next. You, with the blue-and-yellow hair." Dude had a logo with the same colors on his chest.

"Ridge Byte with the Flossing Network, can you tell us about your dental routine?"

I blinked. "I don't brush and I sure as shit don't floss. Teeth are luxury bones and I'm rich as fuck. You, the hot one with the rainbows. Also, you single?"

The girl blushed prettily. "Ah, hello, Violet Shade, from PRSM, the LBGT-QWERTY Tech Network . . . I'm not single?"

"Yeah, I'm not either," I admitted.

"Thank you?" she tried. "S-speaking of relationships, Miss, what's your current status and if I may, what's your stance on two-spirit, lesbian, gay, bisexual, transgender, queer, questioning, intersex, asexual plus issues?"

"I'm very not single and happy about it, and I don't care who or what people fuck as long as it's not with me," I said. I pointed to the next guy.

"Avery Covert, Top Secret News," he said. "What are the samurai around here doing? Initially, there was a push to protect this area, but for the last two days, sightings have decreased substantially, and there are clear signs of some sort of cover-up."

I paused for a moment. Dude was getting to the heart of it, wasn't he? Should I lie? Dismiss it? I shrugged and did as I would with the kittens. "You're right," I said. "There's some shit going on, and I can't tell you about it because we're doing a big cover-up of the whole situation. I wish I could tell you, but I really don't want to, and you're just gonna have to live with that. If it helps any, we're saving the world, probably."

I pointed to the next chump.

"Wendy Gale, Canada-Wide Weather, what are your opinions on modern climate change?"

"I'm a Canadian girl who's only seen snow in movies and TV, but it always looks like it'd be a pain in the ass to handle, so I really don't care," I said. "You, with the army getup."

"Charlie Foxtrot from MNN," the man said. He was standing tall and serious, looking like a poster boy for the army. "You've been working with the armed forces for some time now around this area, what do you have to say about your experiences so far?"

"It's been good," I said. "Lots of professional sorts. Shout out to Major Tinwhistle, Lieutenants Moreau and Juno, and the brigadier general. They're real accommodating and don't fuck around, which is something I can appreciate. I've discovered that I really love artillery too."

He nodded seriously, but he seemed happy with the answer. I pointed to some hippie-looking chick next to him.

"Holly Woods, Nature and Entertainment. Why did you set a lake on fire?"

"Shit was fucked," I said. "The lake was some corpo's chemical dumping ground for super pesticides that cause super cancer or something. They didn't work because the aliens thrived in that shit, so Gomorrah did as she does and now the lake's on fire." I raised a hand. "Myalis, can you send her an infodump on the fuckers?"

Consider it sent . . . because it is.

Holly seemed happy enough with that, judging by her winning smile. "You," I said, pointing to the next guy. We were . . . maybe halfway through, but I wasn't going to stand around here all day, not when I could see more media-types rushing over.

"Word, Buzz, of Politycon. Are you planning to murder any more politicians?"

"Only if they don't keep to their lane," I said. "You?"

"Penelope Scope, The New Montreal Celebrity Investigators. We've noticed that you have a few cat-like body enhancements and have recently set up a charity-like program offering people low-priced prosthetics. Are cat ears going to become available as well? Maybe tails and claws?"

"I wasn't planning on offering anything like that," I said. "Would people even want that? No, don't . . . don't answer that. You, with the fancy tech hair." I pointed to a chick with a 'fro made of green-and-blue tech hair.

"Wanda Lust of the Globe Travelers News Association, have you considered roaming outside of the New Montreal area?"

"Uh, not really, but I have been making friends in other countries lately, so who knows? Maybe I'll fly over to say hi one of these days? I'm sure shit's worse in some places than it is here and they might need a hand."

I pointed to one last guy. He seemed smartly dressed, more of a classic journo than the rest. He nodded his thanks and adjusted a pair of aug-glasses. "Benjamin Lebeau from CNMN. My . . . peers here have brought up a number of questions, but I really wanted to know where you stand with regards to improving New Montreal. You shot the mayor, causing a great deal of political turmoil in a time where such is unwelcome, but you've also visibly put a lot of effort into the reconstruction and repair of the New Montreal sewer system."

"Uh, sorry, Ben, but where's the question?" I asked.

"Forgive me. The question is: What are your policies and do you aim to improve the city, and if so, how?" he said.

I had to take a moment to unpack that, but no more than a moment. To these kinds of jackals, a long pause would only give them fuel to call me slow-witted and stupid. At least, it would be enough for the kittens to do that.

"Right," I said to fill the air a little. "Look, I'm from New Montreal. Born there . . . more or less raised there. It's home, and it's never not been shit. The air stinks, the people are cunts, and it's a giant festering shithole. I don't think I can change that. I'm just one girl, samurai or no. But I've got some friends, like this little brat here, and others, and we're willing to claw and shoot and fuck shit up to keep the city going. I guess that's my policy. I'll fix what I see as broken enough to bother fixing. Don't expect me to turn the place into a utopia. If you want that, you'll need to do your share too."

"Thank you," Benjamin said.

"Yeah. Okay, that's enough, we need to get back to work. Talking to you bunch won't get the aliens any more dead. Yeah yeah, I don't care, move it. Move it! For fuck's sake."

CHAPTER FIFTY-FIVE

CUTTING TO THE HEART
OF THE MOON

Are they hiding something from you?
Top Secret News says . . . yes! Exclusive street-side interview with two
samurai reveals hidden truth! A conspiracy is at play! Subscribe now!
—Top Secret News, 2057

"Hey, thanks, eh? You saved my ass back there," Gros Baton said.

"Yeah, yeah, just don't get too comfy about it," I grumbled.

I didn't mind the kid. He was polite enough. Hell, he was just a good
bloke as far as I could tell. He tried, at least, and that was more than I could
say about a disconcertingly large portion of the population.

My only problem with him right now was that he had his arms wrapped
around my waist.

I didn't have any issues with Rac holding onto me. She was a kid, and a
girl, so it was fine, but I was getting all sorts of squicked out by this guy. I
mean, it was objectively stupid. I was wearing several layers of armor. None
of his disgusting boy germs were gonna escape his hairy arms and get to me,
but it was still uncomfortable.

Fortunately, we didn't have to fly far.

I shot across Saint-Jérome, then down to use some of the taller buildings
to cut our line of sight from the media sorts we'd left behind. Then I gunned
it, rushing out of the city at an angle and slowly curving around westward
until I was aiming more or less toward where the Big Gun was.

A few minutes later, we were being scanned by a dozen AA positions
that looked ready to tear us apart until something pinged us as friendly. I
really needed to upgrade my bike to something that could take a few flak
hits before the inevitable happened, but the inevitable wasn't happening
today, and I landed in the open space before the command structure a few
dozen meters from the Big Gun.

"Alright, enough clinging to me, off, off," I said.

"Yeah, yeah," Gros Baton said as he rolled off the side of the bike. "It wasn't comfortable for me either. Didn't know where to put my hands. Christ, you need 'andles or something."

"Keep talking and I'm getting a sidecar," I said.

"That sounds kinda fun?" he said. "I was thinking I'd get something too, ya know? Une genre de skidoo qui peut voler ou ben quelque chose d'même?"

I wasn't sure what he was saying there, but I kinda got the mental image from his gesturing. "Uh-huh. Just make sure it's got a good autopilot. Real lifesaver, that shit."

"'Kay," he said with a nod.

I checked the time on my augs. I was only twenty-minutes late to the start of my shift, which really didn't explain the "why did you shit on my bed" look Hedgehog was giving me as I got closer to the command center and he stomped out.

"You finally decided to show up?" he asked.

"Yeah," I agreed. "Had to save the kid from the big bad journalists. I think I've given them enough to talk about that they'll leave us alone for a minute."

He sniffed. "There's no such thing. They're insatiable."

"Well shit, I was hoping some of them would at least be a little distracted," I said. "So, how's the gun?"

He uncrossed his arms and shook his head. "It's doing well enough, but we're short on ammunition."

"Can't you buy some?" I asked.

"Tankette has been supplying us, but her ammunition is mostly . . . standard. Her armor-piercing shells have had the best effect so far, but they're not nearly as efficient as some of the more . . . creative ammunition you left behind."

Hedgehog started walking toward the little room at the back of the gun, the one I'd loaded the shells into last time. "Are we out of creative things to shoot, then?" I asked. "I can buy more. Hell, I can buy a lot more, I upgraded my catalogs for just this occasion."

"Good, good," he said. "Phobos has been pounded all night."

"That makes one of us," I said.

Gros Baton choked, then started to laugh until Hedgehog turned and gave us both the stink-eye. "We're talking about the end of the world here. Some level of seriousness would be appreciated."

"Sorry," I said. "Go on?"

"The tesla collider has fired twice more, both times dealing some substantial damage. And at the moment there is a constant swarm of smaller

Keiretsu drones harassing the . . . we're calling them point-defense models. Smaller, space-capable models that can fly around Phobos and who are harming our targeting and attacking any drones."

"Damn, alright. And our shots? What's the damage?"

"Moderate at best," he said, which was . . . not something I was keen on hearing, to be honest.

"Can you give me something more . . . tangible? I don't know, a percentage? An HP pool? A nice round number my small pitiful brain can wrap itself around?"

Hedgehog paused for a moment, then nodded. "We've managed to successfully detach seven percent of the moon's mass from the surface."

"That's nothing," I said.

He made a so-so gesture. "It's more than you'd think? That's several hundred thousand tons of mass. But in order to eliminate the danger that Phobos poses, we'd need to reduce its mass to something like a hundredth of its original mass. If Phobos hits Earth as scattered debris, we'll have won."

Right, right, that sounded decent. "So we're more than seven percent of the way to victory?"

"If you put it that way, we're closer to twenty?" he said. "My AI suggests that it's not a very precise way of looking at things."

"No, that's fine. I just need something ballpark-ish to wrap my head around the whole thing." We arrived at the command room and Hedgehog gestured for us to go in first, so I did. It was just as cramped in there as I remembered. I instantly quieted down when I noticed Tankette on one of the seats.

She was holding a large, quilted-looking blanket, and had her head leaning to the side against one of the consoles. Someone had snuck a pillow under her, and judging by the little hedgehog pattern on its cover, I had a good guess as to whom.

"She's . . . a very heavy sleeper," Hedgehog said, but he was keeping his voice lower too.

"Uh-huh," I replied. "So . . . what worked?"

He frowned, and I had the impression he'd pulled something up in his augs. "The most successful round so far was the deployable monofilament bomb."

"Really?" I asked.

Hedgehog seemed to take offense at the question. He turned toward the consoles behind him and tapped a few buttons. At least he seemed familiar with the Big Gun's controls now. A few moments later, one of the big screens lit up.

It showed a projectile moving across a plotter, the usual thing now for visualising one of our shells zipping out toward Phobos.

Then it cut to what had to be a sensor drone's point of view. The time code on the bottom of the screen slowed down, so we were seeing things one fraction of a second at a time instead of replaying things in real time.

The camera caught sight of the shell and started to zoom in, only for the shell to unfold and break apart.

The casing flew off into the void of space, but what it revealed looked like . . . "Kinda butt-plugish, huh?" I asked.

Hedgehog sighed.

The . . . I was gonna call it a dart for now, was spinning through space at what was probably a ridiculous speed even as six smaller darts flew out of it.

Then it crashed into a rocky outcropping on the edge of Phobos, a sort of mountain that took the impact with barely a puff of dust rising from where the dart hit.

At least, at first. The camera zoomed out, then zoomed right back in as a slice of that mountain shifted. It was a perfect cut, the decapitated part slipping downward slowly before it gained momentum and started a small avalanche. The camera zoomed out again, and it became clear that the dart had basically cut six long slices right out of the mountain, and they were all moving now that they were separate.

"It's hit or miss," Hedgehog said. "The cuts go deep, but just because something is cut doesn't mean it'll detach itself."

"Right," I said. Tons of stone like that didn't just move away so easily. "But the damage is good, otherwise?"

"In combination with the tesla collider? It's significant. It seriously weakens the moon's structural integrity, and the monofilament wires can stretch out for hundreds of meters. It's the widest-range weapon at our disposal right now."

I nodded along. That made sense. Monofilament was small as hell, so it was easy to pack a ton into a single shell.

"Not bad," I said. "But let's see if we can't try something else, huh? I got my hands on a new catalog and I need to test out what sort of trouble I can get up to with it."

Tankette snored in approval.

CHAPTER FIFTY-SIX

LE BAD SUCK

I see you, I feel you. You thought I was dead? You wish I was. But you forgot that I'm It. I will fuck you up in ways that no one's ever fucked someone up before. They will invent words to describe what I'm going to do.

I will turn your corporation into statistics.

I am a broken mirror and my shards are in your throat. I'm going to tear your reflection out of your spine . . . bitch.

—Mad Vlad to Calliope Corp CEO before their bankruptcy, 2045

"Alright," I muttered just low enough not to wake Tankette up. "Myalis, what have you got for me? Keep them under . . . call it one thousand points a shell? We need to fire a fuckload of these."

Certainly. Are we still going for variety first?

I considered it, then realized that I had two others to do the thinking for me. "Hedge, do we go for variety or just lots of what we think might work?"

He frowned, then nodded slowly. "Variety. But please don't grab anything wasteful. We only have a few dozen more shots to make this count. We can try new things—and we're probably better off varying the kinds of damage we deal—but we can't afford to waste effort and shots."

"Got it," I said. "Heard that, Myalis?"

I did. Let's start, then! First, might I suggest something simple to whet the appetite?

"Go on." Was she trying to sound like a fancy server on purpose? Actually, scratch that, she definitely was.

The first is a scrambler bomb. This one detonates and creates a field around itself that shifts items around. It's not quite random, but it might as well be. The scrambler will remain active for a relatively long time after deployment and will continuously move atoms away from their current location and transport them to a random one nearby.

"And that does . . . what to a person?"

It scrambles them, Catherine. That kills people.

"Oh," I said. "How big of an AOE are we talking here?"

"AOE?" Gros Baton asked, but it was aimed at Hedgehog. The man started to explain about video game terms like area of effect and how they ended up co-opted by the military.

The area of effect begins at a kilometer across, give or take a few bus-lengths. Then it shortens over time with the incident of atomic re-materialization increasing exponentially. I must add that this creates a lot of radiation, both as heat and across the radioactive spectrum.

"We won't have to deal with that, the aliens will. Fuck it, add one of those to the shopping cart," I said. "Next?"

Next . . . an electron-suppression bomb would have some interesting effects on the Phobos object. It would give all protons in a large area a negative charge.

"I don't know enough about physics to tell *what* that would do, but I can imagine it would be bad. Add it!"

Fantastic. A riff on a bomb that you've purchased before as a grenade might be interesting; the Full Stop is a device covered by a nearly unbreakable shell. Once activated, it stops moving.

"Why would a device that can't move be good?" I asked.

You misunderstand. It cannot be moved. It is spatially locked.

I shrugged. "What would happen to Phobos if it runs into a spatially locked indestructible thing?"

Hedgehog perked up. "You should get that."

"Alright, add it. Anything else?"

Gluon bombs. I'd explain how changing the environment reactions to the strong nuclear force could be destructive, but by the time you'd understand it, Phobos will have landed.

"Fine, fine, add your glue bomb too."

"That doesn't sound as destructive," Hedgehog said.

"I know, right?" I said. "Next?"

Short-duration black holes?

"Fuck yeah!" I said. "Nothing says 'fuck off' like chucking a black hole at someone."

"That sounds good, yeah," Gros Baton said. "Give them le bad suck."

Now I was second guessing myself. Did I want to be known as the samurai who gave the big mean moon le bad suck? The memes would be ruinous. On the other hand, footage of a small black hole opening up on the side of something the size of a moon and fucking it right up might do wonders in reminding people not to mess with me and mine.

"Okay, add a couple of those to the cart," I said. "Anything else?"

Keiretsu have been spending a lot of time combatting the smaller models encircling the main body of the Phobos object. Perhaps something that would assist them?

STRAY CAT STRUT—BOOK 7

"More than smashing big bombs into the side of the moon?" I asked.

Somewhat, yes. I'd suggest the Bee Bomb. It's packed with a system that allows its interior to be larger than the volume expected from its exterior dimensions. The insides are filled with small self-powered drones. Several thousand of them. On deploying, these drones exit the bomb and dart out toward enemy targets at high velocities. They're packed full of explosives.

"Add it," I said with a nod. It might help our Keiretsu buddies, and it just sounded cool besides. "Is that it?"

Of course not. So far we've only toyed with two of the fundamental forces. But if you want a capstone . . . perhaps the Cryogenic Anti-Thesis Stasis bomb? It'll sap the heat from the area where it lands. The Antithesis generally requires some amount of heat to operate, and the other bombs you've been considering will create plenty. This might reverse that to some degree.

I considered it for a moment before my eyes narrowed. "That spells out CATS," I said.

A coincidence, I'm sure.

I shook my head. "Alright, let's get . . . two of each? That should hold us up until the end of our shift."

Hedgehog, ever the helpful sort, moved to the back and opened up the access door into the shell storage compartment. There were two left, both loaded into their slots and ready to fire.

New Purchases:
Scrambler Bomb x2
Electron-Suppression Bomb x2
Full Stop Bomb x2
Gluon Bomb x2
Black Hole Bomb x2
Bee Bomb x2
Cryogenic Anti-Thesis Stasis Bomb x2
Total Cost: *13,250 points*
Current Point Total: 32,530

Fourteen shells appeared in the racks, each one slotting into place with a satisfying *click-thunk*. They were all slightly different, with shiny exteriors covered in burnished steel.

"That's half a day's worth of shells," I said. "If we're lucky, we won't even need this many."

"If we're lucky," Hedgehog said. He glanced at his wrist, where an old-school watch was wrapped around his arm. "The tesla collider should be firing within the next hour. We'll shoot right after. And then my shift will be over. I'll escort Miss . . . Tankette to bed."

"How romantic," I said.

"She's not interested that way," he said.

I blinked. Did that mean . . . he was? But Hedgehog had a poker face like a marble statue and didn't give anything away.

"Sleeping this way will give her a crick in the neck. You might be too young to understand, but once you hit thirty you'll know that sleeping crooked is unacceptable."

"I know what you mean, yeah. We used to get mil-surplus beds back at the orphanage," I said. "The mattresses were thinner than a slice of burger meat and you were lucky if you got one without springs. Knew one kid that died because of it."

"How did he die from a mattress?" Gros Baton asked.

"Tetanus," I said with a shrug. "Like, half the symptoms of that are shit you get from a bad diet, so it's not like it was easy to tell that he had something wrong going on, at least until it was too late."

Hedgehog just stared at me for a moment. "That's messed up."

"Happens. Anyway, are we good here?"

"We should be. Keep us updated in the group chat as things progress. And please make sure not to leave the site without at least one samurai present. Two is better," Hedgehog said. "The media is sniffing around, as proven by Gros Baton's interaction with them earlier, and that's not to mention the others liable to want what we have here. Any one of those shells would be worth millions to a corp."

Don't give the dubiously-moral corporations access to WMDs. Got it.

I padded over to Tankette's side and touched her shoulder. "Hey, uh, Tankette, time to wake up?" I hesitated and almost called her "ma'am," but that was too formal. "Sweetie" swung the bar all the way to the other side, and "dear" was right out because I wasn't born in the 1800s.

She blinked awake, then looked around herself with a start. "Oh my, did I fall asleep? Hedge, I'm so sor—" She cut herself off with a demure little yawn that she hid behind a hand. "Sorry . . . I guess I'm not fit for staying up all night anymore."

"Been a while?" I asked.

"I'll have you know I used to be able to party from sundown to sunup."

Somehow, trying to imagine Tankette as a party girl felt . . . inherently wrong.

"Uh-huh," I said.

"How do you think I ended up with my first child?"

"I really don't want to know," I said.

She laughed, then stretched her neck to the side. "Oh, I'm going to have a crick all week."

"Best get you to a proper bed, then. Come on, Gros Baton and I will take over while you get your sleep on."

CHAPTER FIFTY-SEVEN

IN SPACE, NO ONE CAN HEAR YOU BUZZ

Top 8 Bestselling AugGames of 2057:
1. *Reality Runners* [AR Collector Game]
2. *The Family* [Samurai Gacha]
3. *Silly Starlight Symphony* [Rhythm Gacha]
4. *Galaga 2* [Fixed Shooter Arcade]
5. *Hope/Punk* [Party Game]
6. *Minecraft* [Sandbox]
7. *Verseforge* [World Creator]
8. *Catastrophe Clicker* [Clicker Game]

—Game News Networld, 2057

I thought being on watch would be boring, and I was mostly right. It did have a few highlights, though.

A dinky little alarm clock went off a few minutes after Hedgehog carried Tankette away. It was one of those small red ones with the two big bells on top of it and the purely analog clockface. I wasn't even sure how to read the time on it, but I did figure out that smacking the little knob on the top shut it down.

"Okay, I'm guessing that means it's time to shoot something," I said.

"Ça l'air pas mal ça." Gros Baton said. "What're we shooting?" He was flicking through a whole menu with all of the loaded shells on one screen, each option highlighting one after the other.

"Good question," I said. "Uh. What's the situation around Phobos?"

I eyed the consoles and realized that there were a lot of blank buttons. I pressed one at random, then some less-stupid part of my brain realized that I'd just pressed a random button on a kilometer-long gun's control station and that was probably a bad idea.

Instead of pushing random buttons, how about you just let me handle things and leave the poor coolant control system alone?

"Yup, sorry," I said as I drew my hands back from all the buttons. "Just . . . can we throw Phobos's status ATM up on the big screen?"

Certainly.

I felt Gros Baton eyeing me, so I half turned to meet his gaze. That gave him the push he needed to ask me a question. He even bothered to ask it in his accented English. "Why do you talk to your AI, uh, out loud?"

"You mean Myalis? How else am I supposed to talk to her? Text?"

"Yeah," he said with a nod.

"Oh. Well . . . isn't that impersonal?" I asked.

He shrugged. "I text my best friends all the time."

"I mean, sure. I don't know. I guess I could, but it feels more natural to talk to her out loud?"

"You could whisper."

"Do I look like the whispering sort?"

He considered that for a moment, then shrugged. "Fair enough," he said. "Looks like the evil moon is busy, eh?"

I squinted at the screen. He was pretty spot-on there. Phobos was sur-rounded at the moment by hundreds of little darting dots. It looked like . . . actually, it kinda looked like flashing a light into a super dark and dusty room. Lots of little particles catching the light and swirling around. "What are those little things?" I asked.

Mostly lower-tier models. It seems as though Phobos has launched several thousand model elevens and a number of model twelves.

Model elevens? Those pterodactyl-looking motherfuckers? That was pretty low on the food chain, all things considered. "Wait, they can fly in space?"

"Why not, at this point?" Gros Baton said.

I mean, sure, but while I might have been lacking any sort of proper education, I was pretty sure wings didn't count for shit in zero-G and with-out any atmosphere. Then again, the Antithesis seemed to have a knack for not giving a fuck about the rules of the universe. "Okay, whatever," I said. There were frequent flashes as Keiretsu drones sniped some of the models away with what looked like laser fire, but the models seemed to swarm around organically, and I saw one drone get taken out by a screen of Antithesis smashing into it.

"Let's load up one of those Bee Bombs," I said. "We can fuck up their screen, give the Keiretsu a chance to get their drones in closer."

"Ça m'semble bon," Gros Baton said as he took the second seat and started to fiddle with the targeting. I had no idea if he knew what he was doing, but I didn't want to show that I was clueless, so I left him at it.

The ammo selector thing was pretty simple. A sort of menu with a flicky wheel next to it that I could roll to switch between options. There was an entry for every kind of shell I'd bought, with the number remaining next to it. I noted that there were a few HE shells that I hadn't bought as well. Probably Tankette's purchases.

I rolled the wheel until Bee Bomb was selected, then tapped the "accept" button next to it.

Behind me, a mechanical arm moved up to the correct shell, then loaded it into a sort of holster before moving it to the Big Gun's breech.

After that, all we needed to do was pick a target. Phobos was pre-selected, which was nice.

"Time to target . . . two minutes? Shit, that's not long," I said.

The satellite thing with the other portal *had* been moving this entire time, and it was slowly getting closer to Phobos. That, and Phobos was slowly getting closer to us.

I wasn't exactly what anyone would call a math whizz, but I understood that the time between shooting and hitting being shorter meant that shit was getting closer together. I kinda dreaded looking at the final countdown between the meeting with Phobos and Earth. So, instead, I looked at the percentage we'd chipped off the moon.

Eight.

Eight percent. That was still a lot, but fuck me if that wasn't nowhere near enough. A small pit formed in my stomach. Then Gros Baton grinned and pointed to the big red button. "J'peux-tu?" he asked.

"Go ahead," I said.

He flicked up the little plastic shield, then slammed a fist down onto the button. Good thing it was made tough.

The usual hair-raising thing happened as the Big Gun fired, followed by the hiss of coolant working to keep the gun intact. "Myalis," I said, once the noise died down a little. "Can you show me how to run diagnostics? I'd like to shoot more than once an hour. Even just ten minutes sooner every hour would be one more shell every six-hour shift, right?"

Ten times six is sixty, yes. I can help you with that. It should be possible, though it will increase wear slightly. Given the time constraints, the increased wear shouldn't interfere with operations.

"So we can keep shooting and shoot a little faster and shit won't blow up in our faces? Yeah, I'm down for that." I reached up and rubbed at the spot where my cybernetic cat ears met my head.

Gros Baton nodded, then pointed to the screen. The Bee Bomb was arriving. It looked like a streak across the monitor as it raced toward Phobos.

We watched in glorious HD as the bomb exploded and sent a thousand pinpricks moving across the screen. They intercepted just as many model elevens in midflight, turning the birds into statistics.

"Nice," I said as I leaned back.

The keiretsu didn't waste too much time. Some drones continued to mop up, and more of them flew right into Phobos, slipping between the cracks that were soon illuminated by laser fire. I wasn't sure what was going on in there, but I figured it wasn't pleasurable for the aliens.

I blinked as I got a notification from Myalis. It had me sitting up a little straighter.

Targets Eliminated!
Model Eleven . . . 278 models
Reward . . . 27,800 points
Model Twelve . . . 41 models
Reward . . . 4,100 points
Total Points Earned: 31,900
Points Distributed to Vanguard: 3,987
Current Point Total: 46,517

Holy shit, that was a lot of points. "We're eating good tonight," I said. I resisted the urge to rub my hands together. Didn't need Myalis switching me from cat shit to raccoon shit. That role was taken already.

Gros Baton grinned. "I'mma buy the loudest skydoo," he said.

"Yeah, you go, bud."

To be fair, though, that last bomb had targeted small, easy to eliminate models instead of the moon. It wasn't actually helping directly except to farm points. That eight percent wouldn't move so easily.

But more points meant I could afford more shells, which was nice. I'd just filled my budget for the next day and a bit. The tesla collider was going to fire soon too, so that would hopefully leave us with a nice gap where we could fuck up Phobos before it would have time to recuperate.

It was going to take some time to fuck the moon up, and I was legit afraid that it would take more time than we had left. But hey, Keiretsu and the Nightwatchmen weren't freaking out as far as I could tell, so that was probably a good sign.

"Right . . . so uh, we've got another fifty or so minutes to wait, huh?"

Gros Baton shrugged. "Ouien?"

"Yeah . . . got any games on your augs?"

CHAPTER FIFTY-EIGHT

KNIGHT TAKES MOON

People still play chess? That game's ancient! Why would anyone still want to play that?

—Livestreamer MonMonMan, 2034

The hours were crawling by, and if the fate of the entire world hadn't been at stake, and if I wasn't making points hand over fist, I might have fucked off already to do something more entertaining.

As it was, Gros Baton and I were on our sixth game of chess. The kid had bought a holographic chess set for like, three points or something.

It hovered between us, the board currently a bit of a mess as our pieces were locked in a contest for the middle. He was winning, of course, but if he made about . . . six major mistakes in a row, there was a tiny chance that I'd make it through.

His pieces looked like tiny medieval people. The knights looked like knights and the bishops looked like bishops. His pawns, for some reason, were teeny-tiny Napoleonic soldiers with itty-bitty muskets.

"Pawn to E5," he said, and one of his lil' soldiers struck one of my knights with the fun end of his bayonet.

My pieces were cats. My king and queen were lions, my knights were bobcats in plate mail, my bishops were leopards with little pope hats, and my towers were . . . towers, with lazy tigers sleeping atop them. My pawns were plain old house cats. What few I had left, anyway.

"Ah, fuck," I muttered. That move had opened up the middle, and once that pawn of his died, his queen would be right up in my king's grill.

And then my phone rang. Or the phone app on my augs went off, at least. I jumped, and blinked at the names. The Keiretsu and the Night-watchmen were calling me at the same time?

I glanced up at the Phobos monitor before I hit reply. Gros Baton and I had smashed two more shells into the moon. An electron-suppression bomb, which had done . . . something? It bored a large hole through the moon and made the radiation sensors the Keiretsu had go absolutely haywire. And right after that, a black hole bomb. That one had been less impressive than I'd hoped. It went off before the moon and gave it the bad suck. Lots of dust and smaller debris was ripped off the surface of Phobos where the bomb went off.

By the time the bomb went all supernova and blasted that end of the moon until it looked like something Lucy had started to cook and promptly forgot about, it looked like a good quarter of Phobos had been powerwashed.

Pretty okay results, all in all. We were up to ten percent, which was a good sign, I figured.

"Yo," I said as I answered the call. I made the universal "I'm on a call" gesture with my thumb and pinkie so that Gros Baton would know that I wasn't just surrendering.

"Ah, Miss Stray Cat?" Doctor Weber said. "Good! It's a pleasure to speak with you again. I heard that you were currently operating the Big Gun's . . . Big Gun, and so I thought it would be a good time for a conference."

"Yeah, sure," I said. "Sup? And uh, hi to you too, Susan."

"Greetings, Stray Cat," the calmer Japanese man said. "Your team has been doing impressive work."

"Aww, thanks! Your drones are pretty kickass too," I said. I'd been seeing them coming in on the Phobos monitor. It looked like the Keiretsu had kicked up production pretty steadily, because the number of drones rushing over was increasing every hour.

They were actually kinda neat? They looked like balls, mostly, with maneuvering thrusters poking out all over the place and then whatever kind of gun they had stuck out of the end. Some of them were linked up to get to Phobos, often tied to a larger booster that would disconnect, then fly over to the moon, where they blew up satisfyingly before the drones started to go around and do their own things.

"Thank you," Susan said. "We didn't call to trade compliments, however."

"Indeed. The situation is more dire than we expected," Radikal said. "Our current projections suggest that Phobos will be within the red zone in forty-eight hours."

"What's the red zone?" I asked. "Beyond the obvious that it's something we don't want."

"The red zone is what we're calling the area of space where an unbroken Phobos will absolutely be able to annihilate life on Earth. Even if Phobos is rendered into pieces no bigger than a car, within the red zone it would still kill us all."

"Oh," I said. "And how close are we to the, uh, orange zone?"

"We're in it," Susan said.

STRAY CAT STRUT—BOOK 7

"Well, fuck," I said. I sat up a little straighter. "So, I'm assuming we have a solution to all of this?"

"We do," Radikal said. "The solution is to continue as we have. The rate of demolition is somewhat exponential. In the next twenty-four hours, the Keiretsu drones should be reaching the kind of critical numbers where they'll theoretically be able to excise the Antithesis near the moon's surface. The next use of the Teslakollisionsgenerator should significantly weaken the moon's structural integrity."

"Cool, cool," I said. "And that'll be enough?"

"It should be. Current calculations show that Phobos should begin dispersal six hours before entering the red zone. At which point our task becomes to further spread the remaining mass out as much as we can so that its entry into Earth's atmosphere is minimally disruptive."

"Anything we can do to help on our end?" I asked.

"Your current push has been quite positive, I would suggest you continue," Radikal said. "Though, if you have any exotic weaponry that might slow the moon down, it would be quite welcome. Otherwise, anything that weakens its integrity should be prioritized."

I leaned over and looked at the shells behind us. "I think I might have something for that. Was gonna load something else first, but we might as well try it? It's called a Full Stop, and it's a sort of spatially locked thingy that we can leave in Phobos's path? I don't think it'll stop the moon dead, but it might slow it down."

"Hmm, that would depend on the size of it, but I can imagine such a thing causing some significant damage," Radikal said. "I almost wish we had attempted a different approach than the Teslakollisionsgenerator, one that would allow for more flexibility."

"Yeah," I said, because what else could I say?

"In any case, fire that device. The Teslakollisionsgenerator is warming up now and should be ready for another strike within the hour. This time we're aiming for the opposite of the usual compaction method."

"You're gonna make the moon uncompact?" I asked. "Like, spread it apart?"

He laughed. "Exactly! Before the larger wave of drones arrive and risk being battered by the moon's expansion. Hopefully this will expose the hives within the moon so that they might be eliminated."

"Is that even a problem at this point?" I asked.

Susan huffed. "Obviously. Though I can see your reasoning in thinking otherwise."

"Yeah, lots of reasoning going on here," I said. "But explain it to me anyway."

He was silent for a moment, and I think that the language barrier saved me a little. "The Antithesis within Phobos is a higher-tier model wrapped around a large hive. Were it to crash on Earth, it would survive."

"Damn," I said. "So we want it dead before it gets around, but we're breaking the whole moon up anyway, so it's kind of a moot point, no?"

"Not quite," Radikal said, and he really sounded like someone who'd earned his doctorate as he "um actually'd" me. "The issue with the Antithesis currently inhabiting Phobos is that it allows the moon to adapt. The wings we saw earlier, the production of small fliers dedicated to eliminating keiretsu drones, and now there's evidence of organic cooling systems below the moon's surface as well as organic reinforcements threaded throughout the structure. According to all of our calculations, Phobos should have been cracked and destroyed by now. The Antithesis is holding it together, and more importantly, encouraging the moon to repair itself."

"Repair itself?" I asked.

"It's producing a cement-like compound and filling gaps," he said.

Ah, well, fuck. "Okay, that does make things more complicated. Will your drones be able to kill it?"

"They will do what they can," Susan said.

"Alright then. Let me and Gros Baton here load up the next shell, then we'll see about spreading that moon out like . . . uh . . ." I froze. None of the metaphors I could think of when it came to spreading things were PG-13. "Anyway, yeah," I settled on saying.

"Thank you, Stray Cat," Radikal said. "If we do happen to fail, it will comfort me to know that I was at least able to work with such talented people."

CHAPTER FIFTY-NINE

THE FULL STOP DOES NOT STOP

While we try very hard to keep inflation at a steady rate—because such a steady rate allows for steady, controllable growth across all sectors—we firmly believe that the currency inflationary rates for foodstuffs might be too elevated.

Five hundred percent yearly increases would mean a very real risk of starvation among the workforce, a workforce that we've yet to automate. Not to mention, this same workforce makes up a vast majority of our customer base.

—Letter from the Union of Corporate Interests of North America, 2042

"Here goes nothing," I said as I gently tapped the "fire" button. My hair stood on end, the room trembled slightly, and the shell was off.

At the moment, it was somewhere in the mid-afternoon, and I couldn't help but feel like that was subtly wrong.

We had just fired what might be the final blow. It was meant to be momentous, something big and important, a moment that would go down in the history books . . . and all I could think about was how I was a little hungry.

"Could really go for a snack right about now," I said.

"Ouien," the kid said. "J'ai un, uh . . . catalog for poutine."

"Wait, just poutine, or is it like, a food catalog?" I asked.

He shrugged. "Just poutine. It was cheaper."

Huh. I knew that catalogs were cheaper the more narrow their scope, but I'd never thought to apply that to food, specifically. "Alright. Is it good, at least?"

"Eh." He made a so-so gesture. "La petit place au coin d'ma rue en fait une bonne aussi."

I squinted and translated that one all on my own. *The local place makes a good one too.* "Well, I'd give it a try, I guess."

"Cool! Tiens," he said, and then just like that, a styrofoam bowl with a little plastic cover appeared in his hand. It was steaming, and instantly filled the room with a greasy, fatty smell. I took it from him and peeled off the cover revealing . . . cheese curds, fries, and lots of brownish sauce.

Somehow this felt like a step down from the usual Protector food I ordered.

Gros Baton handed me a plastic fork, and I shrugged before digging in. It tasted as healthy as it looked. Salty and greasy. The cheese squeaked and the fries crunched. It was pretty good, to be honest, but I just knew this was going straight to the love handles.

We watched the progress of the Full Stop on the main monitor while we ate. The little shell was racing ahead right toward Phobos. A smaller status screen showed the tesla collider warming up for its next big shot, and the Keiretsu had a small army of drones on a collision course with Phobos as well, all timed to arrive about two minutes after the collider did its thing.

"Oh, it's gonna impact," I said as I pointed to the screen with my fork.

"Mm-hmm," Gros Baton agreed before wiping some gravy from his chin. "Fuck 'em up, tabarnak!"

"Yeah! Tabarnak all the way!" I cheered. I had to hand it to the kid, he'd make for a good drinking buddy. Maybe if I was into sports or something, I'd invite him over to watch the game and he'd show up with booze and snacks.

The Full Stop . . . stopped about a minute later. In a blip, It went from moving at fuck-you-fast speeds to being completely still. Though . . . I wasn't so sure. Things were still moving around it. It just looked like it had suddenly changed directions?

"What's it doing?" I asked.

It has stopped. The motion you see now is the relative motion of the sensor equipment and Phobos, but the shell itself is locked in place.

"Locked in place relative to where?" I asked.

Don't you worry about that.

I felt like I *should* worry when Myalis said something like that, but I wasn't going to have time for the whole explanation when Phobos and the shell were just about to collide.

I leaned forward and pressed a button to switch the main monitor to a camera view from one of the spy drones keeping pace with Phobos.

The Full Stop was too small to be visible at the distances we were looking at it from. Phobos, on the other hand, was a zoomed-in mass of rock covered in a lot more craters than had been there a few days earlier. Huge sections of its surface were blackened by soot and char, and there were canyons running across it like the cracked shell of a dropped egg.

A few mountains had been flattened, and chunks of the moon were just outright missing now.

And then Phobos ran into the Full Stop.

The shell struck the moon dead center. Or maybe the moon struck it? In any case, there was an immediate reaction. A cratering ripple that ran across the moon's surface like a splash in a still puddle. Phobos didn't slow down against the backdrop of stars, exactly, but it looked like the entire moon had flinched.

And then it was through, and a scattering of rock and debris came pouring out of the back of the moon like guts out of some schmuck that got blasted by a shotgun.

"Nice," I said. The integrity counter ticked up from nine percent to twelve. That was a pretty big jump, all things considered.

And then the tesla collider came online once more.

Arcs of electricity the size of skyscrapers raced across the moon's surface, illuminating its dark side in bright blues and pure whites. Nothing happened, and I was worried when the integrity counter didn't move. Was it a dud?

Then the moon *heaved*. It was like Phobos had just taken a deep breath.

Chunks that had to be the size of islands slowly moved up and away. The cracks running across the moon's surface widened. I'd expected Phobos to simply explode apart, but it wasn't quite so violent. At least, not from the very long-ranged view we had.

Instead, Phobos broke apart like a diagram of one of those cool blueprint things where every part is shown individually.

"Whoa," I said as the moon continued to expand outward. It was now twice as big as it had been at the start, parts still connected by long, twisting trails of lightning.

The tesla collider stopped, and the steady, neat separation of the moon gave up.

Chunks collided into each other, others went tumbling out into empty space. The moon scattered.

I might have called it a total destruction, except that Phobos was alive, and it wasn't happy to be split apart like it had been. Long tendrils reached out, crashed into the bigger parts of the moon, and tethered them in place. It looked like the middle of the moon was a many-tentacled sea urchin desperate to keep itself together.

That thing, to scale, had to be bigger than New Montreal. I wasn't sure if it was a single model or thousands of them working together, and I was even less sure if the difference mattered at all.

The Keiretsu arrived a minute later. A swarm of drones, larger than any of those they'd sent before. They burned hard in the empty void, a thousand candle flames visible in the dark. Retrothrusters? I wasn't sure and didn't know enough to guess beyond that.

Whatever rockets they used were jettisoned to crash into the semi-disassembled Phobos. Then the drones themselves moved in. It looked like they weren't doing much at first, except that there were occasional explosions of rock and debris across the inside of Phobos's expanded shell.

Gros Baton did something, I think turning on some sort of thermal vision, and then the lasers they were firing became visible. Each drone was like an angry disco ball, sweeping lines of hot fire through the Antithesis meat.

Smaller models were launched by the thousands, then by the tens of thousands. They scattered, some flinging themselves across space, others having their own ways of moving through space.

Drones started to die, but never without exploding violently on death.

I glanced over to the integrity ticker. Thirty-four percent. Had we really taken off a third of Phobos's mass just like that?

"Look," Gros Baton said.

I turned my attention back to the screen, poutine entirely forgotten as an Antithesis swarm was unleashed.

There had to be millions of them. Tiny black specks that shot out of Phobos, opened large wings, then farted their way forward even as they twisted and flapped into a swarm.

It looked like Phobos was tired of waiting. It was sending its own Vanguard our way.

"I'm betting that's not a good thing," I said.

"No shit," Gros Baton said. "My AI says we have a day."

"Great," I said. "Think they know where we are, specifically, or do you think they'll just land wherever the fuck they want?"

"Yeah, non, I'm not gambling on that one."

"Yeah, I figured," I said.

Well, it was time to call up the others and let them know that shit was being flung at the fan again.

CHAPTER SIXTY

RELIGIOUS EXEMPTION

While it isn't the opinion of this author that removing governmental religious exemptions was one of the leading contributors to the fall of Old America, one must admit that the changes to the laws that gave religious organizations the ability to not pay taxes did coincide with other massive changes in the cultural and economic state of the Western world.

However, I posit that the Corporate Tax Exemption—the law allowing sufficiently large corporate entities to avoid taxation outright—was a far greater harbinger of the end of the Old American way.

—Doctor C. Thumbs, thesis, "The Fall of Old America," 2046

"Okay, can everyone hear me?" I asked.

"Mm-hmm!" Grasshopper said.

"You woke me up for this?" Gomorrah replied.

"Ah, yes?" came Tankette.

"Affirmative," Hedgehog said.

"Howdy there," Crackshot said.

"We can both hear you here!" Princess said.

I didn't need to glance over to Gros Baton next to me to know that he could hear me, even if he was still distracted by the last of his poutine. "Okay!" I said. "First, uh, sorry for waking you up or whatever."

"I don't mind," Princess said.

I went right on past that. "But yeah, big news! Phobos isn't out of the race just yet, but it sure as shit ain't looking good." The monitor showed us the moon in all of its fucked-up glory. Honestly, calling it a moon now was a lie. Phobos had given up the pretense of being a lost space rock and was now just a fuck-big alien hive with large chunks of moon being held around it like million-ton shields.

Keiretsu drones were swarming around Phobos, and more of them were arriving every twenty minutes or so. Not to say that there weren't any losses. Space around Phobos was also swarming with aliens. Little fliers zipping around, lumps of twitching alien matter, and a disturbing number of what looked like very organic "spitting" guns that were knocking out drones as they flew by.

Even as I looked, a small chain of itty-bitty explosions ran across one of the bigger tentacles. They seemed tiny on the monitor, but I imagined that each one of those explosions was big enough to take out a house.

We'd given Phobos a brown eye and knocked a few teeth loose, but that fucker was still coming. "Alright, so, time for an update," I said.

"Go on, we're listening," Grasshopper said.

"The tesla collider went off right after we hit Phobos with a new type of round, and the moon kinda . . . exploded. Now it's a big tentacle-y mess. The Keirestsu drones are messing it up as we speak. Since the innards are exposed, that means a lot of damage is being done directly to the hive."

"Is it over, then?" Gomorrah asked. "Or nearly over?"

"I don't think so. We've ripped off a full third of the moon, but that still leaves a neat fuckton of moon behind," I said. "And we've got new problems to worry about."

"Oh boy," Princess said.

"Yeah. So, Phobos didn't seem happy about what we did to it, so it looks like the moon has flung shit our way. Here, I've got some imaging of the crap courtesy of our friends with all the drones. Since the Phobos . . . swarm is basically flying past the Keiretsu drone . . . swarm, we're getting some pretty good images. I think our AI can basically pinpoint exactly where everything is going."

I shot an image onto the main screen, then fiddled with the attachment thing in our chat for a moment before figuring out how to send the same to the others.

Our buddies were sending nonstop drones at this point. It seemed like they were producing them at some stupid rate, something like one new drone every five minutes. Maybe less. They were launching each one soon after it was built, so that meant that there was a string of drones only a few minutes apart from Phobos to Earth.

All of those had cameras and sensors on them, and longish-ranged laser guns.

They were intercepting the Phobos swarm, firing off into the heap as they shot by, then letting the next drone do the same.

"That's a lot of aliens," Grasshopper said. "Far less than an incursion, however."

"Is it?" Crackshot asked.

"Mm-hmm!" Grasshopper replied. "I recall Stray Cat being in New Montreal during the last incursion there? Did you see it in person?"

"Yeah," I said. I could distinctly remember the sky far above opening and aliens pouring out of the rifts by the thousands. "It's not something I'm going to forget so easily. Not anytime soon. But uh, care to explain what you mean anyway?"

"Of course. From what I can see here, this swarm is mostly made up of perhaps four or five different models, most of them third tier and below, though they're variants capable of space flight. A normal incursion comes down with plenty more than this. And there's a wider range of models, usually with a focus on models that can make landfall and immediately start building a hive. There are scouts and . . . for lack of a better term, construction models. The goal of an incursion, insofar as there is a goal we can understand, is to create a beachhead."

"And this is different?" Gomorrah asked.

"It does seem different," Hedgehog said. "This isn't an incursion, it's an offensive."

"Yeah," I said. "Now, here's the tricky bit."

I ran time forward in the recording thing. It was all predictions from here, but they'd been made by the Nightwatchmen, and I trusted them to be pretty good about these.

The swarm moved toward Earth, then split lightly. One large chunk went right at the Keiretsu's orbital drone factory, another toward the tesla collider, and the third, largest group, charged right past and came crashing down toward Earth. Specifically around North America. Even more specifically, toward the eastern end of North America.

"Oh, that's, uh, right on us, isn't it?" Princess asked. "I was never good at geography, but I'm pretty sure that's here."

"Yup," I said, popping the "p." "I don't know how, but they know that we're here, and they're coming to mess us up."

"What's their ETA?" Hedgehog asked. He sounded a lot more alert now than he had been when this started.

"We've got a day," I said. "They're still accelerating. I've got no idea how they'll manage to survive hitting Earth's atmosphere, but I figure if they can pinpoint our location then they've probably got a few tricks to not just burn up and land as a heap of ashes."

"This is rather distressing," Gomorrah said. "What's our next step, then?"

"The fuck would I know?" I asked. "I'm just delivering the bad news."

"You've had longer to think about it," she returned. "And I think we mostly trust your opinion . . . to a limited degree."

"Well thanks for the vote of confidence," I said, reaching up to pinch the bridge of my nose. I had a stress headache coming on. "Look . . . we've been handling Phobos on our own. I mean, for our region, at least. The Big Gun's done what it needed to. We can keep on shooting at Phobos until it's right on our doorstep because each shot peels a little more away and helps some. But this attack right on top of us? Yeah, I don't see why that needs to be *our* problem alone."

"You think we should get outside help?" Crackshot asked. "I'm sure some locals won't mind pitching in. Emoscythe would certainly help."

"Her, and anyone else that's willing to help at all," I said. "There are a few other samurai around New Montreal, yeah? Hell, there should be a lot of others around here. We can get some from elsewhere in too. The global incursion is calming down, isn't it?"

"We'll have to involve the Family," Gomorrah warned.

"Well, tell them that if they don't help they'll have to rebrand themselves as the Orphanage, because there won't be enough survivors to call themselves a family of anything," I said.

Gomorrah chuckled darkly. "I'll talk to them, then."

"I know just about every samurai who lives around here," Grasshopper said. "I make a point of making contact with as many as I can, in case they need help. I can start sending little 'hellos' to all of them, just in case."

"That'd be nice," I said with a nod. "What else? Maybe . . . Ah, fuck, we're going to need to put out a call on social media for anyone willing to help. And to warn people to keep their heads low for the next couple of days."

"Not it," Princess said.

"Same," Craskshot said.

"Pas moi," Gros Baton added.

"I'm not suited for that," Hedgehog said at the same time as Gomorrah said, "No."

"Ah . . ." Tankette said as she was caught out. "I don't know . . ."

"That leaves Cat," Gomorrah said.

I blinked. "No it the fuck does not," I snapped.

"Tankette can help you, I'm sure."

"Aren't nuns supposed to be kind and helpful?" I asked.

Gomorrah was quiet for a few seconds. "My religion demands that I abstain from social media?"

"No it doesn't! You bitch!" I snapped.

But it was too late, wasn't it? That stress headache wasn't going to disappear after all.

CHAPTER SIXTY-ONE

LIGHTS! CAMERA! BULLSHIT!

You should absolutely, under no circumstance, allow someone untrained in public relations do any of the talking when any number of cameras are involved.

—*Politics 101* textbook, ninety-second edition, 2029

I couldn't decide if I was annoyed with the job or not. Why did I land with the "be the face" job? I was crass, rude, uneducated, and lazy. I didn't want to be the one reaching out to others to kick their asses into gear. But *no*, it had to fall on me.

I could have been home right then, wearing nothing but a loose T-shirt, watching shitty reality TV on a screen with more square feet than some apartments, and Lucy cozying up to me, but nope, the Earth needed saving and it fell on me to get the saviors to get their shit together.

Bullshit.

"You, uh, okay?" Gros Baton asked as he heard me muttering.

"Yeah, yeah," I said with a dismissive wave. "I don't know how to do social media shit. I mean, I've been scrolling since I've been old enough to swipe my thumb down, but I don't know if that qualifies me to *make* posts, you know?"

You could listen to music your whole life, but that didn't mean you knew jack shit about playing it. Gros Baton didn't seem to appreciate that distinction much, as he just shrugged. "Fais juste de ton mieux. J'pense pas que tu peux vraiment tout fucker ça." He grinned. "Dans le pire des cas, tire sur un autre maire ou quelque chose du genre. Ça va te remettre à TV." *Just do your best. I doubt you can fuck this up too much. Worst case scenario, shoot another mayor or something. That'll get you on TV again.*

"Oh, fuck off," I mumbled. He was probably right, though. "Okay . . . right. What would work on me?"

Would I pay attention to a news broadcast by a samurai? Probably, a little bit, if only because it was fun to see the material that would later become memes while it was still fresh. Shit, my brain really was rotted.

Right, what would work beyond that? Just sitting at a table and talking into the camera would come off as honest, but also boring as balls. I needed to keep people's attention.

I sent out two texts, both with the same content—one to Gomorrah, the other to Lucy.

Would you be willing to wear a bikini on camera to save the world?

I got two "No"s within seconds of each other. They didn't even ask me to elaborate. So that plan was shot. Well, whatever. Hot chicks only worked on . . . honestly, a majority of the population, but if that failed, I'd need something more impressive.

I looked around. We *were* standing behind a kilometer-long gun that shot into space. That was kinda badass. I nodded, then sent out another pair of texts. One was to the group chat, the other directly to Tankette.

Hey, I need intimidating people to stand in the background of a video while looking cool. Volunteers?

The message to Tankette was simpler.

Can I borrow your tank for like, an hour?

This time the replies were a little more positive. Princess and Knight were down for it. Hedgehog said he would show up, and Gros Baton was already right here. Tankette didn't mind letting me use her tank at all, it turned out. And Crackshot said that he could be over with Emoscythe within the next half hour. Gomorrah was busy, but once she caught on to what I was planning, she let me use her *Fury*, which . . . well, might get a certain demographic of car nuts to pay attention, at least.

The next problem was making things seem natural. Sure, having half a dozen samurai was badass, but . . . we could just be standing there like a bunch of jumped-up dorks. That'd immediately look unnatural and stupid, and if there was one thing that a modern audience would pick up on, it was inauthenticity.

Thankfully, while I busied myself moving my cat mech next to the Big Gun and placing it next to the *Fury* and Tankette's mini-tank, two familiar faces popped up, and I instantly had an answer to my problem.

That answer being "make it someone else's problem."

"Emoscythe!" I cheered as she and Crackshot walked across the compound. Emoscythe looked around the place, seeming curious but not too impressed. She *had* been a samurai for a while, so this setup was probably nothing too spectacular for her.

"It's Emoscythe Mordeath Noir," she reminded me, not unkindly. "And hell, Stray Cat. I see you've taken to wearing the outfit I helped you with."

"Ah, yeah," I said. I was rocking that bounty-hunter samurai look. She, on the other hand, was in full-on gothic lolita, with a poofy yet rather short skirt with a wide fringe . . . thing. She looked one part French maid, one part sickly Victorian child, and with all of the chains and little skulls built into her dress, not to mention the sword by her hip, one part "capable of fucking you up." "Hey, you're the resident PR expert, right?"

"I am," she said without an ounce of uncertainty.

I glanced at Crackshot, who was smiling like . . . well, like one of those pictures of a golden retriever who'd just been given a bone. He looked normal otherwise, though I didn't fail to notice that his cowboy hat now had a little black skull pin on its band.

"Cool, cool. I need to set up this stream thing. I want to show off that we're serious. How do I do that?"

Emoscythe blinked, then looked over the scene. The others were mostly forming into small groups and chatting. "Just let people do whatever they want. If they're visible, then they're visible. I'll try to stay in frame if you wish it, but there's no point in faking things if you can't fake them well."

"Yeah, people can always tell when things are fake," I agreed.

"No, people can tell when the fake is cheaply done," Emoscythe corrected me. "There's a point where the common person's perception stops noticing things. But you won't have to worry about that, I'm sure. What kind of camera are you using?"

"Huh? Oh, I've got a cat drone around here somewhere. They have camera eyes. I think I can use one of those."

Emoscythe did not look impressed. "No, absolutely not," she said. "One moment." She reached a hand out to the side and a box appeared over her splayed fingers.

It was small, made of dark, lacquered wood with thin insets of lighter wood forming a sort of mandala pattern across the top that looked a bit like a skull if I squinted. The front had a nice brassy-looking clasp.

It was, by far, the fanciest samurai order box I'd ever seen. Most of the time the boxes were plastic with maybe a logo printed on, but this was on a whole other level. Emoscythe reached down the front of her dress, then tugged a small metal key out. It was on a long string that wrapped around her neck.

I blinked, then tried not to think dirty thoughts as she fit the key into the box's lock and twisted. The clasp came off with a click, and the top opened of its own volition. Out of it came . . . a doll. Not quite just a doll. Its "face" was a complex array of small cameras and sensors, all black gunmetal, but the rest of it was designed like a small Victorian doll.

It hovered up to eye level and floated there, staring at me . . . kind of menacingly.

"This is a proper media drone," Emoscythe said. "The kind of thing I used to use when I had my drone phase."

"Drone phase?" I asked.

"We all have one," she said dismissively. "Its cameras are better than anything you can afford right now, so don't be shy. And don't worry, the footage will be downscaled to something appropriate for public consumption. We don't need people learning about the random soldiers in the background by scanning one of their hairs from afar, do we?"

Wait, what kind of resolution would allow for that? "Uh, okay," I said. "Thanks."

Emoscythe walked over, then started to fiddle with my outfit. She adjusted my coat, tugged on my scarf a few times, and even licked her fingers and rubbed off a smudge from my helmet, which was gross, but she was scary enough that I let her. "There," she said as she stepped back. "You could do with some makeup, but you're never seen with any so it would ruin the illusion."

"What do I say?"

"Never mind that," she said. "You're a samurai. As I was once told, our job is to say 'fuck it, we ball' and then do what we think is right. Rehearsal never helped that." She glanced at the drone. "You're live in three."

"What?"

"Two."

"Wait, serio—"

The drone's eyes lit up, and I froze for a second. Then my well-honed bullshittery reflexes kicked in.

"Hey, assholes. Just a friendly heads-up; Earth is about to be blown the fuck up in . . . T-minus not very long, so listen up."

CHAPTER SIXTY-TWO

CAT OUT OF THE BAG

Holy shit, guys, have you seen this? No, no, it's on the stream, look, some samurai took it over?

Another? Oh, fuck, they're on all the streams, this is big shit!

Wait, wait, did she just say that Earth is gonna be destroyed?

—Reaction Andy Dandy, livestream, 2057

I swallowed and tried not to let it show when Myalis filled the edges of my vision with the kind of information that the average streamer would die for. Viewership numbers, lists of channels and streams I was on, even a few rapidly scrolling chats that were moving too quickly for me to read anything.

At least I could easily pick out the generic cat emojis.

Another small box showed me what the world was seeing. It was . . . me. Well, my helmeted face, at least. It was a cool helmet, but it was also rather . . . faceless? There was no expression there.

So, to start things off right while the viewership numbers were still climbing so fast that the ticker looked like it might spin itself out of control, I reached up and removed my helmet. The entire time I was aware that the camera was catching sight of the others in the background.

Tankette was by her tank, but also by Hedgehog, who'd just arrived. She was tugging his uniform back on straighter and had licked her thumb to wipe a smudge off his face. He seemed rather put off by the whole thing, but he wasn't fighting her.

From the corner of my eye, I could see Emoscythe next to Crackshot. They were both listening as Princess pointed to the Big Gun and gestured at a bunch of things.

My helmet came off, and I casually let it fall before running a hand through my hair. It was that fancy new tech hair, which was honestly just cheating. I had always liked having longer hair, but as a one-armed cripple, that shit was hard to maintain. Lucy had always helped me get the knots out and brush it down. She liked doing it, and it wasn't like her own frizzy mop of hair was easily brushable.

This tech hair shit? Yeah, it just fell into place, curled just right, bangs where they ought to be and not a knot in sight. It was bullshit and proof that Myalis's space buddies were also bullshit. No one wearing a helmet for so long should be able to remove it to reveal perfect hair.

"Alright," I said as I looked back into the camera. I'd given myself thirty whole seconds to get my thoughts in order and I'd spent none of them actually thinking. Go me. "So, as I was saying . . . you might have noticed if you're the sort of dork to stare at the stars, but Mars is fucked. Planet's been overrun by aliens for a bit."

The chat sped up at that, and now the cat emotes were joined by little red circles.

"So, buncha top-tier samurai went over to Mars to clear it out, because we can't have our neighbor planet be covered in shit that needs killing. So far, all good yeah? But then the aliens flung Phobos—that's one of Mars's moons—at us."

I pointed with a thumb over my shoulder.

"That's the Big Gun. It's a kilometer-long railgun. It fires bullets the size of a man's head so fast you need scientific notation to write the speed down through a portal at the end of the barrel and out of another portal slapped on the side of a spaceship. It's fucking rad as hell."

I nodded, because what else was I supposed to do?

"Anyway, we're not the only samurai who have been fucking Phobos up, but I'll let the others speak for themselves. Look, things were going alright for a good chunk of time here. We were messing Phobos up, cracking it apart bit by bit. Sure, it's a moon-sized mess of tentacles and hate, but we were fucking it up like a back-alley mugger caught by the cops. Actually, we're still messing it up."

I started to walk, because it gave me something to do. No clue what I was supposed to do with my arms and hands, so I let them dangle uselessly by my side. The camera panned along with me, its creepy doll thing shifting as it caught Princess, Emoscythe, and Crackshot in the background, then Knight standing an awkward few steps past them.

"Phobos has mostly been fucked over. We should all be safe . . . ish. If things keep on the way they are, most of it will miss Earth and the rest will burn up on entry. So yeah, you're welcome. Except the alien fuck living in the moon just flung a whole shitload of fliers our way. We've got . . . Myalis, what's the ETA?"

Approximately sixteen hours.

Huh, that was a decent chunk of time.

"We've got sixteen hours or so before they start entering Earth's atmosphere. They probably won't burn up on entering because they're made for this shit. We'll kill plenty, but we're mostly focused on Phobos at the mom—"

I frowned when I was interrupted by a ping. I'd gotten a text. From Lucy. I blinked as I opened it.

Lucy: *Do you prefer this one?*
Lucy: *Or do you like this one better?*
Lucy: *Img . . .1 Img . . .2*

"Hmm? Oh, sorry, I got a text from my girlfriend," I said to the camera with a dismissive little wave. I opened the two attachments, and they both filled my vision. "Oh."

I felt my cheeks warming up before I carefully saved both images and closed them. Lucy had found some bikinis after all. They were cat-themed. She had a tail.

"Uh . . . right, so, uh." I coughed into a fist. "Aliens are going to rain down from the sky to eat everyone. Which is the important thing we should all be focusing on. Stop posting blush emotes, you fucks," I snapped. I was absolutely not blushing. "Some of you are going to die horrifically and I really wouldn't mind it all that much, but I happen to care for some people, so I'd like to avoid that scenario if possible."

I needed to get shit back on track. Fortunately, Gros Baton poked his head out of the Big Gun's command center. "Yo! We're gonna shoot the black hole," he said.

I gave him a thumbs-up. "Cool! Lemme know how that goes. Uh . . . Right, for the rest of you. If you're a samurai in North America, keep an eye on the skies? We think that the aliens are mostly aiming for around this area here, to take out our Big Gun. So what I'm saying is, if you've got the time and the inclination not to turn into plant food, then . . . contact Gomorrah at this number!"

I waited for a moment. Nothing happened.

"Myalis, for fuck's sake, put Gomorrah's contact information on the screen."

Oh, fine.

The information appeared on the screen at about the same time as I got a text from Gomorrah. It was two words, one of which was very un-nunlike.

I chuckled to myself, then stopped when I realized that probably made me look like a creep. "Anyway. World's fucked, but we're working on it, so give us a few and don't lose your shit. I mean, in the worst case scenario, we fail and then you won't have to worry about anything anymore, right?"

The Big Gun started to hum behind me, and I paused, not looking its way as it fired. All along the edges of the gun, steam came spitting out of the vents built into the sides of the barrel, and then there was a *crack-thoom* that made my hair stand on end.

I nodded.

"Yeah, anyway, Stray Cat, out. Good luck out there."

I saluted, then ended the video. The total viewership was in the mid two-digit millions. I took a breath, and when I let it out it was a little shaky. Fuck, that was more than the entire population of New Montreal. And I just knew that more people would be watching recordings of that whole thing after.

"You okay?" Gros Baton asked.

"Yeah, I'm fine," I said. I shook my head to clear it, then reopened those pictures that Lucy had sent me.

She had to know they were arriving mid-stream, right?

Unless she'd been distracted and didn't know.

Either way, I felt like I ought to go see her right about now . . . before the adrenaline wore off . . . and before she changed out of that.

I deserved some amount of stress relief, as a treat, right?

Of course, Gomorrah chose that moment to call me, and it was clearly a group call meant for all of us.

I groaned. Maybe we could just let the world end, and then no one would ever have to deal with team meetings ever again.

STAY-AT-HOME PR MANAGER/GF

"Wow, there are a lot of haters out there," Lucy said. She shifted, reaching down to rub at her calf where it was a little itchy.

The motion caught the eye of the other person in the room, who looked, then immediately snapped her attention away. "Are they saying anything about Delilah?"

Lucy grinned. She and Franny in her and Cat's bedroom. Fortunately, the room was massive, and they'd snuck a couch in next to the kiddie pool in the corner with a good view of the big-screen TV Lucy had acquired with her discretionary funds.

Those funds came from her efforts to fundraise and raise money for the Burlington branch of the Kittens, who were actually doing very well. She was slowly allowing the group to expand into New Montreal. That meant appointing managers—of a sort—and arranging both online and IRL meet-ups and discussion groups. It was fun, busy work, and it was giving her a pretty nice chest of spending money.

A lot of corporations were willing to throw money at the cause. Lucy suspected that it was because they thought it would get them in Catherine's good graces. She accepted the money and promptly forgot everything about those who gave it to her. Morons.

"You wanna see if people are talking shit about your girl too?" Lucy asked.

Franny frowned. "No," she lied.

Lucy smiled, all teeth. Their nun friends might have had a posh educa-tion in their little nun-house, but they lacked some vital skills, like how to lie or properly hide their feelings. "Don't worry, they're not being too mean. I saw her name pop up here and there, but not too much. I think people just associate her with Cat."

"I suppose. They are samurai partners," Franny said. She shifted in her seat. It was a simple, single-person chair with a few plump cushions on it. Franny sat on it as if it was a pew while she worked hard not to look Lucy's way.

If Lucy were a more vindictive, evil woman, she'd flaunt her stuff some more, but there was only so much teasing she could do before even she started to feel bad.

"Might you *please* consider putting something on?" Franny asked.

"Oh, fine," Lucy said. She *was* getting a little cold. And while being all chilled and perky was fun for sending pics to Cat, it was less than comfortable after a while. She padded across the room and plucked a clean-enough shirt off the floor. It was her old "Cat's Got My Tongue" shirt. One of her favorites.

She pulled it on, then returned to the couch, but not before grabbing a blanket from the foot of the bed to wrap herself in. "*Omph*," she said as she flopped onto the couch. "Okay, did I miss anything?"

"In the thirty seconds it took you to cross the room?" Franny asked.

"Hey, this is the internet, shit moves *fast*."

Lucy blinked, and with a small gesture she brought up a dozen screens across her vision. Without a Myalis to cheat for her, she had to arrange things on her own. She'd gotten a few programs to help sort and moderate chats, and now she was using those to pause the live feeds to catch a glimpse of what people had said.

It was thankless work, of course, so she hadn't planned on doing any more than the bare minimum. Honestly, though, she didn't expect that reading even a thousandth of what had been said would be necessary.

She'd been in the middle of said work (after teasing Cat with those bikini pics, of course) when Franny had showed up to help handle the media side of things.

There wasn't really much they could *actively* do, but keeping abreast of people's opinions might be valuable moving forward. Lucy needed to know which memes to capitalize on for maximum success.

[User: Alia, Anxiety Prone]
THE ALIENS ARE COMING! 👽 👽 👽
[User: WakiestWombat]
Can a cow fit into the railgun? Cows a % of c please!
[User: Freija]
Why does Stray Cat have perfect hair? AAAAAA
[User: TwiTwiTwi]
#SpaceHair
[User: OneOfTheSols]
RIP Phobos
[User: Bobble]
RIP Phobos, you were a good moon
[User: FeralSlider]
Flung Phobos at Earth? How???

[User: BlazeBrightly]
Yooo, that's a big gun!
[User: ShortFused]
Kilometer-long railgun? #WTF
[User: DiceyFrew]
She's blushing!
[User: MythologicalSelkie]
Bets on what that message had?
[User: PrinceofHemlock]
Show us the GF pics!
[User: S'tella]
Lmao, gay
[User: FanaticalFirefly]
"Big Gun." Solid name. Very creative. Definitely didn't name it last minute.
[User: WhoNow]
Aliens are coming and soon so is cat!
[User: HarpingLili]
I'm looking up and I don't see aliens #AnotherConspiracy
[User: SaneMika]
I think it's sweet that her GF texted her <3
[User: MamaGoose]
#CatforMayor
[User: Cammie D. Sprite]
One railgun Vs. One Angy moon?
"Hmm, yup, the people on the internet are all weirdos," Lucy said.

"That's not very kind to say," Franny replied.

Lucy scrolled up a little. "This one here wants to eat Cat's hair . . . and this other one wants to lick her toes. Even *I* don't want to do that, and I've definitely licked her before."

"Ah," Franny said. "I think I've just started to naturally filter those kinds of replies out."

"Like ads," Lucy said.

"Exactly," Franny replied. "Just get so used to them that you barely perceive them at all. I don't know if that's healthy or not, to be honest."

"Oh, definitely not," Lucy said with a sardonic laugh. "But whatever. Overall, it looks pretty positive?"

She moved her arm across the air before her a few times, resorting her various feeds. She had no idea how Cat had managed to be on so many sites at once.

Back when Catherine had murdered the mayor, the story was only carried by a few local news channels, but then it had been picked up by a bunch of bigger ones, meme sites, and aggregators before finally the react streamers got in on it and spread it even further out.

This, though? This was being streamed on every major steaming platform, right at the top of their pages. It even interrupted live news broadcasts.

Lucy expected people to comment on it. It *was* rather funny to see newscasters jump and try to handle the screens behind them switch out to Cat's stream, especially with her opening. The AI newscasters were a lot more confused, some of them still looping through the story they'd been covering before.

The stream had also shown up on TV, but Lucy didn't know anyone who actually *watched* TV anymore, so it was kind of just a weird footnote.

Her sorting ended with roughly four piles. At the top left were the most ignorable streams and older forums. The reactions there were muted, though a few of the more science-y bunch were going on and on about the Big Gun and its implications. That's also where she shoved the political echo chambers. They were already working to try and spin the whole thing against each other, but their memes had stopped being funny thirty years ago.

In the top right, she placed the celebrity stuff. Media aggregators and influencer dumps, as well as all the hangouts for the big paparazzi chains. The chats there were split between gushing at the samurai who showed up in the background, speculating about Cat's love life, and yapping about hair, clothes, and possible new fashion trends.

The bottom left was for the people freaking out about the end of the world. It was a small chunk of the overall number, and Lucy couldn't decide if that was disturbing, or if it would be worse if it was the largest chunk.

Finally, the bottom right of her vision was filled with reaction Andies, streamers and quick-media platforms that usually specialized in small, high-dopamine content. They were in it for the spectacle. It was also the corner where Lucy started to sort through the most memes.

The meme trends were wild at the moment because Cat had unwisely fed them all with so much to work with.

"T-Minus Not Very Long" was doing great on some of the more wargamer-ish sites and was on T-shirts already. People were talking about a huge jump in tech-hair prices, and images of Cat's cute blush were all over.

She'd *hate* that.

But memes made the world go round, and memes pushed things from the mainstream core of the internet deeper into the Mesh, where the permanently online sequestered themselves.

Memes were like . . . rain, Lucy imagined. No matter how deep someone was in the underbelly of things, the rain always found a way to leak through the ceiling and leave mold on the walls.

Or something like that. She'd workshop the analogy some more.

"Hey, are you hungry?" she asked.

"Me? I suppose," Franny said.

"Cool! You can help me make something for Cat. I need to talk to her, and food distracts her better than anything else. Plus I want to give the rule-thirty-four artists some time to cook."

Franny sighed. "Of course you do."

CHAPTER SIXTY-THREE

CAT CALLED

The history of telemarketing stretches all the way back to the early days of the Bell telephone, when only the eccentric and rich could afford a phone of their own and therefore made for great targets for sales pitches and cold calls.

As history progressed, the phone became a ubiquitous part of human society. It's no surprise that ads vectored in through that medium continue to be popular to this day.

—On Advertising, second edition, 2049

Gomorrah was not happy with me.

I could tell, because she very pointedly removed her face mask so that I could get an unobstructed view of her glare. Also, the first thing she said when she arrived was "I'm not happy with you."

"Did you get a lot of calls?" I asked.

"I had to get an answering machine catalog," Gomorrah said. "Your little prank has cost me fifty points."

"Oops?" I said. I wasn't actually remorseful, but I could pretend to be guilty like the best of them. "But hey, some of those calls are good, right?"

She sighed, but nodded. It had been a couple of hours since my broadcast. Most of us here were just chilling around the Big Gun, cheering whenever it went off and taking in the occasional update from Gros Baton about the progress around Phobos.

Things were actually looking up on that front. Phobos had been fucked up pretty hard, and it wasn't being allowed to recover at all. The constant swarms of drones were leaving their mark. Death by ten million cuts was still death, and we were helping by ramming the moon with the occasional miniature black hole or web of monofilament.

The points we were earning helped too, though it wasn't that much, all things considered. A nice, steady trickle every fifty-odd minutes.

I'd seen some recent images of the moon. It was fully split now, and some of the bigger chunks didn't even have tentacles keeping them together. Keiretsu drones with large thrusters were pushing the bits apart. It looked like they were moving at a snail's pace, but that didn't matter. A one-degree change out there meant a whole lot to us down here. It would be enough for those chunks to miss Earth entirely.

The next use of the tesla collider would probably be the finishing blow. We'd crush what was left of Phobos, and then all that would remain was the cleanup.

So, in a way, we'd won.

Woo.

Hurrah.

All that jazz.

Actually, sarcasm aside, the mood was pretty upbeat. Princess and Knight were prattling along to Emoscythe. Tankette was taking care of a food tent nearby, wielding a ladle like a king might a scepter. Crackshot and Hedgehog were close enough to the entrance of the Big Gun's control room for Gros Baton to join in on their conversation. Rac was . . . somewhere, and Grasshopper was off doing her own thing elsewhere.

I had listened in for a bit, and . . . it was really disgusting the kinds of things guys would start talking about when there wasn't a woman around. Not that I would start flinging stones from my glass house or anything.

The area was starting to fill up as well. The idea of keeping the Big Gun secret had flown out the window with my broadcast. There was too much background stuff. Some geoguesser would spot two trees and know the exact coordinates down to the centimeter. It was only a matter of time.

So if secrecy was out the window, then the best protection came from numbers, and that meant a huge influx of troops.

Major Tinwhistle's engineers had gotten back to work, setting up barracks and defenses. The ground was being reinforced and extra concrete was being poured out into molds for barricades.

The order of the day was AA. The incoming swarm was made up of fliers. Gunning them down before they hit the ground or even got close was our best bet for keeping the Big Gun and the area around it safe.

"We received some calls from several local samurai," Gomorrah said. "And several from some that aren't as local. I've gotten offers from some less-close samurai as well. Dreamer and Teddy from Calgary, Gray Goo, Myriad, Bloodhound, Magpie, Zenovir, Hard Rain, GroundWire, Speed Demon, Cassy the Clown, and several others from Big Top, Gaea, Legion . . . the list goes on. I've also gotten some . . . unhappily worded messages from the Family saying that they'll be willing to assist us with the logistics."

"Logistics?" I asked. "What sort? Are we going to be spreading people out?"

"Ideally, yes. It looks like this will be the epicenter of the . . . pseudo-incursion, but Antithesis will be landing all across this hemisphere." Gomorrah reached up and rubbed her nose. "It's a lot. We need to cover a huge area. There might be a few samurai who can do that, but they're not around, so scattering as many samurai as possible makes sense."

"Alright," I said with a nod. "And the Family's taking charge of that?"

"They are. And I'm looking over every one of their choices now. They're annoyed that we didn't give them a proper heads-up and forty-eight hours of lead time before dropping that announcement."

Well, at least she was saying "we" and implicating herself in the whole mess. "They do understand that forty-eight hours is too late, right?"

"Do logic and common sense ever stop you from being irritated by something?" she asked.

I didn't have to think about it for long. "No," I admitted. "That's a fair point. But you'd think they'd be better. Plus it's like, a whole-ass company. We're talking about them like they're one person."

"Sometimes it's just like that," Gomorrah said, and she didn't elaborate any before sending me a message. I opened it without checking. If Gomorrah wanted to send me viruses and shit then I would be in rough shape already.

It opened to a map of our hemisphere, centered more or less on where the Big Gun was located. There were pins all across it in an array of colors with little icons next to them indicating who was where.

There was a grasshopper for Grasshopper, a tank for Tankette, a crown for Princess, and so on. We were all squished in so close together that there was some serious overlap in the icons.

There were also, I noticed, "ghost" icons. Those were sometimes linked to a more solid copy of the same. "Are these location markers?" I asked. The ghost icons and the rest were scattered across a wide area, covering most of the northern end of the country and a lot beyond as well. Even some over the bigger lakes and out in the ocean.

"That's where the Family wants people. Each location forms the meeting point of a set of three equilateral triangles. So we'll be equidistant from each other except for a few areas of high importance, like right here."

"Makes sense," I said. Then I took in the scale of things. "How many points are there on here?"

"Not including the areas of greater importance? A hundred and twelve."

"That's not a lot of points," I said. Not for the amount of area we had to cover, which was massive.

"We don't have a lot of samurai," she said.

"Oh," I said. Right, this was all-hands-on-deck in a big way. Then the map updated and I noticed the triangles getting very slightly smaller, and some icons already hovering over their designated locations were being asked to move inward. "Did we just get more?" I asked.

"This is with the current crop of volunteers," Gomorrah said. "And then, only those who are explicitly working with the Family. I'm, or rather Atyacus, is working to keep in contact with those who called me directly who aren't affiliated and don't want to be. That's only a dozen or so samurai, so far."

"Makes sense. I'd be more willing to call someone directly than deal with a corp I don't trust."

"Yes, it turns out that your fumbling around actually had some benefits."

"As planned," I said.

Gomorrah crossed her arms. "No. Not as planned. I refuse to believe that. In fact, I know otherwise. If anything, this is me looking very hard for a silver lining to your goofing up."

I laughed. "Sorry," I said. "So, are we stationed right here?"

"This is where it might be the worst," Gomorrah said.

"And where we'll make the most points for defending," I said. "And where we literally have an army and no one civilian-like around for kilometers. We can afford to go all out."

"And we'll need to," Gomorrah said. "What have you prepared so far?"

"Uh," I said.

Her eyes narrowed. "You *have* spent the last two hours or so preparing, right Catherine?"

"How upset would you be if I did nothing but fuck around and chat instead?" I asked.

"Not upset. Disappointed."

"Ah," I said. "Well, that's no fun. But it's also the truth, so at least you know that I'm honest with you?"

"You're nothing but a pest, Catherine," she said. "We need AA set up, and soon. I'm thinking several larger guns. We need the ability to strike at small, distant targets. These enemies will have come through the atmosphere, so either they'll be weakened or we'll get the ones so tough that it didn't slow them down ,and that'll mean a whole other level of problem."

I nodded. She was right, we were probably dealing with mid-twenties enemies here. These weren't model ones with a few burnt-up feathers. They'd be genuine threats. "I'm sure we can get something going that'll give them all a proper earthly welcome."

She nodded. "Good. Then we need to get ready to deal with those that survived the landing and any hives they might awaken on the way down."

"We're not finishing this tonight, are we?" I asked.

CHAPTER SIXTY-FOUR

ANTI-ANTITHESIS-ANTI-AIR

Orbital defenses aren't an option anymore; they're a necessity. I understand that there are political frictions involved with planting weapons past low Earth orbit, but for the safety and security of our nation and people, we must prepare to receive the alien threat as far from land as possible, and that means installations in outer space!
—General Whitaker to the US Congress, 2023

"Hey, boss, what's the plan?" Gros Baton asked, leaning lazily against the doorframe of the Big Gun's command room. His call had caught the attention of the others.

I looked around. We were all here, it seemed, with one extra, even, in the form of Emoscythe. Tankette was still making her way over while wiping her hands on a small tank-patterned towelette. She was close enough to hear, though.

A quick check of my augs showed me that it was a few minutes shy of six in the evening. When had the time flown? Also, had I skipped lunch? I couldn't remember if I'd eaten anything since that poutine earlier, and that was like, last night.

Right, people were expecting shit from me, and I couldn't just sit here and bitch about being hungry, even if I really wanted to. "Alright boys, girls, and Grasshopper," I said.

Grasshopper giggled, so I figured that one had landed.

"We've got more news, which sucks because I'm tired of this constant cycle of having to deliver news, then something weird happening, then having to deliver more news again right after. It's a boring circle. Fortunately, the boring circle will be busted up soon. The Family has their panties all knotted up, but I think they're getting their shit together too. They're laying out a grid of samurai to keep an eye on the skies and knock the aliens down."

"A grid?" Hedgehog asked. "What kind, and what are our numbers?"

I checked the thing Gomorrah had sent me. "We're up to a hundred and forty-eight samurai volunteering, which is pretty decent. The spacing is . . . awful. We're covering the entire hemisphere, which means a lot of space between points on the grid. The bigger cities mostly have locals staying in them to keep them safe, and they usually have their own AA, so there's that."

"There are hardly all that many cities in this hemisphere," Crackshot said. "I reckon NM's the biggest here, then Quebec to the east, and a few more south of us, but the north is wide open. The west has some pretty big gaps too."

"It's a problem, yeah," I agreed. "The nice thing is that no one sane lives in the north, so fuck it. If the aliens crash there, that's on them. They can eat snow or whatever."

"They'll need to be taken care of," Grasshopper said. "Just because a problem isn't right in front of you doesn't mean that it doesn't exist. The Antithesis will have to be dealt with, even if they're not landing right on top of us."

"Well, that's where we're lucky," I said. "Because they definitely are landing right on top of us. Got the projections from our German pals. They did the math and we're right smack-dab in the center of the shitshow, and it's probably safe to say that this is where most of the aliens will be coming. We have almost a day before it's raining plants."

"So what's the plan?" Gros Baton asked. He pointedly looked up to the sky, where it was a bit overcast. "Tire le ciel?"

"If Phobos is already fucked, we can probably use the Big Gun a few times to shoot into the swarm," I said. "Does Earth have any orbital defenses?"

"A few, yes," Gomorrah said. "There are some stations in orbit that belong to various samurai. You'll recall Deus Ex's station."

"That's the kind of thing I was thinking about, yeah," I said. I could still remember just . . . going into space on one of Deus Ex's planes and arriving at her station. I was pretty sure it was in low Earth orbit, not space, but I was also sure that I was the last person who should be discussing the difference between one and the other. "Her station had guns on it, right?"

"She's taken it to Mars," Gomorrah said.

"Wow, top-tier samurai are amazing," Princess said.

"Yeah, it's a whole other thing," I agreed. "And Deus Ex isn't the only samurai with a station, right? There have to be more? And if they left them behind, then that might knock some aliens out before they hit the atmo."

"I wouldn't gamble on a few stations being enough," Hedgehog said. "Though this entire incursion and the Phobos situation might be the last kick that the governments and corps need to start building real orbital defenses. They've been talking about it for thirty years."

"Budget issues?" I asked.

He nodded. "That, and public perception. Some people said that the orbital stations would be used for mind control, and I don't think the smarter people out there had the time or patience to correct the idiot majority."

"Ah, that's rough," I said. It always sucked when the conspiracy theorists got in the way of progress. And it sucked extra hard when they turned out to be right. "So were there really mind-control systems that were gonna be put on those orbital stations?"

Hedgehog gave me an unamused look. "They were to assist with advertising. They're not mind control."

"Uh-huh," I said. "Anyway, setting that aside. I think that whatever we have in orbit can help, but it's unlikely to be anywhere near enough to completely stop us from being attacked on the ground. I'm not even sure if any AA we buy will be enough."

"To add to that," Grasshopper said, "it's very probable that upon entering the atmosphere, the Antithesis will scatter signal pheromones. That might well trigger any still-dormant hives into awakening, but the last global incursion might have actually saved us there."

"How so?" I asked.

She gestured vaguely around us. "Because most hives were already awakened by similar means."

Which meant that they were currently attacking or had already been wiped out. The Phobos Antithesis wouldn't find too many locals to help them, but just because we'd wiped out a number didn't mean that we'd taken them all out. This entire expedition had started as a way to go out and cull more, and there was no lack of the fuckers around.

"Okay, so we're going to have to shoot them down, then probably deal with a local surge or something?" I asked.

"That sounds accurate," Gomorrah said. "Since we have time to prepare for it, we might be able to gain additional support from New Montreal to defend this area."

"More troops?" I asked.

She nodded. "And artillery. We're within range of the bigger pieces in the city, and well within range of any of the missile launch systems."

"Right," I said. "So primary focus is anti-air to knock the fuckers out, and then ground defenses second?"

That seemed reasonable enough. The discussion turned toward just how much air defense we wanted. We'd all been earning a fair few points, and this next fight would earn us a few more, but our pool wasn't infinite.

In the end, Hedgehog and Emoscythe ended up being the ones leading that discussion. They both had more experience than the rest of us, one in military matters, the other with direct combat experience against the Antithesis.

The plan was simple. Fill the air with so much high-velocity lead that we wouldn't even be able to see the plants before they came crashing down. Missiles were okay too.

Soon enough, we were all buying up some AA for ourselves. There were plenty of catalogs that had *something* capable of shooting into the air.

Tankette bought a large rack that fit onto her mini-tank, then she got a set of multi-barreled guns on a turret that hovered on top of that. Princess and Crackshot combined some of their catalogs into a sort of . . . very pretty, boxy building with a single barrel sticking out of the top.

Grasshopper and Emoscythe both got their own small buildings, towers that were very much opposites. Squat and rounded for Grasshopper, with a sort of boffer gun atop it, and tall and angular and dark for Emoscythe. I was pretty sure that Emoscythe had done that on purpose, tailoring her design to . . . un-complement Grasshopper's so much that it wrapped around to matching.

Gomorrah just bought a large missile launching system. She said it was like a HIMARS, and I pretended that I knew what that meant.

Gros Baton supplied a heap of ammo for the rather plain-looking installation that Hedgehog bought and dropped by the command center of the Big Gun.

The others spread their things out a fair bit, placing them around the Big Gun but not all clumped together.

That left me with a spot of my own . . . which I now had to figure out how to fill.

CHAPTER SIXTY-FIVE

SKY'S THE LIMIT, BUT I CAN REACH

Wow. Insurance is such a scam.

—Lord Burninator, at his criminal trial
for mass arson, 2032

"So, what're my options when it comes to AA?" I asked Myalis.

Presuming from context that you mean anti-air and not Alcoholics Anonymous or automotive insurance, then we do have quite a few options. In fact, you have options for all three.

"Wait, all three?" I asked. I had walked off on my own, feeling a little awkward for being away from all the others, but it wasn't all that bad. I'd be rejoining them in a minute or five.

Indeed. Technically, as a Vanguard, you could subscribe to any number of insurance services. The companies offering them make the information about their low-premium samurai-tier policies as easy to find as possible. As for the alcohol, I have substances that are so addictive that you'd never have time to be addicted to alcohol to begin with.

"You are far less reassuring than you ought to be sometimes," I said.

I find it amusing.

"You think you're so cute," I muttered.

I'm adorable. Now, shall we talk anti-air options? You have fifty-one thousand, one hundred and seventeen points at the moment, which is a very respectable amount of buying power.

I glanced over to the others. They were mostly crowded around Tankette's updated tank with a few further out. Crackshot and Emoscythe were sitting in a rather nice wrought-iron bench that had definitely not been there minutes ago.

"That's . . . a lot of points. Shit, I'm close to the big leagues, aren't I?"

No. You're still some ways away from that. However, you certainly are edging your way out of the more beginner tiers. Now, what kind of budget are you looking at?

I rubbed my chin for a moment, then nodded. "I think two thousand or so? I know I have a lot more I could splurge here, but that doesn't feel right for a one-and-done kind of event. I'll want something that I can move back to our home and slap onto the roof, though. So it needs to look pretty intimidating? As for weapon types . . . maybe something that fires larger rounds so that I can load it full of explosives?"

That's a clever idea. How about a Mark Six Heavenly Striking Tiger Automated Anti-Air Platform? It would come to one thousand nine hundred and fifty points. A few shy of your stated limit. The system is autonomous, with very competent long-ranged tracking capabilities, and it's designed to fire 30mm shells.

Those were some chunky bullets. "Will they go far enough?" I asked. "Ideally we can hit them while they're still, like, nearly in space?"

That complicates things slightly. But I could have the barrels reinforced, add a water-cooling system, and elongate the receiver to compensate for those additions. It'll allow you to fire the same projectile but with a larger propellant charge. You might still want specialty shells to reach that far up, whereas lower targets can be taken out with more traditional rounds. All that would increase the cost by two hundred points.

That was a smidge over my initial budget, but not by so much that I'd mind. The gun was probably going to earn that point cost back, and then some. "Alright, do it," I said.

Not so fast. This gun is rather large. Placing it right in front of you wouldn't mean that it can't be moved, but it might be best to lay it down in its final intended position.

Ah, that made a heap of sense. Myalis was pretty good with the deliveries of stuff. She'd never dropped anything on my toes before, and I'd come to trust her with that kind of thing. "Lemme ask Hedgehog where he wants it, he seems like the one to ask." It was him or Emoscythe, but she was being cute with Crackshot and I wasn't gonna cockblock my guy.

Hedgehog was happy to help. He explained the rough idea of the current layout, going on about overlapping fields of fire and combined arms and firing intervals. He didn't want our flak to mess up our missile fire, and there were issues with several of our things interfering with our targeting.

The army was putting up more of those balloons, with powerful sensors strapped to the top that pointed into the sky to better identify incoming fliers, and we were going to piggyback off that a little.

The army also had its own AA. A mix of rather simple "big gun that shoots up" and surface-to-air missiles specifically designed to track and hit Antithesis.

The army had a lot of gear for taking out swarms of model ones, even far from a base or a fixed location. They were a minor threat on their own, but in big enough swarms they were definitely a problem. They also had some weapons platforms for bigger fliers. But what they didn't have was weaponry designed to take a flying Antithesis out from over a dozen kilometers away.

The strange truth was that warfare had become a much more evenly-matched game in the last few decades. Range was still king, but when the enemy always rushed to come to you, it made things much easier overall.

Since the thing I was aiming to buy had decent range and seemed like it wouldn't have great traversal, Hedgehog insisted that I place it more or less in the middle of the camp that was forming up around the Big Gun.

He called over one of Major Tinwhistle's assistants, some sergeant engineer who bobbed his head in understanding and then literally took off running. Ten minutes later, we had dudes digging a hole, then filling it with cement and rebar, and basically setting down a platform for my AA gun to sit on.

It only took a few minutes for it to set. It was some sort of quick-drying concrete mix, and the engineers were attacking it with what were basically industrial hair-dryers to get it to set even faster.

The engineers placed some large metal plates over the whole thing, then backed off and kind of just lingered there. It looked like they wanted to be the first ones to take a peek at my new toy, which was fair, I supposed.

"Alright, I'm ready," I told Myalis.

New Purchase: Mark Six Heavenly Striking Tiger Automated Anti-Air Platform

Points Reduced from . . . 51,117 to . . . 48,967

The gun appeared with barely a whisper. Myalis had obviously calculated it so that it arrived with no space between its feet and the metal plates the engineers had set down.

It was pretty big, the size of an old-school SUV, with four long barrels covered in metal shrouds sticking out of the business end of it.

Of course, all four shrouds were shaped like pouncing tigers, with the barrels sticking out of their mouths, and the boxy remainder of the gun had my familiar neon cat logo slapped onto the sides.

There was a space in the rear that someone could easily walk into, with access to several ammo hoppers that were currently filled with 30mm shells with cases longer than my forearm.

The turret spun around, then aimed straight up, the moment so quick and sudden that I jumped in surprise.

"Looks good," I said. "If a bit gaudy. What's up with the name? It sounds like the protagonist of some Chinese web novel."

"You've read a novel?" Hedgehog asked.

"I mean, I've seen ads," I said with a shrug.

The name fits the naming rules.

"What naming rules?" I asked.

The ones I made up.

I narrowed my eyes at nothing in particular. I could almost feel Myalis laughing in the back of my mind. "For someone so smart, your sense of humor is weak." She didn't rise to that bait, leaving me stewing in silence with my new super AA gun.

Tilting my head back, I looked up and into the sky. It was a little overcast, but it seemed as though the clouds were lifting in a few spots, enough to see the sky, at least. It was just dark enough to make out some stars past the incredible light pollution put out by New Montreal.

No aliens, though. Not that I'd probably be able to see them until they hit our atmosphere. Still, it was strangely unnerving to look up, feel so tiny, and know that death might be raining down on me at any moment.

I shook my head and pushed those thoughts away before marching off to meet the others. We'd chat a little more, and then I wanted to head back home for the night.

The world might end tomorrow, but that didn't mean I couldn't spend the rest of today with Lucy and the kittens.

Besides, I was learning not to hinge too much on mights. I was a samurai; defeating the odds with superior firepower was what I was meant to do.

CHAPTER SIXTY-SIX

POINTS ARE PRECIOUS, BUT EXPLOSIONS ARE PRICELESS

The High Mobility Artillery Rocket (HIMAR) system is a weapons platform designed to carry mid- to long-range rockets onto and out of the battlefield so as to be able to assault an enemy position from a tactically advantageous angle without preexisting defensive infrastructure.

While the HIMAR system proved its worth in the early 2000s across several theaters, its real accomplishments were during the early 2020s incursions, in which undefended areas were made the target of saturation bombardment by HIMAR systems in order to eradicate Antithesis threats.

—History of the HIMAR, 2031

"That's not enough gun?" I asked.

"Obviously not," Gomorrah said. She had her hands on her hips and was looking about as amused as usual. She was also standing next to my . . . what was it called again? The Mark Six Heavenly Striking Tiger Automated Anti-Air Platform? "What's the rate of fire on this thing?"

"A lot?" I tried. It had four barrels. That was four times more gun per gun.

Gomorrah just rolled her eyes. "Atyacus says that it fires two hundred and forty rounds a minute. That's a decent number, but it's nowhere near enough to counter the sheer volume of Antithesis we're going to be dealing with, especially as some of them will take multiple strikes to take out."

"Ah," I said. "So what, I need an even bigger gun?"

"Or more of them," Gomorrah said. "I bought six HIMARs. One will stay here, another is heading to New Montreal, and the other four are going in every cardinal direction to provide a wider umbrella of fire. They're loaded with sixty precision rockets each."

"That feels low," I said.

She shrugged. "They're reloadable. I'll be sending a truckbed full of extras with the five that are heading out. My point is that we, and by extension Grasshopper and Emoscythe, can't afford to be cheap here, Catherine."

Oof, she was using my whole name, which meant she was being serious. "I'm assuming it's because we're the big guys around here?"

Gomorrah finally removed her hands from her hips. "Essentially. We're the highest-tiered samurai in the area. Grasshopper and Emoscythe notwithstanding, but neither of them are built for combat exclusively."

I assumed she meant "built" in the sense that they weren't only focusing most of their points earned into combat-related stuff. Grasshopper, I knew, poured a lot into education and information and even some into infrastructure. Emoscythe did fashion and mass media misinformation and propaganda stuff.

They weren't combat specialists the way that Gom and I had somehow managed to become.

The newbies were . . . well, they were doing their own things. Gros Baton didn't seem to have picked any specific path yet. Hedgehog was definitely heading in a "combat" kind of direction, and I suspected the same for Tankette, though she felt more like a support and logistics kind of person. Princess and Knight . . . actually, I had no clue for either of them. Crackshot was probably going to keep up his current "kill things dead from afar" shtick.

Yeah, looking over at the newbies, it was clear that they were still scrounging things together. The Big Gun had given them all a massive boost, though.

"Okay," I said. "That's fair. Let me chat with the major. I'll see about buying a few more of these guns that we can slap around."

Gomorrah nodded. "Do you want me to buy you some trucks for them?"

"Are they expensive?" I asked.

"A cheap land-based car is only about four hundred points for me," Gomorrah said.

"That few?"

"*Cheap*," she repeated. "No easily replaceable parts, good construction quality but poor materials. Battery-powered, but not designed to be recharged, and not exactly comfortable to drive. They do have stable bases and are strong enough to carry something like your AA platform to a destination, though."

That made sense, though it was a little weird to think of something as large as a car as cheap. The sheer bulk of it made me think "expensive," but then a lot of stuff about cars was expensive in relation to just owning the damned things, right? The fuel and permits and parking and all the rest. The actual car was just plastics and some metal and a motor. Maybe some tires or whatever.

"Alright," I said. "I'd appreciate that. Lemme chat with the major. Maybe I'll get five more gun platforms as well and like, a trailer-full of ammo." I paused. "And some smaller cat bots to make sure that all stays in our hands. Just in case."

"That might be wise," Gomorrah said. "Though I don't worry too much about that. You'd have to be mentally unwell to steal explosives from a samurai, especially explosives designed to be detonated from afar."

"Sounds like a good way to clean out the gene pool," I said. "Anyway, yeah, lemme hit up the major. I'll be back in a bit."

Gomorrah seemed pleased with herself, if the way she sauntered off was any indication. I watched her go for a moment before turning back toward the rest of the camp, in particular the small mobile base slapped down in the middle of it.

The major was there, sitting behind a desk beneath an awning that extended from the side of the mobile base. She glanced up as I squeezed past the guards standing nearby.

"Major," I said.

"Samurai Stray Cat," Tinwhistle said as she stood. "Can I help you with anything?"

"You might be able to, yeah," I said.

"Oh, thank God," she said, and her shoulders slumped. "Ever since your broadcast went live, the army's been breathing down my back."

"Trouble?"

She groaned. "The brass, and by that I don't just mean the brigadier general, but the actual top brass, are blowing smoke up my ass right now."

"I don't know what that means and I'm not sure I want to," I said.

She snorted. "A mere major in the position I'm in right now is seen as . . . somewhat above my rank. They'd rather replace me. But by all reports we did really well here, and they don't want to rock the boat. So instead they're nagging at me nonstop."

"So . . . is this a bad time to ask for a favor?" I asked.

The major shook her head. "God, no. This is the best time. More samurai work is a valid excuse to foist all this paperwork onto some poor schmuck that isn't me."

One of the major's assistants raised his head further in, and I had the distinct impression he was the poor schmuck in question. "Right, well I've got some work for you, maybe. I'm about to buy a few more of those big AA platforms and I was hoping you could spread them around. I'll probably get some cat bots too, to guard them, but more guards couldn't hurt."

Major Tinwhistle frowned a bit. "I can help with the installation and the transportation as well."

"Gomorrah said she'd get me some cheap trucks to move them around," I said. "Anyway, I'm sensing a 'but'?"

"My boys are engineers. Not guards. We're all armed well enough, and we've got some stationary weapons sitting around that we can lay down in a pinch, but we're not the ones you'll want guarding your machines. I'll pop a question over to the lieutenant."

"Think he'll be okay with lending us some guys?" I asked.

"Oh, of course he will. The army being seen so close to this many samurai is a PR miracle. The brass are losing their shit right now about that part of things. I'll bet you that recruitment numbers double in the next six to nine months. Especially if we can get footage of our people in green fighting next to you lot."

Fair enough. Some hot military-types fighting the aliens next to a few samurai always looked great. Slap on some phonk and aftereffects, and young men and women across the country would race to sign their lives away.

I looked back and noticed a small row of five extremely nondescript trucks parked not too far from my platform. "Cool! I'll buy the guns. Just have them set up before nightfall, yeah?"

"Can do, ma'am!" Major Tinwhistle said. She was out and shouting orders a split second later.

I walked back to the trucks, checked to see if they had enough room on the back, then chatted with Myalis for a moment. A few seconds after we came to an agreement, there were five distinct *thunks* and the trucks settled down a little.

New Purchase: Mark Six Heavenly Striking Tiger Automated Anti-Air Platform (x5)

Points Reduced to . . . 38,217

"Alright," I said. "And now . . . cats and ammo."

The cats were cheap enough. A semi-decent drone was a hundred-point investment. I needed ten, which did sting a little, but I swallowed my cheapness and made the purchase.

New Purchase: Personal Use, Security Systems, Model Y (x10)

Points Reduced from . . . 38,217 to . . . 37,217

And then, while the boxes were still appearing and the mechanized cats were still climbing out of them, I checked on the next set of purchases. Three thousand points' worth of ammunition, split between high-velocity armor-penetrating sabots and timed-explosive flak rounds.

New Purchase: 30mm Anti-Air Ammunition (Various)

Points Reduced from . . . 37,217 to . . . 34,217

That stung a little too, but it left me with several dozen large boxes, the sort that would require two strong guys to lift, filled with pointy-tipped shells with my grinning cat logo stamped onto their sides.

If all of this wasn't enough to give the aliens a warm welcome, then nothing would be.

CHAPTER SIXTY-SEVEN

THE QUICHE OF COMMITMENT

Quantum Quiche: A Synth-Cuisine Delight

Ingredients:

- 1 package Quantum Crust (Patented multigrain blend, infused with omega-3 nanobots for optimal crunch)
- 2 cups SynthFarm™ Bio-Enhanced Egg Substitute (High-protein, low-cholesterol formula for the health-conscious consumer)
- 1 cup Neon Cheese Shreds (Vegan, dairy-free, and bursting with flavor synthesized from the finest algae)
- 1 cup Mutant Greens, spinach, kale, or a mix (Genetically modified for maximum nutrient density; no Antithesis byproducts)
- ½ cup Cyber Seasoning Blend (A proprietary mix of salt, pepper, and spice, guaranteed to elevate your taste experience)
- ½ cup Holo-Vegan Cream (Plant-based and shelf-stable, perfect for a creamy texture without the guilt)

Instructions:

1. Prepare the Quantum Crust: Preheat your preprogrammed oven to 375°F (190°C). Unwrap your Quantum Crust and lay it in a 9-inch pie dish. Prick the bottom with a fork (for optimal heat circulation) and pre-bake for 10 minutes.

2. Craft the filling: In a large mixing bowl, combine the Bio-Enhanced Egg Substitute and the Holo-Vegan Cream. Whisk vigorously until the mixture achieves a perfect vortex of creaminess.

3. Add the Neon Cheese and Mutant Greens: Fold in the Neon Cheese Shreds and your choice of Mutant Greens. Sprinkle in the Cyber Seasoning Blend to taste. This is where flavor meets the future!

4. Assemble the quiche: Pour the filling into the pre-baked Quantum Crust. Use a silicon spatula to ensure an even spread—precision is key.

5. Bake to perfection: Place the quiche in your trusty oven and bake for 35–40 minutes, or until the center is set and the top has that golden glow of a neon skyline.

6. Cool and serve: Allow your Quantum Quiche to cool for 10 minutes before slicing. Serve it warm, or chill it in your fridge for a refreshing cyber-snack.

—Quantum Quiche recipe, *Quick Cooking with AI!*, 2055

The anticipation was killing me. All the prep, the big spending, the whole ordeal with showing my face to the world . . . and yet there was still plenty of time to sit on our thumbs and wait. The Antithesis were at our doorstep, but they hadn't knocked yet.

We fired the Big Gun a few more times, alternating between taking some final potshots at the remains of Phobos and firing back toward Earth with Bee Bombs and guided explosives to tag some of the bigger chunks of the incoming swarm. The soldiers, especially the growing crowd of new faces, cheered every time the gun fired.

I didn't expect the cheering to last until morning.

In any case, I went around, made sure everyone was alive, then said my goodnights and headed out. If the aliens were going to do me the courtesy of showing up tomorrow, then I could at least spend the night at home.

When I arrived, I found Lucy waiting for me just inside. She greeted me with a hungry kiss, then whispered some of the sexiest words I'd ever heard.

"There's a warm quiche in the oven."

"I don't know what that is, but I'm starving, so please tell me it's a kind of food."

Lucy laughed and dragged me into the living room. I took off my coat as she darted to the kitchen, then bullied the kittens a little. Bargain had spilled soda all over the sofa and turned it into a sticky mess, and I had to tell him off to get him to clean it up. It was a good couch, so nothing hard to clean, but I didn't want to sit in sticky crap regardless.

The kittens seemed to be in a good mood. Junior even told me that I hadn't looked *that* stupid on screen, though I had interrupted a livestream she'd been watching, which was unforgivable.

Apparently, I was worse than midroll ads, which was quite possibly the worst insult I'd ever had pointed at me.

Lucy delivered the quiche. It was some sort of . . . egg pie? She said the veggies in it were actually real, organic veggies she'd had delivered that morning and cut up herself, and the eggs were from chickens.

It tasted pretty good, especially spiced with hunger. Lucy sat on the arm of the couch and toyed with my hair while I complained at length about everything.

"That is a lot of points," she said once I told her how much I'd spent on AA platforms. "But I don't think it's *that* bad. You'll probably make them back, right? And it's not like they're not reusable."

"I know," I said. "Still feels shitty, though. The ammo's expensive too."

"Can't we make some here? I'll see if Rac wouldn't mind checking on the fabricator while we make a few rounds. Can't take more than a few minutes each."

That was a good idea, actually. I was probably not using that machine to its full extent. Still, the rate at which we'd burn through ammo and the rate the fabricator could make more wasn't anywhere close. Unless we had weeks to stockpile, it really wasn't worth the effort.

"Probably best to leave it as it is. We'll have to see about setting up a bigger fabricator at some point. Maybe on one of the lower floors?"

"At this rate, the entire tower will house half the samurai in New Montreal," Lucy said.

"That means it'd be safe, right?" I asked.

She smiled, then leaned way down to give my cheek a peck. "I guess so," she said. "You did well, by the way, with the whole livestream."

"Urgh," I groaned as I let myself fall to the side. It allowed me to crash into Lucy, who laughed as I let my head rest on her lap. "That was embarrassing. It's all Emoscythe's fault. She pulled that shit on me without any warning."

"That's okay. I think you did better with the . . . spontaneity than you would have done if you had time to think about it," Lucy said.

"Is that a commentary on my ability to think?" I asked.

"Yes."

I huffed. What was with it with people thinking that I couldn't think well? I could think as good as the next thinker! "It was a mess. I was talking so fast. I'm not even sure what I said."

"It did come off as a little stream-of-consciousness," Lucy said. "But that's okay. It's a really hard vibe to pull off on purpose, so it felt authentic, and that's important. Besides, it worked, right? The call went out?"

"Yeah. Gomorrah showed me this map from the Family. They're spreading everyone out. There's like, almost two hundred samurai who mobilized."

"That's a lot of samurai," Lucy said. "Like, legitimately a lot of them. I don't think two hundred samurai show up to most small incursions."

"Eh," I said with a shrug. "I think more show up than you'd think. It's just that a lot of them aren't . . . celebrity samurai? More discreet sorts, you know?"

"I suppose," Lucy said. "You're more of an expert on that than I am."

I shrugged half-heartedly. "Myalis, is two hundred samurai a lot?"

It is a rather large number. The most Vanguard that ever participated in an incursion on Earth with the exception of large assaults like the ongoing Mars project and global incursions, is four hundred and thirty-two during the Second Battle of Zurich in 2051.

That was a chunk, holy shit. I didn't envy whichever poor idiot had to handle the logistics of that.

"Four hundred is a lot," Lucy said. "Guess you'll have to try harder next time."

I stuck my tongue out at her, and she laughed and tried to poke it. "There will be no next time," I huffed. "If Gomorrah, or God forbid Emoscythe, ever try to put me in front of a camera again, I'm going to do nothing but swear the entire time."

"I don't think that would actually tank your rankings in a meaningful way," Lucy said. "You're not exactly striking hard in the pre-teen demographic."

"My rankings? Oh! That popularity poll thing?"

Lucy nodded. "You're in the top three thousand now, by the way!"

Huh, that was . . . something. Way ahead of where I'd been just a week or two ago. Then again, the mayor thing, and that big broadcast . . . yeah, that was a lot of my face going around. I shouldn't have been surprised that I had gained some amount of infamy, but it still felt weird to even think about.

"So, how's it feel to be dating a celebrity?" I asked.

"Ohh, can we go to one of those red-carpet things? I want to hang off your arm while wearing something very skimpy," Lucy said.

I laughed. "Sure. Maybe after tomorrow, though? I've got this feeling that my samurai buddies wouldn't be impressed if I went to some movie premiere instead of helping."

"I see and understand your argument, and in my magnanimity, I accept," Lucy said as she tilted her head back and tried to sound snobbish.

I relaxed. This was nice. The kittens were mostly ignoring us and making a racket, the TV was on across the room with the volume too high, my breath stank of eggs, and my leg was asleep because of the weird way I was sitting, but it was still nice.

"Did I ever tell you that your legs are squishy?" I asked.

Lucy snorted. "My legs are not squishy."

I shook my head. "Squishy."

"No!"

"Only good for being used as a pillow," I said.

Lucy looked down at me, then reached over and tapped my nose with a finger. "Idiot," she declared. She didn't shift or kick me off, though, so it was my victory. I closed my eyes as she started to play with my hair again, her long fingers rubbing at my scalp. If I could purr, I might have, cat allegations be damned.

Tomorrow was going to be a whole ordeal. We'd have to gun down ten thousand aliens and hope that we took out enough of them to keep the chaos in the area to a bare minimum. There were people and orgs in the region who wanted to make a big name for themselves, and I was going to have to be there to keep tempers calm.

But tomorrow was tomorrow. Right now, I had a warm Lucy to cuddle and a full stomach, and that felt like enough for the moment.

Then Lucy leaned down and started to whisper some *ideas* into my ear, and I found that my post-food nap mood was set aside. There were other, more fun things I could be up to.

CHAPTER SIXTY-EIGHT

LATE, LOCKED, AND LOADED

Fear isn't the mind killer.
Stress is.
—*A Corporate's Guide to the Modern World*, second edition, 2035

"Is it possible to be bored and stressed at the same time?" I asked the ceiling.

Lucy shifted next to me. Her nose pressed up against my arm, and it was cold on the end. She pulled herself a little closer, as if she wanted to steal my warmth. "At the same time?" she asked. Her voice was husky and rough from having just woken up.

"Yeah," I said. "Is there a word for that?"

"I don't know," Lucy said. She yawned. "Make one up?"

"Hmm. Bored and stressed . . . Bressed?"

Lucy sniffed. "Never mind. Don't make up a new word."

"Did I fail to imbress you?" I asked.

Lucy laughed, and that laughter clearly woke her up some. She poked me in the short-ribs. "You are so . . . you."

"Don't make it sound like an insult," I said.

"I'm not," she said before stretching up. She pressed a kiss against my cheek. "I love you . . . you."

I flushed a little, then returned the kiss. "I'm not so bored anymore," I murmured.

"Oh-hoh? Horny and stressed . . . Hressed? Horssed?"

"Let's not," I said with a laugh. I snaked an arm around so that I was holding Lucy closer, even if I knew that would lead to the entire arm falling asleep sooner rather than later. "I have to go in a bit."

"In a bit isn't right now, though," Lucy said.

"That's true," I said. I cuddled in a little closer. "Later, then."

"When do you have to go?" Lucy asked. "We still have some time, right?"

"Eh, I guess about one, maybe two or so?" I said.

"Cat."

"Yeah?" I asked.

"It's two-thirty."

I blinked, then checked the time in my augs. "Ah . . . fuck me."

"Well, we hardly have time for that now, do we?" Lucy said. She wriggled about for a moment, then pushed me off with a shove. "Up, up! Get dressed and all that, I'll run and prep some breakfast."

"Oh, fine." I said as I allowed myself to be rolled off the bed. There wouldn't be time for a shower, but that didn't mean I couldn't spray myself down with deodorant and find some moderately clean clothes from the floor heap to wear.

Lucy darted out of the room, and I soon heard her banging things together in the kitchen. I took that moment to open up my messaging apps, only to discover a few hundred pings aimed my way. Gomorrah wasn't amused, but she was also not my mom and if I was a little late, then . . . no one would die, probably? Not if I was only a little late.

Putting my armor on was a bit of a chore, but I wasn't about to leave the house without it, not today. Then I shrugged on my coat and made sure to sling on a few guns and grenades. I had a bandolier full of explosive fun, my Laser Pointer, and my old Trench Maker in a thigh holster. Basically, I was armed for war, which was just about what I expected to encounter.

Lucy's idea of a quick breakfast was a small plastic box filled with stuff. One of the boxes gear I bought came in, repurposed as a lunchbox. There were toaster tarts, a ketchup sandwich in a ziplock baggy, and a fistful of granola bars.

"Thanks," I said.

"If I had longer, I'd have made something better," she complained as she brought over a plate with some warm toast on it. There was butter covering it and a slathering of real peanut butter on top of that.

"This is fine!" I said as I grabbed the plate and bit into a piece of toast. It immediately smeared peanut butter on my face, but whatever. I took three big bites, wiped my face clean with the back of my hand, then pressed a kiss against Lucy's lips. "Gotta go," I said after swallowing thickly.

"Bye! Have fun killing aliens and corpos! Don't die! And I love you!"

"Love you too!" I shouted as I ran toward the entrance hall. I grabbed my helmet, then was out the door and into the pouring rain a moment later. The weather was not being very cooperative. It would have been better for us if the skies were clear, but that was a rare occurrence.

As I took off northward on my bike, I noticed something strange. A lot of rockets were rising out from around the city and slowly climbing up and into the cloud layer far above. There were several loud pops that must have been pretty big explosions, but I didn't see any light or any other signs of anything bursting above.

I checked my messaging app and found an explanation as I scrolled up a little. The rockets were a gift from Forró, a Brazilian samurai whose gimmick included weather fuckery.

My concerns about cloudy skies were apparently unfounded. By the time I was halfway to Saint-Jérome, the clouds had turned thin and wispy, and there were great big holes where I could see the blue of deep sky above.

I flew around the Big Gun site. It was hard to tell from the ground, and when I left the night before it was late enough that I couldn't see it well, but the site had expanded a ton. Trenches had been dug out in a wide circle, trees had been chopped down, and large areas had been cleared of bushes and weeds and the grass had been mowed down.

Any Antithesis coming to the site from the ground would be seen from some ways off, and that wasn't saying anything about the defenses. Palisades were up over the trenches, and there were these quick-deploy towers up every fifty meters or so.

Within the defenses was a full-fledged army base. The temporary buildings were looking less temporary every day. We had to have a thousand or so soldiers here now.

The Big Gun itself was off to one side, the camp spread out around it but still giving it plenty of space. Unsurprisingly, the more samurai-ish vehicles were all parked in a row by the base of the gun.

I came around and landed my bike next to my mecha. I had barely landed before I saw Gomorrah making her way over.

"I should have expected that you'd be late, even today."

"Hey now, would you rather I be late, or early and grumpy because I didn't get enough sleep?"

"You should have had plenty of time to get eight hours of sleep and still make it here before noon," she said, rather waspishly.

"Well, some of us actually get laid sometimes, so life just has to make space," I said.

She sniffed, then chuckled while shaking her head. "You're lucky I'm so lenient," she said.

"What does that even mean?" I asked as I finally got off my bike. "Is everything ready?"

"As ready as we can manage," Gomorrah said. "We had a few more samurai join in at the last minute. People like you who don't understand the concept of professionalism. Otherwise though, the overall plan hasn't changed."

I nodded. More samurai joining wasn't unexpected at all. I checked on that map the Family was keeping up and saw that the total number of samurai joining in was in the low two hundreds. That was a good number. Still spread way the fuck out, but that was fine. It meant a good amount of points for everyone involved and hopefully less risk.

"Do we have anything in store for when things go to shit?" I asked.

"There are three rapid-response teams," Gomorrah confirmed. "Mostly samurai who can get somewhere quickly without any fuss, and some PMCs as well. If the Antithesis land in bigger numbers than expected anywhere, then they'll be able to respond."

I nodded and started to make my way to the others. Tankette was around . . . Maybe I could grab something warm to drink from her? This felt like a "walk with a coffee" moment. "Are we still expecting the fucks to mostly be concentrated around here?"

"More or less, yes," she said.

"More or less?"

"The swarm is dispersing. It's still concentrated, but their trajectories have gotten complex. The Big Gun has mostly been firing backward into them and taking out larger clumps. They're about to reach the outer range of what few orbital defenses we have."

So, we'd still have to deal with a lot of the bastards. That was probably good, because it would be embarrassing if, after everything else, there weren't any that showed up and we all just found ourselves sitting here with big AA guns and nothing to shoot at.

Mostly that would be embarrassing for me, the one who'd asked people to help.

"I think this'll be a nice day," I said.

CHAPTER SIXTY-NINE

NICE

If you don't want to be diagnosed with pyromania, just . . . burn the therapist.
—Attributed to Gomorrah, unconfirmed, 2057

For all that Gomorrah wanted me to show up at the crack of dawn, and for all that I showed up . . . past that, there were still several hours to wait before anything actually happened.

I ended up sitting over with the others in the main space next to the Big Gun's little command bunker. It was comfortable enough, and I got to chat with Gros Baton and Crackshot. The kid and I mostly double-teamed Crackshot, teasing him about his relationship with Emoscythe.

From the way he spoke about it, my favorite cowboy was entirely whipped by his hotter, older mistress, and he was loving every second of it. He had a goofy smile on, even as we poked fun at him, and the blush that stretched across his nose and made his ears glow was quite cute.

I mean, he was still a disgusting boy, but I could see what Emoscythe saw in him. That kind of honest and entirely earnest charm was endearing.

It was a solid two or three hours after I arrived at the camp before an alarm went off. All three of us jumped in our seats and glanced around. The alarm was one of those old-school wailing sirens. It made the kind of noise that was more appropriate for a horror movie than anything else. It screamed, and with it, the soldiers around the camp started running.

"Sounds like shit's about to go down," I said.

"Yeah," Crackshot said. "Bet we'll be filled in eventually." He reached up and adjusted his hat, then pulled his rifle off the ground behind him where he'd left it while we chatted. It looked more or less the same as I remembered, though maybe the barrel was a little shinier, and there was a sticker of a chibified Emoscythe stuck onto the stock.

"Ah, criss," Gros Baton said. "Ca commence, hein?"

"Yup," I said. I moved outside, then tilted my head way back and took in the sky. Those rockets earlier, the ones that cleared things out and made the sky as cloudless as I'd ever seen it, were well worth whatever they'd cost.

The sky was so blue it almost hurt to look at it, but there were now teeny-tiny speckles of something darker above. I squinted. My fleshy eye couldn't see shit, but my better one twisted my vision, and it felt like I was looking through a digitally stabilized telescope for a moment before my field of view narrowed and zoomed way in.

Those tiny flecks and lines I could see weren't solid. They were . . . beams or something, flashing out in the dark of space. It was hard to make anything out past the dome of blue overhead. "That has to be the orbital defenses," I said.

"Looks like it," Crackshot said. He tugged his hat on lower to shield his eyes from the sun, at least a little. "I reckon space is a good ways up there. Even coming down pretty fast, we'll have a while before the aliens are close enough to shoot."

"Maybe they'll all die first?" Gros Baton asked.

"Doubt it," I said. "We're not that lucky."

Turns out, I was unfortunately right. The siren stopped after a minute, leaving the entire temporary base in a state of high tension. The soldiers I could see were either fiddling with their weapons or keeping their eyes on the sky.

I checked the group chat, where some of the others were complaining about the sudden alarm. Hedgehog and Gomorrah were posting updates, though.

Gomorrah: AT spotted in close orbit.

Gomorrah: Moon bases have launched interceptors toward the AT swarm.

Gomorrah: Intercept in ten.

Hedgehog: Army sats have a lock-on. They're sending telemetry down.

They were nerding out in the chat, trying to see who could post the most incomprehensible military jargon. I mostly glazed past those and focused on the bits that were helpful to read.

Gomorrah: AT are 8,000km out.

Gomorrah: They'll be in our out-range in five minutes.

"Five minutes," I said as I closed the chat up. "Time to grab a drink."

"I don't know, it'd feel weird to grab a drink while waiting for the sky to fall down on our heads," Crackshot said. "Weather's nice for it, though. This is ideal barbecue weather."

"I think Gomorrah's feeling the same way," I said with a grin.

I went back into the Big Gun's command room and fetched my helmet and coat. I probably shouldn't have left without them, but when we were just sitting around it felt weird to be fully kitted out. I sent a message to my mech as well, calling it back to more or less where we were.

The mech stomped its way over, then sat down nearby. Gros Baton used that as an excuse to lean against the mech's front while still keeping an eye on the sky.

I did the same. I couldn't pick anything out with the naked eye, but there were plenty of little black specks when I zoomed in closer. They were spreading out now. It almost looked like . . . dropping milk-substitute into a cup of coffee or something. The small specks were spreading out, growing . . . more?

Nah, that wasn't quite right. It was more likely that there were just more of them coming close enough to be seen.

I checked the chat again, just in case there was something interesting that popped up onto it.

Hedgehog: AT count coming in. 24,452,485 individual targets.

Fuck me, that was a lot of aliens. To be fair, the vast, vast majority of that was going to be made up of chaff, and as I looked into it some more, it turned out that "individual targets" meant . . . stuff. Some of that stuff was angry aliens, and some of the stuff was just debris. Bits of blown-up aliens and probably some chunks of Phobos and drones that the swarm had rammed through and carried with them.

Basically, anything larger than a basketball and heading in an earthly direction was flagged as a "target" regardless of anything else. It would either be watched as it melted through the atmosphere, or we'd have to shoot at it afterward.

The chaff was providing some good protection for the wider swarm, though. There were some targeting AI things trying to specifically ping off the actual aliens that kept getting false positives.

I continued to stare at the sky until the swarm finally hit the upper atmosphere. Then it really started to put on a show.

Warnings about the incoming apocalypse might have been ignored before, but what we were seeing now would be much harder to dismiss.

The sky was filled with raining fire.

Tiny specks of darkness came down with their own personal fireballs. Streaks filled the sky as objects coming in far too quickly melted and left nothing but blurry lines across the sky. It was a meteor shower of burning alien corpses.

Unfortunately, some of those aliens were making it through.

Hedgehog: Visuals on surviving AT.

He sent images, a few dozen that loaded in an instant. Distant shapes, unfurling wings, monsters taking flight in an atmosphere for the very first time. The systems calculating their trajectories went nuts for a moment as the aliens mostly just tumbled in the thin upper atmosphere.

Debris continued to shoot down around and past the falling Antithesis, some narrowly missing the larger monsters.

Some of that debris opened up into more of them, or into entire flights of smaller models that twisted and tumbled through the air on stubby wings.

I was twisting my head left and right, trying to work out the cricks that were starting to form, when some nearby AA guns fired.

There were several earth-shaking booms, and I was able to barely follow the smoking streaks rising up far, far into the sky above. The shells climbed until they were even with the aliens, then burst into what looked like tiny little splotches from the ground, but they must have been massive way up there.

Gomorrah: Firing.

Her HIMARS-like launcher opened up, a volley of hissing missiles rocketing out of skyward-pointed racks, then angling upward slowly. Those were easier to follow. The rockets were fast, but not nearly as quick as a shell.

The rockets must have had some guidance to them, because they split up and spread out. I saw others on the horizon, growing upward like the stems of massive flowers.

Then they reached their apex and bloomed. Flowers made of rolling fire.

"This shit's making me feel poetic-like." I said as I continued to stare at the sky.

"We'll see if you still feel that way once they start landing," Crackshot said.

"I think so. Killing shit makes me feel artsy," I said.

CHAPTER SEVENTY

I JUST WANT THE SKY ON FIRE

"You know that saying 'There's always a bigger fish'? Well, it ain't true. Eventually you hit whales and there's nothing bigger.

But with the Antithesis? The Anathema? Yeah, with them, there really is always a bigger fish."

—Back Grounder, during Samucon panel interview, 2038

I'd never considered it before, but the sky being on fire really was quite pretty. I think it was the red and oranges contrasting well with all of the deep blues. Then there were suddenly long streaks ripping through the boiling balls of fire above, tiny black specks unfurling into massive Antithesis forms.

I zoomed in on one of them, trying to take in as many details as I could. It looked like a model . . . twenty-two? Those big pterodactyl-looking ones. I remember almost getting messed up by one when I was a brand-new baby samurai.

This one's body looked a little larger, and its wings were stubbier and covered in strange ridges. Feathers? Meat flaps? I wasn't sure from so far away. It could have been anything. Maybe some sort of biological thing that allowed the bastards to fly their way through space?

They were followed by more aliens dipping through the screen of fire that Gomorrah had put up. Some were smoking and charred, but plenty of them seemed fine.

"They're low enough now," Crackshot said.

"Low enough for wha—" I began.

I was interrupted by the jackhammer thumping of massive guns. I looked over, and the gun emplacement I'd bought was opening fire along with a few others. A round sent up every second, alternating between barrels one after the other.

I tilted my neck back again to see what that was amounting to.

The rounds were . . . not smart, exactly, but they did have some guidance to them. I wasn't surprised when the alien I'd marked out earlier had a face-to-shell meeting that ended with a small explosion that turned it into so much scrap biomatter.

"Looks like things are going alright," I said. There were a lot of shells going up now, not just my gun, but from a few dozen others. Machine guns picked up the fire, as well as a few missile launchers and flak cannons.

Unfortunately, there was also a lot of sky to shoot at. Blanketing the entire sky would be a whole ordeal. I squinted as more black specks started to appear above. Guns turned, tracking software picked out ranges and trajectories, rounds were planted into stranglers, but there were more and more of them, and after a solid two or three minutes of nonstop firing, I was starting to notice when the crisscrossing lines of tracer rounds were targeting aliens that were much lower to the ground.

I almost jumped out of my skin when a corpse splattered to the ground a dozen meters away from me. It was smoking and riddled with holes, its body looking like it had passed through a strainer and then got the shit kicked out of it, but it was recognizably a model twenty-two . . . or a quarter of a model twenty-two.

More bits of aliens were starting to rain down around us, as well as tiny bits of shrapnel. Gros Baton was the first to dart into cover, crouching down under my mech as a chunk of metal pinged off its side.

I ran over to join him, and Crackshot moved over to the entrance of the bunker. "We're going to have some of this for a while," he said in a shout. "We can't afford to be hiding when they finally make it close!"

"You think they'll make it close?" I asked.

"Don't be overconfident, yeah?"

That was a fair point. Assuming that we had enough to take them all out was asking for them to swoop in and wreck a few guns, then things would slowly tilt the other way and we'd be dealing with angry flying aliens all over the place.

"Hey, get to cover," I said to Gros Baton. "I'm hopping into the mech."

"Correct!" he said with a little salute. He zipped out toward the bunker with his coat pulled up over his head, as if he was avoiding some rain.

I ducked to the side and sent the right order to my mech's computer. It lowered itself down with the front popping itself open to make room. I grabbed on, pulling myself up and into the cockpit. It took some reshuffling once within to tuck my coat away but soon enough I was in the seat and plugging myself in properly.

There was that familiar moment of disorientation as my augs' many screens were shuffled away and replaced by all of the system messages, alerts, and the usual heaps of quick-glance information I needed to operate my mech.

My feet settled into place on the pedals and I wiggled my fingers loose before grabbing onto the controls.

My ammo counters all read full. My targeting system was pinging off debris and bits of aliens above as they came into range, and the mech's comms system was sifting through piles of reports from across the country and from two dozen PMCs and governmental agencies, not to mention the Family and some smaller samurai groups.

"Alright," I muttered mostly to myself. "I'm ready to kill shit."

Killable things are on their way.

"Hell yeah," I said.

Myalis was, as usual, spot-on. The aliens raining down from above soon grew from one or two quick-moving stranglers to a full on rain of bodies. The AA guns around the compound started to twitch, more rockets went screaming up, and now when they detonated it was close enough to kick up dust off the ground.

Gomorrah's fire-based explosives were going off less than a kilometer above, and that was close enough to warm the ground up. The humid patches left by the last bit of rain started to steam, and I saw soldiers ducking for cover between the blasts.

The rest of the AA continued to shoot through the fireball, and for good reason, as aliens continued to tumble through.

"Northeast sector!" someone cried over the comms. The mech's systems had picked it up and flagged it as high-priority. "We've got—Fuck!"

I aligned myself with the gun, then turned to face north. There, on the far end of the camp, a large model was climbing up over the dirt-and-sandbag wall surrounding the camp. A few soldiers were backing away from it, sparks going off as they emptied their rifles in the general direction of the Antithesis.

It was a big bastard, as tall as my mech when it stood on its wings, with a long, narrow face that had something approaching a beak. It stabbed down and just barely missed skewering a soldier who had leapt out of the way.

Smaller models were hopping off its sides and back. Model ones? They seemed a bit thinner than the usual birdlike models I saw, but also much ganglier, with longer wings and bodies.

I didn't waste any time locking my Gatling guns on the big fuck and opening up. The twin *brrrrs* of my guns roaring was soon accompanied by the musical tinkle of hot brass cases clinking off the ground.

The bigger alien stumbled back, my guns punching several hundred holes across its chest and wings and ripping into its head.

Just to be sure, I lined up a shot with one of my bigger guns and my index twitched over the trigger. A single 105mm shell punched a hole through the alien's middle large enough to crawl through.

It slammed down onto the ground, very dead.

I turned, scanning for more, and it didn't take long for me to find stuff to shoot. The Antithesis were mostly getting their shit kicked in by all of the

AA installations we had around the area, but a few, because of blind luck or because they were just that tough, were making it past all of the defenses.

They mostly came sweeping down with punctured wings, covered in scorch marks, and often with missing limbs from close calls.

I took it upon myself to finish them off. It was impressive what a 105mm high-explosive shell could do to ruin some alien fuck's afternoon.

"Haha! Bienvenue sur Terre, motherfuckers!" Gros Baton was shouting as he shot a pair of large LMGs upward. I don't think he was aiming so much as just . . . shooting a whole lot in the general direction of the aliens. It was working, though, and I think his enthusiasm was encouraging the nearby soldiers too.

Yeah, we had this shit in the bag.

Big target incoming.

Big target? I looked ahead, then blinked as something huge burst through the wall of fire Gomorrah had going above us. It was still a solid couple of kilometers away, but it was so massive that it felt closer. An alien large enough to swallow a city bus whole, its body covered in gaping, bleeding holes and licks of fire, but its wings were still beating, and it was still coming down right on us.

"Ah, okay then," I said.

Maybe 105mm wasn't enough after all?

CHAPTER SEVENTY-ONE

SHE WITHOUT SIN DROPS
THE FIRST SHOE

Whenever you think you have a clear and precise idea of what the Antithesis are capable of, a new model shows up that breaks that preconception.

It's very much possible that these creatures are not beholden to the same physical limitations that make life on Earth possible. Or perhaps it would be safer to say that they have found ways to circumvent, through blind chance or guided evolution, the laws that make for the foundations of our biological sciences.

—Doctor Evelyn "Dagger" Hargrove, 2034

"Myalis, what in the fuck is that?" I asked.

My mech's targeting software had no issues locking onto the big flyer above, probably because it was the size of a literal barn with nothing between us and it except for zipping tracer fire. I watched as lines of light machine gun fire stitched themselves across the alien's underside.

That is a model thirty-one. It's a space-capable flying model that can serve as a light transport and rapidly birth new hives. It can also produce its own sub-model type.

"It can make whats?" I asked.

The fat fuck above seemed to contract in on itself, then it shifted around, its wings sort of gorging outward until they became larger. It looked a little like one of those manta rays, but with a mouth at the front large enough to swallow a sedan.

Then more mouths opened up all along its sides. They had disturbingly human lips, and from the look of them, each one was covering a hole large enough for someone to crawl into. The model swelled some more, and then there was a loud spitting sound.

Large gobs of mucus shot out of the mouths all along its sides, each one flung in a different direction.

"What in the fuck," I muttered even as my mech's targeting locked onto the spit balls. They . . . turned in midair? I let the mech start shooting at them with its Gatling guns, but I marked the nearest to be left alone.

It swung around, the snot stuck to it peeling off as it flew. I squinted at it, then recoiled when it kind of stretched out.

It was an alien, not some lump of mucus or just a projectile. A small, cross-shaped bird thing with horizontal and vertical wings. Four long, thin tentacles trailed after it like streamers, and as they twisted and flicked, the little flying alien spun in the air and changed directions.

It came crashing down sharply, and I shifted my mech to have a better view of it.

The model's "wings" ripped off its back, turning into four long, multi-jointed arm things that it started to use to scamper about. Its tentacles were snapped out toward a nearby soldier who screamed and jumped away.

I walked over and stomped it flat with my mech's forepaw. "What the fuck was that?" I asked Myalis.

A model thirty-one-slash-one. It's the model thirty-one's primary offensive tool. A sub-model that the larger flyer can create and spit out. They are some-what unwieldy, but still quite strong. Fortunately, they are quite ill-suited to combat in a gravity-based environment. Their excretions and tentacles allow them a great deal of maneuverability in space, at least within relatively short ranges.

Yeah, fuck all of that. I flicked on the comms to the general channel that was being used for tactical shit. "Stray Cat here. Put a higher priority on the model thirty-ones. The big fucks. They can summon smaller aliens. They don't seem that strong on their own, but we don't need them spread-ing around."

I got a few "yes ma'am"s and nodded to myself as I refocused above. The model thirty-one was in a rough shape already. It had tanked a few more bigger strikes and the constant AA fire was ripping it apart.

Sure, it was a model in the thirties, which made it scary as fuck, but it was also taking on the full might of an entire anti-air network. I aimed my 105mm guns up and took a few potshots, then I aimed my railgun up and got a lock. It was somewhat awkward. The gun had piss-poor traversal, and it was in my mech's chest, so I had to stand with my forelegs on a small building, but I managed.

A single loud thump from my railgun and there was a hole punched through the model thirty-one from chest to back. Its armored sides could only take on so much, it seemed.

That spelled the end for it. Its big sacs deflated, and after spitting out a couple more of those thirty-one-slash-ones, it came crashing down about two hundred meters out from the edge of the base around the Big Gun.

I glanced at the sky. There were still lots of aliens coming down, but I had a minute to spare. Rushing over and around some tents, I came out of the side of the base just in time to see Tankette rolling her tank in the same direction. "Just making sure it's *dead*-dead," I said as I linked to her.

"Oh, that's good," she replied. Her speech was hard to make out over the rumble that came from inside her tank. "I was coming over to do just that."

I shrugged, and we both sat in comfortable . . . not-silence as we laid into the alien corpse. I switched out the ammo in my 105mm guns for some incendiary rounds to light it on fire after a bit. "Keep an eye on it," I said before stepping back toward the base.

Things were okay, more or less. A glance upward revealed a dozen more model thirty-ones, as well as plenty of big fliers moving around them as escorts, but for the most part we had some time before they got too close. Better yet, they weren't all able to withstand our AA fire.

Plenty of them were imitating the Hindenburg at the moment, turning into burning sacs of organic goop that melted even as they came plummeting down out of control. The heavy thumps as they struck the ground were a good sign. I figured that terminal velocity was as good a weapon as any.

"Any updates?" I sent out.

Surprisingly, or maybe not, Gomorrah called me a few seconds later. "Cat," she started.

"Hey," I said as I settled back and allowed my mech to take care of the lock-ons and the next few shots. At most, I moved around a little to help line things up. "What's up?"

"Things are going . . . well enough. We're not too far from our best-case scenario for this engagement. At least, the Family's idea of a best-case."

"That's good, no?" I asked. "Best-case is the best case, let's go! Woo. Hurrah." I kept tracking some of the bigger models with my mech's eyes. The nearer ones were taking a fair bit of damage, but they were getting closer, and because the fire was focused closer, it meant that the ones behind were dropping lower with less damage taken. I was seeing a pattern forming, and I wasn't sure I liked it.

Then the sky filled with rocket trails, some coming from nearby, others from way off near New Montreal, and the higher-flying models suddenly had to deal with massive explosions all around them.

"It is good, yes," Gomorrah said. "Except that we now have an issue, and it's a worst-case-scenario kind of issue."

"Ah. You know, the moment you called, I figured you were waiting with a shoe to drop on my head," I said.

"I'm surprised you even know that expression," Gomorrah said.

"When you're from a place like where I was raised, you get to learn all of the expressions that have to do with shit getting worse," I deadpanned. "What's the sitch?"

"We had a suspicion that the Antithesis would be dropping signal pheromones across the atmosphere," Gomorrah said. "It was one of the Family's bigger fears."

"Why? We're already in the middle of a global incursion."

"Because with prevailing winds, there's a very real chance that those signal pheromones will stay up there for weeks or months. It means trouble over a much greater timeframe."

I . . . had a hard time caring when the current issue we were dealing with was right in our face, not weeks or months away. "Who cares?" I asked.

"All the people who don't want to die in a week?" Gomorrah asked.

I rolled my eyes, then paused and did it again. Did . . . did my mech just roll its eyes too? Why was that even programmed in? "We can take care of that later. Unless there's anything we can do about it now?"

"There might be some weather control systems that would pull the pheromones down. It won't be worth doing until we've finished clearing out the swarm, however. A reduction in visibility now would be ill-conceived. In the meantime, expect all nearby hives to awaken and converge. We know what they'll be producing."

"We do?" I asked.

Gomorrah sent over a package. I opened it, then stared. It was a scientific report titled "A Field Analysis of the Pheromones over the North American Hemisphere and Their Indicators and Possible Meanings."

The rest of the document was page after page of text, with a few graphs to break it up. It didn't even have the common courtesy to be in dark mode. "What's this?" I asked.

"The pheromones will be summoning flying-type Antithesis from any available hives. We can expect a surge in model ones in the next day, extending out to . . . whenever we get around to eliminating the hives that received the message."

"Well, that'll be something," I said.

Could be worse, could be better. We'd handle it. In the meantime, I wanted to see if I couldn't snipe more of those bigger fucks with my railgun.

CHAPTER SEVENTY-TWO

BEHOLD MY CATLIKE GRACE

Grace isn't just about looking good while doing the impossible. It's about making sure everyone else knows you're better at it than they are—and maybe stepping on a few necks along the way. Figuratively. Mostly.
—Attributed to Emoscythe Mordeath Noir, early 2050s

The next twenty minutes were kind of boring. Even the constant drumming and thumps of multiple AA guns turning the sky into pin-cushion land was something I could get used to.

And then, on the twenty-first minute, things stopped being boring, but in the bad way.

I got a call. It was flagged as urgent, and it was coming from Grasshopper. "Where's the fire?" I asked as soon as I answered.

"Hello, Catherine," Grasshopper said. "Are you busy right now?"

I stared ahead, where I was moving my mech so that I could line its railgun up with a target some two klicks above and away. "No?" I said.

"Oh, fantastic, because I have a bit of a disaster that I'd appreciate your help with," she said.

I took the shot, then stepped back, allowing the railgun to cool off while I gave Grasshopper my full attention. "Alright, what's the disaster?"

"I've made a lot of friends in the wider samurai community, as you may be aware, and I always keep an eye out on new up-and-comers, just in case they need a helping hand!"

"Uh-huh," I said. Gosh, I loved Grasshopper, she was a sweetheart, but holy crap was she ever bad at getting to the point.

"In this case, a whole lot of samurai have answered the call. There are Vanguard peppered all across the country working real hard to keep people safe and destroy as many enemies as possible. A lot of these are newer, however, and I've been keeping an eye on them, just in case."

"I'm following so far," I said. "Is one of them in trouble?"

"Just so!" she said. "I'd give you a gold star, but we are in a bit of a hurry, I think. There's a . . . rather reserved samurai who has been a Vanguard for some time, but she usually keeps to herself. I only met her a couple of times, and I always had the impression that while she was competent, she would really rather work alone. I named them, you know!"

"You want me to pop over and check on them?" I asked.

"Yes please! I'd appreciate it. They're closer to you than I am, and I'm currently watching over a small group of new friends who could really use the help. Her name is Shy, by the way. I'll have Bybyt send her coordinates over!"

"Bybyt?" I asked. Didn't that mean "bug" in French?

"My AI friend! Did I never introduce you? Oh, you'll love them, they're quite friendly! Anywho, toodles! Thank you for trying to save my friend's life!"

Grasshopper cut off the call and left me stranded there in a heap of confusion. I shook my head when I received a ping. Coordinates, from Bybyt the AI. As well as a small introductory digital postcard, because of course Grasshopper's AI would be just as extra as Grasshopper herself.

"Myalis, can you make sense of these numbers? And . . . if it's far enough, I'm going to need a carrier to get my mech from here to there."

Certainly. These are standard coordinates. Vanguard Shy is some seventy-nine kilometers northwest of your current position. As for carriers, I have some options.

"Nothing that's shaped like a cat," I said.

I have fewer options, but some remain. You could purchase a small transport vehicle for approximately nine hundred points. It will be capable of lifting your Nyanzerfaust and moving it. It has no defensive capabilities, but the mech's own weaponry should suffice against lighter opponents.

"As long as it can go seventy-ish kilometers quickly and then survive the trip back, I'll be happy. Get me something that's not too loud, though. I don't need to alert the entire area that I'm around."

I blinked as a large vehicle appeared nearby. Myalis had decided against summoning it in a box, which was probably for the best since I didn't want to get out of my mech to figure that out. The carrier was built on four skinny legs, with a large turbine mounted on each corner so that they could tilt a little. There were those long glowing slat things that all hovercars had as well.

It didn't take a genius to figure out how it worked. My mech fit right under it, and there was a large clamp that came down right over the back of my mech's neck and hooked on. I shifted the mech's paws so that there was one standing on all four of the pylons on the corners, and then the entire thing was linked into the mecha's control system.

I . . . did not know how to fly very well, but the carrier had an auto-leveling system and was otherwise pretty simple, control-wise.

"Point me in the right direction, please," I said. Myalis threw up some pointers on my augs, and I nodded. "And can you tell the people ground-side not to shoot me out of the sky? Maybe also send a message to the group chat explaining what I'm up to. I'll be back in a few."

Sent and sent.

"Thanks," I said. "So, what do we know about this Shy samurai?"

Unsurprisingly little. Her records reveal that she has been a Vanguard for two years, and then the records remain rather sparse. A few showings at some minor incursions, including in the very incursion where you became a Van-guard, but no record of any large high-tier kills.

"Okay," I said. Maybe Grasshopper was spot-on with that name. Shy seemed to be living up to it. "Any idea what her specialty is?"

She is either actively hiding her specialty, or she doesn't seem to have a clearly visible one yet.

Yet? After two years? I had something going on after an afternoon. Then again, I was probably not a very good yardstick for measuring shit by.

The very helpful little distance readout projected before me ticked down until there were only a dozen kilometers left. The whole "moving in a straight line from A to B" thing really cut down on how long it took to get places, and the skies farther out from the Big Gun weren't nearly as busy with AA fire, which made for much smoother flying.

When the coordinates counter hit zero, I came to a full stop and scanned the area. It was a small town, the same sort of bumfuck nowhere that Gros Baton had lived in, but without the benefit of a coordinated community and a local samurai to keep the plants at bay.

This town had twenty or so homes on a T-intersection, and the only two larger buildings were an old pub and a fire station that looked like it doubled as the town hall.

It didn't take long for me to spot some Antithesis. A flight of model ones was zipping across the town's only intersection toward a few packed-together homes.

No, not just model ones. There were a few of those thirty-one-slash-ones too, the weird plus-sign-shaped freaks with the tentacles, and they were doing a good job of keeping up with the model ones.

Now, if they were all heading *that* way, then there had to be something calling them in that direction.

I flew over, and soon discovered something running across a wide back-yard. Footprints on unmowed grass, and my thermal sights were showing *something* running away from the widening flight of aliens.

The something turned and there were a few quick muzzle flashes before a few aliens were evaporated out of the air.

That only took out a few of them, however, and the motion revealed that what I had thought was some sort of invisibility suit was more like a cloak. From above, it was great. From the ground? Probably not so much.

The model ones rushed upward, flipped, then shot out toward the lone samurai. The bigger tentacle-y flyers shot ahead, their tentacles coming around like whips.

I disengaged the clamp holding me in place.

If the aliens expected to have a multi-ton mech crash into the ground between them and their prey, then they sure knew how to act surprised. I especially liked to imagine that their emotionless monster faces had a flash of regret on them before I opened up with my cannons.

The blast alone was enough to pulp the nearest of them with nothing more than displaced air. The few actually struck by twin 105mm rounds . . . didn't make it.

Then I let loose with the twin shoulder-mounted Gatling guns, spraying the space ahead of me with a very tactical figure-eight motion right through the middle of the swarm before I allowed the mech's self-targeting to take over to pick out stragglers.

"Hey," I said through the mech's exterior-mounted speakers. "You good back there?"

I glanced through the camera mounted on the back of my mech and found a slack-jawed young woman, her face covered in splotches of white and brown and her eyes opened wide.

"Yeah, that's how people ought to look when they see me," I said. "Grasshopper said you might need a hand?"

CHAPTER SEVENTY-THREE

IT'S ALWAYS THE QUIET ONES

What about . . . Quiet? No, that's too on the nose, hmm? Oh! Lady Shy-lance? You'd need to pick up a lance for that.

Ah! Just Shy, then?

—Recording of a conversation between Samurai Grasshopper
and a wall, 2056

"You good?" I asked, checking my mech's scanners. There were a few living Antithesis around, but they were flopped onto the ground, with hefty chunks of their bodies missing, and I figured that the whole "living" thing would rectify itself soon enough.

I refocused on Shy. My guns were relatively silent . . . ish, all things considered, but they *had* shot right next to the samurai, and I didn't know if she had ear protection.

If she was shy by default, I couldn't imagine how she'd be if I blew out her eardrums.

Stepping back very slowly let me see the woman a little better. Shy was a thin twenty-something in an all-black outfit wearing something like a long poncho with a hood and a sort of cloak bit at the back. Her suit was armored, from what I could tell, and her face was partially exposed. She had these sorts of large goggles on, which still let me see her wide-eyed stare. Her skin seemed a little strange? Motley. At first I thought she had burn scars like me, but it didn't seem like that. That one thing where people's skin was two-colored, maybe? It started with a *V*, but I couldn't remember the name.

"You good?" I repeated.

She looked down, as if checking herself, then let go of her gun. It hung off her side by a strap while she tapped herself all over real quick. Then she paused and shyly, slowly, looked back up. She nodded.

"Uh, yeah, good," I said. "Can you talk? Or like, sign?"

Shy blinked, all without meeting my mech's face with her gaze. Then she reached down toward her neck and . . . tugged up a piece of cloth, covering the few parts of her face that had been exposed.

I wasn't getting the feeling that she'd be chatting with me anytime soon. Then I got a ping, from Myalis.

It seems as though Vanguard Shy wishes to forge a connection between her AI assistant and myself. I'm ambivalent about it.

I shut off the mech's microphones so that she couldn't overhear. "Is that dangerous?"

No.

"Uh, you sound sure of yourself," I said.

Her AI is a thousand years too young to pose a threat to me. In any case, this isn't too unusual. Vanguard who work together frequently sometimes do this. I've been in contact with Atyacus quite frequently, for example. Asking for this level of connection outright is a little strange, but not dangerous or a threat.

"Okay?" I tried. "So, what would that even do?"

Every Vanguard AI is already networked together, to some degree or another. This would merely allow you to hear what this Vanguard wants to convey through her AI assistant. In this case, in the form of text and sound-based communication.

"Would you say yes to it?" I asked.

It's harmless, so I don't see why not. I suspect that this Vanguard has communication issues and her AI is willing to assist.

I considered it for a moment, but then gave up on thinking. If Myalis said it was safe, then I could probably trust her. If the day came that I couldn't, then I was fucked anyway. "Sure, patch them in," I said.

Patching!

There was a small blip, and then text appeared at the bottom of my vision even as someone else spoke up. It sounded like they—he?—was standing right in front of me and talking with a rather posh-sounding accent. *"Greetings! I am Latyns, Lady Shy's personal AI assistant. It's a pleasure to meet you, Vanguard Stray Cat."*

"Yeah, pleasure's all mine," I said. "So, any reason why Shy set this up?"

"Ah, indeed. Lady Shy is somewhat averse to speaking aloud with strangers, and so I have been tasked with translating her wants to you directly."

"Right," I said. I looked over to Shy, who was . . . muttering something under her breath. She looked up for a moment, met my mech's eyes, then nodded her head low in what was almost a bow.

"Lady Shy thanks you for your assistance. Without your timely aid it was possible that she wouldn't have survived this encounter with the model thirty-one."

"Wait," I said. Then, realizing that I could ask her directly instead of going through her AI, I flicked on my mech's mic. "Wait, you downed a model thirty-one?" I asked.

Shy nodded slowly. She half-turned, then pointed back the way she'd been running from. I saw her jaw move a little before Latyns piped up again. *"Lady Shy shot the alien out of the sky some half a kilometer away from here. The model was injured already, but her final strike took it down. It is not yet dead, however, merely incapacitated."*

I could leave Shy here. Let her finish off her kill now that there weren't as many flyers around, and she'd earn herself a nice heap of points for her troubles. On the other hand . . . I could already hear Grasshopper nagging me for not keeping an eye on the girl.

"Want me to give you a ride over to the thirty-one?" I asked. "You can hop on top and I'll run over to where it landed."

Shy seemed to consider it, then muttered something too low for me to pick up. Was she subvocalizing?

"Lady Shy would appreciate the assistance. She has some equipment that had to be abandoned at haste by the location where the model thirty-one crashed. She has two concerns, however."

"Go on," I said.

"First, the Lady worries that your vehicle and presence might be somewhat loud."

"I can be quiet too, you know?" I said. A flick of a switch activated the mech's stealth functions, and it suddenly grew a lot quieter. Then it went fully invisible. Well, almost fully. Some panels were open at the moment, and the insides weren't covered in the same stealth-screen coating shit that made the entire mech transparent at will, but it was stealthier than just standing there as a giant mechanical tiger.

I saw Shy's big, expressive eyes blink. *"The Lady is impressed. Her second concern was one of comfort."*

"Comfort how?" I asked.

"Why, she wonders if two people will fit within your mechanized unit's cockpit."

"You want to sit in my mech?" I asked.

Shy stared.

"Where else would she find herself if you were to carry her?"

"I mean, I was thinking you could hang on to the side? Or like, ride the mech on top? Like . . . a really big horse?"

Shy started up at me. She had some really pretty eyes under those tech-goggles. Grayish blue, and very soulful. Also, very disappointed.

"You know, for someone so shy, you seem real eager to get in here with me. Usually people wait for a few days before getting it on with all the skinship."

Shy leaned back onto her heels, then quickly shook her head. *"Lady Shy wishes to clarify, with great enthusiasm, that you are inherently incorrect in your assumptions."*

"Uh-huh."

"She has decided that walking back is acceptable."

Before I had time to reply to that, Shy spun around and started running back. She quickly faded from view, her poncho-cloak turning her invisible. So, another stealth specialist, then? Not that I had really been leaning into that lately. Stealth was cool when you were punching up, but once you had big guns it kind of took a back seat to just exploding your enemies.

Shy was a pretty quick runner. I might have lost sight of her, but Myalis painted an outline over her current position, so as I bounced up and after her, I was able to keep up without squishing her underfoot.

I split my attention between moving forward and keeping an eye on my mech's readings of the area. Spending time playing mechanic hadn't been a waste. I knew more about how to pilot this machine than ever before, and that really let me use the whole of it.

"Model ones ahead," I warned. "Might be a few of those flyers the thirty-one spits out too."

Shy's hand appeared from out under her poncho and she gave me a thumbs-up.

Right, working with her was going to be interesting, and maybe not in the fun way.

We shot past the backyard of an old farmhouse, then Shy leapt over a decrepit wooden fence into a spot filled with younger trees. It had probably been a field just five or six years ago, but now it was well past overgrown and starting to become a forest of sorts.

My mech crashed through the smaller trees. Fortunately, they were mostly leafless, so it wasn't all that loud, but it wasn't too subtle, either.

The aliens caught on quickly enough. We were going to have to ditch the stealth stuff, unless Shy wanted me standing atop her again to keep the birds off.

I didn't want to make a habit of it.

CHAPTER SEVENTY-FOUR

I HAVE THE SHY GROUND

That's NOT how recoil works. Hell, that's not how physics works.
No, I don't care that you're a samurai or whatever. While you're human,
in this universe, you obey the laws of physics, dammit!
—Professor K. Dick, Physics dept., MIT, 2033

I tried to be somewhat subtle as I moved through the woods. Shy was ahead of me, and she caught on soon enough that my mech was on the wider side of things. That meant that she mostly picked out a route with fewer trees, or at least more room between them whenever possible.

I was still crashing through the woods, rustling branches and breaking saplings with loud snaps. There was subtle, and then there was multi-ton mecha subtle.

At the end of the day, there was really only so much that could be done.

Shy half-turned, and I could only just make her out from the very slight shimmer in the air where she stood. Her camo was good, but it still warped a little when contrasted against a complex surface, like fallen trees and piles of leaves.

She raised a hand out from beneath her poncho, a finger raised in a 'one-moment' kind of gesture. I paused, lowering my mech down a little so that I wasn't poking out of the canopy as much.

A flight of model ones swooped by overhead, their little raven-like heads tilting this way and that as their too-many-eyes scanned the woods.

Looking past them, into the wider sky above, I could make out distant tracer shots still leaving marks across the sky. There was the occasional *pop* and *bang* of flak bursts going off. Sometimes I could hear the whistle of a rocket reaching up into the atmosphere. Those would be accompanied by a small spark, like a tiny second sun, for just a moment as something was fucked up way out above the atmosphere.

The number of aliens coming down from above seemed to be slowing down? Maybe? I wasn't sure. The amount of shots going up certainly seemed to have dwindled a fair bit.

Shy gestured me forward, and I followed. The flock of model ones had moved on. It seemed as if they were patrolling the area for a bit before heading off toward the south west a little. The same direction as the Big Gun.

I had to get back there sooner rather than later if I wanted to help.

Shy led me around in a wide arc, and I realized that we were slowly heading back toward a roadway, one with an old stone bridge over a small creek. There were some things discarded on the roadside.

One of those things looked a lot like a gun. A big one. Shy ran over to it, then knelt down while swishing her poncho out so that it covered most of the gun. I could still see part of her though, hands quickly moving over the blocky receiver, checking it over for damage and pulling back the bolt.

"What's that gun?" I asked.

Shy glanced up to me, then back down. I almost caught her saying something before her AI filled me in. *"Lady Shy has two specialties. Stealth, which keeps her hidden and discreet, and her weapon specialty is shotguns."*

"Shotguns?" I asked. That thing was longer than I was tall. "That's a shotgun?"

Shy looked up to me and spoke for the first time that I could actually hear. "Punt gun."

What the fuck was a punt gun? Shy answered by reaching down to a small case on the floor and carefully flipping the lid with the end of a boot. It revealed space for three shells, but two were missing. The one remaining was about as big around as my wrist. Shy picked it up with both hands, then opened a slot on the side of her gun and shoved the shell in.

She cocked the gun by pulling out a small lever from the side. Then, sitting down on the ground, she tugged back with her entire body, like a rower tugging back on a paddle.

The gun clunked.

She stood up, patted down her pants, then lifted up the entire gun, seemingly with little difficulty. "How much does that thing weigh?" I asked.

"Lady Shy's rifle weighs eight kilograms. It's mostly made of aluminum and titanium to keep its weight down."

"And that fires one fuck-big slug?" I asked.

Shy shook her head. I actually got a second word out of her. "Birdshot."

She'd taken down a model thirty-one with birdshot? That was ballsy.

"What do you usually use?" I asked. "When you're not punt-gunning things?"

Shy reached into her poncho and pulled out a smaller gun. Smaller as in only as long as her forearm, but it still had a barrel wide enough to fit a few fingers in. "Four-gauge," she said. The gun had a weird stock, but I didn't have time to examine it before she disappeared it back under her poncho.

I turned my mech around and scanned the area. It wasn't hard to spot where the model thirty-one went down. A few of its flyers were spinning circles above and there was a bit of a trench blown through the forest leading toward where I suspected it was lying.

"Let's finish this job, then I need to head back to the Big Gun, to keep it safe."

Shy nodded. *"Lady Shy understands and appreciates your need to move quickly. She also appreciates your assistance in this matter."*

"Yeah, no prob," I said. "Want me to clear the skies while you get close to the big guy and finish it off?"

Shy nodded sharply, then took off running toward the edge of the bridge. I was wondering what she was planning when she jumped up with surprising ease for someone carrying such a big gun.

Two shotguns slid out from under her poncho, held facing downward by mechanical arms that had to be attached to her back.

Then they fired and launched Shy into the air with their recoil.

"The fuck?" I muttered. Physics wasn't supposed to do that.

It seems as though she's invested in a device that lightens her own mass considerably.

So that her own shotgun shots could yeet her through the air? That . . . was not the smartest thing I'd ever seen. "Couldn't Shy buy a jump-jet pack for like, way less?"

I don't question the purchases of others.

Yeah, fair enough. I realized that I was falling behind. Shy's arc through the air was shifting. She was coming back down, her cloak and poncho fluttering around her as she came in for a hard landing. Then her guns blasted again. They were pretty quiet, though they did blow two holes into the earth behind her.

I took off running to catch up, which didn't take long. Sure, she had super-jumps on her side, but I had a big mecha.

I caught up even as I started to lock all of the flyers above into my mech's targeting software. Shy landed nearby, then nodded to me once. *"Lady Shy is going to head upward as soon as the skies are cleared and take the finishing shot."*

"Got it," I replied before flicking my Gatlings on. I checked my ammo counter and nodded. A few hundred rounds left. I'd have to order up some more soon, but this would be enough for now if I stopped the guns from free-firing and set them to only take precise shots.

I switched my 105mm guns to flak, then fired twice.

The burst ripped into the swarm, then my Gatlings started to spit out rounds, a couple per second, each one smacking a bird out of the air.

Shy knelt down close to the ground.

I checked ahead. The model thirty-one was right there, pushing itself up on the ends of its wings. Its body was riddled in long rents and a few holes. Two in particular looked like someone had attacked it for a couple of hours with a knife and great enthusiasm.

Shy's shotguns went off and she flew upward into the air. Her legs kicked at the same time, giving her that much more speed. She hung in the air, poncho and cloak fluttering behind, legs splayed out, big gun aimed downward.

There was a blast like the sky ripping itself apart, and Shy *zipped* away.

At the same time, a hole a few feet wide opened up where the model thirty-one's face had been.

I cleared out the sky, then turned toward the direction where Shy had been flung. "Hey! You good?"

"Lady Shy could use some amount of assistance."

Frowning, I ran over to where I'd seen her disappear. It didn't take too long to find her. Her poncho's stealth only worked when it covered her, and at the moment the poncho and Shy herself were both tangled in the branches of a tree.

"You need help up there?" I asked.

"..."

"Yeah, figured," I said. "So uh, I'll help you down, then leave you to it, alright?"

She slowly raised a thumbs-up.

CHAPTER SEVENTY-FIVE

THE WORTH OF A HUMAN

Studies indicate that 11 to 20 percent of veterans who served in front-
line roles experience PTSD in a given year. Likewise, 15 to 35 percent
of Antithesis conflict veterans experience PTSD within a year of their
departure from the front lines.

Data for the samurai/Vanguard is limited, but self-admitted cases of
PTSD among that group suggest that only 1 to 3 percent of samurai/
Vanguard suffer from PTSD-like symptoms.

Whether this is due to the process by which they are chosen is
uncertain.

—VA-PTSD.rd.gov, "Prevalence of Post-Traumatic Stress Disorder in the
Combat Populace," 2046

"Alright, you good?" I asked as Shy landed on the ground.

She patted her knees clear of dust, then shifted the hood of her cloak
back up and over her head. Her clothes were . . . a bit of a mess, to be honest,
but that's what happened when you were flung into a tree.

At least she was partially armored. She had a padded undersuit beneath
that poncho, with some harder-looking plates over the chest with a few little pockets here and there. Basic tactical gear stuff, and all very obviously
Protectorate-made.

"*Lady Shy wishes to reiterate that she is well.*"

"Yeah, that's good," I said as I backed my mech away from the tree she'd been
stuck in. I'd used the mech as a sort of ladder to give her something to climb
down. There were plenty of handholds in the gaps where the exterior armored
plates met. "Look, I can't sit around here for much longer. Will you be okay if I
leave you behind, or do you want to come back with me to the Big Gun?"

I didn't have a fantastic idea of how dangerous this area was, but I
guessed that it wasn't *that* bad. There hadn't been many flyers coming down
from above. Those that I did see were all shooting out in the same direction
I'd come from, and most of those were way, way up in the air.

Unless Shy here tried taking massive potshots at them, she was probably going to pass unnoticed. That meant she could probably pick out the targets she wanted.

The model thirty-one had probably been a target of opportunity for her.

I was . . . way newer as a samurai, but I'd been in the thick of it from the start. Shy here was a more normal sort, and it seemed like she'd chilling out at a lower, more reasonable tech level for a longer time. She probably had a whole life that didn't involve samurai shit.

Couldn't fault her for that. She was here now, doing her thing. Shy hopped on the spot a couple of times, dislodging a few small branches stuck to her poncho, then checked on her guns, each one rising up from under her cloak so that she could look them over. The way they moved was fluid and fast, and I suspected that she was wired into the controls for them directly.

I saw her mouth move behind her scarf a little. *"Lady Shy is thankful for your intervention, and more so for allowing her to eliminate that higher-tier model. Having said that, she doesn't require any additional assistance."*

"Cool," I said. I called over that mecha-carrier. It was hovering not too far from where I'd been dropped off. A few model ones had zipped around it, but it wasn't biological enough for them to nibble at and it wasn't hostile, so they treated it as just an obstacle and mostly left it alone.

I was sure that wouldn't be the case if a bigger, smarter model flew by, but for now it was safe enough. The carrier turned, then started moving my way at a slow, careful pace.

"If you've got any problems, just gimme a call. Your AI buddy can ping Myalis, yeah?"

Shy nodded once. She pushed her shotguns down, then gave me a small bow. Then she kind of just . . . stood there for a moment. I could feel the awkwardness wafting off her like a weird smell before she turned and scampered away. She went invisible, but that didn't hide how weird she was.

"That girl's a little strange," I muttered after shutting my exterior speakers off.

Most Vanguard fit a set of criteria that don't comply with normal human behavior. It's natural, therefore, for them to stand out as a little strange to the average person.

Normal, huh? I shook my head, then moved myself over to the side a little so that I was in a clearer spot for the carrier to come down and grab onto my mech.

Once I was clamped in, I angled toward the Big Gun and shot off in that direction. I had Myalis connect with the tactical net that we were using to coordinate our AA. In theory, we wouldn't look like a juicy alien target, but I didn't want to test it.

I was pretty sure my mech could eat a few rounds from the smaller AA guns without any real issue, but if one of those bigger rockets slammed into me, I'd be a cooked cat before long. My own 30mm guns probably had enough juice at this altitude to punch right through whatever armor my mech had, or at least mess it up.

Better safe than punctured.

On approach, I noticed a long train of Antithesis rushing toward the south. They were spread out in a long line, and most of them were flyers— model ones, a few model elevens—but there were plenty rushing along on the ground as well.

The line ended some hundred meters from the Big Gun, where a few fireteams with machine guns were ripping into them. I noticed Hedgehog, Princess and Knight there, along with Tankette in her tank. A constant barrage of mortar fire was punching holes in the formation.

I flew around. As much as I might have been tempted to land in the middle of it all, it did look like the newbies had things in hand at the moment. Dropping in now would only disrupt things, and I might get blasted in the crossfire. Better to leave them the work, and the points.

Instead I aimed for the inside of the camp and swooped in for a landing. A few soldiers were spooked, but they calmed down when they realized that it was a giant robot cat, not some large plant alien swinging down to make a meal out of them.

A quick check with Myalis revealed that Gomorrah was nearby, in one of the command rooms, though she was on her way out.

I opened the cockpit of my mech, unhooked myself from the controls, and hopped out. "Hey!" I called out.

Gomorrah changed directions slightly, heading closer to me. "You're back," she said. "Grasshopper's friend is okay?"

"Yeah. She told you about it?" I asked.

Gomorrah nodded. "I saw you leaving on the tactical net, so I asked. You should have reported it in, but that you didn't isn't too strange."

"Yeah, Shy—the samurai who needed a hand—wasn't in a terrible spot, but she was out on her own. I left her there on her own too, but I think she'll be able to figure things out."

"Good," Gomorrah said. "Things are pretty stable here. We have some Antithesis resistance moving this way, but . . . it's well organized."

"And that's good?" I asked.

"They're marching in what passes for neat rows for them," she said. "It makes it easy to rip them apart with artillery. Once the skies have cleared out some more, we'll have the air force in to reinforce us, and that'll be it for them."

That was pretty good. "So, some samurai need help?" I asked. "How's the situation overall?"

"Three casualties," she said.

"That's it?" I asked. I was sure there had to be more. Were they way underreported? With this many jugheads running around with guns and grenades, I couldn't believe that only three had died.

"Samurai casualties," she clarified.

"Ah. Are we not checking the other casualties?"

She shrugged. "Not to put too fine a point on it, but they don't quite matter as much. Not when we need every force multiplier we can get. Besides, it's hard to keep track of millions. Keeping track of some two hundred samurai is comparatively easy."

Something twisted in my gut at that, and it didn't take a bachelor's in ethics to figure out what was wrong with that entire thing. "That's kinda fucked up, Gom."

"I know," she said. "But right now, there are more samurai defending small towns and remote villages than PMCs or soldiers. I mean . . . there are more towns being defended by us than by the armed forces. They need numbers, logistics. We don't. Every one of us lost means another small town or frontier lost. It's . . . a difficult calculus if you think of every number as human, so we can't afford to."

"That's a big ask, isn't it?"

"I think it's why my religion considers us saints. It's that much easier to think of each samurai as larger than life that way." She started walking again. "I need to replenish the ammunition in some of my AA platforms. Then I'll be flying out to assist some samurai who might need it. I'd suggest that you do the same."

That sounded like a decent idea. I stretched my neck back and looked up into the sky.

It was still raining aliens, but at least it was petering out, and the clouds were returning. Soon it would be overcast as usual.

CHAPTER SEVENTY-SIX

A GIGGLE AND A ROCKET

The UFO craze started a little before the Cold War took off, and it was mostly concentrated inside the United States. Unsurprising, as at the time, the US armed forces were testing several devices that seemed alien to the lay person, and rumors of extraterrestrial sightings only masked the presence of these planes and drones.

UFO sightings gradually faded into a strange hobby for the crackpot and the conspiracy theorist until the early 2020s, when there was a sudden and powerful resurgence, one that the armies and intelligence networks of the world looked upon with growing concern.

Then we met aliens, and they weren't peaceful little green men.

—*UAPs and UFOs, the Declassifying,* 2035

I checked up on the newbies, just to be sure, but they really didn't need my help.

The team had grouped up atop one of the defensive structures around the Big Gun compound and were pretty much just having a blast messing up the Antithesis whenever they came into range.

Someone had given Princess a rocket launcher. Gros Baton was helping her load it up between shots, then she'd stand up on the wall and fire it out in the general direction of aliens that needed blowing up. The rocket was guided, which was the only reason it hit anything.

It was a little concerning, hearing her giggle so much between shots. I think she mostly liked the way that the backblast made her poofy princess dress whip out around her.

Hedgehog had picked up some new gear. His spiky armor looked different—more LED lighting, sharper spikes—and Knight was . . . just kinda chilling with her sword on her lap, waiting for the aliens to get within stabbing range.

Yeah, they didn't need my help, so I pulled back and checked on that Family-curated map of local samurai. It looked like a few of the dots had moved around a little. Some tightening in around cities, some dispersing out a little. I bet it was a real pain in the ass to herd this many samurai.

"Hey, Myalis, any areas where shit's going wrong?" I asked. There was a sort of heatmap overlay available, but I couldn't make sense of the lava lamp of colors blobbing around it. There were comments and expert analyses as well, but it was couched in the sort of technical jargon that would take me a while to parse through.

Indeed. This area here, within ten minutes' flight of your current location, has been flagged as high-risk.

A widening red circle appeared on the map northwest of the Big Gun's location. Mont-Tremblant? It was a bit past that, actually, but not by too terribly much. The map showed three grayed-out icons.

"Why are these grayed out?" I asked. Most of the other samurai icons were bright and easy to spot, except in places like where I stood, where too many of them crowded into one spot and they were all shrunk to fit.

The Family was using some generic icons for a lot of samurai, but some of them, of us, had custom logos. The three in the area looked like . . . a toe, a horse piece from a chess set, and a red dot with an L in it.

The three Vanguard in this area have failed to report in. Two are confirmed dead.

"What the fuck," I muttered. "Two of the three Gomorrah mentioned as dead are here?"

No. When she spoke earlier, all three of these Vanguard were alive and well.

So, in the space of . . . what, ten minutes? Three samurai had died. I licked my lips and zoomed in on the map a little. They'd been relatively close to each other, all arrayed out in the more mountainous range in that area. Probably for good visibility.

"What took them down?" I asked. This could be the aliens, or it could be some corpo fucks that saw an opportunity and jumped on it.

I opened a second, third, and fourth screen in my augs and quickly typed in the samurai's names. There was a wiki that kept track of things, pictures, debut dates, armaments, shit like that. At a glance, Cavalier and Track Pad Lad weren't too impressive.

Cavalier was a newer samurai, a guy who started after the global incursion, so on par with the newbies. Track Pad Lad had been around for a couple of years, but his thing was tech stuff. A sort of hacker samurai? His profile showed him very present online, but not so much in any recent incursions.

So not a super strong samurai either.

ToeJam was different. A tall, gangly-looking sort of guy, dressed like a suit from the eighties. Lots of augmentations, but they were subtle. Dude had been a samurai for a year and a bit, but he was all over the place. Incursions in the states, one in Brazil, one in Columbia. He was pretty popular in his little niche, and seemed like the kind of guy who got into trouble and then exploded himself out of it.

He was the only one not confirmed dead.

There have been few concrete reports. The Family seems curious as well, of course. A squad of elite Family troopers are on their way to investigate now.

Myalis highlighted a small trio of moving dots flying across the map from New Montreal. No samurai, so probably just a rapid response team of some sort?

"I'm going to link up with them. Can you let the Family know? If it's corpo fuckery, then we'll blow some heads off. If it's the Antithesis . . . then we'll know when we get closer, I guess." The aliens were rarely anything approaching subtle.

Message sent. It seems like you won't be alone. A Vanguard is heading to investigate as well.

"Who?" I asked.

Myalis zoomed my map out and added a line going from the south of New Montreal out toward Mont-Tremblant. The samurai's icon looked like a little shield thing.

Their name is Invincible.

"Well, that'll help," I muttered.

There wasn't any point in waiting around. The team sent by the Family was halfway there already, and they were moving pretty fast. So I checked the carrier again and took off upward.

The AA around the Big Gun site hadn't exactly gone quiet, but it was now only taking potshots at a few lingering aliens above. The swarm was spread out, but it looked like we were just dealing with the tail end of it now. Which made the dead samurai all the more suspicious.

We were so close to what I'd call a total victory, so how had these three gone and messed themselves up?

I checked what I could on the way over. The Family had good records of where alien bits had crashed, because it only made sense to track as much of that as possible. Mont-Tremblant wasn't far, not when you were coming from space and that kind of distance meant nothing, so aliens aiming for the Big Gun who were only a couple of degrees off sometimes veered toward Mont-Tremblant. More veered toward New Montreal, probably because they could see the city from orbit.

In any case, the Family's tracker showed a few coming in close. There was a whole little city up on that hill, with its own defenses and such. The samurai there had been taking out fliers that came too low since the sky started to fall.

There were records of aliens tumbling down around the area, and . . . that's all I really had to work with.

I was sure given a few hours I might be able to figure something out, but I also had a cheat that I could use. "Myalis, do we have any clues as to what actually went down?"

Are you just asking me because you're too lazy to look yourself?

"I'm not," I said indignantly. "I'm asking because you're able to figure this shit out in seconds while it'll take me hours, and we don't have hours before we arrive."

Hmm, I suppose that's fair. Let's see . . . The distribution of Antithesis in the area matches projections. It's probable that the threat that took out the Vanguard in the region was Antithesis-borne.

So, another alien fuck. Got it. I could handle that.

I ended up encountering the Family agents halfway. They were riding in a quadcopter. It was an armored box, with heavy-duty landing gear and a few small turrets mounted to the sides and bottoms of short, stubby wing-lets. The kind of thing that was probably significantly more expensive on fuel than the average hovercar, but it was also armored and a whole lot faster.

There were three of them, flying in a tight formation, so I placed myself at the rear of their flying V and enjoyed the turbulence of their backdraft.

Fortunately, it didn't take long to make it to Mont-Tremblant.

The small mountaintop city wasn't much to look at. A few skyscrapers, some resorts for the rich, and some artificially snow-covered hills for people still into skiing all year round.

There was also a lot of smoke. Craters dotted the area, and several buildings were on fire.

It looked like the local samurai hadn't gone quietly.

That left me with a bad feeling in my gut. Something bad had gone down here while all of our attention was elsewhere, and I was going to have to find out what.

CHAPTER SEVENTY-SEVEN

DEAD SAMURAI TELL NO TALES

Samurai are our saviors. Our heroes. The people we follow, the madmen and women who force the world to change.

And sometimes they die.

—President of the United States,
Silver Hoop's eulogy, 2035

The Family squad ahead of me landed on an open roadway. Three quadcopters came down with military-grade precision in the center of an intersection with their fronts turning so that they formed a sort of triangle.

I brought my mech carrier up and into the center of that formation, then let the clamps go. There was a heavy thump as my mech landed, but I was strapped in well enough that I barely felt it.

The choppers opened up at the rear and each disgorged a fireteam out onto the road, men and women in all-black armor with just a few small patches for identification.

I felt like I was getting used to working with soldiers, but these people moved differently.

I'm not sure if I could point it out, exactly, but it was ... tighter? More practiced? They glided out of the rides, guns sweeping around as they scanned everything. They all had identical equipment, at least as a base. Small, stubby SMGs strapped to their sides and a much larger rifle as their primary.

I couldn't see anything about the soldiers, though. They had face-covering helmets with nubs for night vision and thermal sensors, and full-body armor on. They looked like the kind of troops elite corporations would use to send a message.

They formed a circle around my mech, every other soldier dropping to a knee and facing outward. The worst part was how damned quiet they were about it.

Incoming message. The squad leader wants you to connect to their group communication network.

"Let's do it," I said.

A moment later, someone spoke up. Male, from the voice, scratchy and rough. "Samurai Stray Cat," he said. "I'm One. Good to have you here with us."

"Pleasure's all mine, One," I said.

I had no idea which one of them One was. The soldiers had little patches on them, but there weren't any easily readable numbers. At least, not from my angle. "Are you here for the same reason as we were dispatched?" One asked.

"Yeah, probably. Three samurai downed in this area. ToeJam might still be alive, and the other two are apparently dead. I intend to find out what happened. If it's aliens, we kill them. If it's some corpo-meddling, uh, the same."

None of the soldiers reacted to that, not even a twitch or a nod. I did notice that a couple of them had some cybernetics. A pair of metallic legs here, some arms that bent in strange ways there.

The quadcopters rose up, then shifted away as one. It looked like we might have some air superiority as long as they hung around, but they were also moving far enough above that it might take a moment.

I sent my carrier out to wait near them, and that left me and all of my silent new soldier friends standing around in absolute silence.

"Acknowledged, Home," One said. I had the impression he wasn't talking to me. "Samurai Stray Cat, our missions align. We're moving to the last known location of Samurai ToeJam to secure him and proceed with medevac. Teams Bravo and Charlie, scouts to LKL of Cavalier and Track Pad Lad. Go!"

Two soldiers knelt down and dropped their packs to the floor, as well as their rifles. In seconds they'd pulled out long hooded cloaks and wrapped them around themselves. I heard the faint click of buckles being clipped together, then they went semi-transparent.

It wasn't nearly as good as what I had, or even Shy's invisibility, but it wasn't bad, and it looked like it wasn't Protector tech either.

The two took off in a rapid sprint in two different directions, and the way they moved and bounced up onto rooftops . . . Yeah, they weren't running on human 1.0 hardware.

The rest of the soldiers formed up into three small groups. I had a seven-man squad ahead, and two six-men ones on either side. "Moving," One said, and they all started to walk forward down the road.

I pushed my mech to move after them, then quickly activated some of the sound stealth stuff I had. My mech had "ears" on the exterior, to let me have a good sense of what was going on around it, but even with that I could only barely tell that there were people there. They moved at a slow, careful walk, their center of gravity held low, their guns pressed to their shoulders.

I'd seen army soldiers clearing Saint-Jérome out. They wished they could move with this much smoothness.

"Do we know where ToeJam is?" I asked.

"No," One said. "Tacnet suggests he's one hundred and fifty-five meters ahead. Eyes peeled."

Well alright, Mister Tightwad. I wanted to grumble a little, but this guy had his shit together, and so did the rest of this bunch. Honestly, looking at this group kind of made me feel antsy. Their guns looked good, their armor was top-shelf, and they looked like they knew what they were doing.

How would this bunch match up against the average samurai? Probably pretty well. What set us apart was that I had access to all the toys. Cool toys were one hell of a force multiplier, but I was still feeling like . . .

I guess it was like when I played something like ping-pong against the kids. We'd had a table for a bit at the orphanage where I grew up, and I got semi-decent at it. It was fun playing against the little shits and showing off, even if they had the advantage of two arms and sometimes bigger, less-shitty paddles. This was the other way around, I supposed.

Now I had the big paddle, currently in the form of my fuck-you mecha, and they had the experience.

Well, whatever. I kept my eyes peeled, like One asked.

Mont-Tremblant was a nice place. The apartment buildings we were walking next to were all modern, square things with flat roofs and large windows opening up to a pretty nice view of some hilly landscape.

A few of those buildings looked like they'd been fucked right up by something large. I saw some flying model corpses splattered here and there too. There'd been some fighting in this area, but it looked . . . pretty light? I wasn't an expert, but from personal experience, heavier fighting usually involved a lot more property destruction.

"Confirmed," One said. "Charlie scout has found Track Pad Lad. Confirmed KIA."

"Fuck," I muttered. "Any idea what did him in?"

There was a decently long pause before One replied. "C-Five, tell us what you can about the mark's condition?"

A second voice joined in, the scout that I presumed was C-Five. They sounded feminine, a little, but I might have been off the mark. "They've been dead for at least twenty minutes. Possible exsanguination. I see several lacerations across their chest, armor was penetrated. Arms are both broken, legs might be as well. Lower torso was crushed."

"Fuck," I said. A shiver ran down my spine. It was . . . clinical, but I could still imagine it. "Their gear?"

"Mark's gear is still present. Armor is heavily compromised. Weapons . . . seem intact. Mid-caliber assault rifle and unknown Protector tech. Can't divine the state of their electronic gear."

I nodded. If it was all still there, then I could probably rule out a corporation being at fault. Plus, no mention of bullet holes or explosive damage. Rents and crushing was more an Antithesis way of doing shit.

I was still walking along with the soldiers, so I noticed when they all suddenly tensed and stopped moving.

"What's going on?" I asked. I did a sensor sweep, but nothing strange came up.

"B-Five is down," One said.

B-Five had to be the other scout, the one who'd been sent to find Cavalier. "Where?" I asked.

My map pinged, and I found two pins had been added to it. One was the location of Track Pad Lad, the other Cavalier's last known location. B-Five's location was also there, a little dotted line showing them traveling over, then circling around the body before moving in . . . then getting thrown way the fuck back.

Unless they'd gained a lot of speed all of a sudden, it looked almost like they'd been ejected out of the area.

"Change in objective," One said. "Alpha Medic, take Alpha Two and Three, rendezvous with ToeJam."

Three of the soldiers, including one with a slightly bigger pack that had a discreet red cross on it, took off at a fast jog.

"Alpha squad, on the samurai. We're keeping her safe. Bravo, vanguard, Charlie, take point."

The group rearranged itself in an instant and I had to do a little step-dance to get my mech facing the right direction. I wasn't liking this whole "not being in charge" thing, but as the group started forward with a bit more pep in their step, I figured it might come in handy to have a bunch of dudes with guns around when shit went down.

CHAPTER SEVENTY-EIGHT

YOU ARE BEING HUNTED

Stay safe out there, okay?
—Cavalier's wife, 2057

Cavalier's last known location was just ahead, near a sort of . . . I think it might have been a resort? There was definitely a restaurant to one side, with a large patio that was partially covered, as well as a dining room inside. To the side of that was a parking lot and then a fancy store that looked like it exclusively sold skiing gear. Both were connected at the rear to a long, low building with a covered walkway on the exterior.

From the look of the cars left in the lot, this was the kind of place that was a little expensive for my blood.

The entire area felt crooked. Probably because it was on the side of a pretty steep hill, and the ground was pretty sharply angled.

The group of soldiers I was tailing slowed down, then one of them in the group ahead raised a fist, and they came to a complete halt. I did the same, taking the moment to scan the area.

It didn't take long to see what had caught their attention.

There was a mechanical horse in the parking lot. It had been left on its side, bits and pieces of its mechanical innards flung around and its armor-plated side ripped apart.

That wasn't the only sign of a fight. Several cars here were dented and crushed. Windows shattered, tires punctured. It looked like something big had crashed onto them, but whatever that was, it was gone now.

"Samurai Stray Cat," One said. His voice coming out of nowhere made me jump a little in my seat.

"Yeah?" I asked.

"Our tech operator noticed some light scrambling over our secured comms. Can you confirm?"

I frowned. Scrambling? As in, someone trying to fuck with our communications system? I had a thing for that. Buried somewhere in my augs was an app thing that would let me check signal strength and whatnot. "Gimme a moment," I said.

He's not incorrect. There is a faint amount of interference. Look.

Myalis popped open a screen, and on it was what looked like the wave . . . thing of the conversation I'd just had with One. She highlighted some bits, little parts that looked slightly off.

"I don't have the degrees to figure that out," I admitted.

It's very light. Faint, even. From experience, I believe that you're in an area with a physical signal jammer in the air, but the quantity has decreased enough to make it negligible. I'm impressed that anyone even noticed.

I nodded. That could have been something one of the samurai here used, maybe? I could see a few reasons to want to jam signals. "Looks like your tech guy was right," I said to One. "There's some sort of signal jammer thing. Myalis, my AI, says it's a physical jammer."

"Understood. Switch to AP."

The soldiers took turns, two by two, to pull out their magazines and replace them with new ones. AP? That had to mean armor-penetrating, but why?

We continued our approach, but this time at a slow walk. The soldiers spread out a little until there was nearly a meter between each of them and they had formed up into a sort of grid. I stayed in the center. Moving so slowly was actually kind of awkward in my mech, but it was doable.

"Approaching, one contact, friendly," One said.

There was a whistle and I looked up in time to see a black speck in the distance grow much closer. As it did, it also grew louder until the form resolved itself into a man. A man covered in an entire fuckload of armor.

He had two large turbines stuck to his back on a pair of metal wings. They shifted and twisted, blasting air out in different directions to stabilize his flight. It threw up dust and snow-covered leaves until he kicked the flight system off some five meters above ground and came crashing down.

His knees barely bent.

"Invincible! Here to bring the pain!" he said.

Invincible was wearing as much armor as one of Tankette's tanks, but it was enveloping him in the form of a thick suit. His head was encased in a steel half-dome with slits on the front, and his arms and legs were almost as thick around as my mech's. The suit made him eight feet tall, so I imagined that the actual Invincible was probably buried deep in there.

"Yo," I said through my external speakers. "We, uh, were trying to be discreet."

I don't know how, exactly, but with just a few subtle shifts, Invincible managed to look a little embarrassed. "Oh," he said.

"Yeah," I replied.

"Samurai Invincible," One said. I *still* didn't know which soldier he was in the bunch, and at this point it would have been humiliating to ask. "Adding you to our comms channel. We recently lost a unit in this location while they were investigating the loss of Samurai Cavalier."

Invincible half-turned, then he spotted the wrecked mecha-horse thing. "I see," he said before stomping closer.

I moved up, just a little more. Not so much that I broke formation, though. I hadn't noticed because of the angle we came in at, but that horse had a rider. Most of the rider was still there.

I wasn't easily disgusted, but I still felt a little queasy at what I saw there. The lower half of some guy in plate armor was stuck in the saddle. The body left off about halfway up the waist. "Fuck," I whispered. That had to be Cavalier. Or their lower half, at least. No sign of the rest of them.

Two of the soldiers moved up, one of them sweeping the area while the other knelt down next to the body. They inspected it, calmly and professionally, then raised their head up and said something that I couldn't hear.

"Understood," One replied. "No signs of modern weaponry use. They died from a bite."

"*A* bite?" I asked.

What hell could bite a person clean in half like that? Through plate armor and all? "I'm calling the choppers in closer. We might need close air support."

"I'm picking something up," Invincible said. He stomped toward the building, heedless of the rest of us behind him. "I've got some pretty good scanning tech. There's something warm in there."

"Form up!" One snapped.

The soldiers ran ahead, some of them moving to place themselves behind cars, others taking a knee at the rear. I moved up as well, skirting around Cavalier's body as I followed Invincible forward.

I was just about to ask if Invincible was certain when the man froze up for a moment. Then his arms opened up, revealing small barrels that aimed out below his forearms. "Bug!" he shouted.

I looked ahead just in time to see a set of four large eyes opening *inside* that big ski shop. Then the front of the store exploded outward. There was a split second, just a fraction of a fraction, shorter than a blink, where I had time to process what I was seeing.

I'd once fought a model twenty-three back in Burlington. That thing had been a T-rex on steroids. Big fucking head, lots of muscle, fuckloads of mass to throw around, and it had been *mean*. Mean but kinda stupid.

What I was looking at now was a little larger, but also a lot more sinuous. The little monkey part of my brain that got spooked when it saw anything snakelike was shitting itself. And then I made out the fact that this thing had eight legs behind it, long spidery ones that blended in almost too well with the background.

I didn't like it.

I liked it even less as it rushed out of the storefront.

The soldiers opened up on it, as did Invincible.

The nightmare fuel monster's neck snapped out like a striking cobra and it clamped its teeth around the samurai and *squeezed.*

I heard the whine of metal bending even as Invincible screamed, barely audible over the constant roar of gunfire.

I shook myself into action, leapt forward, and swiped at the thing's neck. Somehow, the soldiers shifted all of their aim in time to miss me while still punching rounds into the thing. My claws struck nothing but air as the massive spider-monster scuttled back into the shop and tore through the back wall.

The gunfire stopped.

"Reload," One ordered. "Charlie Four is down."

I glanced to the side. One of the soldiers looked like his chest had been punched through by something big. He was just slumped there. When had that even happened?

"What the fuck was that?" I asked to anyone who'd be willing to answer as I scanned around me. There was no sign of the fucker, just one dead soldier and Invincible crunched up a little.

That was a model thirty-three. It is a hunter. You are being hunted.

CHAPTER SEVENTY-NINE

MORE THAN THE MACHINE

This is a world where your value as a human doesn't contribute to your own happiness, but to the wealth of others.
It's inevitable.
The only thing you can do is make them as miserable as you.
—Mario Russo, the CEO Bomber, 2029

"Eyes open!" One snapped. It was the first time he'd sounded actually concerned. "Medic, check on Charlie Four."

A soldier ran over to the dead man on the ground, but . . . yeah, there wasn't much that could be done there. That dude was very dead. Then they surprised me by taking apart the upper chest section of Charlie Four's armor. A few disconnected bits later, and the medic had Charlie Four's head entirely removed and was placing it into a foldable bag.

A cyborg? Not just a minor one either, but a full-body conversion? Fuck, that was something I didn't see often.

I shook my head and refocused. The Family's guys might have been the most badass fucks I'd ever seen, but that didn't help us now. One of them had still gone down to that model thirty-three and it didn't look like we'd hurt it much.

"Invincible, you okay?" I asked. I was practically standing on top of him.

"Yeah . . . more or less?" he grunted as he tried to sit up, then fell back down. "Oh, fuck, I think I broke a rib. One sec . . . yeah, my AI says I broke two, and my clavicle, and some bones in my hand."

"You'll live?" I asked.

He muttered something that I couldn't make out, and a box thumped to the ground next to him. Then the back of his armor opened up slightly and a small four-legged drone fell out and ran over to the box. It returned with what looked like a Nano-Regenerative Suite that it climbed into his armor with. "I'll live," he confirmed.

That drone wasn't a bad idea. "Myalis, gimme . . . six cat drones. Cheap ones. We need to find where that thing went. And maybe . . . can you equip them with a little surprise? Some HE bombs or something?"

Certainly. Six cat drones coming right up.

They were delivered in three boxes with flaps on the sides. No one chose to comment on how they looked a little like a cat carrier. The sides opened and a gaggle of little cat drones darted out. They had small cylinders on their backs, covered in yellow-and-black warning stripes.

One of the screens in my mech flicked over to a six-square view of what the drones were seeing. "One, you got visual on that thing?" I asked.

"No," he replied. "We're bringing our quadcopters down to get a better picture of the area. Our electronics aren't picking anything up."

I frowned. There was some fuzz in his speech, like he had a bad mic or something. "Myalis, is it me or is there something fucking with the comms?"

You're correct. There's more interference than there was previously.

I looked around, and finally noticed that there was probably more dust in the air than could easily be attributed to the alien crashing through the walls of that shop. The damned thing had spewed out dust all over, then, something that messed with electronics? That seemed possible. It could also be something to help its stealth. I'd noticed it going all chameleon on us when it pushed out the back of the store.

"Can you give me a rundown of a model thirty-three's abilities?" I asked.

Certainly. They're generally considered a hunter-type model. They have higher-than-average intelligence.

"For an Antithesis?" I asked.

No. Just in general.

"Ah."

They have relatively decent stealth capabilities and can regulate their temperature as well as turn their skin different colors and textures. Not so different from some octopi. Other than that, the model has an average amount of strength for a model in the third tier, with average durability but excellent self-healing abilities. Given a few hours, a model thirty-three that is near death can essentially regrow itself.

Well, damn. "We need to find this thing fa—"

One of the screens to my right went dark. A split second later I heard a loud *boom*, and a plume of dust rose out from maybe a block away.

I switched to the same channel as One and the other soldiers. "Looks like it found one of my drones," I said.

My cat drones moved in closer and came upon a street with a new crater blown out of the middle. There were a few bits of alien goop around, but no big corpse. The five remaining drones started to run around the area, searching front yards and scanning the fronts of ritzy apartment buildings.

One spoke up. "Let's move into the area. This position isn't defensible. I'd rather keep moving."

"Got it," I said.

"Yeah, sure," Invincible replied. He sounded a little shaken up from it all, but I didn't blame him. That had been a close call. If that thing had a better set of jaws or his armor hadn't been as good, then he'd be mulch right now.

The soldiers formed up again. The quickest way to the next block over was just down the street, then around and up another steep street. The block was higher than where we were, with a guardrail overlooking the shops and resort in some spots.

The troops moved at a slow, careful pace, guns pointing ahead, steps measured and deliberate. I could almost imagine them breathing slowly and steadily. They were pretty brave, I'd give them that. Their guns looked decent, but they'd barely scratched that big thing. If I was them, I'd be about to quit unless I was given a rocket launcher.

The quadcopters flew in closer until one was hovering just a couple dozen meters above. The other two stayed a bit farther back.

I noticed motion on one of my drone cameras, then faster motion as it was picked up and *thrown*.

"Careful!" I shouted.

The cat drone was flung into the air, right at the quadcopter. It . . . harmlessly flew past. I was expecting a big explosion, but I supposed that bombs were generally a little safer than that.

The choppers above were able to trace the area the drone had come from. Within seconds a trio of missiles were screaming across the air to ram into the side of an apartment building with an explosion that burst windows and scattered concrete.

The soldiers dipped to a knee as debris flew past, then the choppers opened up with some machine guns, peppering the space where the model thirty-three had been with massive figure-eights.

Another drone went dead, and I realized that it wasn't where they were shooting.

But it was closer.

"Left!" I shouted.

I turned, scanning the area. It was one of the troopers who saw it first, a vague form in the dust that was rushing our way. He opened fire on it only to be rammed aside by a long, sinuous tail tipped in bony barbs.

I ripped into it with my Gatlings, and then it was right there in front of me.

I stepped back, out of the way of its snapping jaws, then swiped out with my forepaws, the claws on it hissing as their mini–Void Terminus blades swallowed the air.

The monster shifted to the side so fucking fast it was almost just an afterimage.

Invincible fired his under-arm guns, then grunted as he was rammed aside to land on his ass.

The troopers opened fire in earnest, but their gunfire cut off quickly. The damned thing was in the middle of our formation, and we were all in each other's crossfire.

I hopped back and to the side, lining up my 105mm guns even as my mech's railgun warmed up.

The moment the crosshair was lined up, I fired.

In that same moment, the monster leapt.

A single shell caught it in the lower stomach, between two of its rear legs. The other rammed into one of the buildings down the road and blew it up.

Alien giblets were tossed all over the place, but the fucker landed on its remaining five legs and then shot toward me.

I gasped as its massive jaw clamped down around my mech's head, then winced as a dozen damage alerts rang out.

My Gatlings turned, and I opened up on its face.

I saw its eyes pop like overfilled water balloons, but the moment my Gatlings had passed, they started to regrow.

Myalis had severely under-described its healing.

I reached up with one paw even as the model thirty-three lifted my front off the ground. I buried the paw into its guts, and I could tell that its insides were being siphoned through the portal-tipped claws.

We'd see if it could live with no insides!

"Samurai Stray Cat!" One shouted. "The edge!"

The edge?

Then I realized what he meant as the alien gave a shove and my world spun over. I was falling backward, the guardrail doing fuck and all to stop me from tumbling back.

But I grabbed the bastard anyway, unloaded both 105s into the sky with a spray of alien innards, then pulled it down with me.

The crash shook my everything. Fortunately, it was only one floor down.

Unfortunately, the model thirty-three was still chewing on my mech's head.

"Fucker!" I yelled as I opened up with the railgun.

I couldn't see, but I was pretty sure it now had a hole in its middle large enough for me to crawl through.

And yet it was still alive and eating me. I struggled. One Gatling was just gone, ripped off at some point. My 105s were throwing up warnings. My tail was caught. My forelimbs were scrambling against the alien's underside . . .

Then it bit down *harder*. I screamed as teeth started to poke through the walls of my cabin.

Fucker was trying to eat me!

My mech went on the fritz, because it wasn't designed to be a fucking chew toy.

But I knew exactly where the bastard's head was, didn't I?

"Myalis, is the head weak?

Its brain is in its head, at the very rear, near the neck joint.

I unstrapped myself after moving my mech's legs to hold on tighter. I almost stumbled out of the control seat as things shook. The walls ground down, Antithesis teeth moving in a few more millimeters.

But I knew, more or less, where its brain was. My drones gave me an okay picture from the outside. It didn't look good, but . . .

I pulled my sword up, unsheathed it with some difficulty, then pressed the tip onto the front of my cockpit even as I shifted myself around so that I had one foot over my headrest and the other bent down before me.

"Fuck you!" I roared.

The cockpit filled with the hiss of the void.

I pushed.

The sword stabbed through my mech's armor like it wasn't there until the hilt met the glowing inside of my cockpit.

The alien froze up.

There was a long, long moment where I wondered if I'd just stabbed my own mech for nothing. Then the teeth clenching slowly loosened, and I shut my sword off in a hurry as that meant nothing was holding my mech in place anymore.

CHAPTER EIGHTY

NO COUNTRY FOR OLD CATS

Die young. It's not worth it, being old.
—Slogan of the Young Bloods, PMC group, 2051

"Myalis, is that thing dead?" I asked.

Death confirmed. Points deposited.

"How many?" I asked even as I allowed myself to slump back. There was some crap on my seat that dug into my back. Oh, and I could see the sunlight through the walls of my mech, which meant that shit had been way closer than I liked.

You received two thousand points for the elimination of that model thirty-three.

That was it? Then again, a chunk of that was split with Invincible. Maybe even ToeJam, if he'd damaged it and survived. Which meant that big fucker was worth a *heap* of points.

Probably less than what it would cost to fix my mech.

There was a shushing followed by a pop over the comms. "Samurai Stray Cat?" someone asked. Young, male, still kind of gruff-sounding.

"Who's this?" I asked. I hadn't switched channels. Unless something got knocked around?

"This is Two. One is injured and I'm taking command in his stead. Can you confirm that you're well?" Two asked.

Very imaginative names, this bunch. "I'm alive," I said. "And not injured. My mech's another story. The alien's dead, but feel free to empty a few more rounds in the fucker if it so much as twitches."

"Understood. Samurai Invincible and our team are coming around to assist you."

I grunted, then reached over and grabbed one of the screens that showed my drone's visuals. From above, it looked like . . . well, like I'd tumbled down the side of a short cliff with a fuck-large spider-velociraptor and crashed through the roof of a store.

I shifted until I was sitting back down, then I reached over and tapped into my mech's diagnostics.

There was more red than I'd ever seen before. But . . . well, the mech was made tough. I knew, because I'd opened it up a few times and fiddled around with its insides. I also had a passingly decent idea of exactly how much of a pain in the ass fixing all the errors being thrown up would be.

I got my feet into place and grabbed the yoke, then started to extricate myself from the alien's body.

It was larger than my mech, kinda. The thing had a relatively small central body, but its legs went on for days. I chopped off a leg with my mech's claws to get it to let go, and then all I had to figure out was how to climb out of the wreckage.

We'd fallen right through the roof of . . . was this a snowmobile dealership? There were a few crunched up next to some ATVs. The lights in half the shop were down. There was almost enough room for my mech to stand there.

Crawling my mech down onto its belly, I made for the exit, then shoved right through the safety glass.

Once my mech was out, I had it stand up tall and pulled the latch to open the cockpit.

Fuck-all happened.

"Yeah, figured," I muttered. The cockpit was all chewed up. Something was probably jammed into something else and now it wasn't opening up like it should. I bent down a little, then gave the roof a few swift kicks. Something crunched and the top moved up a little.

Enough that when I pulled the release again, it screeched upward and opened most of the way before getting caught on something.

I cursed as I left the cockpit and sat up atop my mech.

It looked like the alien had gone for the face. Honestly, that was for the best. There were lots of delicate, probably expensive sensors in there, but it was otherwise mostly for show. Then it had tried chewing on the mech's neck, the top of it, where on an animal there would be a lot of important nerves and the start of its spine, and on my mech I had my cockpit.

There were punctures in the armor large enough for me to fit my thumb into. Armor meant to take small-arms fire like rain off a windshield. A few bits were crunched in, and I winced as I ran a hand over a plate that was bent almost in half.

That was going to be a bitch to replace.

I saw some of those Family troopers making their way over. Just a few of them though. A look upward showed the rest of them camping out up the road. They were taking care of their injured as one of those quadcopters came down gently nearby.

"Do you need help, ma'am?" one of the troopers asked.

"Nah, I'm good," I said. I continued to climb over my mech, checking it over from above. The side-mounted guns were mostly fine. I had a few errors thrown up about them, but that was probably just some damage from the fall.

I'd need to check into it. I did grab one sensor mounted over the gun and gave it a shake, only for it to wobble. It was . . . not supposed to wobble. I groaned, then allowed myself to slide off the side of the mech to land in a crouch.

I was still connected to it via my augs, so I had the mech turn on its camo, only to wince harder. Lots of scratches and dents and places where the optical coating was screwed up.

By the time I was finished going around it twice and poking what was pokable, I heard Invincible thumping his way down the road. "You got scratched up too?" he asked.

I glanced back and up. The dude's armor was partially peeled back, revealing the kind of square-jawed face that would fit right in on a meme post about Chads and virgins. The bloody gashes and bruised cheekbones kinda added to it.

Frankly, I found it a little off-putting, but even I could admit he was traditionally handsome. "I'm alright," I said. "Might have a new bruise or two, but I'll live. My mech . . . eh."

He nodded. "That's gonna cost a point or two to replace."

I let out a sigh. "Yeah, I'm afraid that's what it might come to." I could sit this one in the garage and tinker with it, though. Maybe build something for like, a very specific loadout?

"Shit happens," Invincible said. He reached down to a plate on his chest and tapped it open, revealing a small compartment. He pulled out a small cardboard pack, bit something out of it, then tucked it away and reached for one of those old-timey hotel-style match boxes. He lit up, then grabbed his fresh cigar and gestured to my mech with it. "You gonna scrap that?"

"Nah, I'll keep it to fix," I said. "Second, I'd love to chat but . . . any of you know if ToeJam is alright? And the troopers up there? Shit happened in a blur and I didn't see if anyone was too badly hurt."

One of the soldiers, whose voice I recognized as Two, spoke up. "Three minor casualties. One fatality," he said.

"Well, fuck," I said.

That was a lot of dead to one rampaging alien.

Actually . . . that one alien had fucked up three samurai, played with Invincible here like he was a chew toy, and took just about everything I had to put down.

I shuddered. It was hitting me, suddenly, how close I'd come to adding another notch to the number of samurai it killed.

"Myalis, can I have something real incendiary?" I asked.

A few moments later, the corpse was burning up. So was the back of that shop, but I figured they probably had fire insurance, and I handed out a couple of anti-fire 'nades to the troopers, in case shit got out of hand.

It might have been a slight waste of points, but I wanted to make sure there wasn't anything left of that piece of crap.

One of the quadcopters came down further in, then shot off in a hurry in the general direction of New Montreal. "ToeJam has been evacuated," Two said. "There's a second team coming in to gather our KIA and secure the area. The Family wishes to offer its gratitude for your assistance."

"Yeah, no prob," I said.

"That's what family's for," Invincible said with a dark chuckle. He puffed out a little more smoke, then dropped the cigar and stomped it flat. "Nice meeting you, Stray Cat. I'm gonna get back to a safe space, have my bones checked, then head out again."

"Alright," I said. "Nice to meet you too. Uh, see you around."

He nodded seriously. "It's a small world."

Weird guy. I glanced at my mech, then the area. It was . . . safe-ish. So sticking around wouldn't be helping anything. And heading back out . . . well, that wasn't gonna happen with my main weapons platform in this kind of state.

"Fuck me, I'm gonna have to spend points again, aren't I?"

Hurrah.

I rolled my eyes at Myalis's sarcastic cheer, but I had the impression she wasn't displeased about it.

CHAPTER EIGHTY-ONE

TOUCH ME . . .

And so we discover that technology is sufficiently advanced, that what we understood was but a mere fraction of the whole, and that our instincts are nothing but fumbles in the dark.

What a time to live in, when there is so much to see in a world where mankind is introduced to the first true light, even if it may be of another's making!

—Professor Le Guin, 2038

I ended up asking the Family if they could spare a ride back to the Big Gun. My mech was loaded onto the carrier, with a bit of difficulty, and sent off toward home. I'd given the carrier instructions to park itself out on the porch, for ease of access later. I would move the mech into the garage when I got home and could supervise it a little. Maybe it was time I bought a mechanic's catalog and a few jacks and . . . one of those big fork things that they used to lift cars up, but for mechs.

I'd expected the Family to let me ride in one of their quadcopters, but instead they flew over a speedy little APC strapped on with some jet engines. It landed nearby, and I waved goodbye to the troopers still securing the area.

It was back to the Big Gun for me.

Sitting down in the otherwise empty APC felt strange. I was drained. Maybe it was the adrenaline finally sinking, or the long-ass day finally starting to weigh on me, but whatever it was, I felt like I hadn't slept in three days.

I wasn't physically tired, just . . . my brain felt a little buzzed out, and not in a pleasant way.

I stifled a yawn as the APC came in for a landing and I stood up and grabbed onto an overhead handle for stability.

There was a moment where I got a good view of the Big Gun site from above. The wave of aliens rushing toward us looked like it had petered out to nothing, but not without leaving some signs.

There was a trench of craters and burn scars a few kilometers long reaching from the base way out into the countryside. It was filled with small bits and pieces of aliens.

The newbies had been having fun, it seemed. A few larger corpses were tossed around there too, but nothing even in the twenties.

The *Fury* was parked nearby, so the moment the APC set down, I hopped off and started to search. I hadn't thought about what might have happened to Gomorrah, to my friends, while I was busy with that thirty-three, but what if that hadn't been the only samurai-killer out there today?

My shoulders slumped a little in relief when I found Gomorrah, mask off, sitting near the Big Gun's command room. She was talking to Emoscythe, and both of them were holding paper coffee cups.

"Cat," Gomorrah said when she saw me. "You're back late."

"Huh? Oh, yeah," I said. "Did you hear what happened?"

She frowned faintly, then shook her head. "No? I just returned."

"You look like you've seen a ghost," Emoscythe said. How she knew that when I was still wearing a helmet, I had no idea.

"I had a close call. Two samurai died to one alien, and a third was messed up. Got there and, uh, ran into one I'd never seen before."

"Thirties or higher?" Emoscythe asked.

"Fuck me, I don't know if I could handle something higher than the thirties now," I said honestly.

She shrugged. "Saturation bombardment cures many ills. What did you run into, exactly?"

"A model thirty-three," I said. "Weird spider-dino looking fucker. It chewed my mech up pretty good. Injured this other samurai I'd never met called Invincible."

"I heard of him," Gomorrah said. "He's Family through and through. I don't think he's from New Montreal. Somewhere further south. New York, maybe."

I shrugged. "He got injured a little too. But he'll live."

"Close calls happen," Emoscythe said. "It's why we're paid the big bucks. The little Antithesis? Any properly organized army could take care of them. It's the bigger ones that need special attention, and that's why we're always valuable and tolerated. The praise and fame and such is just good PR on top of that."

"Sure," I said, because who was I to deny her? "How about you?" The last was directed to Gomorrah.

"A few newer samurai needed some help. The larger flying units need special attention to be taken out, sometimes. Gear that not everyone has access to yet. In any case, it wasn't anything too bad?"

"Yeah," I said with a nod.

Gomorrah stared at me for a moment. "I've got things here handled, Cat," she said. "Go home."

"Huh? Nah, I'm sure there's still shit to take care of," I said. I still hadn't gotten any news about Phobos, or, like, the wider situation. What if I was needed on some flank somewhere? Or another mean fuck like that model thirty-three showed up?

"It's fine," Gomorrah said. "I've got it handled. Come back in the morning. At a reasonable hour for once, and we'll see what needs to be done. I imagine we're going to need a massive debrief."

"And a funeral," Emoscythe said. "Heroes deserve to be put to rest in glory and with all due honor. No one wants to die and be forgotten, even if they're dying for a respectable cause. And it's just good optics. We'll need a cenotaph worthy of the event."

"Cenotaph?" I repeated.

"An empty tomb," Emoscythe explained. "A monument for the lost. Something physical and tangible that marks out the space where they were. There are a few dotted across the world now, honoring common people who rose up, soldiers who picked up arms, and samurai who made the final sacrifice in order to keep one more human alive." She smiled. "I always enjoyed them."

"I'm sure they make for great places for a date," I said before I sighed. "Yeah, I uh, I might need a few hours of shut-eye, I think? Been running on fumes and not enough sleep and there's been a lot to stress about."

"It should be better now," Gomorrah said. "There isn't a moon being flung our way anymore. Things should return to something approaching normalcy in the coming weeks."

"The curse of living in interesting times, eh?"

"You said it," Gomorrah replied.

I patted her on the shoulder, then gestured toward my bike, still parked off in one corner. "I'll get home then. Call me if there's an emergency?"

"I'll do that, don't worry," Gomorrah said.

We didn't exactly say goodbye as I trudged over to my bike and climbed on. I just sat there for a moment, not even turning it on.

Do you want me to call ahead to Lucy?

"Huh? No, it's okay," I said. The question was enough to kick me into gear. I turned the bike on, then rose up and over the Big Gun site. I did a quick turn around the space, just making sure, but most of what I saw were soldier types sitting back and resting, some of them shoveling up shell casings and others just laying back on the ground, their fatigues covered in sweat.

I aimed south, toward New Montreal, and kicked the throttle down. I made good time, but it was one of those flights where as soon as I arrived home I wasn't sure if I'd really registered anything between A and B.

I brought my bike down on the top floor landing, sliding in under the awning just as the sky started to open up again with another New Montreal downpour.

I didn't know if that was a good sign or not, but I was too tired to question it as I walked in.

Lucy was by the entrance. She was glaring. "What happened?" she asked.

I shucked my helmet off, then tossed my coat onto a rack by the door. My guns and such I dropped nearby. One of the robotic cats showed up and picked them up in its mouth, then wandered off with them. It was probably for the best that someone was making sure none of the kittens got their hands on a rifle.

"Hey," I said at last, trying on a smile.

Lucy came closer, got onto the tips of her toes, then gave me a kiss. "Hey," she said.

I melted a little, but that was before I noticed that Lucy was holding something. It was a bottle, with one of those spray nozzle things at the top. "What's that for?" I asked.

"You almost died," she said.

"I was fine," I said.

Lucy raised the spray bottle, and before I could react, spritzed me in the face.

"Ah! Lucy, what the fuck?"

"I'm sorry, Cat, but it's for your own good," she said. She legitimately sounded sorry too.

"What's for my own good?" I asked.

"You're point-pinching too much, Cat. I won't lose you because you're unable to buy stuff to keep yourself safe."

"I've bought plenty of stu—Ah! Stop it!" I squeaked as she spritzed me again.

"Not until you take better care of yourself, Cat! It's for your own good!"

Somehow, we ended up on the floor, then in bed, then on the floor again.

CHAPTER EIGHTY-TWO

TILL I CAN GET MINE

Generally, over the course of a samurai's lifespan as a samurai, you'll see them shift a lot in their purchasing patterns, though some stick to a single pattern.

There are some who never have any points remaining, as they spend them as soon as they gain them. Others save up, or try to reach a certain ceiling, then once they've reached it, they cease all expenditures until they're ready for the next leap upward.

—*On the Spending Habits of the Samurai*, sixth edition, 2054

The next day was . . . quiet.

It wasn't like I could afford to do nothing, but nothing is exactly what I did. I think I slept a solid ten hours, grabbing Lucy close and not letting her go, even when she complained sleepily about having to get up.

I couldn't sleep without her next to me, and . . . I didn't want to admit it, but maybe that close call had rattled me a little. Having Lucy in my arms reminded me that I was alive. As long as Lucy was breathing, then I'd be living too.

I still woke up early, at the kind of hour that Gomorrah would have praised me for. I got up, finally letting Lucy waddle off to the washroom with some grumbled complaints that had me smiling, at least a little.

After loading up on coffee as a decent replacement for breakfast, I slipped on some bunny-eared flip-flops and made my way down to the garage. I'd ordered the cat carrier to bring my mech down there, with the help of my repair drone.

My mech was waiting for me in the corner of the garage. I stared at it while gently sipping at my coffee. "Yeah, still looks fucked," I said.

It is in dire need of repair. But I am rather confident that you could do it. It would take a lot of time, and a lot of effort, but you could manage.

"I guess," I said. I started to circle around the mech, eyeing it from different angles and making a mental tally of what needed replacing. It was . . .

not as bad as it could have been. The legs had a few scratches, but they were superficial. The frame was intact, and the body was mostly fine. A few bent bits here and there, but nothing expensive. The head was . . . fucked beyond repair. One of the Gatlings was just gone, and I wouldn't trust the side-mounted guns.

So, just one big chunk to replace, which would probably require taking apart a lot of the front of the mech. I'd need a sort of jack to lift the head off. Maybe I could sell it off to the Family or something? There were a few decent sensors and such tucked into the head that someone might be interested in.

"Myalis, how many points am I sitting on?" I asked.

Current Point Total: 72,417

That was . . . a hefty chunk of points. "How much was the mech again?"

You paid twenty thousand points for the Mark IV Mechcatular Nyanzerfaust.

I had enough to buy three more mechs just like it. But that would be silly. "Okay," I said. "Well, I don't want to lose this one, it's been good for me, but Lucy *will* get out the spray bottle if I don't upgrade again to be safer. This baby was good against stuff up to the twenties. I think I'll see about fixing her up and using her for that kind of thing."

A reasonable choice. It also has some degree of automation. You've used it from afar a few times to serve as a guard.

"Yeah, that's a good point," I said with a nod. "Alright, here's what we're gonna do. Do I have a catalog that has garages in it?"

You have a Defensive Structures Catalog that does feature a few structures capable of serving as garages, but they're more designed to be placed outdoors as temporary housing for vehicles.

"Yeah, I'm looking for something I can shove in here," I said with a gesture to the garage's rather bare wall. It was pure cinderblock and concrete, painted over with some thick off-gray paint. This floor was one level below the offices where the prosthetics shop was set up, and one level above Gomorrah's floor. The far corner actually had some walls up, and it looked like Gomorrah had finished setting up that car lift.

Otherwise, it was a lot of empty space, most of an entire floor's worth, though a few hovercars were parked off to one side. People visiting the prosthetics shop, maybe? There wasn't much else for anyone to do here.

"Okay, what can I get for a couple of hundred points? I just want a nice space to park my mechs, plural, with space for tools and maybe a jack and some crawlspace underneath."

Hmm, I can see two ways to go about this. Indoor Garage Catalog for two hundred points would get you what you need: a space to place your mechanized vehicles as well as your bike, with plenty of storage, tool cabinets, lighting, and even some small equipment to maneuver larger parts around.

"But," I said leadingly.

But there is another, slightly more expensive option, from a Sun Watcher catalog. It's called the Sun Watcher Vehicular Bay Catalog, and it features a wide selection of tools and utilities to create a modular vehicle bay, one specifically designed for quadrupedal mechanized vehicles. Though of course there could still be room for more common vehicles. It would come in at a hefty four hundred points, but you might save on equipment costs moving forward. This catalog has a lot more in terms of automated machinery for the repair of mechanized vehicles like your own.

"More Sun Watcher stuff, huh?" I muttered. Well, Lucy was threatening to spritz me still, so why not? "Okay, I like that one. Let's get it."

New Purchase: Sun Watcher Vehicular Bay Catalog

Points Reduced from . . . 72,417 to . . . 72,017

I nodded. "Right, okay, now we need to actually get something . . . Let's aim for one with like, three bays? One for repairs, two for just parking mechs and shit in? Maybe just take up this one outer wall, though?"

Certainly. And your price range? Keep in mind that the more you spend here, the easier time you'll have with the installation. Given enough points, I can install the bay directly into the structure of the overall building.

"And I'd want that because . . . ?" I asked.

Because your home isn't resistant to everything. This way there will at least be two sections of the building entirely resistant to most human weaponry.

Well, that wasn't a bad idea.

"Let's call it . . . uh . . . I guess it's three bays, so three K? But no, I want one of them to be decently equipped. Maybe make it . . . five thousand points?"

Damn, it almost hurt to say that.

Okay, Catherine. A three-bay garage unit, coming right up!

New Purchase: Sun Watcher Three-Vehicle Bay with Mechanized Repair System

Points Reduced from . . . 72,017 to . . . 67,017

I always expected a big flash or something impressive when I bought something large. But instead the bays were just . . . there. There wasn't even any displaced air, just the sense of something moving, and suddenly the space before me was filled up and I was stepping back from a wall.

A good chunk of the floor was now taken up by a curvy building of sorts, or section, I guess, since it reached from floor to ceiling without any visible gaps.

The walls were chrome, with a slight bluish tint to them, and where they turned, they did so with smooth, gentle curves. It reminded me a little of those modern building fronts corpos liked so much, only . . . this was done better. Organic, without really pushing it into the weird.

"Nice," I said.

There were three doors at the front, and unlike normal garage doors, these looked like they were designed to slide apart down the middle, each half slotting into the wall next to the entrance.

The doors opened with a faint hiss and the hum of an electric motor, moving aside to reveal . . . Well, one of the bays was just that, a bay. A large, mostly empty space. The floor had been replaced, and I noticed a few drains in the ground. The back wall had cabinets made of the same chrome-y metal and there was a station to one side that looked like it had a built-in pressure washer.

There was a row of hooks, a wall designed to hold dozens of tools, and a couple of long metal workbenches at waist height.

Honestly, it looked like it would be the kind of space where working would be *fun*.

The second bay was identical to the first, but the third was different. The repair bay reminded me a little more of something you'd see next to a Formula 1 pit stop. There were liftable platforms on the ground, controls on the walls, and several large servo arms hung from the ceiling with different sorts of hands mounted to their ends. I saw what looked like grinders and welders, some small enough that I imagined they could be used to snip a hair off someone's head while others looked like they were designed to peel off tank armor.

"Okay, yeah, that's a good start," I said. "Now . . . I think I need a new mech, and I can feel this one hurting my wallet already."

CHAPTER EIGHTY-THREE

CAT OF ALL TRADES

The future of mechanized warfare is not walking mechanized vehicles. It will never be walking mechanized vehicles.

Legs will never trump tracks! You fucking pissants!

—WarLightning forums, 2028

I think, before you start spending points on a new mech, you should decide what you're looking for in a vehicle.

I frowned at that. "What do you mean?" I asked. Wasn't I just looking for a bigger, better version of my last mech?

Generally speaking, most weapons can be divided into two broad categories: specialized and general use. A handgun is a general-use weapon. It can use different ammunition and it's almost always good to have on hand. A marksman's rifle isn't as useful in most situations, being too heavy and cumbersome to use; however, in its specific niche use, it is far better to have than a normal handgun or even a common rifle.

"Alright," I said with a slow nod. I could see where she was going with this. "And my previous mech was . . . what, a sniper rifle?"

Somewhat. Thinking in strict binaries won't be good for you. Think of it more as a sliding scale between the two extremes. The Nyanzerfaust is a decent all-around platform with a very specialized main weapon and secondary armaments that have lots of versatility. I would say that it leans more toward the "Cat of all trades" side of things.

"Was that a pun?" I asked.

I am the final arbitrator for what is funny.

I groaned and rubbed at my face. "Sure, whatever. Just get to your point."

My point is, do you expect to use the Nyanzerfaust again in the future?

"Yeah," I said after thinking about it for just a second. I was a bit attached to it, and it wasn't *that* fucked up.

In that case, it might serve as a decent platform for general use. If you purchase another platform that can do everything the Nyanzerfaust does, but better, then you'll never need it again. Seeing as how that might be wasteful, why not purchase something more specialized instead?

That sounded . . . not too bad. "So, a sniper mech? Maybe a melee mech? Maybe something way tankier, so that I can take on big fuckers without worrying when I get chewed on?"

That would be three separate specializations. How about all of them?

"Isn't that just generalizing again?"

I mean why not purchase multiple mechanized platforms and a unit to transport them to the location where you want to use them? A carrier of decent size could ensure that you have an arsenal of platforms available. You could also buy a single highly modular frame and switch out its specializations as you go.

I leaned up against one of my new garage's walls as I thought about it. A fuck-huge flying carrier that transported a half-dozen mechs like my current one, all ready to be deployed and with different sets of weapons to fuck enemies up in new and refreshing ways. It sounded awesome as hell.

Having one mech that could switch out guns and shit on the fly . . . also sounded pretty awesome. "Okay . . . both sound kinda cool," I admitted.

I would suggest the carrier option.

"Why?" I asked.

The increased modularity is worth it, in the long run. The cost of the vehicle to carry mechanized units might be somewhat steep, assuming you want something armed and armored and comfortable, but once you have such a vehicle, you can continuously upgrade your arsenal by buying new and improved mechanized vehicles. Those not in use can be stored here. The carrier option would also give you the potential to carry large amounts of materials to a site, or ever smaller combat or scout drones.

I was nodding along by the time she was halfway through. "Okay, but I need to see what this carrier thing will look like. And it needs to fit in here." I gestured vaguely at the entire parking garage. If I was gonna have something like that, I'd want it to be parkable at my place.

Certainly. Let's get you some options across a range of prices. There's a holographic projector in the mechanical bay that we can use.

Like Myalis had said, there was a smaller projector inserted into one of the workbenches. It looked like the kind of thing meant to display parts or schematics, but as I got closer and my augs connected with the garage's interface, the little projector came to life.

A swirl of lights later, and there was a hovercraft on display.

Seeing as how you have both a Class I Armored Assault Vehicle, and a Class I Mechanized Warfare Platform Flight Systems catalog, I will limit purchases to items that don't require any new catalog unlocks.

"Thanks," I said as I leaned in closer.

The hover . . . tank, thing, was a rather boxy-looking car. It was thin and long, with a fat nacelle at the rear for its engines and two gull-wing doors on either side. Each one looked large enough to fit my current mech through.

The schematic had the doors open and close, revealing tight little bays on the interior where a pair of mechs could stand. Landing pad "feet" unfolded from below, and there were even little ramps that slid out from under the openings for the mechs to get in and out easier.

The front was a blunt-nosed cockpit, with little more than a seat and driving controls. It . . . did look a little less angular on the sides, but not by too much.

All in all, it reminded me of one of those hovering delivery vans, but way longer and slightly beefed up.

This is a model that would only cost you four thousand points. It's a capable vehicle, with decent speed and acceleration capabilities and room to store two mechanized units. It is also perfectly street-legal. Unfortunately, it is unarmed.

Not too expensive. The 3D model I was looking at was colorless, but I could imagine a big black boxy thing coming in and dropping off a few mechs. It looked a little too . . . normal, though.

"Alright, next one up?" I asked. "I do need guns."

This next one is based on an ancient Sun Watcher gunship.

The 3D render was replaced by a new model, and I perked up a bit at the sight of it.

This one was much stubbier. Not as long, but way fatter. It had a sort of protruding cockpit in the middle, with two large angled gates next to it. That meant that the entrances for the mechs were all forward-facing. The spine of the ship was actually lower than the two boxy containers for the mechs.

Myalis had the model spin a little, and I took in the shape of it. From above, it was almost coin-shaped, with a protrusion for the cockpit at the front.

It had small winglets, but there was no way it was aerodynamic enough to fly. "Weird-looking thing," I said.

It's ancient, as I said. But the design features a roomy interior and it's well-armored for its size.

Myalis had the diagram blow apart, showing the inside. The cockpit was actually pretty large, like the inside of a big SUV, and there was a walkway from it to a cargo hold that had a bed and a small living space. I could access the two mech holding spaces from there.

A longer, slightly more expensive version is also available for sixteen thousand.

The model stretched out, this time adding two more mech holds and a much larger living space. The original version had an underbelly turret and a pair of smaller guns on top. This longer version doubled that until there were six hardpoints spread across the carrier.

Room for four mechs was pretty nice, actually, and the living space was decent.

"I think . . . I like bigger," I said.

Fantastic! Then you'll like this next one, at least until you see the price tag.

The image disappeared, and then was replaced by . . .

"Is that a spaceship?" I asked.

It is not technically capable of reaching space.

The carrier was long. Twice the length of a semi-trailer, and about three times as wide, but still relatively low. It had three bay doors on each side, all of them numbered, and below that, six large mechanized legs.

The damned thing was bristling with small guns that stuck out of rounded pods on its sides and top and bottom. Myalis had them wiggle around, showing their firing arcs, then the legs retracted back in and the bay doors opened.

The thing looked like it belonged in a sci-fi movie.

The model opened up, showing the interior. There was a conference room, a bathroom, two areas with tight little bunk beds, and a bridge. The entire middle section had room for six mechs next to the bay doors, and two more tucked further within.

This model would cost you a neat thirty-seven thousand points, but it is quite capable in combat all on its own and can carry up to six mechanized units the size of your Nyanzerfaust onto a battlefield in relative safety.

The model reassembled itself, then spun. It looked intimidating. Of course, the front of it had a slightly . . . feline look to it, but not enough that anyone could outright say it looked like a cat.

Yeah, I could work with that. "A few changes . . ." I started.

CHAPTER EIGHTY-FOUR

MODERN GODDESSES

There hasn't been a single damned creative idea in years. It's the same thing, over and over again. Sequels of sequels, mashing ideas together that have been done to death.

A creative person comes, creates something new, and then the corporate dogs rip it to shreds and parade the corpse around for all to see!

I give *Inside Out 7* a 6 out of 10.

—NeonMovieReviews, 2039

"What's this one even called?" I asked as I gestured to the mech carrier.

The changes I'd asked for weren't too extreme, I didn't think. It mostly came down to adding sofas in the little command room in its center and an integrated minifridge. At least, at first. I started to have fun with it after that.

The centermost space, designed to hold two mechs, was replaced by a small mobile garage. Nothing too complex, but enough that I could maybe fix a few easy things on the move. Myalis helpfully added a docking port for a repair drone as well, which was sensible.

The ship . . . Was it a ship?

I frowned. This was way too big to just be called a car, or even a truck. It had more in common with a ferry than either of those. Yeah, ship felt right.

Anyway, the ship had plenty of guns strapped around it. Six twin-barreled machine guns, on ball-shaped turrets that had wide angles of fire, and a single-barreled 105mm gun on an angular, flat turret at the top. Below were two large pods that could tilt in and out of view, each one able to hold sixteen rockets or small guided missiles that could be reloaded from the interior.

It had less armament than a modern main battle tank, sure, but it could also fly and was armored up the tits.

Myalis shifted the design a little, making it somewhat less boxy. The armor gained more of an angular look to it, sharp edges and all.

"Okay," I said. "Lay it on me, how much would this thing cost?"

Currently, with the modifications you've brought to it, the Catbox *will cost you—*

"No," I said. "We're not calling it that."

It's an objectively good name.

"It's objectively stupid," I replied. "Come on, we need a name with a bit of . . . you know, oomph to it. Something cooler and . . . stronger?"

And you expect to come up with this name yourself? I will defer to your greater erudition in the matter of nomenclature and your obviously superior vocabulary with regards to names with appropriate gravitas.

I rolled my eyes. "Don't be a bitch. We just need a cooler name than *Catbox.* The Nyanzerfaust has a silly name, but it's got some syllables to it, and Gomorrah has her *God's Righteous Fury,* which is a name that has hairs on its chest."

Felis Aegis?

"Lucy would like that. But it's too cutesy," I said.

I see. How about the Clawhold? *Or perhaps the* Iron Pride?

I passed my tongue over my teeth. Yeah, those were a bit better. "Not bad, but like, for a gun or a shield or something. It doesn't feel right for an entire . . . you know." I gestured to the hologram of the ship.

I see. Then perhaps something with a bit more fur on its chest? How about the Bastion of Sekhmet?

"Who's that?" I asked.

Myalis took over the hologram and showed me some old Egyptian-looking art. Some lady in a skirt with a cat head and one hell of a headdress.

A warrior goddess from ancient Earth mythology, specifically ancient Egyptian. She has a lion's head and is one of the solar deities.

I rubbed at my chin. Was it cool to appropriate another culture's imagery just because it was kinda badass-looking?

Probably not.

Would it annoy Gomorrah and did it sound rather badass?

Yeah, it did.

"Alright, I'm down for that. The *Bastion of Sekmeth.*"

Sekhmet.

"Sure," I said with a nod. "And this is gonna cost me . . ."

Forty-two thousand points.

I needed to sit down for a minute. Forty-two big ones. That was . . . a large chunk of what I had. Way more than half of my total points. Sure, it was for something *big,* and there were good chances that I wouldn't be replacing that for a long time, but . . .

I chewed on my lower lip. If I was a smarter sort, I might consider a pros and cons list, but that'd never been my way of doing things. Did I want this thing? It seemed damned useful. It would be a hell of a thing to show up to problem locations with. I'd spent a decent load of time in mobile bases recently, PMC and army ones. This would be the same, but flying, and it would be mine.

Did I want it?

Yeah.

"Alright," I said. "But why's it so damned expensive?"

Mostly the cost comes from the technology required to ensure that it stays afloat without breaking apart under its own mass. The sheer size is also a factor in its cost.

Right, I couldn't argue that too hard, it *was* a big thing. "Go ahead, Myalis," I said.

New Purchase: The *Bastion of Sekhmet*

Points Reduced from . . . 67,017 to . . . 25,017

Oh boy, seeing my points drop by that much made me feel dizzy for a second. I took a deep breath and then flinched as the air in the parking garage *whumped* past me.

There was suddenly something huge taking up a hefty chunk of the room. A wall of flat black steel and armored panels.

I blinked dust out of my eyes, then looked up at my new toy.

The *Bastion of Sekhmet* was larger than I'd expected it to be from the hologram. It looked like it was just a few centimeters from scraping against the ceiling.

Legs larger than my old mech's were deployed around its base, all six of them clamped onto the floor. I hadn't asked Myalis about color, and the hologram had been that glowy blue that holograms tended to be. The *Bastion* was a flat, light-absorbing black, except where its armored panels had sharp edges. There, it was covered in gleaming gold panels and backlit by pale blue light.

I started to giggle to myself as I walked around it. It took a while. There were, as I'd noted, six large doors, slightly angled, with golden numbers embossed onto them. Each was more than large enough for me to walk my old mech into.

"Ah, shit," I said as I finished my circuit. My Nyanzerfaust had been like, twenty thousand points. I wasn't sitting at much more than that now, and if I spent what I had left I'd be point-broke.

. . . Fuck, did I just buy a mech carrier without the points to fill it with mechs?

Don't worry, Catherine, I'm certain we can buy you at least one new mech.

I frowned. "Are you reading my mind again?"

You're predictable.

I wanted to disagree, but she was probably right. "Let me give the inside a tour first," I mumbled. My augs connected to the *Bastion* automatically, which was nice. I could open up any of the gates from a rather simple interface, and there were controls for the guns, the ship itself, and all sorts of knickknacks like the lights and stuff from a simple set of menus.

I opened gate six and stepped back as an unfolding ramp came down and gently touched the ground.

"So, mechs," I said as I stepped in and started to look around. The bays weren't entirely cut off from each other, but they weren't sharing a large space either. There were thin walls with bracing between them, and folded-up robotic arms designed to cling onto any mech parked in here so it wouldn't bounce around.

I have a simple suggestion for you. Since you seem to use your Nyanzerfaust as a scout relatively frequently, why not purchase a frame more capable in that regard? A lighter, faster-moving frame, with better stealth capabilities and a more powerful suit of sensors?

"And cheaper than something all-purpose?"

By a certain number of points, perhaps.

Uh-huh. A stealth mech wouldn't be too bad, and something faster might be fun. It didn't sound as safe as what I had already, though. Then again, if it was meant to serve a different purpose, then did it matter?

I walked deeper into the *Bastion*. There was a wide corridor down the spine of the ship, large enough for a mech to walk through to the garage-like installation at the very rear of the vessel. Myalis, took over one of the projectors in that room, same as the one in my other new garage, and tossed up an image of a mech.

It was another cat-shaped frame, only this one was lithe, with the proportions of a cheetah rather than an overstuffed lion like my Nyanzerfaust. It was low to the ground, but then it stood up in the hologram.

I eyed it over as it spun slowly.

A central cockpit behind the head of the mech was fitted with a seat designed to be laid down onto. Two small holes on either side of the chest by the front for missiles, a tail that could elongate itself into a sort of barbed whip, and claws like on my last mech.

The mouth opened up to reveal a small turreted gun, and there were two more mounted on the flanks that could unfold a pair of long, articulated arms that let them aim in every direction. They were still rather small, basically belt-fed machine pistols.

"Yeah, that's something," I said. "But . . . I want enough points for another upgrade to my wetware too. To keep Lucy happy."

CHAPTER EIGHTY-FIVE

M.E.O.W, THAT'S RIGHT!

There's no such thing as cyberpsychosis. That's an urban legend started from the prevalence of certain pieces of literature and video game media.

There is, however, cyber-dysmorphia, the discomfort brought about by having a limb or body part replaced by a synthetic one.

Strangely enough, some people are more comfortable when their synthetic replacement has less in common with their organic parts. The separation being clearer and more obvious makes it far more comfortable to handle than if the replacement prosthetic is poorly designed to look like the part it's meant to simulate.

—Lecture by Professor Wells, 2046

There's actually another option, as far as mechanized units go.

"Oh?" I asked. I was still looking at the smaller, lighter mecha that was apparently within my now very much reduced price range. "What's that?"

Since you want to prioritize protection, what about a heavier, more armored frame? It wouldn't have the stealth capabilities of your previous machines, but it would make up for that by being significantly harder to damage.

"Throw it up on the projector," I said with a gesture to the spinning image of the fast scout mech.

It flicked away, and was replaced by a whole new cat-shaped mech.

This one looked . . . fat? Like an overfed house cat. It was one chonky boy, with relatively short legs mounted on pistons thicker than my thighs that could shift the entire thing upward.

This motherfucker was armored, though. Big plates of curved armor, looking like something off a World War II tank. The fuck-off large gun on its back reinforced that image some. It was mounted in the center-rear of the mech, in a large, bulbous turret.

"How big is that gun?" I asked.

155 millimeters.

I nodded, then looked over the rest of the cat. The "paws" were massive things, with fat wheels beneath them, those sorts of not-quite-ball-wheels that some robots used, only these looked reinforced. They'd have to be to support all that weight on them.

This unit, the Mechanized Exploration and Operations Walker Mk IV, is designed to endure maximal amounts of damage, both kinetic and explosive, as well as from acidic attacks. The cockpit has a self-regulating environment, capable of being closed off from the outside world for years at a time.

"Damn," I said. "What about other guns? I mean, that big one's . . . big, but I wouldn't wanna use it on a model one. Bit of overkill, you know?"

Of course.

The model shifted, and some of the armored panels slid open to reveal spaces where gimbal arms could move out of the mech. Two at the front, two at the rear. They held small machine-pistol-looking things.

Again with the low-caliber guns, but . . . yeah, they'd work against anything below the twenties.

Another pair of sections at the front moved back, revealing two holes by the front "shoulders" of the mech, on either side of its neck.

These are a pair of seventy-five-millimeter cannons. Small, but respectable. Their traversal is extremely limited, however. The mech has a self-detonating ERA system. Explosives that you can detonate the moment an enemy nears without damaging the mech itself.

Holy shit . . . that was kinda rad.

I narrowed my eyes. "Wait, what was its name again?"

The Mechanized Exploration and Operations Walker.

"The . . . MEOW?" I asked. "Myalis, what's the other mech's name?"

The Cybernetic High-Efficiency Exploration and Tactical Assault Hybrid.

I sighed. "Yeah, of course. How much do they cost?"

The MEOW Mk4 comes in at a respectable seventeen thousand. The CHEETAH at a slightly lower sixteen thousand five hundred.

I worked my jaw as I thought about it. Myalis had the hologram split to show off both mechs at once, including their price tags.

The difference was . . . not much, honestly. I made more than that in an hour. A good day of work would give me more total points than either mech cost, and viewed like that, it wasn't a terrible deal either way.

But I didn't have the points for both, even if I was rather tempted to *get* both. My brand-new *Bastion* deserved to be filled with lethal amounts of mechanized warmechs. I had ideas for others too, but I imagined that it would be better to hold off for a bit.

"Damn," I muttered.

Having a difficult time deciding? How about we focus on something else for a moment? You mentioned a passing interest in self-modifications?

"Huh? Oh, yeah." I looked around, then found a convenient seat on top of a workbench pressed up against one wall of the garage. "So, I've done the skin thing, my hair, which is more cosmetic I guess, and I've got some organ shit. That leaves, uh, muscles and bone, right? Like, if I want a baseline improvement across everything?"

That's a sensible way of looking at it. Yes, I think I would suggest either a skeletal or muscular upgrade if you wish to continue improving yourself physically. Do you have any preference?

"Muscles would be nice," I said as I flexed my one bicep. "But . . . eh, I don't need to be much stronger, and I want to survive better. Not so much be faster or stronger or whatever. So . . . bone? How would that even work?"

There are plenty of methods to replace your skeleton. I believe most of these methods fit on a sliding scale of intrusive to unintrusive, depending on how brave you're feeling about full-body transplants.

"Right," I said, stretching the word out. "That's way too far. Got like . . . really good vitamins? Space milk for stronger bones?"

I think I can offer something better than calcium. How about bone sheathing?

"What?" I asked.

A bone sheath is a covering placed over your natural bones, usually made of a material that's tougher than the bone itself. It's essentially bone armoring. Good sheathing can extend between bones as well, filling in the gaps of your ribs, for example, and creating a more solid connection where you have ligaments.

I nodded along. "That makes some sense. How much tougher are we talking here?"

Not that much, I'm afraid. Common human bone sheaths use titanium alloys as a base, but I'd suggest a graphene-magnesium alloy. Quite light, relatively durable. Harder and stronger than your current skeleton, though don't expect your bones to suddenly be unbreakable.

Right, I imagined that unbreakable would either mean thick and heavy as shit, or something very alien in nature. "And installing this?"

A simple procedure! A spool is inserted through your skin at the base of your spine and a small army of nanomachines carries strips of the alloy through your body and welds them together over your bones during the course of two to three days. That would be the least intrusive option.

"Huh," I said. "And I won't feel it?" I asked.

You'll weigh about four kilos more.

"I thought this shit would be lightweight?" I asked.

Catherine, lightweight isn't weightless.

"How much?" I asked. I was ready to flinch at the answer already.

Seven hundred and fifty-six points.

That was . . . not that bad, actually. "Cheap," I said.

That's assuming you don't mind taking something that will require some time to install itself. It's nowhere near the cutting edge of what you could have, but I believe that it's your best current option before moving into the full-body-replacement territory, in which case saving a few points may well be worth it.

Yeah, that made sense. "Okay . . . yeah, let's do it."

New Purchase: Graphene-Magnesium Bone Sheathing

Points Reduced from 25,017 . . . to . . . 24,561

New Purchase: Nano-Regenerative Surgical Suite

Points Reduced from . . . 24,561 to . . . 24,261

A decently large box appeared before me, about as big around as a basketball, though it was a little flatter.

I opened it, and discovered a sort of plastic . . . bin thing, with a large strap running around it. "Is this . . . a fucked-up fanny pack?" I asked as I lifted it. The plastic shell was hard-ish, with some squishy padding on the interior.

Place it around your lower waist, beneath your clothes. I'll alert you once it's ready to be disposed of.

I frowned but did as Myalis said, tugging up my shirt to expose my stomach and back, then biting the hem to hold it in place while I fit the pack on. The belt was wide but just large enough that I could buckle it on the front.

"Feels weird," I said. It wasn't *that* heavy, but it was certainly obvious that it was there.

You'll only need to wear this for a few days. It's hygienic enough, and you can shower with it on. Tense up for a moment.

"Huh?" I asked, then I tensed up as several pin-like things poked me in the back. "Ouch, fuck!" I snapped.

There, incisions complete! Congratulations on your ongoing bone-improvement procedure!

"Thanks," I said flatly.

Have you come to a decision with regards to the mechs?

"Hmm . . . not yet. Lemme ask Lucy what she thinks. Plus she'll wanna have a look at the *Bastion* too. It's kind of a big thing, right?"

Lucy would help, because she was the best, even if she didn't know jack shit about this kind of thing.

She'd probably pick the one that she felt was cutest, or the one that would keep me safer. Eh, either way was fine by me.

Delilah stood on the edge of a field. To her left were rows upon rows of flowers. Small, red things with black centers. Her hand trailed down to her side and she gently pinched one of them. She imagined that it was soft, but her gloved hands hid any such thing from her.

Behind her was a clearing, a wide space hidden by a raised hillside where cars and transports were parked. The media was here, because of course they were, but they were being polite. Professional. Somber.

It was raining.

That was almost always the case, but it felt especially appropriate now. Rain, and a biting, humid cold that clawed at her exposed face.

She'd worn a habit today, one she'd bought from Atyacus for the occasion. Black on black, with a white coif and a short bandeau, and a long veil that masked her hair and cut into her peripheral vision, turning the world into a dark-sided tunnel.

It was fine. She pulled her hand away from the unfelt flowers and glanced up.

There were other samurai here. There were a lot of other samurai here. A full quarter of the Vanguard who had participated had shown up. Some members of the German and Asian groups, the Nachtwächternetzwerk and the Keiretsu, had come as well.

Officers, from the various PMCs who had assisted and from the army, politicians, some people who had been on the front lines and who were here for their own reasons. It was a busy place at the moment.

She wasn't with them. Instead she was here, away from the main group, enjoying a field of poppies that hadn't been here just hours ago. A gift from one of the samurai who understood more about symbolism and meaning than Delilah herself did, but she could understand the thrust of their actions, and appreciated it all the same.

Seven losses, among the Vanguard.

Seven dead samurai.

More than was lost in most minor incursions. More lost in a single day than humanity had lost since . . . well, last week, when the global incursion began in earnest.

The rate of attrition was terrifying.

Normal people had died as well. By the thousands. Some of those flying models had crashed into small towns and poorly prepared cities. A vault, designed to shelter thousands from ordinary incursions, had been crashed into and collapsed. Even now first responders were pulling survivors from the wreckage and cataloging those who hadn't made it in time.

Delila took a deep breath, then flicked her eyes to the side. A menu came up, showing her the time, weather, and a few other necessities.

"She's late," she muttered.

As per usual.

She huffed, very slightly. Her friend . . . her best friend—as terrible as that particular thought was, what with Franny being, well, more than a friend—was perhaps the least punctual person Delilah had ever had the misfortune of meeting.

"She'd be late to her own funeral," Delilah said. She tilted her head back a little, letting some of the drizzling rain smatter across her lips and cheeks.

Myalis suggests that Vanguard Stray Cat is on her way. ETA two minutes.

"Thank you," Delilah said. She wasn't sure what kind of relationship Atyacus and Myalis had, but she sometimes had the impression that there was a level of . . . respect there. From Atyacus to Myalis. Did the AI have superiors? A hierarchy? She didn't think so.

Delilah folded her hands back into her sleeves and watched the poppy field sway as she just let her mind . . . not think too much. It was something she used to do a lot, usually while working on some chores. Dishes, sweeping, anything that didn't require thinking.

She supposed that she should have been praying, but she wasn't in that kind of mood at the moment.

She was pulled out of her thoughts at the sound of an approaching rumble. Another large hover vehicle coming in? There had been a number of those, people visiting the site and samurai landing nearby. Fortunately, the space they'd chosen was quite large, and while there weren't proper parking spots, there was plenty of room.

Delilah glanced up at the incoming vehicle, then she did a slight double take.

It had cat ears.

Or at least, the way that the forward section's metal plates were laid out gave the impression of ears. Subtle, but also very much not. The hovercraft was large, far larger than most she'd seen besides mass inter-city bulk transports.

It came in low and fast, then did a half-spin, tilting onto its side as its thrusters slowed it down enough that it could come to a safe landing over the field next to several news vans. Large mechanical legs folded out from beneath the ship, and it came down onto them with a series of hissing clanks.

Delilah started walking over. By the time she arrived, the large ship was fully parked, and she could see some vague movement behind the thick panes of glass in the cockpit at the front.

It took a few long seconds before one of the doors started to open. It was a large bay door, with a stenciled 3 on it. The 3 had cat ears.

Catherine stood inside, with Lucy next to her.

The girls were both in dresses. Somber black ones, though Catherine was still wearing combat boots and clearly had a handgun strapped to her thigh. And her skirt was a little short, but Delilah decided to look past that.

"Hello," she said.

"Hey," Catherine replied as she clunked her way down the ramp. "You look the way you usually do when I'm late."

"I wonder why," Delilah said, her voice flat.

Catherine grinned, unrepentant and amused with herself. "So, uh, funerals. Lucy told me I *had* to dress up for it, but I think she just wanted me in a skirt."

Lucy smiled smugly next to her idiot. "Hi, Delilah," she said sweetly. "Nice to see you again."

"Hi, Lucy," Delilah replied. How did such a sweet young woman end up with such an idiot? Truly, God worked in mysterious ways. "We should head up the hill. Things are going to start soon."

"Right," Catherine said. She stretched up onto the balls of her feet, then fell back on her heels. She always had this tendency to stretch this way and that. It was strange, as if she couldn't just stay still until she grew serious.

Delilah nodded, then allowed herself to fall into some small talk as they made their way over. Yes, Franny was fine, and she was at home. Yes, she was fine with Catherine adding to the parking garage. Maybe her *Fury* would need repairs one day, so it was a nice addition. No, she didn't think Catherine's new mobile mech-deployment platform was too much. Though, yes, it was big.

They made their way around the hill and began to climb up it. Someone had carved steps into the ground, and there were thin stone plates atop each step now. Marble, Delilah guessed. That hadn't been there earlier, but she couldn't guess which samurai was responsible.

On reaching the top of the hill, Delilah noticed Catherine's cocky smile slowly dwindle.

There were seats laid out in rows with a few corridors between them. Room enough for a couple of hundred people, and a lot of that seating was already taken up.

Politicians, media, army officers, and samurai were mingling. Some of the samurai stood out on account of their unique gear and clothes, but a lot of them had dressed up, or down, to better fit the mood. Black was uncommonly common at the moment.

Before them was the cenotaph.

The memorial stone was a massive thing, bought by a West Coast samurai called The Dirty Earth Man. Despite that samurai's name, the cenotaph itself was . . . pretty.

At its center, a black stone obelisk rose twenty-five meters high. It was about a meter and a half wide and thick, with a tapered top that had some sort of metallic cap above it that gleamed a deep bronze.

Names were carved into the surface, each one no taller than a finger's width. There were thousands.

Next to the obelisk were two forms. They were vaguely humanoid, but abstracted, made of pure white stone. Each had one arm wrapped around the obelisk, while the other stretched outward, one gripping a bronze sword, the other raising a bronze shield.

"That's a lot of names," Catherine said.

"A lot of people died," Delilah replied. It was trite, but it was also the truth.

"Fuck," Catherine muttered. "We could have done better, huh?"

Delilah was tempted to nod, to twist the knife, but . . . well, that wouldn't be fair. "Maybe. But I don't think you should look down on what we accomplished. We destroyed Phobos. We warned people. We set up defenses. Think of it less as people dying, and more as people we saved."

Lucy patted Catherine on the shoulder. "You did good," she said.

Catherine frowned. "Yeah, yeah, I know."

Delilah glanced at the time again. "Let's find a seat," she suggested.

They made their way through the rows of chairs toward the front. There were a few seats free at the very front. Unsurprisingly, the people there were familiar. The Saint-Jérome team. Princess was in a more somber dress than usual, and Knight was in a black pantsuit next to her. Crackshot was still in jeans, but he'd worn a nice button-up, at least.

Hedgehog was in a military uniform with any identification stripped off, and next to him was Tankette in a very humble gray dress.

Delilah took a spot next to Tankette, and Catherine and Lucy gathered up on her other side.

There were some hellos and greetings traded, and several samurai in the row behind them reached out to give their greetings too. A man called

ToeJam, a samurai she wasn't familiar with, walked over to thank Catherine in a low, hushed voice before moving back.

The event started in full a few minutes after they arrived. A man in a dark suit walked up to the podium set up before the cenotaph. He adjusted his tie, cleared his throat, and then . . . launched into an uninspired speech.

The man was from the Family, and while his job was important, Delilah couldn't help but feel like he lacked the gravitas necessary to make a good showing here.

The media ate it up, of course, though they did so silently. Corporate journos and a few influencers were crowding the very back of the space. She imagined that a few of them were tempted to make a scene, but . . . well, there were too many samurai here to make that worthwhile.

So many of that sort wanted to go out with a bang, but death-by-samurai wasn't the way to do that. It was far too likely that a samurai would just erase all traces of their existence out of spite, so they behaved.

The speaker asked for a minute of silence, and everyone bowed their heads and waited.

At the end of that, he asked the crowd if anyone had anything to say.

Delilah was surprised to see Emoscythe step up onto the small raised dais that served as a base for the obelisk.

"Hello," the darkly dressed samurai said. Delilah was impressed to note that she wasn't wearing her usual samurai garb. It was something close, of course, a variation on gothic fashion, only this was far more subdued, more . . . respectful, maybe? She wasn't sure how someone conveyed that with clothes alone, but here it was.

The woman seemed to take a moment to gather her thoughts, a moment that everyone willingly gave her.

"For those of you whose hearts have been blackened by the events that brought us here today, know that your suffering isn't a lonely one," she began. "We stand beneath a crying sky in a sea of ashes. This sky is ours once more, as it was once before, but only through the sacrifice of blood and lives. We are still here. We are still breathing. We are still mourning."

Delilah found herself swallowing. There was a lot more emotion there than in the platitudes of the Family's man.

"The cost of life is heavy. Heavier than steel and grief. It's the weight of absence that you feel now, dragging you down. There are those who should be here with us now, and who aren't. They were innocents, they were fighters, they were heroes, they were normal people we failed to protect."

She half turned, glancing up at the obelisk.

"This will be here to remember them by, but it's just a symbol. If you truly want to honor the dead, then live as if they meant something. Our friends, families, and heroes should be more than names carved in stone.

They should be what makes us take the actions that will allow us to have a future where we can look to the stars without fear."

Emoscythe nodded to the crowd.

"Thank you."

She stepped off the stage and came to take a seat by Crackshot.

Delilah nodded to her. That had been better than the rehearsed, likely AI-generated speech that the Family's man had made.

He politely asked if anyone else had anything to add.

No one said anything for a few long seconds, then Catherine sighed.

"You don't have to," Lucy muttered.

"Feel like I kinda do," Catherine said before she stood up. Delilah almost reached out to tug her back. Catherine was . . . well, she was a lot of things. It was complicated. She was, most of all, not the ideal public speaker.

But she still had a bit of a gift to her, the ability to inspire despite her sheer crassness.

Catherine walked up to the podium and glared at the mic, then looked up and scanned the crowd. Delilah had known Catherine for long enough to read her expression, even past the mask she wore. She was a little nervous now, but drowning in . . .

Whatever the crazy lesbian version of machismo was.

"Yeah, I'm not great at this kind of thing," she began. "Honestly, Emoscythe said it better than I can, but . . . but sometimes something's lost when you're trying to be pretty about it."

She reached up, running her flesh hand over the edge where her cybernetic arm started. The scarred skin was all gone now, but Delilah could remember the red, welted flesh that had been there recently.

"We lost a lot of people. Too many. I'm not even talking about the samurai. We're . . . It's kinda fucked to say it, but we're made to die, aren't we? We fight it. We fight against the way we're all inevitably going to die, but that doesn't mean we'll ever win. I'm talking more about the normal people."

Catherine nodded, and it felt like she was finally finding her stride.

"I don't care much for the cowards. I care a lot more for those that fought back. Fuck dying, but you're going to anyway, right? But out there, there's people that picked up guns and knives and . . . wrenches and sticks. They saw that they weren't gonna make it, and they decided to spit in death's face and give the aliens a final 'fuck you' before they went down. Those are the people we fight for. I hope that those kinds of people make up a lot of the names on that rock behind me."

She shifted, glanced back, then dismissed the cenotaph.

"This city, this world, is held together with duct tape, spit, and spite. I've seen it. Sometimes I'm not sure if the worse enemy we have is the Antithesis or each other. But I don't think it matters, because we're still here. We're still fighting. We don't owe the people who died a bunch of crying. We don't owe them pretty speeches. We owe them working together. We owe them pulling ourselves up and fighting. For ourselves, for our loved ones, for a future that isn't shit, where people don't die by the thousands, and where we won't need to make hard choices about who lives and who doesn't!"

Catherine blinked rapidly. There were tears in her eyes.

"So . . . yeah. We'll keep fighting. Not because we're heroes, but because we can. We're gonna die anyway, and given the choice, I'd want to go down fighting."

Catherine nodded, then stepped off the stage.

Delilah closed her eyes. She'd only have a moment to think before she'd have to interact with Catherine again, a moment to think about how her best friend might just be the nexus for something that she wasn't sure anyone would be able to control, because the people sitting in rows upon rows behind her? They were cheering.

Catherine might be an irredeemable moron at times, but she had the animalistic charisma of a cult leader, and a drive for war that might send them all spiraling into something dark. Glorious, but dark. And every urge in Delilah's body wanted to be there, burning humanity's enemy at the front.

ABOUT THE AUTHOR

RavensDagger is a Canadian writer who wants to make people smile. The best way to do that, he has found, is by pecking away at the keyboard and hoping for the best.

RESPAWN YOUR CURIOSITY
follow us on our socials

 podiumentertainment.com

 @podiumentertainment

 /podiumentertainment

 @podium_ent

 @podiumentertainment